# THE ALCHEMIST'S TOMB

JASON LEE WILLIS

# THE ALCHEMIST'S TOMB

A NOVEL BY

## JASON LEE WILLIS

Lura
Publications

**Lura Publications**
**803 Silver Street East**
**Mapleton, MN 56065**
**www.lurapublications.wixsite.com/books**

Publisher's Note: This book is a work of fiction. Names, characters, places, and incidents are products of the author's imagination or are used fictitiously. Any resemblance to actual events or locales or persons, living or dead, is entirely coincidental.

While the real life events of Joseph Nicollet and Pierre-Charles LeSueur were closely followed in previous books, the characters in this book are only loosely based on the real life figures and should not be considered historically accurate.

Book Layout © 2024 BookDesignTemplates.com

**Library of Congress Cataloging-in-Publication Data**
**Willis, Jason Lee, author.**
**Eckman, Raven, editor.**
**Bunkowske, Caryl, editor**
**Anderson, Mark, designer.**
**The Alchemist's Tomb / Jason Lee Willis. – First edition.**
**Summary: A Scottish noblemen and his friends embark on a global search for an ancient treasure and secret tombs.**

eBook ISBN: 978-1-971362-01-4
Softcover ISBN: 979-8-9903790-5-3
Hardcover ISBN: 979-8-9903790-9-1

**[1. Historical Fantasy – Fiction. 2. Maritime History & Piracy – Fiction.**
**3. Thrillers – Fiction. 4. Action & Adventure – Fiction.]**
**Library of Congress Control Number:**

*Dedicated to the cellar monster that lived at my
childhood farm in South Dakota.
You were persistent, but you never got me!*

# Author's Note

As the fourth and final "element" in the Alchemist Chronicles, *The Alchemist's Tomb* will pick up where *The Alchemist's Map* left off following the death of Joseph Nicollet. While William Drummond Stewart really was baptized in St. Louis with Joseph Nicollet as his sponsor, most of the details in this story are invention. And yes, Stewart really did bring Antoine Clement with him on a clandestine trip to the Holy Lands, but that doesn't prove the Philosopher's Stone is real either. Like my other novels in the Alchemist Chronicles, this story will be rooted in history with equal parts fantasy.

Just like the other stories are inspired by Indiana Jones, *The Davinci Code*, and *National Treasure* romps through history, this story combines my love of Bram Stoker's *Dracula* and Fredrick Manfred's *Lord Grizzly*. Yet my storytelling style requires that the fantasy elements *could* be possible, so that means I enjoy the real history as much as my creative twists.

If you want to learn what's true and what's make-believe, check out my website for insight: www.williswrites.com

I'd like to thank Julie for first bringing me to Transylvania and the following year to the headwaters of the Columbia River near Sinclair Pass. Hopefully the reader will enjoy these trips as much as I did. Next, I want to thank Raven for her curiosity and insight during the developmental edit of the novel, and then Caryl for helping to tighten and polish the story. I'm indebted to this team.

102/2
J. N. Nicollet
Philadelphia May 8th 1843.
Henry D Rogers
Philadelphia
Prof. of Geology. Univ. of Penn?
May 8. 1843
Monsieur J.M. Nicollet
Astronome, Geog: &c &c
Philadelphia 8th May 1843.
Oct 11th Septr 1843
Henry D. Rogers Professor of Geology
University of Pennsylvania
Philadelphia 8th May 1843,

# PART ONE
## A WORLD WITHOUT NICOLLET

# PART ONE

# PROLOGUE

WASHINGTON, DC

July 24, 1843

Joseph Nicollet stopped abruptly and turned to face the sidewalk behind him. A few strangers looked directly at him, but not one adjusted their plans. No one pulled a knife. A gang of thugs did not rush from an alley. Despite his fears, danger did not present itself.

Convinced, he slid his hand into his vest pocket, where he felt the key to his office. Safety was just a short distance away.

On one side of the street, the offices of the US Corps of Topographical Engineers loomed. Inside, many friends and colleagues toiled on maps of the frontier, but his time making maps was over—at least publicly. On the other side, a red brick two-story building sat a few yards off the street. Aside from an address, the building's purpose remained undeclared to the public. Nicollet pivoted on his heels and continued to the front door.

Once he pushed through the double doors, a young clerk looked up from the front desk of the lobby, but recognizing Nicollet's familiar face, he smiled and nodded and went about his business. The building housed a governmental pension distribution center, but a friend-of-a-friend had allocated storage space to Nicollet for his project.

Even though the walk from his apartment had not been exerting, Nicollet perspired and his hands shook. After being stuck in Washington for three years, Nicollet feared the coming expedition would be stopped—which is why he kept it a secret.

He trotted down the stairs to the basement, looked back over his shoulder, and unlocked the solid door. At the center of the large room, eight tables had been gathered to create a large island, leaving him with just enough space to circle the entirety of North America; for he'd assembled a collections of maps to bring the continent to life in front of his eyes.

He lit the closest lantern to confirm nothing was amiss. The central map remained immaculately clean. The smaller tables along the walls contained his personal collections of artifacts and notes from his previous expedition. The contents of the outside tables were diverse, ranging from books, to scientific equipment, to geological samples. He walked over to the other side of the room, lit another lamp, and studied his risky plan already set into motion.

A dozen hand-carved figurines stood upon the map. Nicollet knew as many artists as he did scientists, so finding a sculptor to make the figurines had been easy. When he returned from the frontier in 1840, he commissioned the figurines and enacted his plan. His own figurine stood alone above Washington DC, where it had been for far too long. On the other side of the map, he adjusted the locations of his friends from recent correspondence.

In the Rocky Mountains, his apprentice John C. Fremont captured the attention of a nation as he explored the untamed west. *My red herring.*

Far to the north, near the disputed Canadian border, William Drummond Stewart's figurine, along with Antoine Clement's, searched for the headwaters of the Missouri River. Just south, also in Montana, Jesuit priest Pierre-Jean DeSmet served at a mission for the Sailish Indians. *They draw the eyes of my enemies while I am stuck here.*

Nicollet walked to the north side of the table, inspecting the territory now known as Minnesota. His official governmental map, still in the process of publication, drew attention to the southern part of the state, where he boldly labeled it THE UNDINE REGION.

Pawns like David Faribault and Jim Taopi would soon be on the move, leaving no one to draw attention to the northern part of the state, where Lake Manitou waited for his return. *Two more months, and my part of plan goes into action.*

A sharp knock on the door caused Nicollet to jump out of his skin. The pension office workers rarely interacted with him, so his heart raced as his eyes searched for a weapon. A second knock drew him away from thoughts of defense, and reluctantly, he approached the door.

He placed his foot a short span from the door to serve as a doorstop, reached for the handle, and opened it an inch or two.

A handsome young man with a fop of hair swept across his head stood smiling in the dark doorway. "Professor Nicollet?"

The friendliest face on the 1836 expedition had been the one who tried to murder him. Nicollet defensively kept his foot against the door to say, "I'm busy."

The young man held up a wrapped package with a red ribbon and bow.

"Do I know you?" Nicollet asked.

"No, I haven't had the honor, sir. I'm Julian Glissant, an assistant to Auguste Edouart. I've been in town for the past few days trying to deliver this to you, but—"

"Ah, the Philadelphia silhouette artist. I'd completely forgotten," Nicollet felt the hairs on his neck relax. "Yes, yes, come in." Nicollet opened the door widely, but not in naivety, but so that anything that happened could hopefully be heard by the clerk at the top of the stairs.

Glissant looked around the room, puzzled. "Is there a place I can set it?"

"Set it on Florida," Nicollet pointed to the corner of the map.

"I was given instruction to ensure the art has not received blemish" Glissant said as he began to unwrap the package. "It's been a challenge locating you, sir. I've been to four addresses associated with your name."

"Ah yes. Wealth has not aligned with fame, unfortunately, but my friends often offer their hospitality. How is it you found me here?"

Glissant swallowed hard and did not provide an answer.

A terrifying sign.

The young man continued to unwrap the package. "A fellow by the name of Jean…um…Jean-Louise. Uh, you'll have to excuse me, I didn't pay close attention."

*I was followed here,* Nicollet realized. *Am I in danger?*

With a flourish, Glissant slid out an actual portrait instead of a hidden weapon. Relieved, Nicollet stepped closer to study the two dark figures silhouetted against a tan canvas. In the portrait, Nicollet stood facing Henry Darwin Rogers, the geologist he'd met months earlier back in Philadelphia.

"Do you like it, sir?" Glissant asked at his shoulder.

"Yes. Yes. I look thin and healthy. Auguste could have added a few more inches to my height. But…what I don't understand is why it has been delivered to me here."

"Edouart wanted to make sure you were pleased with it."

As requested, Eduoart drew him holding a map of the lost island continent of Atlantis. "Yes, but this was supposed to be sent to a friend of mine." *John C. Fremont.* "It was meant to be a gift to him." *In case I died trying to retrieve the Philosopher's Stone from Lake Manitou.*

Nicollet felt a chill run down his spine.

The plan had been discovered.

Glissant showed far too much interest to be an actual assistant and his forced smile slowly crept away.

*He's here to kill me.*

Nicollet felt his knees weaken and sat at one of the chairs along the edge of the massive map. His time on the frontier had taught him he had no predatory or self-defense skills. He took his eyes off the young assassin, choosing to focus instead on the portrait. The convention in Philadelphia had been an excuse to privately meet with Henry Darwin Rogers, an expert on thermal springs and geology. Rogers blindly offered his insight into Nicollet's unique collection of vitriol samples and his theories on how geological catastrophes and upheavals had formed the coal fields of the Appalachian Mountains chain.

That had been their first guarded conversation.

But after Nicollet invited him for drinks at the hotel bar, the two men had unguarded conversation about the Great Flood of Genesis, the Epic of Gilgamesh, and a discussion about the Lost Continent of Atlantis. For his part, Rogers enthusiastically vetted Nicollet's numerous theories about human civilizations, empires, and kingdoms existing prior to recorded history. On a whim,

Nicollet and Rogers posed the following day for silhouette artist Auguste Edouart, who captured the likeness of the celebrity scientist. After, Nicollet commissioned Edouart to include him holding a map of Atlantis in his hands—a clue left for his wayward apprentice.

Before Fremont and his friends scattered to the wind, Nicollet posed a theory to them about the legendary Philosopher's Stone, including who made it, when it was made, and why its location mattered.

Now, with his back turned to the assassin, Nicollet gazed upon the island civilization. "'But at a later time, there occurred portentous earthquakes and floods, and in one grievous day the island of Atlantis was swallowed up by the sea and vanished.' Am I about to sink into the sea also?'"

Noting the silence, Nicollet turned to face the young assassin.

Glissant's lips tightened, and his cheek constricted in an attempt to hide a smile. "I'm just a messenger."

"And what is your message?" Nicollet watched for a knife or pistol to be drawn, but Glissant held steady.

"My master wanted to make sure the address was correct. He believes you might've made a mistake in the shipping."

*Am I a paranoid fool? Is this young man truly a servant?* "Cherry Grove, Kentucky," Nicollet said emphatically. "It's the Benton estate—the childhood home of Jessie Fremont."

"I'm glad I came. It turns out you did make a mistake in the shipping address."

"I did?"

"Shouldn't this work of art be sent to Scotland instead?"

Nicollet stifled his gasp and swallowed hard. His eyes betrayed him for a moment as they glanced up past the drawing of Atlantis to the far off figurine of William Drummond Stewart at the headwaters of the Missouri River. "Who are you?"

"As I said. I'm only a messenger sent to confirm—"

"Who sent you?"

"I don't mean to alarm you, Professor Nicollet. I am only a friend of a friend who wants to ensure that your efforts do not go to waste. It would be a shame if a misstep was made at the end of your journey." Glissant looked out over the grand map as if he understood everything about it and the coming expedition.

*A friend of a friend?*

Nicollet thought back to over a decade ago when the chaos of the riots became the July Revolution. A friend had stepped out of the shadows to save his life from a secret society that wanted him killed for his knowledge. The same friend then set him on the quest for a lost treasure. "Are you saying that Fremont is being watched?"

Glissant walked around to the other side of the table, stopping to look at the Minnesota territory—the intended destination for Nicollet's covert expedition. "Your life has been in constant danger for several years now, yet by all accounts, you've succeeded beyond our wildest hopes."

Nicollet sighed in great relief. "I thought you'd come to kill me. Are you here to stop me?"

Glissant shook his head. "Only the Creator can determine the best path, and you must follow His will, but…" Glissant glanced to the west, to Stewart in the north and Fremont in the south. "Even the mighty civilization of Atlantis fell into the sea, a symbol that even the greatest will one day end. As much as we'd like for you to go to Rome and personally share your discoveries, our sources know what you are planning next."

"Should we send the portrait to Council Bluffs?" Nicollet asked, eyeing the figurine of Jesuit Missionary Pierre-Jean DeSmet. "Obviously, DeSmet told you about the plans for my next expedition. Surely, he could be trusted."

Years ago, when Nicollet was just a boy, his family risked everything to save a group of Jesuit priests from the mobs of the French Revolution, but it hadn't been the Society of Jesus who saved his life from the mob in the subsequent July Revolution, it had been a clandestine organization independent of the Catholic Church—the Periphery. "The Jesuits do have a curiosity about the old legends, but we are concerned how they would behave if someone other than DeSmet did in fact come into possession of…your portrait."

"Is there something you need to tell me about my young apprentice?"

"Captain Fremont is a loyal friend, but our enemies watch his every move. His popularity grows, and so does attention given to him. If he were to receive anything from you, it would be known, especially a portrait with such…obvious…value."

The Periphery challenged him to find the physical location of an ancient map. "My governmental map—it is set to be published with some fairly obvious value written upon it." *The Undine Region. LeSueur. Lahontan. Blue Earth.*

"Let me speak plainly: The Order of Eos, the Priory of Ormus, the Jesuits…they've known about the Undine Region for centuries now, so your map will only appear as an independent confirmation of their theories. And if you happen to return to the Undine Region and determine that the Philosopher's Stone was not lost off the coast of Bermuda but in fact, remained hidden away in some secret cave, little would change. However…" Glissant walked back around the table, stopping beside Nicollet, to point his finger directly upon the Island of Atlantis. "Neither our enemies nor our allies have been able to sift through the centuries of tainted knowledge to correctly discern the purpose of the Stone."

"Surely you don't believe this portrait reveals such secrets?"

"We understood your reference. Those who search for the Stone have their own theories about its purpose, and this portrait will only enflame their curiosity. It proves to us that you were the right man for the job when we plucked you from the riots in Paris. Your success in scouring the frontier has alarmed both your allies and enemies. By holding the map of Atlantis, you propose a theory to whoever looks upon it."

"And what does the Periphery believe I'm referencing with my portrait?"

"Atlantis…Hyperborea…Thule…the tales all go back to the same legend, don't they? With a portait of you holding such a map, you're suggesting to both enemy and ally that the quest is not just about finding the Philosopher's Stone but also about finding the resting place of the man who made it."

Nicollet nodded. "I met a wise old man out on the prairie who vexed me with this very thought: what is the purpose of the Stone? So when I found a haunted place out on the frontier where an

ancient spirit slumbers, it made me realize is not *what* they are searching for, but instead, *who* they are searching for that truly matters."

"And you are determined to test your hypothesis, Professor Nicollet?"

"To my dying breath."

"Young Fremont is noble, but he is too close to your enemies to continue the quest," Glissant said, studying the map. "We do not know what DeSmet and the Jesuits would do with such knowledge, and those in Minnesota do not have the resources to act if your theory is correct. So we must insist that you send this portrait to Scotland."

*The Periphery worries about me dying.* "You want Captain Billy to be Plan B if I die?"

Glissant rolled his eyes. "We know about Stewart's baptism in St. Louis and subsequent trip to the Middle East. We also realized you've used him as another red herring, sending him far up the Missouri to confuse your enemies. If Atlantis does fall and in a day sinks into the ocean, we'd like him to possess this portrait. Lord Stewart's dedication to you is known, and his independent wealth could make him a formidable asset in the days to come. Let him continue your work."

Nicollet looked over his elaborate extraction plan to acquire the Philosopher's Stone and to discover the location of a lost tomb, and the audacity of it all temporarily stole his nerves. "Yes, send it to William."

Glissant immediately began packing up the portrait while the forlorn Nicollet sat in a chair. The young man finished and nodded his head to Nicollet. "May the Grace of God fall upon your endeavors."

As soon as the young man left, Nicollet felt a bit of optimism. Instead of focusing on his many mistakes, he thought of the brief time he'd spent at Lake Manitou. Everyone from the Periphery to Chagobay wanted him to solve the mystery, but fear of the unknown made him hesitate.

Had he acted a few years earlier, he might've failed, but thinking about the quest for the past few years gave him clarity.

Succeed or fail, the Periphery would still be there. Stewart would continue the quest.

But Nicollet didn't plan on failing.

In just a few more weeks, he'd return to the frontier to test his ultimate theory.

# CHAPTER 1

FLORISSANT, MISSOURI

1852

Xavier Clement lifted the splintered log onto the chopping block and carefully balanced it. Although his shoulders ached, he wanted to prove to his older brothers that he was man enough to care for his elderly father, which meant chopping enough wood to keep the farmhouse warm through the frigid month of January.

His axhead sank into the log three inches and remained stuck, forcing him to lift ax and log a foot off the chopping block and hammer it down until the wedged blade forced itself deeper into the wood grain and the log split. He was thankful his brothers didn't see his dearth of skill and strength.

When he bent down to pick up the two pieces of wood, he saw a single rider approaching. The Clement farm was tucked away along the Missouri river, which meant there were few travelers on the dead end road.

*An unexpected guest*, Xavier realized, hoping that it meant a big supper and bigger stories.

The rider approached slowly and stayed on his horse to ask, "Is this the home of Antoine Clement?"

Xavier didn't know the rider. The thin man with a dark beard looked miserably cold in a jacket far too thin for the weather. Xavier reckoned the fellow had ridden out from St. Louis. "It is. Is my father expecting you?"

The rider shook his head. "I carry an international dispatch intended for your father. Is he inside the house?"

"No, he's stacking wood in the barn," Xavier said, pointing to the structure on the edge of the trees. "Who's it from?"

"Do you know the name Baron William Drummond Stewart?"

Xavier nodded enthusiastically. Although his parents openly despised the Baron for stealing away his eldest brother to the frontier, Xavier had read all about the Baron's adventures into the wilderness in old newspapers and pictured his brother with his hunting rifle alongside the nobleman.

The rider smiled. "Finish chopping your wood. I can find my way to the barn."

The house had been built on a small hill to protect against spring flooding, and several acres of land had been cleared for raising crops. Crossing frozen ground on his horse, the rider spanned the distance in a few gracefull gallops.

Xavier had last seen his oldest brother four years ago when the famed sharpshooter went from hunter to soldier to fight in the Mexican War. Any news was welcome, and he eagerly jogged after the rider to find out the contents of the correspondence.

"Antoine Clement!" the rider shouted out from his horse when he reached the barn.

Xavier's father slowly rolled the big front door of the barn open and stood in the opening.

Still foolishly holding onto the ax with both hands, the boy was breathing too loudly to hear the conversation.

The dispatch rider held out a letter, and when his father stepped out to accept it, the rider pulled out a pistol and fired three shots into his father's chest.

Xavier felt as if his own chest received the impact of the bullets.

His father fell back and the dispatch rider fired three more shots into his father's still body.

The rider still hadn't noticed him, but the horse sensed danger approaching and began to turn. Still in a full sprint, Xavier pulled back the ax and let out a gutteral cry of anguish and rage.

The startled horse reared up, lost its footing, and fell. The rider remained trapped in the saddle as the horse fell on his leg and hip, breaking the rider's bones from the weight.

His father's blood covered the ground. The killer hadn't missed a single shot.

Seeing Xavier approach, the killer tried to twist his broken body to aim his pistol. The pistol clicked on an empty chamber.

Xavier swung the ax.

Splitting a man's head was much easier than splitting logs.

Despite the twitches from the killer's body, Xavier knew the man was also dead.

"Father," he muttered to the still air and took several steps closer to his slain father. "Help! Help! He killed father! He killed father!"

In the distance, help came too late. His mother and sisters emerged from the house while his older brothers Joseph and Basil appeared from their log cabins on the edge of the farmstead.

The letter floated on the ground near Xavier's feet. He tossed the ax and snatched the letter. Instead being addressed to Antoine, the letter was addressed to Lawrence Barkwell of St. Louis—the killer—and instead of coming from Lord Stewart in Scotland, it had come from a place called Oxford House. Although Xavier caught only bits and phrases, he clearly noticed "how to find Antoine Clement's property near St. Louis."

His mother's scream drew him away from the letter.

His brothers sprinted to their slain father.

Before any of them reached Xavier, he had the mystery figured out. No one in their right mind would hurt an eighty-year-old man, but his oldest brother—Antoine Clement Junior—had made many enemies during his time on the frontier.

*He meant to kill my brother…but why?*

# CHAPTER 2

OPATIJA, CROATIA

1852

An hour before dawn, Pyotr Petrov woke naked, tearing the sheet from his bed and immediately dropping to the cold floor. His hands spread wide to caress the stone and his arms began doing push-ups before his clouded mind fully woke. He quickly found his rhythm of a push-up per second, and within several minutes, he'd done several hundred lifts.

He counted each one.

After ten minutes, he flipped over. His toes caught the edge of the bed, and he began his routine of sit ups, followed by squats and pull ups. His body glistened with sweat but his lungs maintained a steady breathing flow. He quickly toweled off, dressed, and stepped out into the darkness.

After a few steps, he sprinted.

His mind now fully cogent, he plotted an erratic path through the city of Opatija. He took alleys, side streets, main streets—all at full speed. The more obstacles, the better. He lept benches, hurdled walls, and climbed fences, all while maintaining the fastest pace he could manage. When he reached Kvarner Bay, his piston legs slowed, and he took in great gasps of air to fuel his weary muscles.

The town began to wake prior to the sun's appearance..

His routine ended on a dock in the marina. He fell to his belly, reached down to the water, and splashed his face until he was refreshed. Cleansed, he walked steadily to the new Hotel Scarpa.

Like all the other workers, Pyotr avoided the grand entrance and walked around the magnificent building to the rear entrance. The kitchen staff already toiled over breakfast and none of them took notice of him as he entered. He kept a steady pace on his way to the cloak room, and very discreetly, he slid a knife from the counter and tucked it along the underside of his forearm.

None of the other waitstaff had arrived yet. He quickly changed into his simple uniform and tucked the blade away. However tempting it might have been to shove the steel up through the chin of the headwaiter, Pyotr knew the blade had been procured for another. The good news was he would soon to be dismissed from service at the resort.

Instead of waiting for the breakfast shift to begin, he slipped out of the hotel as quietly as he'd entered and found his way down to nearby the water.

The shore of Kvarner Bay was rocky with walls of green rising right from the watery depths. However scenic, it was not Ibiza, Majorca, or Sardinia, yet the deep water of the bay allowed the wealthy and elite to sail right up to the isolated city to be served and pampered. The rugged coast also allowed Pyotr a place to hide.

Two days earlier, after a ridiculous shift of training, he confirmed his target. Yesterday, after flashing dimples at the ladies for the day, he listened to enough breakroom gossip to know where his target stayed. Pyotr wasn't fool enough to wait in a closet to stab the target to death in bed, so he quickly formulated another plan for the assassination.

He walked past the stone patio where rows of chairs waited for the sunbathers to arrive. Its concrete steps allowed swimmers to enter the deep waters and escape the hot sun. Past the large patio, bungalows were tucked away along the hill, connected by a series of trails back to the main building. Pyotr stepped off the trail at the third natural grotto and hid discreetly in the bushes.

*Waiting is my favorite part of the hunt.*

From his position, Petrov watched the sunrise in the east from the opposite side of Kvarner Bay. The waters became busy with boat traffic and soon, the small coastal village also came to life.

Somewhere, back in the kitchens, his absence was certainly noted and he'd lose a job he never desired.

Had a stranger strolled into the resort, security would have intercepted, but he, having gone to the effort of being hired as a waiter, now belonged.

Noise came from the bungalow—the visitors finally woke.

From the height of the sun, Pyotr estimated it to be late morning. Finally, the dark-haired man—his target—emerged from the bungalow followed by two others. The two younger men, already deep in conversation, came down the steps and headed for the main building of the resort. His dark-haired target, however, came down the steps, crossed the path, and took the stone steps down to the secluded pool.

The area was a natural grotto with rocky walls, dense foliage, and a window to the bay. His target held a Bible in one hand and a saucer of coffee in the other. The man dressed modestly: a white cotton tunic and white pantaloons over a pair of dark bathing shorts. He had arrived nine days ago on a two week vacation and had quickly established a predictable routine. Pyotr Petrov had arrived three days ago, first going to the prison, and then to the local police station to ensure the coming narrative would make the newspapers all the way back in Scotland.

Pyotr watched the man sip his coffee for a few moments and counted the time it would take for the other men to be seated at the nearby restaurant. When his target finished his coffee, he set the cup aside and held the Bible with both hands as he silently prayed. Then he ripped off his cotton tunic, slipped his pantaloons off, and stepped down into his private bathing pool. Once the man dove into the water, Pyotr stood up from his hiding place and advanced on the man's belongings.

His target emerged ten yards from shore, and after a breath, he submerged again.

Pyotr picked up the man's Bible and waited.

His target wiped his face clear of water and paused when he saw the interloper standing in his private grotto.

"Excuse me," the man called out in English in a soft voice. "Those are my belongings."

"Lord Stewart?" Pyotr questioned just to confirm his assumptions.

The target swam back a few strokes until he could stand. "Do I know you?"

"Are you Lord William Drummond Stewart of Perthshire?"

"What?" The man's face grew agitated. "Yes, I'm Lord Stewart."

"Then this is now mine," Pyotr said, turning with the Bible still in his possession to draw Stewart in.

"Excuse me! Where do you think you're going with that? That is my personal Bible."

Pyotr didn't run. He could hear Stewart angrily sloshing through the water. His thievery ended once he heard Stewart emerge from the water. Flashing his dimples, Pyotr turned and extended the Bible to the thin Scottish nobleman. "I'm only teasing you, m'Lord."

He'd read that Stewart had thinning black hair and a mustache, which had obviously been shaved for his sojourn away from home. As soon as Lord Stewart snatched away the Bible, Pyotr knelt down, not in obeisance, but to find his long dagger tucked into his boot.

In one quick motion, Pyotr punched the blade into Stewart's left ribcage. With the Bible clutched in both hands, Stewart offered no defense for the second and third stabbing.

William Drummond Stewart collapsed.

Even though the dagger hit lung and heart, Pyotr leaned in until he was almost nose-to-nose with his victim.

"The Goddess Columbia sent me to give you this," Pyotr said, kissing the dying man upon his forehead before running the blade of the dagger across the man's throat.

Pyotr Petrov dropped the blade, turned, and dove into the water, swimming out of the grotto before anyone was the wiser.

# CHAPTER 3

GALVESTON, TEXAS

1852

Frank Penny pulled out a tin of beeswax, scooped a bit into his fingertips, and carefully applied it to the tips of a mustache, spinning the strands until the tops were as sharp as horns.

He took once last look at his reflected image in the general store window, adjusted his tie, and brushed off his golden vest. As he walked across the street, the red tassels on his pants created a whooshing noise, and if his golden vest and mustache didn't draw attention, his pants certainly did.

Feeling like a million dollars, Frank burst into Galveston Jail whistling one of his favorite songs.

"Hello there, young fella," the man behind the desk greeted him. "What can I do for you?"

"Is Sheriff McGuffin in his office?"

"And who would like to know?"

"Frank Penny. My father is Ebenezer Penny of Allen's Landing. Sheriff McGuffin and my father fought together during the Texas Revolution."

Frank didn't even have to finish the next sentence for he heard boots in the hallway. "General Penny's boy?"

"In the flesh, sir. My father says we've met but I was only a wee lad at the time."

"If you don't look like your father! I hear your father's businesses are doing well. I still can't believe they're calling the city

Houston rather than Allen's Landing. So what brings you down to Galveston?"

"First things first," Frank began and pulled a satchel off his hip and over his head. He opened it and produced a leather wallet stuffed with money. "My father would like to make a contribution to the sheriff's department and your reelection campaign."

"Now I understand why you're armed to the teeth," Sheriff McGuffin said, noting the two pistols on each hip and the big Bowie knife strapped to his leg.

"It's a dangerous world out there. My two dimples must make me look like an easy target, so my pistols will show folks I'm a serious fellow."

"I see," Sheriff McGuffin said, inspecting the leather wallet. He accepted with a grin. "It's hard to believe a man as young as yourself served in the war."

"Yessir. I rode with the California Lancers."

"So I deduced from your golden vest. You can wear it proudly from what I hear."

"It so happens that I'm also here on another matter connected to the Mexican War."

"How so?"

"My father hired a private investigator to track down a fellow I once served with who didn't come home after the war. Rumor has it you're holding a fellow by the name of Bill Brunia, a halfbred."

"The ogre?" the desk clerk interjected. "Yes, we've got Bill Brown serving two years for crippling three men in a bar fight."

"You might not believe it, but that ogre was one of the best marksmen in the war. He served with valour but had issues with drinking. He is a dear friend of my father's friend, and it turns out he's come into an inheritance."

"Bill Brunia?" Sheriff McGuffin asked, holding the wad of money.

"My father would like me to bring him home so we can clean him up and set him on a better path."

"How much of his sentence remains?" Sheriff McGuffin asked the clerk.

"Five months, but he eats enough for two grown men, so the way I reckon, I'd sooner be rid of him than keep him."

"I don't know if I dare turn down an order from General Penny. It warms my heart to know your father still remembers me."

"I believe it was Shakespeare who described men who served together in war as a 'Band of Brothers.' Bill Brown is like a brother to me."

"Then I'll release him into your possession."

"Could I first speak with him? For all I know, you've got the wrong Bill Brown in there."

"Absolutely, come. I'll bring you to him."

The Galveston Jail consisted of three cells. "Tough times, indeed," Sheriff McGuffin said before turning. "Give me a holler when you're ready."

"Brunia," Penny said loudly enough to get the ogre to stir. "My father pieced the name together. Brunia was an alias you used during your time in the Minnesota territory. What was the other? Missabay? And Bill…that's short for William."

Frank Penny had never met Antoine Clement, Jr., but he'd seen the paintings of the hunter made by Alfred Jacob Miller. The ogre in front of him appeared to be in his forties with long black hair and the copper skin tone of a Metis.

"You've got the wrong man," he said to Penny. "Can you picture me on a horse prancing around in a gold vest?"

"No, but I can picture you alongside William Drummond Stewart out on the frontier. I invented that part of the tale. But some of my story is true. Are you Antoine Clement?"

"Who? I don't know what you're talking about kid. My name is Bill Brown."

"Look, if I wanted to, I could have come in here guns-a-blazing. Even now, I could pop a few slugs in you and shoot my way out of here. Before you are released, though, I need to confirm your identity."

"Fuck off," he muttered and rolled onto his back to face the ceiling.

"Apparently, you have unfinished business at a place called…hmm…" Frank pulled out the letter for a quick reference. "at a place called Lake Manitou."

"Who are you?"

"The son of a friend of a friend. We've never met, so let me properly introduce myself. I'm Frank Nicollet Penny. My father met the real Joseph Nicollet in 1833, but that was a year before I was born. I've been tasked with finding you and bringing you back to Scotland."

"Why would I want to go to Scotland?"

"Your enemies are hunting you. In a case of mistaken identity, your father, Antoine Clement Senior, was killed in cold blood at his farm in Florissant, Missouri."

"What?"

His reaction was all the confession Penny needed. "A random killer put six bullets into your father believing it was you. You're one of the world's most wanted men, apparently, with a large enough bounty that'll make men chase you to a Galveston jail. I'm lucky I found you first."

"But father is an old man."

"Once again, a case of mistaken identity, and desperate men will do desperate things when your name has a small fortune attached to it."

"Who did this?" Clement asked, rising to his feet, filling the space in the jail cell. His father had told him the man was a giant. Now he understood.

"The same men who poisoned Professor Nicollet, likely. Afterwards, you took revenge on the men responsible, didn't you?"

"They killed my father?" Clement repeated.

"Yes, and you can have your revenge if you come with me. What do you say?"

"Get me out of this shit hole," Clement muttered, "Tell me more about the men who killed my father."

△<br>20

# CHAPTER 4



Karl Andreas Geyer passively endured most funerals, but this one was different. He honestly loved the man who was being put in the ground.

Outside the carriage window, the old forest reflected the gloom in his heart. The road followed the Tay River, a sign the journey was coming to an end. Since arriving in Edinburgh, civilization had all but vanished with rugged mountains and tall trees filling the window.

*Why did Stewart travel all the way to America when he had this in his backyard?*

Geyer held many mysteries in his heart, which is why he'd finally found the motivation to leave Meissen, Germany after so many years in social isolation.

"Are we there yet?"

Geyer flinched, almost forgetting his young wife Emma had accompanied him. Twenty years his junior, Emma kept her vestal figure after five years of marriage. When Geyer had returned home after a decade on the American frontier, he'd been a lean explorer in his mid-thirties with his pick of any maiden in Dresden. Just like his botanical collection, he'd carefully studied the landscape, finding the most beautiful flower in the field. Even now, after sleeping for two hours in a carriage, Emma's blonde curls, alabaster face, ruby lips, and inquisitive blue eyes remained the ideal qualities of her Germanic stock.

Geyer, however, had not aged as well in five years.

"We've been there for the past twenty minutes," he answered and then yawned. "That last village was the gate to the estate."

Emma's eyes widened. "Are we really staying in a castle tonight?"

He grinned at her enthusiasm. "Mind you, it won't be like German castles. Do you see those monstrous old oak trees in the distance? That's the last of Birnam Woods."

"From *MacBeth*?"

"Yes, from *MacBeth*. Unlike castles in Germany, this region of Scotland is for those who wanted to get away from the trappings of civilization. This region has remained untouched to act as a hunting preserve for the lords of Europe to visit." It'd also stayed the same since he'd last visited Stewart on his return from America.

"Ah, did the real MacBeth live near here?"

Geyer chuckled. "No, Inverness is still another seventy miles north of here."

"So Malcolm hacked down branches from Birnam Woods and carried them for another seventy miles. What is the point in that?"

"You'd have to ask Shakespeare, my dear, but I'd guess that there was symbolism in the untouched woods of Birnam. Perhaps there are still witches hiding behind those big oaks."

Emma sat up and stared out the window, which reminded Geyer that she was still a child at heart.

Emma loved his stories more than she'd ever loved him, and in recent years, he'd run out of stories to tell. During their courtship, she'd prop her chin upon both hands and listen to him describe the wild Indians, the grassy plains, the towering Rockies, and the roaring rivers. After marriage, she'd pry more tales from him, making him wonder if she kept an investigative journal hidden away in the house for each name and place he'd been. Despite the warm fire of nostalgia, the painful flames of memory became too much. One day when she pressed him about Nicollet, he snapped, "Enough!"

The trip to Scotland was his last chance to save his failing marriage.

"It's beautiful," Emma kept repeating, her hand gripping his knee as she leaned out the window for better angles. Having seen both sides of the Atlantic, Geyer agreed. The estate was right out of dream, with manicured lawns, rows of pruned trees, sculpted shrubs, and centuries of disposable wealth planted in polished marble monuments. The carriage stopped in a courtyard where the L shaped castle filled both windows.

Servants came hustling out of the doors. An even broader smile graced Emma's face, and when the door opened, she almost burst from the carriage and spun like a ballerina once on solid ground.

Geyer groaned as he slid forward in his seat, waiting for a young footman to appear. "I have a weak knee," he said with a pained smile. The footman nodded in affirmation with a training that hid the reality of the situation—Geyer had grown obese. Using the young man as leverage, Geyer kicked his foot out to the step and paused long enough for another footman to appear. Together, the two young men balanced him as he stepped off the rail and then also served as cushioned brakes as he lurched forward. Geyer heard the carriage shift as he stepped off.

He felt all their eyes upon him as he caught his breath.

*They can all go to hell. I've traveled the world with great men.*

Emma quickly regained the spotlight as she naïvely clapped and jumped with joy.

Two figures stepped from the main doorway of the castle.

One he knew by reputation. Lady Stewart wore a red velvet dress cut low enough that her cleavage threatened to spill out as she descended the stairs. According to the stories he'd been told on the prairie, Lady Stewart was the furthest thing from being a lady. Born in the gateway village of Perthshire, Christina Battersby began life as a peasant. Once puberty arrived, the voluptuous maid caught the eye of young William Stewart, and in every possible corner of the estate, the two young lovers explored their sexuality together. Even after William's tastes evolved, the two remained close. Their secret relationship, however, was exposed when she got pregnant with his child.

Instead of rejecting her, William Drummond Stewart stood with her, which brought the wrath of his father and older brother. The second son soon found himself banished to America, leaving

Christina to raise their son in shame in Edinburgh. When Stewart's father and brother died, and William inherited the estate and title, he stood behind her and elevated his former lover to the Lady of Murthly.

"Welcome," Christina Battersby Stewart said with an authentic smile. The voluptuous former maid now had wide hips and a double-chin from a life of luxury, but her eyes still laughed and her dimpled cheeks remained a testament to her youthful beauty. "We're honored to host you. Would you prefer refreshments or to retire to your room?"

"Oh, I could use some refreshments," Emma said before turning around to receive Geyer's approval.

The second figure also needed no introduction, even though Geyer had never interacted with Jamie Anderson. The four-foot-tall dwarf stood beside Lady Stewart, who greeted Emma warmly, and with just a glance at Jamie, unspoken orders were relayed. Jamie stepped forward with an extended hand, shaking hands with Geyer while saying, "I'm to bring you to the Hunting Lodge."

And off Emma and her luggage went into the castle.

Fortunately, Jamie Anderson kept a slow pace over the great western lawn. His short legs allowed Geyer to keep pace easily.

"You're the German Botanist, aren't you?" Jamie asked after a few yards of silence.

"Yes, I explored half of a continent with both Stewart and Nicollet." Almost a decade after Nicollet's death, it still pained him to say the man's name.

"Ah, I guess that explains it."

"Explains what?"

"I've met many of Stewart's friends."

"And?"

Jamie opened his mouth but instead of answering, he smiled, commenting, "You have a lovely wife… As lovely as a doll. I'll be your host during your stay, and if there is anything either of you needs, I can certainly provide it."

*Is he insinuating sex?* The "fool of Murthly" had been Stewart's companion since the Battle of Waterloo. After the Napoleonic Wars, Captain Billy returned with his young French friend, who had no official role at the estate other than collecting eggs and stealing the virginity of the maids. Although French, Jamie now wore a black kilt and black socks.

"Mrs. Geyer and I are happily married," Geyer insisted.

"Of course you are, and I am sure you're tired from your travels. I've entertained noblemen here at Murthly Castle for the past twenty years, so I understand what it means when a man remains a bachelor until his forties—and then takes a young bride."

"I'm not sure what you mean." Geyer looked up, realizing how far removed the Hunting Lodge was from the main castle.  Even though William had been Lord of Murthly for almost two decades now, his bitterness toward his family led to him claiming the Hunting Lodge as his preferred home, leaving the trappings of wealth to his guests.

"You've lived an exciting life, no doubt, and after a trip across the channel, these accumulated years of travel would even leave Hermes exhausted. A young woman like Mrs. Geyer, however, has youthful needs."

"Stay away from my wife," Geyer nearly shouted. He felt his ears turning red from agitation.

"Of course. Of course. I didn't mean anything, but I know trips to a wild estate like Murthly can bring out a certain wildness in guests who crave adventure. Even for those who would only like to watch something adventurous."

"I'm here to pay my respects, not to seek an adventure."

"Yes, yes. I know. I know. I know all about your adventures on the frontier as a discreet traveling companion. I'm just letting you know that I'm also a very discreet traveling companion."

"Mr. Anderson!"

"Lord Stewart told me to show you all courtesies, and I obviously misread those instructions. I'll stay away from your wife," the dwarf finally relented, and the two continued the half mile trek across the lawn until reaching a small stone building with a large sign: Warning! Keep out!

"This is the Buffalo Hut," Anderson said, stepping inside to grab a large pitcher of water. Without asking, he poured a glass for his guest and then another for himself.

Geyer quickly guzzled the water. "Buffalo Hut?"

"When Captain Billy returned from America the first time, he brought back two Indians and a small herd of the North American Bison," Anderson explained. "This was not only a safe place to hide from the beasts if caught out in the field but also a home for the Indian shepherds. While Captain Billy was abroad, the bull and cows tripled the size of the herd in just a few short years, but one spring, the big bull broke down the fence and killed the gardener. The whole herd was put down after that. Did you ever see a buffalo while out on the frontier?"

Geyer sudden felt more of a man. "I did. Joseph Nicollet and I came across a herd that might have been a hundred thousand in number. We climbed up onto a massive boulder and watched the beasts flow around us. It was the day we met Chief Wahanantan of the Yanktons."

Jamie Anderson studied him for a few moments as if he could discern lies.

Geyer didn't need to lie.

"The Hunting Lodge is on the other side of the ridge, down by the river," Jamie said and began walking across the second field.

Geyer could see both the river below and the single three-story turret of the lodge peering through the tallest pines. He'd always known William Drummond Stewart came from a wealthy family, but now he finally understood why the wild Scot had been so irreverent around the St. Louis elites. His hunting cottage was grander than the finest estate west of the Mississippi River.

Including the shooting tower, the hunting lodge was three stories high with three visible rooms on the second story and a large living room and kitchen on the main floor. A few horses were hitched to the post near the front door, and smoke came from the big chimney, a sign of other guests for the funeral.

Both Geyer and Anderson were breathing heavily when they stepped up onto the porch. To give himself time to catch his breath, Geyer asked Anderson a question, "Is Fremont attending?" All of Nicollet's companions had unfinished business still, but in the nine years, Fremont had become a celebrity.

"No, the former Senator is returning to his California ranch to placate dissatisfied constituents," Anderson explained, showing off his girth of gossip and vocabulary in one statement. "But others say it is to pan for gold. You knew the Pathfinder, didn't you?"

Fremont seemed only a boy in those days. "I knew him well. I'm sure he'll be a great leader for the people of California."

The dwarf opened the door.

The mounted heads of two dozen exotic beasts lined the dark walls of the massive living room, and swords, rifles, and pistols decorated a stone fireplace. Pine furniture and decorations brought memories of Joseph Renville's cabin out on the headwaters of the Minnesota River.

Three strangers already waited in the lodge.

One—a lean, handsome man in his thirties—sat in a chair nearest the fire with his feet propped up on an ottoman and a thick book in his hands. With black eyes and a black beard, he glanced up, looked at Geyer and Anderson for just a moment, and then returned to his book without so much as a nod.

Geyer rebuttoned his jacket.

Another—an even younger man—was passed out on the couch with a half-dozen empty bottles, a large cowboy hat, and a pair of colt pistols on the nearby table. With sandy hair and a smooth face, the boy appeared to barely be out of puberty.

The third man was stocky—in his sixties without a stitch of hair upon his head but with a thick goatee upon his chin. He groaned as he rose from his plush chair. He grabbed a notebook and a large coffee cup before walking over to Geyer. He stopped in front of them, glanced down at his notebook, and read aloud, "Karl Andreas Geyer, the gardener from Zabeltitz."

Jamie chuckled, repeating the word in broken syllables, "Zabel tits."

"Sergeant Lewis Cairns, formerly of the Cold Stream Regiment of Footguards," the older man said with a crushing grip on Geyer's hand.

"And I'm the gardener," Geyer surrendered to the diminished title.

"Sergeant Cairns once tried to kill me," Jamie explained, "and I don't think a day goes by that he doesn't regret it. This gruff old billy goat is in charge of security at the estate. Together, we're the eyes and ears of Murthly."

Sergeant Cairns ignored the fool. "I can assume you heard about the details of the murder in Croatia. After the funeral and dedication tomorrow, there is going to be a briefing. You are to be here immediately after supper."

News of murders came in the same letter as the news about the funeral service. Even in Germany, it was not safe to be an associate of Professor Nicollet. "How long is this briefing going to last?"

"There will be entertainment for your young wife back at the castle—"

To which Jamie Anderson grinned widely and Geyer grunted.

"The situation has grown a little complicated, which we referenced in the letter, but we are not prepared to sit back and let these vile attacks continue. We're prepared to go on the offensive, which is what the others are talking about down by the river. Come, they'll want to know that our illustrious botanist has arrived."

Sergeant Cairns stepped out the backdoor of the lodge, where a scene of previous revelry remained strewn across the back porch. A narrow path through the trees led to the river, and at a landing built along the shore of the river, two ghosts sat on large adirondack chairs.

One ghost had been murdered by an escaped prisoner while vacationing in Croatia.

The other ghost had died a few years earlier during the Mexican War.

"Lord Stewart," Geyer rushed forward to hug his old friend. Looking over William Drummond Stewart's shoulder, he looked into the eyes of another old friend. "Mr. Clement."

# CHAPTER 5



Antoine Clement understood the pain of loss, and he buried it deep down while the others wept openly in the pews of the chapel. Instead of allowing the memories of the dead to soften his heart, he used the pain to harden his resolve for vengeance.

He stood along the back wall of the Chapel of St. Anthony the Eremite as the private ceremony neared its end. Though the stone building was centuries old, William Drummond Stewart had poured the last of his disposable wealth into refreshing the sacred structure with burgundy paint for the walls, yellow paint for the tall, two-story windows, and light blue for the tiled trim. Designed by architect James Gillespie Graham, the ornate ceiling now had refinished, varnished wood beams, and above the altar, a massive mural painting showing the conversion of Constantine. The curtains were the same color as Joseph Nicollet's green velvet vests—a frivolous show of love.

At the front of the renovated church, Jean Nicholas Nicollet's little body was ready for reburial in the place where the old chapel met the new chapel.

Everything fell apart after Nicollet's death. While William Drummond Stewart threw himself into the designs of the new chapel, Clement had thrown himself into a bottle of whiskey after his brother Francois Clement also died in a freak accident. His grief sent him to Mexico, where he could murder and drink to his heart's content—all under the guise of war. He quickly sobered up in a Mexican prisoner of war camp, and following the Treaty of Guadalupe Hidalgo, was released in 1848, only to end up in a Texas jail after a night of drunken rage. A young Frank Penny showed up with a letter and wad of cash to bring Clement back to Scotland, but Antoine insisted on visiting his family in St. Louis before making the voyage across the Atlantic Ocean.

The assassin meant to kill him—not Antoine Clement, Sr. His father had been a lowly trapper who saved all of his money to return to St. Louis. He'd never threatened the lives of some of the most powerful men on the continent—that'd been his son's handiwork. Yet his father had been killed in cold blood by an assassin.

Now, because of what happened to Stewart's brother, Clement knew he'd finally be unleashed on his enemies.

*The same men who killed my father are the men who killed Nicollet. We should have killed that entire family in Detroit…*

*Now, I'm going to be part of another war.*

Although Nicollet had been dead for almost a decade, William Drummond Stewart insisted it was time to bring the scientist's body to a better resting place. It was the plan back in 1845 when the renovations began, but following the murder of his younger brother Thomas Drummond Stewart in Croatia, plans were hastened.

The louder that Stewart wept up in the front row, the more that Clement feared the coming reaction.

When he was just a boy, Antoine Clement allowed his heart to creep all the way up into his throat as he wailed for the death of his mother, Starlight. She was the daughter of a powerful Cree chieftain, who gave her to Antoine, Sr. as a business alliance. Even as a child Antoine, Jr. was large compared to other boys his age, earning him the nickname Brunia and Missabay from his mother. He was only five in 1811 when she died. He ended up staying with his Cree relatives for the better part of a decade until his father rescued him and brought him to St. Louis in 1821. His father re-married Mary-Elizabeth Dumont, raised three more children, and farmed until an assassin murdered him in the barn.

*Revenge won't bring my father back, but it will help me forget the past,* Clement thought as Nicollet's private funeral continued.

"Oremus," MacPherson began, drawing Clement's brief attention. Just as he knew several other languages, Clement had attended enough funerals to know Latin. Hearing the Rite for Burial reminded him of his slain father. "Per Christum Dominum nostrum."

The small congregation echoed "amen" together.

Ross MacPherson finished the ceremony, reciting the Latin ceremony as if a legitimate priest. The square-faced, bearded official, although still in his mid twenties, had a receding hairline. Like the rest of Stewart's "band of merry men," MacPherson was a flawed genius. Over the past few weeks, MacPherson and Stewart endlessly debated scripture and drank until one relented or grew sick. Young MacPherson did not, however, wear a priestly collar. A few weeks earlier, the new chapel had been publicly dedicated by Bishop Carruthers. The burial of Thomas Drummond Stewart followed. For all the world knew, Nicollet still rested in a grave in Washington DC, and all of the invited guests knew the importance of keeping the fact a secret.

The idea of a priest asking for Nicollet's soul to be delivered from evil agitated Clement. While he'd been a sinner for most of his life, and Stewart even more so, he couldn't think of any unChristian thought, word, or deed from the little scientist. In fact, Nicollet's grace had hit Clement upside the head like an oar and his life had never been the same since.

*This chapel suits a man of his greatness.*

The ceremony's ending caught Clement off guard, and before he knew it, two-dozen people were flowing past him, offering condolences and kind words. Those in attendance knew what Nicollet meant to Clement. He'd gone from being Nicollet's protector during the 1836 expedition to running across the world like an errand boy. He shrugged it all off since he needed his hatred to fuel revenge for his father and Nicollet. Finally, Stewart and Geyer approached with their wives.

"We'll meet in the Hunting Lodge after supper," Stewart said.

*As if I'd forget.* Clement sullenly nodded.

Clement was tasked with placing Nicollet in the tomb. Clement had been a poor Indian his whole life, so he didn't mind being treated like a servant, especially when the task involved Nicollet. Stewart was far from racist, sexist, or classist, so there was no offense in the request. Stewart knew Clement better than any other man did, so he also understood how Clement detested social gatherings.

Four hired men came out from the older portion of the chapel to begin slipping straps and winches into place.

Ross MacPherson, the collarless priest, waited up front. Like Clement, he didn't belong to the same class as the guests. "It sounds like Nicollet was an extraordinary man. I wish I could have met him."

Clement grunted and assisted the workers in moving the coffin to its final place.

He almost killed the effeminate Nicollet the first night they met, but later, took on the secret identity of Brunia to protect him on his expedition to the headwaters of the Mississippi River. A jealousy always existed, and still existed, when William Drummond Stewart turned from a wild rapscallion into a devoted disciple of Nicollet. While Clement also became a disciple of Nicollet, the Professor always showed fear around him yet beamed with joy when speaking with Stewart.

Because of the recent murders, Clement and Stewart were about to be further separated.

The new chapel was almost as grand as the tombs for the ancient pharaohs. While Nicollet was traveling over the prairies searching for clues about the Philosopher's Stone and other legends, Lord Stewart had taken Clement on a reconnaissance trip to the Middle East. They visited Jerusalem, Egypt, and Ancient Babylon to further reinforce the theories that drove him to the headwaters of so many rivers.

If Nicollet had lived, Clement would have rejoined Nicollet to finish the quest near the headwaters of the Mississippi.

Nicollet's casket lowered into the floor of the chapel, and in just a few minutes, the workers would replace the stones and rebuild the elevated altar. Although Nicollet was not a priest, bishop, cardinal, or pope, he was the most "Christian" man Clement ever met, and in his estimation, worthy of such a tomb.

"Are you familiar with St. Anthony the Eremite?" MacPherson asked as both watched the casket being covered.

"I didn't learn about the saints growing up in Hudson Bay."

"From all the stories Stewart told me about Nicollet, the parallels between the two are striking," MacPherson began and then explained.

St. Anthony was a monk from Egypt, and in the early days of Christianity was considered to be one of the first monks on record. Like Nicollet, he was chaste. Like Nicollet, he had a strict diet. At the age of 35, St. Anthony withdrew from the "habitations of men" and went deep into the desert on a quest for enlightenment. During this time in the wilderness, St. Anthony found himself tested by the Devil. Armed with only the power of prayer, Anthony defended himself from long stretches of boredom, laziness, and the phantom apparitions of beautiful women sent by the darkness to tempt him. Instead of behaving like Job, St. Anthony went on the offensive, searching for the evil that plagued him—finding it in a cave. Although Anthony took a beating from the discovered demon, the attacks stopped, and when the monk returned from the wilderness, he was healthier than when he'd departed.

The workers sealed the stone altar.

MacPherson took a step away and finished his story. "Upon his death, St. Anthony was given a secret burial."

*Rest in peace, Professor Nicollet,* Clement silently prayed and began walking out of the chapel with MacPherson at his side.

*Your journey is at an end.*

*My journey is just beginning*

# CHAPTER 6



The fire roared behind him, sending a wave of heat to where the men gathered in a large circle of chairs and couches. William Drummond Stewart was nervous about how to begin, but the faces of so many friends galvanized him to find strength amid the emotions of the day. *Am I worthy of carrying the mantle of Nicollet?*

He cleared his throat and began. "I was just a boy when I discovered my uncle belonged to a secret society. Mind you, many lords belong to dozens of organizations, clubs, and societies, but my Uncle William belonged to a unique secret society known as the Order of Eos."

The room hung on his every word, some politely nodding along. Antoine Clement sat at his right hand while Karl Andreas Geyer sat at his left, and both nodded in affirmation.

"Despite my fascination with my Uncle William's occult collection, it was decided by his friends in the Order of Eos that I was too reckless to be trusted with any more knowledge than I had gleaned from my covert trips to his library. The family determined I needed to join the military to help set me on the straight and narrow.

Sergeant Cairns chuckled at this.

So too did Jamie Anderson.

At this, Stewart also grinned. "After I defeated Napoleon," Stewart jested, "and old age defeated my Uncle, my fascination with the occult legends housed in Logiealmond took a sudden turn when my aunt was murdered trying to sell a map to an American branch of the Order of Eos. Having once seen the map, I knew the tale of a secret treasure on a lost continent, so I gathered up my allowance, and much to the relief of my elder brother John, I set off for the Gulf of Mexico to explore untamed frontier."

"The Al Marrakk Map, according to the lore, was created by King Solomon himself when he was determined to find a legendary object that could transform matter. Of course, most of you know my obsession with the Philosopher's Stone, but my recent obsession fixates more on the alchemist who created the stone.

"In his research, Solomon learned the old Alchemist lived prior to the Great Flood, but the details about this king and his lost kingdom were confusing. The geography described was either a mythological invention, or it described a world changed by the Great Flood. Either way, wise Solomon could not deduce where to send his crew. And then, in his infinite wisdom, Solomon realized that while the continents and kingdoms might have changed, the stars above did not. Even in the earliest days of civilization, men used the stars for navigation, and he came across astronomical references to what we now know as latitude. The Kingdom of the Alchemist was located in the north, along the same line it had been prior to the flood or passage of time. So Abbaron and his crew went out to the far side of the world to search for the lost kingdom and the lost treasure."

Stewart walked over to a library to play with some of the sculptures. "Of course, the mission failed, producing only an updated map of the lost continent, and Solomon had to turn to making his own version of the Philosopher's Stone, which is the strange substance known as shamir. Somehow, these tales of yore found their way into my Uncle William's library. After the murder of my aunt, I knew it would be a race to find the right headwaters ahead of my enemies who not only sought the 'true' Stone but also the land in which it was buried.

"I did not understand the vastness of the American continent, however. Even though I had a general idea of the "line" of the Alchemist's Kingdom, it felt like folly once I got there. I lost heart, focus, and all drive. Then, of all the people in the world, Jean Nicholas Nicollet showed up in St. Louis. Before I departed

Scotland for America, I had sent Sergeant Cairns to investigate my aunt's murder, and while he cleared Nicollet of any wrongdoing, Nicollet had been one of the last people to see her alive. So, you must understand my misgivings."

"I knew with one glance that Nicollet wouldn't hurt a fly," Sergeant Cairns declared and those who knew Nicollet smiled and nodded.

"Now, I believe, just like the natives believed, that Nicollet had been divinely sent to find this sacred treasure. In St. Louis, Nicollet and I compared our versions of the stories, and like a coward, I sent him off into the wilderness to test those theories."

"I watched over Nicollet for an entire year," Clement added defensively. "The little fellow was safe under my watch."

"And I watched over him for the two years after that," Geyer said proudly to the others, "while you and Stewart traveled to the Holy Lands, I was his constant companion until he returned to civilization. Who knew politicians were more dangerous than the savages we faced."

A sharp glance from Clement ended Geyer's point.

Stewart continued, "The man was a genius, but his nine lives were not enough, it would seem. We soon had more answers than questions, but one question bothered Nicollet the most: what are we supposed to do with the Philosopher's Stone if we do find it?" Stewart referenced a collection of letters he'd received from Nicollet, which he took out for his guests to study. In recent days, he'd sent out his own correspondence to collect men for the next stage of the adventure.

Stewart walked over to Clement and put a hand on his shoulder. "In 1839, Nicollet returned to the frontier to find answers to this question. Antoine and I went on a trip to the Middle East to learn more from wise King Solomon. As many of you know, in the fall of 1843, it was our plan to acquire the Philosopher's Stone. Instead, Nicollet was killed. While it has taken me almost a decade to recover from this loss, I am now prepared to finish what I started the day my aunt was murdered."

Stewart reached down for a drink, his opening preamble finished. He went through the checklist of details in his mind, but for the most part, he covered everything he needed to say to the men gathered together for the next quest. Without Fremont, Faribault, Taopi, or even DeSmet, Stewart had to collect a new crew of loyal men.

On the couches and chairs opposite where he sat, his crew of experts had patiently listened to his words, even though most had already been given clues about the audacious plan.

He cleared his throat and continued. "Once, out on the frontier, somewhere in the Rocky Mountains, we encountered a pack of wolves. The wolf pack followed us for a few days, waiting. Under the cover of darkness, one of the wolves crept into the camp, grabbed hold of one of the hunters by the foot, and pulled him out into the darkness to be devoured by the pack. Another time, a hunter found himself alone on the edge of the camp, and when he ran from the wolf facing him, three other wolves ran him down faster than he could cry for help. So when I found myself staring into the eyes of a wolf while holding my cock as I pissed early one morning, I let go, grabbed my knife, and charged right at that bastard. Now, I was never going to catch that wolf, but I kept running and running and running until it bolted away. I am a predator. I'll not be prey."

*Am I all bluster? I used to be a predator.* Stewart ignored his self-doubt and focused on a full explanation of the new quest.

"Once again, I am being hunted. These bastards caught Nicollet by the foot, and then they went looking for Antoine Clement, murdering his father in a barn. Most recently, my younger brother Thomas was killed when he checked into a resort using my name. If we meekly sit around camp, the wolf pack will take us out one at a time. So it is time we start hunting wolves."

Stewart reached down and took a drink. The solemn eyes of the gathered men both inspired him and terrified him. *They are here. Most already know your theories. It's time to find out if they are as loyal as I think they are.*

"I am going to wage war on the Order of Eos and the Priory of Ormus," Stewart finally declared. "I'll hack down any branch of the tree that I can find, uprooting it from the ground when I'm finished. To do this, the wolves must think we are on the run, so I'll be traveling with my wife, along with Mr. and Mrs. Geyer, on an extended Mediterranean Cruise. We'll be accompanied by my loyal companion Jamie Anderson and two new friends, Ross MacPherson and Frank Penny."

Stewart nodded to those he spoke of and then turned to the others. "Meanwhile, Antoine Clement will accompany Lord Wesley Erskine on a vacation to North America to kill the men who killed his father."

Karl Geyer raised his hand, waiting meekly for Stewart to acknowledge him. "Yes?"

"Pardon for the interruption, but who is Lord Wesley Erskine?"

"A figment of my imagination, but no one in North America will know better. Sergeant Lewis Cairns will be playing the part of this wealthy nobleman, with Antoine acting as his valet. Professor Corey Morgan will be joining them to serve as technical adviser so that Antoine kills the right wolves on his hunt."

"I don't understand—"

"Professor Morgan is one of the world's foremost experts on Norse mythology," Stewart said as he walked behind one of his newest friends, "and after this past year in my family library, he is also the world's foremost expert on the origins of the Order of Eos. In seeking answers to Nicollet's death, we kicked the hornet's nest. Delhut could not keep his mouth shut and obviously gave our names to the assassins who killed Clement's father and my brother. After we deal with Delhut, Professor Morgan is going to make sure Clement knows every branch and root of the Eos family tree."

Geyer shook his head but did not ask another question. Stewart studied the man, noting that he had grown fat, and perhaps, even cowardly. *He's not the man I once knew.* He looked to see if anyone else had questions before explaining more to Geyer. "Meanwhile, you and I are going on a cruise. It'll appear as if we've lost nerve and gone into hiding, but we only dress ourselves as the sheep. We're going to search for the proverbial Lion's den and—"

"Could you please avoid the grandiose hunting metaphors and speak plainly to me," Geyer interrupted.

*He's still the voice of reason. I don't need him to be a warrior. I've got Penny for that.* "Why did Nicollet hesitate?" Stewart asked.

Slack jawed, Geyer sat back. Clement narrowed his eyes in contemplation. None of the others personally knew Nicollet.

Stewart expounded. "He'd found the Philosopher's Stone hidden in a cave. He only needed to reach out and take it, but instead, he hesitated, ignored it, and distracted his enemies with other possibilities. And what did his enemies do? Both Eos and the Jesuits went rushing off to the headwaters of the Missouri River, scouring through the Rocky Mountains for vitriol. Nicollet knew there was more to the quest than just the Philosopher's Stone."

Stewart walked over to the far wall of the Hunting Lodge and pulled the fabric off his framed image of Nicollet holding an image of the lost island of lore.

"Professor Morgan, tell us what the Order of Eos is after."

Professor Morgan, who'd been leaning forward to study the portrait, leaned back in the sofa and rolled his eyes before beginning. "At the heart of it, they believe they are going to resurrect a fallen god who will restore the old ways, elevating the faithful above all other tribes of mankind. They believe the earth had endured a series of cataclysms, and that after the last great battle, four gods were buried alive as a broken earth collapsed around them. The recent discovery of the Philosopher's Stone has motivated them, and now, knowing the key will not remain hidden for long, they seek the tomb of this fallen god. Nicollet's bluff had led them to believe the tomb is located in the Rockies."

"Thank you, Professor Morgan," Stewart said. "But there are always two sides to a coin, and the mythos of the Order of Eos is interpreted differently by others." He cleared his throat. "Mr. MacPherson, share what the Jesuits are searching for."

Unlike the arrogant body language of Dr. Morgan, Ross MacPherson shrunk in the spotlight. He clasped his hands between his knees and slouched forward to look at his shoes, revealing his receding hairline. "There is a theory held by some in Rome. It is based on a passage from *The Apocalypse of St. John*, commonly known as *The Book of Revelation*. When John is shown the future, he witnesses a seven-headed dragon, and when he asks the angel about the meaning of the creature, the angel explains to him that the seven heads represent seven kings. Assuming that the prophecy was given to him around the year 95 AD, during the reign of Emperor Domitian, the angel declared that five of the kings had already fallen, one king was currently alive, and the seventh king had not yet been born. Th—"

"These Seven Kings," Stewart stole the final point, "will lead to an eighth king, the Antichrist himself. Nicollet shared his theory about the Eos belief and the beast in the Book of Revelation having connections," Stewart said, holding the bundle of letters. "This portrait was sent to remind me about Nicollet's theories. Karl, tell them Nicollet's theory about the Big Dipper."

"He was an astronomer, so he was always talking about stars, but his story about the Big Dipper certainly caught my attention," Geyer said, reminding him more of the Karl he knew on the frontier. "He believed the seven head of the dragon connected to a prophecy thousands of years older than *Revelation*. His theory is that the seven represented the seven kings preceding the Antichrist," Geyer explained. "And the Polestar Merak pointed to an eighth star, Polaris."

"The coming Antichrist," Mr. MacPherson finished.

"I'm sorry, gentlemen," Jamie Anderson interrupted. "Being born a dwarf left me a little bitter toward my Creator, so excuse me if I'm not versed in scripture, but are we trying to kill the Antichrist?"

Several of them chuckled, but MacPherson remained serious. While Professor Morgan knew the occult lore, MacPherson had been a devout priest. "Now you understand why Nicollet hesitated until he could get more information. If Nicollet's theory is correct and the Philosopher's Stone as some supernatural key capable of unlocking the End Times, then I cannot allow it to fall into the hands of the Order of Eos, and subsequently, I cannot allow them to find the tomb of some ancient king. That I cannot abide."

"But what do you intend to do?" Anderson pressed.

Stewart looked to Clement for affirmation. "We're fairly positive we know where the Philosopher's Stone is located." Clement nodded. "But we don't know if Nicollet's theory about fallen, buried kings has any merit. Tell him, Ross, what the Jesuits are doing."

MacPherson resumed but remained unsteady. "While the scholarship is not orthodox, there is a little known belief about the identities of the fallen kings who make up the seven-headed dragon. It is based on the interpretations found in Daniel. Yet the most disputed theory is that the first head, the first king, belonged to a man who lived prior to the days of Abraham, and prior to the days of Noah…"

"A preflood king?" Professor Morgan clarified. "Sounds like an Eos legend."

"The original Alchemist," Stewart answered when MacPherson hesitated, "the king who made the Philosopher's Stone. His was the kingdom sought after by King Solomon, albeit for different reasons. Nicollet hesitated to claim the Philosopher's Stone because he knew it was a tool meant to unlock the tomb of this fallen king. He even found references to this king in the legends of—"

"Wishwee and the Legend of No Soul," Geyer interrupted, suddenly reclaiming a bit of his former self. "I remember Chief Sleepy Eyes telling us about it. I also remember Nicollet sharing another legend about the Wintermaker, and how this sorcerer gathered up all the Summerbirds to try to stop the seasons from changing."

Professor Morgan answered, "Put simply, there is an uncertain truth at the center of all of these legends.

Mr. MacPherson nodded in agreement to his peer. "While this isn't a commonly held belief in the Catholic Church, the Jesuits believe the tomb of this fallen king must be found in order for the End Times to begin. Failure to find this king and his key is to forestall the prophecy and plunge humanity into unending darkness—a defeat by Eos."

"'Let there be no more delay, cried the angel,'" Stewart muttered loudly. "Or as the Anishinaabe put it, humanity will be given a choice between certain destruction and an Eighth Fire of harmony," Stewart countered.

"So what are you proposing exactly?" Geyer asked.

"First, revenge," Stewart returned to stand near Clement. "But this time, we won't hesitate. Clement will claim the Philosopher's Stone, and by God's grace, he'll then do his best to locate the legendary tomb of the Stone's creator," Stewart then stepped closer to Geyer. "While Antoine and company head west for America, you and I will put on the fleece of a sheep and flee to the east, but not for the purposes they might suspect. It appears our friends and enemies are interested in collecting fallen kings (or gods), and while all their attention is currently fixed on North America, we're going to take control of this prophecy. I mean to possess either or relic or a king. Once secured, I'll hold the entire prophecy as ransom"

Stewart explained pieces of the plan to his two crews, and he watched them all recoil at the magnitude of it—but none of them flinched. Clement nodded in approval.

"We're tomb raiding?" Geyer asked aghast.

"First, we'll make a stop in Rome," Stewart answered, "but then…have you ever visited the Nile?"

# CHAPTER 7



Seventy miles south of Murthly Castle and the Chapel of St. Anthony, another ancient chapel is found just outside of Edinburgh. Rosslyn Chapel was founded by Sir William St. Clair in 1446, although the family's connection with this part of Scotland extends back further to 1070.

The family is descended from Rognvald 'the Mighty', Jarl of Orkney and Romsdahal in Norway, who was born in 835 AD. His son, Rollo, signed a peace treaty in 912 with King Charles of France in the town of St Clair-sur-Epte, from where the family takes its name. King Malcolm Canmore of Scotland granted the family land where the barony of Rosslyn was established. Throughout the generations, the family held a strong presence in Orkney, Caithness, and Fife. A number of castles were built for them, or acquired by them, in those areas.

None was as mysterious as Rosslyn Chapel.

Curiosity drove Pyotr Petrov to investigate all the stories for himself. After all, he was more than just an assassin; he was a reaper sent to cut away heresies supported by both Eos and Christianity. Whispers about the notorious Knights Templar, a secret bloodline, a severed head, the holy grail, and secret documents centered on the old Sinclair stronghold.

With crossed arms, Petrov studied the exterior of the building for a moment. Its pillars, windows, and spires were impressive, but not any more special than the architecture found in his home country of Bulgaria. Belogradchik Fortress, for example, was older, larger, and more impressive—having been built on a mountain top rather than upon flat ground like Rosslyn. The grand plans of the Sinclair family withered and rotted after the death of their bold patriarch, and Rosslyn remained a monument to "what could have been."

Petrov, seeing little activity, entered the chapel.

The Gothic chapel did impress inside. Even without a tour guide, Petrov found the unique features. In places, the symbolism was Christian, with angels, devils, dragons, and Jesus teaching silent parables to the worshiper. Elsewhere, the symbolism was far more…pagan.

Petrov knew the rumors about the final days of the Knights Templar, how some survivors of the great purge of 1307 found refuge in the outlaw state of Scotland, which was in open rebellion against England. While most Templars fled LaRochelle in a fleet of ships for a mysterious island destination, Robert the Bruce and the Sinclair family hosted hundreds of exiled knights, who in turn, helped Scotland win its freedom—for a short while. From the ashes of the Knights Templar, the Order of Eos rose, with its gaze fixed on the west.

Petrov's gaze also turned west and landed upon a curious sight: *The corn pillar?* Petrov studied the arch on the chapel's south side, where "proof" of a trip to the New World was found in the depictions of the North American vegetable. It was one of the only details allowed to support the unwritten accounts of the expeditions.

He scoured for more obvious motivations for hating Eos and the Sinclair, yet the ornate building only gave him a rich history of a significant Scottish family. It was easier to hate Christianity for imposing its will into every aspect of modern culture, but Eos—despite being equally superstitious—eluded him. His superiors never explained why his targets needed to die. He just killed whoever needed killing and put his faith in his Lady.

He stepped back outside, stretched for a few minutes, and then continued his morning jog before the rest of Scotland woke.

He was a killer, not a scholar, and his mind forgot all about Rosslyn Chapel as soon as he turned his back to it. Ahead, the port city of Edinburgh reminded him of his mission.

Instead of guilt, he felt embarrassment for what happened back in Croatia. The fool had used his brother's name to avoid attention. Thomas Drummond Stewart had been a devout Catholic since birth, and he'd climbed the ladder of rank, with the next step that of Cardinal. On vacation with several friends, Thomas had wanted to avoid drawing attention to his priestly state, but instead, drew the attention of Petrov.

*Too young, too handsome, too predictable.*

Pyotr Petrov shamed himself when he failed so miserably, and even thought about taking his own life, but he knew the only way he could get back into good grace was to do the job himself for another assassin stole the glory. Back in Croatia, he'd been patient and carefully crafted a narrative so that another victim took the blame for the murder. He could've slinked off to the shadows but instead went to Scotland on the off chance he could set things right himself.

*William Drummond Stewart must die.*

The estate of Murthly was guarded, and in recent weeks, filled with visitors. Luckily, Stewart had stayed put long enough for Petrov to arrive in Scotland. Stewart would react one of two ways, Petrov figured. He'd either hunker down in his castle, which made him a sitting duck, or he'd flee Scotland, which is why Petrov watched the port.

His morning routine ended with a jog down to the port, to check the state of Drummond's sailing yacht. Preparing the vessel for travel meant stocking the galley, rigging the ship, and preparing a crew. Once again, the ship sat quietly, unprepared to leave dock.

*Good, I'd like the challenge of killing him in his own castle.*

With each passing day, it meant the attack at Murthly was more and more likely. Soon, he'd aggressively scout the ground and castle.

Upon returning to his rented room, Petrov dropped to the floor for another hundred pushups and sit-ups before he gobbled down as many calories as his stomach could take. Just like it took patience to achieve such health and conditioning, being an assassin meant putting in the effort one day at a time.

His muscular body almost leapt out of his skin when a hard knock came on his door, but he didn't react with panic. *No one is*

*hunting me—so act like it*. Even though weapons were nearby, he didn't bother grabbing any. He opened the door without any hesitation.

A freckled teen stood in the doorway, huffing as he tried to catch his breath. He swallowed hard before saying, "They're gone."

"The guests have left?"

"Yes, but so did the Stewarts. The lights of the castle stayed on late into the night, as if they were having another party, but the kitchen staff showed up at the village with a wagon of food they were throwing away. Lord and Lady Stewart and several of their household left."

"But the stables..."

"None of the carriages left or else I would have seen them," the teen insisted. "They did not leave Murthly by road."

Petrov felt his muscles constrict in rage, but he did not lash out at his purchased spy. He'd have to check the truth of the matter for himself—wary of the situation being a trap. Having personally scouted out Murthly Estate several days ago, he knew to place the boy in the little village, where news and gossip openly spread.

If Stewart didn't use any horses from the stables or even his own sailing yacht, then there was only one way for more than a dozen people to depart: Stewart fled on the River Tay. It was the least logical option and meant instead of taking his own private yacht, Stewart would be booking passage, most likely in Dundee.

Stewart knew he was being watched.

*The chase has begun*

THE END OF PART ONE

# PART TWO

## THE MEDITERRANEAN

# PART TWO

# CHAPTER 8



William Drummond Stewart had been in perpetual motion for twenty years, and even after a night in one of Rome's finest hotel rooms, he still felt the room moving. Of course, a few weeks sailing from Scotland to Rome didn't help, but it was more than just the recent trip.

He rolled out of bed feeling old.

His youthful enthusiasm could be coaxed into returning with just a cup of cappuccino, but his body could not be so easily fooled. Sure, he'd taken plenty of abuse during the Napoleonic Wars and his time on the frontier, but it was more of a dull ache in his bones that he felt waking up. His body simply did not want to go where his mind told him to go.

He dressed plainly, poorly even.

The razor scraped off all the gray hair on his cheeks, chin, and upper lip. His hair—once his pride and joy—now daily mocked him in the mirror. After combing it across his scalp, he set a cream-colored felt hat upon his head to hide the bald spot and to add a few inches of height to help his fragile ego.

For good measure, he tucked his new Colt "Pocket Police" revolver into his jacket for safe measure.

*Time to declare to the world that I'm a lunatic.*

He stepped out of the hotel room, locked the door, and took one pace across the hall. After knocking and a short wait, Christina answered. "I didn't think we had anything going on until noon," she said. She, too, looked worse for wear and had yet to recover from their quick departure down the Tay River and subsequent trip across the Mediterranean.

"We don't. I'm just going for a stroll. I'm taking MacPherson with me. Frank will be down in the lobby if you need anything."

"A stroll?" Christina had known him long enough to detect a lie but she seemed too resigned to argue. "Care to be more specific than that?"

"I've got a covert meeting with the Pope."

"Fine. Leave. Get killed in some back alley." And she closed the door.

Karl Geyer stepped out into the hallway, fully dressed. "Well…I wish you well with the meeting. The hairs on my forearm are standing on end. It's hard to imagine such a thing exists."

*It might not exist.* His brief relationship with Nicollet left him with keys to unknown doors. Today he meant to open one. "I hope I find out. Mr. Penny will stay here in the hotel with the women. Have you seen Jamie yet?"

"I don't know, I just stepped out myself."

*We're not even competent enough to wake on schedule.* Stewart huffed, stepping around Geyer to loudly rap on the dwarf's bed chamber.

"Perhaps he's already in the lobby," Geyer offered when the door remained closed.

Another door opened—Ross MacPherson.

The young bearded man stepped out, also dressed in casual clothing, a sign he'd listened to Stewart's plans.

"Ready for a cappuccino?" Stewart asked. Stewart eyed the thinning hair and full beard. *One day you'll need a hat also.*

MacPherson checked his buttons. "I'm a little nervous, actually."

"So am I," Stewart admitted. "If the stories are true, this will be like meeting Santa Claus or the Loch Ness monster. We'll see how the cappuccino goes. Is Anderson sleeping or is he out still?"

"I heard him leave around midnight, but I fell asleep and didn't hear him return."

Geyer shrugged to MacPherson.

*This isn't a good start.* Stewart knew he could trust Geyer with any task or any secret. While Emma Geyer was an unknown factor, he knew Christina would keep her under wing. Ross MacPherson's enthusiasm seemed predictable, and Frank Penny's machismo could be harnessed, but Jamie Anderson had a mind of his own. "Perhaps he is in the lobby with Penny."

"Let's go find out."

In the lobby, Frank Penny waited, wearing his Texan cowboy hat. It was decided before the trip that the young, hired gun did not have nearly enough acting chops to hide his identity, but since he was a nobody from nowhere, a traveling Texan might distract eyes from the known members of the party. As a result, he sat upon a couch, legs spread wide, wearing a leather vest with holsters on his ribs.

"Frank, have you—"

Curled up on a big chair in the corner, Jamie Anderson slept.

"Is he drunk?" Stewart asked.

"Just tuckered," Penny said. "He was out much of the night."

"I'm half a man and need much less sleep," Anderson said without opening his eyes. At Stewart's sigh, he groaned and rolled to his feet. "I'm ready when you are."

"I'm worried you're not taking this seriously," Stewart chided, stepping closer to tower over him.

Anderson shrugged. "Not serious? I spent the past few hours scouting the route and making observations. I'm hours ahead of both of you. Would you like to know the future or shall I let Geyer experience it firsthand?"

Three decades of buffoonery balanced against Anderson's loyalty. *Okay, I was wrong.* "Penny, the ladies will be in your care."

"One Penny is worth a hundred other men," the youth quipped, tapping the hilt of his revolver.

Stewart extended his hand to Geyer and shook it firmly. "Good luck on your tour. I'm looking forward to your report once we all convene back here. Have a good morning." He turned to his own escort. "Ready Mr. MacPherson?"

"No," MacPherson said and then chuckled. "But let's go see about that cappuccino."

The two groups separated.

ONCE OUTSIDE, STEWART turned back to see Geyer and Anderson heading in the opposite direction. The Templum Gentis Flaviae was only a few blocks from the hotel in the shadow of the Coliseum. But like most of Rome, each block was an archeological treasure chest. Although Geyer's trade was botany, his meticulous nature and attention to detail would turn his three hour private tour into two days worth of particulars. While his scientist friend could catalog every aspect of the trip, Jamie Anderson's discerning mind and curious nature would complement the tour.

Those answers to Stewart's questions would have to wait for a few hours. He and MacPherson were about to meet with one of the men who set Nicollet on his quest decades earlier.

"Is this it?" Stewart asked as Ross MacPherson looked around the facade of the block. Four tables and a single door were the only identifying features of the inconspicuous cafe.

"It is. Do we just sit down?"

"Apparently," Stewart said as he reflected on the instructions originally intended for Nicollet.

Stewart watched with bemusement as Ross MacPherson's head pivoted like a curious prairie dog. In the course of a year, the defrocked priest's physical attire had changed. He wore a long, beige leather coat and a turtleneck sweater that met his thick beard. *Youthful vanity for a bruised ego.* Any movement on the street captured his attention as if the second coming of Christ was about to happen. After a few minutes of sitting, a haggard young man who looked hungover stepped out the door to take their order.

"I'm a thirsty wolfpup in need of a suckle," Stewart crisply said in Latin before finishing the secret request with, "I'd like a demitasse of Kapuziner." MacPherson's meaningless order followed.

When the waiter stepped back inside, MacPherson asked, "So how does this work?"

"For all we know, we'll get a cup of cappuccino and return to the hotel. Relax, Mr. MacPherson. This could be a wild goose chase."

"I think it's real," MacPherson insisted.

"Is this your first trip to Rome?" Stewart asked.

"Oh, no. I've been here hundreds of times…in books. I studied it long before you came into my life. It seems so much more expansive and cleaner, I must admit, but the density of the architecture is stunning."

"Everything is hidden in plain sight, isn't it?"

"Indeed it is."

The haggard waiter returned, setting two saucers down with near disdain. Stewart wondered if it was a performance or if the gatekeeper truly was a hungover waiter. The response to their request did not come immediately.

"Does seeing Rome change your view of the Church?" Stewart asked after slipping the drink and cleaning the film off his bare lip. He still missed his distinct mustache.

"Well, Rome isn't Vatican City, is it?" MacPherson said. "The river seems to separate Christianity and Paganism. The Pope is over there, and our fellow is somewhere around here."

*He avoided the question.* The brilliant young scholar from the Edinburgh Theological Seminary had been a priest for only three short years. Then an affair with the wife of a prominent merchant flared up into an entire scandal, resulting in the defrocking of the promising young priest. Having endured scandal aplenty, Stewart offered sanctuary and friendship. Stewart tested countless theories in his debates with the handsome young priest.

Now, the young man followed him on an insane hunt.

"So have you read the legend behind the founding of Rome?" MacPherson asked.

"Anderson tried explaining it to me, but I don't recall the details."

"Surely, though, you're familiar with the two popular legends from mythology about how the city was created?" At Stewart's nod, MacPherson continued. "The tale of the Trojan War has Aeneus leading the survivors to Italy, where he established a city right here. The other tale interests me even more. It tells of two babes, Remus and Romulus, and how they were raised by a she-wolf. Romulus, of course, is where the name Rome derives. Have you read tales about werewolves?"

Stewart scoffed, scanning the crowd for Nicollet's contact. "Go ahead. Pass the time."

"The most popular legend comes from the wild region in Greece known as Arcadia and the legend of Lycaon, who Zeus turned into a wolf. And there are other stories from the Norse and the Black Forest of Germany about men periodically transforming into wolves. My favorite is the tales from Romania involving Zalmoxis, who was a shapeshifting god the Getae people worshiped."

*If MacPherson ever gets taken prisoner, he'll wear the torturer out in an hour with his ramblings.* "What is your point about werewolf legends?"

"There is a possible connection between the Getae, Romulus, and…" he lowered his voice to a whisper, "and the Periphery."

Stewart nodded but also rolled his eyes.

"Aren't you at all the least bit stimulated by the thought of meeting with a secret society that has existed for thousands of years?"

Nicollet had told Stewart about his encounters with the Periphery. Hours ahead of an assassination by the Carbonari in the riots of the July Revolution, a Periphery agent using the name Giocca rescued him, sending him off on a quest that eventually led to the various headwaters of the Mississippi River. Now, instead of Nicollet, Stewart came to Rome with more questions than answers. "I worry about what they think of our plan. If they want it stopped, they'll simply let our enemies know where to find us."

"The Periphery will be our ally in the coming fight," MacPherson naively boasted. "It's rumored that these are the same people who came to the aid of Moses during his darkest hour."

"Excuse me?"

"Werewolves. Shadows. Caves. The man who rescued Moses was a priest of God, but neither Hebrew nor Levite. Reuel, according to historians, was from a tribe of people associated with caves. The Troglydytae, as Heroditus described them, spoke a secret language and existed for centuries prior to Moses. That puts the Periphery at almost four thousand years old."

*Nicollet would have loved talking with this man.* "Doesn't the obvious symbolism worry you the least?"

"What? The Periphery implying 'The Men of the Shadows'? To be a covert benevolent force, you certainly can't blow trumpets in the streets." MacPherson insisted.

"Nicollet should be spending his golden years in a secluded library, instead he is in the tomb I built for him. Don't be swayed by the grandeur of Rome, Ross."

Thirty minutes of silent waiting ended with a tall, elderly gentleman walking directly toward them from the streets. He paused, sighed, and muttered, "That's my table." He looked around in agitation at the other choices before again muttering "Tourists."

*Is this Nicollet's man?*

The elderly gentleman pulled out a metal chair from a nearby table, hesitated, then loudly dragged it over to their table, declaring, "This is where I meet my friends each day. Do you mind if I join you, so that after you leave, I don't have to worry about another group of tourists taking the spot?"

"We're meeting someone also," MacPherson protested. Stewart placed a hand on MacPherson's arm to stop him from saying more.

"Yes, I know."

Stewart studied the man. The stranger was a tall, and perhaps once quite athletic, but the deep wrinkles at his eyes and the corners of his mouth revealed a man in his seventies or eighties. His eyebrows were almost absent, but his thin mustache still had flecks of hair that was once ebony. His hairline was hidden by a black fedora kept remarkably clean. He extended a big hand, wrinkled with age spots that tried to crush Stewart's hand in it when they shook. "Conrad Simmons."

"William," Stewart answered tartly. "But my friends call me Captain Billy."

Simmons turned his gaze to young MacPherson. "I'd hoped to meet the Metis. His reputation made me curious about what the man was like in real life."

"He is out on errands," Stewart answered in reference to Antoine Clement. *This is the same man Nicollet told me about. This is the one who sent him on the quest for the Philosopher's Stone. A seminarian in*

the 1790s would now be near eighty, which matched the man's age. "You were a friend of the watchmaker's son?"

"And the watchmaker himself. I owe my life to the entire family for sheltering us from the mob. Because of him, I've led quite a life, even reporting directly to two popes. I'm now retired, but when your letter arrived, I requested to meet with you personally. Any friend of the watchmaker's son is a friend of mine." The smile then vanished and his brow narrowed skeptically. "This fellow, however, I'm not so sure about."

"Ross MacPherson." MacPherson extended his hand but dropped it when Simmons shook his head and leaned back.

"I know who you are. You seem to draw a lot of attention to yourself. Stubborn. Willful. Insolent. Driven by ego. Throughout your schooling and years in the seminary, you relished challenging authority. Was it for ego or simply to get to the heart of the matter?" Simmons asked rhetorically. "It makes no difference now, does it? You were caught having an affair with a noblewoman, which led to a few other accusations. It seems your sexual appetite was as large as your academic appetite."

"The accusations were—"

"An attempt to remove you from your position. Lord Stewart saw through the ruse, which is why he has armed himself with such an impressive weapon in his arsenal. Throughout the known world, there are corrupt priests sinning on a daily basis, and most of the time, it is overlooked. Do you ever wonder why *your* behavior was noticed?"

Having lost countless arguments to the young man, Stewart found a grin creeping onto his face as the brash young academic squirmed in his seat. All MacPherson could do was shrug weakly.

"You stuck your nose into areas the Church didn't want you questioning. Adultery is easily explained, but Orthodoxy is much more difficult to defend, and you were seeking answers for questions that dare not be asked. Luckily for you, Lord Stewart was already asking himself the same questions," Simmons concluded and turned his hot gaze away from the defrocked priest. He levelled his gaze on Stewart. "Have you heard any news from the frontier about Father DeSmet? He's all but stepped off the map into the wilderness."

"Father DeSmet mourns the loss of Nicollet in much the same way as I do. He's dedicated himself to the welfare of the Indian out on the frontier. He knows what is coming," Stewart said, thinking of his dear friend. Clement would likely find a way to meet with him. *Will DeSmet forgive Clement his mortal sins?*

"We tried to save the Professor," Simmons boldly claimed. "On several occasions, we tried to pull him from the waters, knowing he was drowning, but he was determined, wasn't he? Unfortunately, his enemies were even more determined. Is that why you've come? To learn more about your enemy?"

Stewart shook his head. "No, I know more about my enemy than I want to know. Nicollet delayed when he came close to the truth. I want to discuss what gave him pause."

"Delayed? What are you implying?" Simmon's eyes narrowed.

"They might've killed Nicollet, but he did not fail in the task you gave him. We believe he found the Philosopher's Stone yet did not claim it. Why? Who knows what would have happened if he lived, but in death, he let me know his theory about the Stone and the maps."

"You received his portrait, didn't you? We knew you'd likely pick up the torch to continue the quest." Simmons noted and asked, "And what is his theory?"

"The Professor realized that the quest for the Philosopher's Stone went beyond the creation to the creator."

"All I asked him to do was investigate the tales surrounding LeSueur and Lahontan, and by the time he died, he was studying the mysteries of Atlantis."

"What do you know about the 'Philosopher' who created the Stone?"

"Not much. My speciality was dealing with modern threats to the Church, which I how I learned so much about Freemasons, the Illuminati, the Carbonari, the Order of Eos, and even newer threats. I know the Order of Eos was eager to let Nicollet lead them to the figurative needle in the haystack. As much as I regret saying it, perhaps his delay was for the best."

"So you can confirm that this quest goes beyond just acquiring the stone?"

"Your family had roots in the Order of Eos. You likely know about their obsessions better than the Pope himself does."

"Yet we didn't go to the Vatican City, did we?" Stewart asked and glanced over at MacPherson, who'd barely moved a muscle and nervously kept his hands under the table. "Nicollet boldly championed the comission given him by the Periphery, and if I am going to continue his mission, I need to understand what I should do if I find something of…great value."

Simmons laughed heartily. "When God looked down upon the earth in the early days of the Christian Church, he didn't pick the most righteous follower; no, he found a murderous investigator named Saul traveling on the road to Damascus. What happened to Captain Billy following his baptism in St. Louis? I see Saul in front of me, yet I hear Paul."

"Oh, I'm more 'murderous investigator' than saint. My younger brother was destined to become a Cardinal, yet he was killed by the same enemies who killed Nicollet. I know what Eos believes; now I need to understand what the Periphery believes."

"I'm afraid I don't have those answers," Simmons said, "but I know a man who does. Luckily, the old man wants to meet you."

# CHAPTER 9



Ross MacPherson kept his mouth shut as he trailed Lord Stewart and Conrad Simmons on their tour through the Capitoline Museum. The finest art and sculptures in Europe were gathered upon the Capitoline Hill in a complex that had few rivals on the earth.

He took note of the steps that arose above the city by several stories, although once he reached the top, the complex had a flat plateau upon which the Piazza del Campidoglio had been built. Everything was bright and open—and blatantly pagan, which surprised him.

Although statues of Constantine, the first "Christian" Emperor of Rome, had been one of the earliest stops, MacPherson could only contrast the Vatican with such a shrine to Rome's pagan past. Neither Simmons nor Stewart seemed too interested in it all. The two talked about the construction of the new museum by Michaelangelo.

Seeing public nudity, even if in polished marble, made Ross's mind fixate on Lady Lithgow.

The accusers had been liars, but his affair with Lady Lithgow had been very real. It started with her earnest questions—or so it seemed. She seemed impressed by his knowledge, and he liked to show off, so the two lingered in an act that could only be viewed as righteous. Then the relationship became a friendship, and he became a listener whenever she had troubles. Becoming a shoulder to cry on became an offer for tenderness, and in one sudden wave of emotion, he was caught up in a moment that led to other moments, and then a pattern.

Within the span of a year, his career came crumbling apart.

*If I'd shown a bit of restraint, I'd still be back in Scotland.* His regret and guilt suddenly abated in the magnificence of the museum.

About the same time his career in the church ended, his acquaintance with Lord Stewart began. He'd heard all about the sexual exploits of Captain Billy spanning his military days to his time out on the frontier with his mountain men. His relationship with Antoine Clement was discussed, even though MacPherson only saw ashes and embers of what had once been a fire. Stewart's wild days had gone by the wayside, and he was left with yearning to understand the mysteries of the Bible. Once Ross's scandal broke, Stewart offered a place to hide from the spotlight. While Stewart's comfort was far from lonely Lady Lithgow's, his was a genuine curiosity rather than an elaborate seduction.

Lost in thought, MacPherson wasn't ready for Stewart to shake hands with Simmons, who abruptly walked away from the tour without providing them with any of the answers.

*What was the purpose in meeting Simmons? Another gatekeeper perhaps?*

Stewart kept walking as if he knew where to go. Finally, MacPherson saw their destination. *Ah, there it is at last—the infamous she wolf.*

The metal statue was almost comical. The she-wolf held little realism to an actual wolf and showed a rigid posture and impassioned expression as she stood over two infants stretching to suckle from the its teats. Scholars described the she-wolf statue as dating all the way back to the first century. "So what do we do now?"

Stewart walked around the statue, noting everything except the wolf. "Now we just wait and see."

While they waited, MacPherson took in the ambience of the museum. For almost two thousand years, Rome had been one of the epicenters of the world, so it made sense for a secret society to have a headquarters in such a place. During that time, Rome had endured much political turmoil and invasion, but the ancient part of the city, along with the statue, endured.

*So what does this have to do with the men who tried to kill Stewart?* MacPherson wondered and turned from the art to the crowd.

An old man came toward them, sweeping the floor as he approached. Stewart froze and watched.

*"The old man wants to see you"….is what Simmons said to us.*

The custodian did not seem older than Conrad Simmons, and if anything, was a few years younger. Shorter and stockier, his beardless cheeks were smooth with just a few wrinkles in the corner of his eyes, which took notice of them since they outright were staring at him. The custodian finished pushing a small pile into the dust pan, set the broom down, and leaned against the base of the She-Wolf.

"First time in Rome?" the custodian asked.

Stewart gasped a little, leaving his mouth agape. Then he stepped back, falling onto the ground like a peasant caught stealing from his master. Seeing Lord Stewart grovel was so sudden and out of character that MacPherson almost chuckled aloud.

*Who is this old man?* While he assumed it was some high ranking member of the Periphery, the humility shown disarmed him a bit.

The custodian was not flattered by Stewart groveling on the ground. "Rise. Quit acting the part of the fool. I am a fellow servant. Kneel before God, not me."

MacPherson looked around to see if any other visitors were amused by the comical scene. Fortunately, the moment was private.

"Yes," Stewart said, still averting his eyes and rising to his feet. "I am…we are…honored to be allowed this meeting with you."

"Boredom got the better of me. In your recent letters, you wrote that you had important matters of theology to discuss. Do you still have questions?"

"I do."

"Splendid, but there are many visitors to Rome, so let us find a more comfortable spot."

The comfortable spot was a stone bench in the middle of the museum plaza. Dozens of people milled around, but none of them paid attention to the three sitting down.

"So how can I help?" the custodian asked. Donning the attire of a servant, the man was meticulously groomed, and despite looking to be about seventy-five, he appeared strong and healthy.

Stewart took a deep breath, glanced at MacPherson, and asked the first question. "Are you familiar with the lost continent of Atlantis?"

The custodian chuckled. "I am, but I am hardly an expert."

Stewart continued, "There are many other cultures besides the Greeks that speak of an island, continent, or civilization that was destroyed in a single day by a catastrophe. The point of Atlantis is that a civilization existed long before the one we know."

The custodian's eyebrow raised. "You speak of the Great Flood of Genesis. Is that why you have come to visit? As I previously stated, I am hardly an expert on matters of antiquity."

Stewart smirked like he did when playing cards. "I think you might understand antiquity much better than I. I'm not interested in the flood but instead in a man who existed before humanity's most recent cataclysm. From what I can tell, the Order of Eos is interested in this fellow as well, and over the centuries, I've found as many references to him and his creation, which we call the Philosopher's Stone."

The custodian hummed. "In recent years, I've also developed an interest in the legend of the Philosopher's Stone. I mourned the death of Professor Nicollet and I fear my interest in this ancient relic led him to an untimely death."

Ross tried to guess the identity of the custodian. For a brief moment, he thought it might be an undercover Pope Pius IX until he remembered the Pope's bulldog face in contrast to the custodian's leaner, darker complexion.

Stewart shook his head. "Nicollet was relentless. Death was the only thing to stop his insatiable curiosity, which in turn, has become my newest quality as well. I wish we could be here today to hand you the Philosopher's Stone, but instead, I only have these two items to offer," Stewart declared, motioning to MacPherson to retrieve the satchel.

Feeling a bit in the dark as to the custodian's true identity, MacPherson released a sigh before pulling the strap over his head and handing it to Stewart.

Stewart paused after unlatching the buckles. "Many men have died attempting to acquire these. My dear friend died because of this. My aunt died because of this." Stewart produced two tubes from the satchel.

The custodian took possession of the tubes. He held them with a slight grin on his face, as if he could see through them. "Are these the two maps that have caused such a ruckus in recent years?"

Stewart nodded. "*The Al Marrakk* map was made by King Solomon himself, who sent an expedition to the far side of the world to search for an ancient treasure meant to aid him in the construction of his temple in Jerusalem. While they searched, Solomon grew impatient and turned to dark magic to create his own version of the Philosopher's Stone. The doomed expedition eventually found its way back home, and a second map, made by Abbarron, was created that chronicled this journey to the far side of the world."

"And the race to find the ancient king's tomb began anew," the custodian summarized Stewart. His face suddenly bore pained guilt. "I know of many men who have died trying to acquire these maps. Some went on my behalf. The agents of the Periphery keep me informed. It hardly seems as if you need my help at all. You've solved a great puzzle on your own."

MacPherson knew Stewart wanted to ask about the Seven Kings theory and watched patiently as Stewart measured his words. "What can you tell me about the Philosopher's Stone maker?"

MacPherson felt himself sitting on the edge of his seat. Although he didn't know the identity of the old man, he knew Stewart had pulled every string at his disposal to get this audience in Rome. He assumed he'd been brought along in case Stewart had private questions or to help translate Latin into English.

The custodian's brow wrinkled as if weighing his words. Finally, he relaxed and opened the end of the *Al Marrakk* map tube. "I think the answer has been in front of you the whole time. Symbolism is often elusive until the meaning is explained."

The custodian unrolled the map of the world created by King Solomon—MacPherson knew it well already. Half of the map showed the known world in the year 1000 BC with the most detailed area showing the Holy Lands. "Sir, that is a very important document."

The old man winked playfully. "If Joseph Nicollet indeed found the resting place of the Philosopher's Stone, then these maps are now worthless, aren't they?"

MacPherson nodded at the logic.

The old man studied the stars along the outer border of the map, and finding the northern side of the map, quickly identified the North Star. "In Solomon's wisdom, he knew the kingdoms and empires had changed but the stars remained the same. His navigators used stars to find the ancient land where the Stone was buried.."

"Yes, it's what Nicollet used to calculate the approximate latitude," Stewart commented.

MacPherson saw it and quickly interpretted the symbolism. "The Big Dipper has seven stars. Do they represent the Archangels?"

The custodian's scoffing chuckle made MacPherson wish he'd kept his mouth shut. He'd heard Stewart's fears about seven evil kings leading to the ultimate evil: the Antichrist. Yet nowhere in known scholarship did MacPherson find any support. So Stewart insisted on coming to Rome for answers.

"To the Greeks, the seven stars combined to make the image of a beast, a bear. These seven stars point to an eighth star, which then makes a smaller yet significantly more important beast."

A gasp escaped MacPherson's lips as the custodian hit the nail on the head: *The Red Dragon and the Antichrist.* He looked to Stewart who nodded in affirmation.

Stewart turned to the custodian. "I became so fixated on the legend behind these maps that I couldn't imagine the whole picture. Nicollet understood the whole picture. His imagination not only allowed him to picture the creator of the Philosopher's Stone but also its ultimate purpose." Stewart turned to MacPherson. "Can you explain our theory to him?"

MacPherson swallowed hard. "The Bible is filled with countless sevens, but in the Book of Revelation, there is a seven-headed dragon—a beast from water. When St. John asks the angel the meaning of the seven heads, he is told that each head represents kings: five who were dead, one who was alive, and one who had not yet been born. These seven kings would precede the worst of them all, the figure known as the Antichrist, who is the 8th." MacPherson then put his finger on the map to illustrate. "The Big Dipper has seven stars, and the two pole stars point to the eighth, which is, um, the Antichrist."

Stewart breathed a sigh of relief, a sign MacPherson stated it correctly. "Does he have the interpretation correct?"

"It's different in Aramaic, and translating it into Latin and then into English certainly didn't help matters, but yes, that is basically what it says." The old man smiled and patted MacPherson on the shoulder.

MacPherson suddenly felt like a child who'd been given a large lollipop.

"We also have come to you about the application of this theory," Stewart added. "The Order of Eos stands in opposition to the Catholic Church in thought, word, and deed, and from what I've discerned, they are searching not only for the Stone but also for its creator."

"Hmm," the custodian vocalized loudly. He scratched his chin like a man who'd once worn a beard. "Earlier, you asked me about the Philosopher's Stone creator, and King Solomon's map included the seven stars for the reason we just spoke. Solomon knew his recent history and how the Sons of Darkness—Eos as they are now called—searched for an even older king, a king that existed before the 'most recent cataclysm,' as you put it." The custodian put his finger near the bottom pole-star. "Merak—the Loin of the Beast."

"Is that the name of the ancient king who made the Philosopher's Stone?" Stewart asked. "Merak?"

The custodian shrugged. "Perhaps. That's what the ancient Phoencians called him, which is where the name of your map comes from: Al Marrakk. The ancient Hebrews called this man Lamech."

"The father of Noah?" MacPherson asked.

"No, the offspring of Cain."

Stewart stiffened his back and looked around the sheltered square where they sat.

*What agitated him?* MacPherson wondered.

Finally Stewart muttered, "Veritas Caput."

"Indeed," the custodian said. "The truth about the head. We learned that your friend Professor Nicollet began researching the legends of Atlantis in the months before his death. Just like the name of the Stone's creator changes in the telling, so too does the name of his ancient kingdom. That is when we knew Nicollet was searching for the first star of the seven-headed beast."

"Merak," Stewart repeated. "The map was in our family library for two centuries and I never understood the meaning of its name: Al Marrakk. I supposed Nicollet put it together the moment he read the name."

"His keen mind went to the core of the mystery faster than all of Nebuchadnezzar's collection of magi here in Rome could," the custodian added.

"So the Philosopher's Stone was only proof of where 'the head' was located. If you found the Stone, you'd also find Caput Mortuum. So the Jesuits were trying to find 'the head' before the Order of Eos could find it. The Stone was inconsequential."

The custodian shook his head. "You are right about the Jesuit interest. Our agents work within their midst, and since rumors of the blue vitriol came to light, we've been sending men out into the frontier to stay ahead of Eos. But you were wrong to say the Stone was inconsequential. Just as the Seven Kings have a part to play in the eighth king—the Antichrist—I believe that the Philosopher's Stone might be a key in bringing about the End Times."

*Perhaps Stewart is not a madman after all,* MacPherson decided. *Our theories are all being confirmed.*

Stewart bent down as if he might be sick and breathed heavily while looking at his toes. He groaned a bit. "Tell me: if Nicollet had found the Philosopher's Stone, what should he have done with it?"

The custodian shrugged. "It matters not," he said and looked up to the open air of the courtyard within the museum. "The Lord will use either saint or sinner for his mysterious purpose."

*It matters not?* MacPherson recoiled. *So what are we supposed to do now?*

"You just stated that the Philosopher's Stone is a key to bringing about the End Times," Stewart angrily repeated.

"'Might be key," the custodian wryly corrected Stewart. "I'd have to see it to know for certain."

"So you counsel that we bring it to you here in Rome?"

The custodian again shrugged. "Across the Tiber, the Pope tries to shape the politics of the world, but on this side of the river, we trust that the plans of God—even the End Times—will arrive as they were meant to arrive. The Periphery exists to nurture the flock, especially those in need. Yet the great cosmic clock is ticking down. You might be far too young to hear it, but an old man such as I can hear it ticking away to the inevitable."

"So you counsel that we do nothing?" Stewart asked.

"Of course not. You are men of action, and I have a hunch that after our brief meeting, you'll be racing around the world trying to thwart the Sons of Darkness."

Stewart collected himself and stared at the man with steely resolve. "And how would I thwart the Sons of Darkness?"

"For their plan to succeed, the Philosopher's Stone is key, and with it, they will be searching for more than just the elusive king known to Solomon as Al Marrakk. If you look into their northern tales, you'll find that the Northmen also believed in ressurrection, albeit much different than the resurrection of the Christ. For their evil designs to come true, they will be looking for all seven kings." The custodian pointed to the symbol of the Big Dipper on the map still spread before them.

"Then, for my part," Stewart said, positioning himself in front of the old man, "I will thwart these Sons of Darkness."

"And I'll be at his side," MacPherson added, caught up in Stewart's earnest bluster.

With levity on his face, the old man rose. "If you mean to call down fire from the sky to consume your enemies, you might be surprised how your prayers will be answered," the custodian said. "Is there anything else you need to ask me today?"

MacPherson reviewed. They'd wanted to learn more about the creator of the Philosopher's Stone and they now had multiple

names. They wanted to know what to do with the Philosopher's Stone, and now they knew to bring it back to Rome. They looked for confirmation that the Order of Eos searched for fallen kings, and the rumor was affirmed. They even knew how to get revenge against Eos—by stealing any of the corpses sought by Eos. Stewart shook his head, but MacPherson's hands dove into the recesses of the satchel.

"If there are indeed Seven Kings," MacPherson began as he searched for the right piece of paper. "What can you tell us about those who came after the flood? Beyond Merak, who are the other kings written in the stars?"

"I also pondered the Seven Kings prophecy after I heard it. If you seek answers, I'd look for them in other places in scripture."

"Ah!" MacPherson interrupted. "Here is our list." In his enthusiasm, he handed it to the custodian, who looked it over and nodded. "How did you come up with these names?"

Stewart answered, "Many were suggested to me by Nicollet."

"May God's grace guide you on your journey, but I fear many of the tombs have already been plundered by the Sons of Darkness. The Periphery will not interfere in your quest and will watch your efforts with great interest." The custodian stood and collected the two maps. "Do you still need these?"

Stewart shook his head. "As you said, they are worthless if Nicollet indeed found the resting place of the stone."

The custodian tucked them under his arm, found his broom leaning against a nearby wall, and went back to work sweeping. He disappeared around the corner.

"That was strange," Ross said under his breath.

"You have no idea how strange," Stewart said. "Once we are far away from Rome, I'll tell you more about the rumors about the Old Man." He stood up, got his bearings, and began walking back in the direction of the hotel.

As they reached the threshold of the Capitoline Museums, Ross turned back for a final glance. Without Stewart saying it, Ross began postulating the identity of the old man, who seemingly served incognito as a great puppet master. As a boy, Ross read about strange rumors of immortality found at the end of the gospel of St. John, and as a young man, he'd also read the stories about the legend of the wandering Jew.

*Is that why Stewart was so unnerved?*

Yet after the meeting's conclusion, the hairs began to stand up on the back of his neck.

*No…such things are impossible.*

In the distance, he saw the custodian drop the two maps in a trashcan and continue sweeping.

# CHAPTER 10



Karl Geyer's heart beat heavily in his chest. Granted, much of it came from the exertion of the tour, but his heart also raced knowing he was on a secret mission for Lord Stewart. Between his own panting and Jamie Anderson's short legs, their private tour went block by block. *Perhaps I'm too old and out of shape for adventures.*

The hired guide waited for them to catch their breath. Geyer moved to stand under the Arch of Titus as their guide began his narration. "This arch was built as a monument to Titus, the general who defeated the Jews following their violent revolt. You can see one of the only contemporary depictions of King Herod's Temple upon the surface."

"I've seen this same thing in Paris," Jamie Anderson declared.

"It was built by Napoleon after he crushed the Catholic Church," Karl Geyer explained and then muttered, "Two enemies of God."

The guide hesitated at Geyer's comment.

"Who had this Arch built?" Geyer asked.

"Emperor Domitian, Titus's brother," the guide explained.

*Perhaps Nicollet was right about the Seven Kings,* Geyer thought, swallowing hard while trying to maintain his composure. Based on their behavior out on the frontier, the Jesuits were sure to be spying on them, Stewart insisted earlier, but they were more interested in Stewart than his lesser companions. So Geyer and Anderson went on the secret fact-finding mission. Stewart and MacPherson put together "The Nicollet List" of kings from history that fit clues found in scripture as well figures known to the Order of Eos. King #1 had been the namless "Philosopher" from the Philosopher's Stone legend, and while there was dispute with several candidates, consensus was reached for King #6. "Domitian," Geyer bluffed. "Never heard of him. I'd like to learn more about him. Lead on."

The guide nodded and led to what remained of the Templum Gentis Flaviae. Anderson huffed and followed behind.

While Stewart and MacPherson sought confirmation about their theories, Geyer and Anderson had a much more specific task: locating a tomb. Geyer had always been more of a scientist than a theologian, so the details of the theories caught him off guard a bit. Yet he had the gist of it. The first king lived in an ancient kingdom, which is where Clement and company had been sent. One king had been alive in the year 95 AD when St. John wrote the *Apocalypse*. The seventh king had not arrived yet and would appear shortly before the End Times began in earnest. Nicollet beleived that king had been Napolean based on the evil chaos he'd sown upon Europe. MacPherson vehemently disagreed. Yet all three theologians agreed upon Domitian.

When they reached the designated spot, Geyer reached into his pocket for a wad of Stewart's money. "I think my friend and I are going to forgo the rest of the tour in favor of some refreshment at the little cafe over there. We thank you for your wonderful hospitality."

The wad of money sent the tour guide scurrying.

"So now what?" Anderson asked as he played along and found a chair. He immediately began rubbing his legs.

"We eat and drink and keep an eye out for spies following us."

"The Jesuits?"

"Most likely since Eos doesn't know our destination was Rome," Geyer repeated Stewart's earlier comment. Since vanishing from Scotland, they hadn't made a public appearance until today. "However, Eos could still have embedded spies watching, so we'll play the part of tired tourists for the better part of the hour before continuing."

Anderson had no problems with that, and after ordering, he leaned back and even napped. "So tell me the truth," Anderson said as he grew bored of napping. "Is Stewart a lunatic? Is he following an even greater fool in this Nicollet fellow?"

"Nicollet was one of the greatest men I've ever known in my life," Geyer began angrily. Back in 1843, he'd been one of the sheep ready to orchestrate the heist before wolves killed their shepherd. Now he felt as if he owed Nicollet his life and that he had to prove the professor correct. "I would've died for that man. He was also one of the kindest, most brilliant men I've ever known, and if his theory about the creator of the Stone and the Seven Kings is true, then I have even more motivation to continue."

Anderson wrinkled his forehead as his mouth opened then closed. "I see." He turned to his cup and finished his beverage. "Thanks for the insight, but Stewart and MacPherson were yapping so quickly that I'm not sure I understand what we're about to do next. What are we doing?"

"Checking to see if a grave is occupied or empty," Geyer answered bluntly. Stewart trusted the dwarf, but Geyer still disliked him.

"Yes, yes," Anderson said, procuring the directions given to him by MacPherson. "I've got all the dirty little details written down, but cut to the end of the madness: what are we really doing?"

Geyer swam in the theory's details himself. "Apparently, our enemies—"

"Eos."

"Yes, Eos. Apparently, our enemies believe they will be able to summon their god if they gather together seven fallen kings and ressurrect them with the Philosopher's Stone."

"Resurrect? How's that supposed to work?"

"That's why everybody and their mother were searching for the Philosopher's Stone: it holds some secret ability to bring the dead back to life."

"And their talk about the Antichrist?"

"The flipside to this prophecy seems to match many of the details, except instead of a fallen god, they'll be summoning the Antichrist."

"But why do we care if Jesus shows up at the end of it all and brings us a happy ending filled with flowers and butterflies? Isn't our mission just delaying the inevitable?"

"Stewart wants revenge for the death of his brother, so he wants to hurt Eos by stealing control of their prophecy."

"By stealing a corpse," Anderson scoffed.

Geyer chuckled at the absurdity of it. "I'm also a little fuzzy on his intentions. He and MacPherson talked on and on about Fate, Free Will, and Predestination. As the good guys, we're hoping to keep these corpses and relics out of the hands of the bad guys for as long as possible."

"I understand. Every man is destined to die—the End Times. Yet it depends on Free Will whether the man exercises and stays fit or whether he eats himself to an early grave. In this metaphor, Eos would be the fat man."

Geyer thought for a moment of flipping the table over and choking the dwarf. As a young man, Geyer had accepted a challenge from one of Chief Wahanatan's braves and almost won a wrestling match. Compared to that man, Anderson would be easy. "Yes, Eos would be the fat man."

Anderson smirked, shaking his head as he studied the instructions in front of him. "And, um, *this* bit of folly?"

"Domitian is King #6 on their list, so while we're in Rome, we've been sent to look for his tomb."

"Monsieur de Arch." Anderson scoffed as he read the coded name aloud.

"You heard the tour guide," Geyer said as he rose from his seat at the table. "After killing a million Jews, you build an Arch to honor your triumph over God. Emperor Domitian seems a likely villain, doesn't he?"

Anderson grumbled and groaned and slid out of his seat with disdain. He checked his glass only to find it empty. "And if we do find a body?"

Geyer chuckled. "It means somebody is very wrong."

"Then let's go find out," Anderson said.

Directions in hand, Anderson led Geyer around an immense building before finding the alleyway described in the instructions.

Sure enough, they found a small entrance that led under the building.

"Why isn't the Texan doing this? He's young and stupid," Anderson complained.

"And also too big," Geyer said, producing the rope ladder which he began securing to posts and pipes in the alley. "Don't worry, I'll make sure you get out."

"There are days I wish Stewart would've left me for dead. Today will likely top all of them."

Geyer dropped the ladder into the cavity leading under the building. *No jokes about my wife today, are there?*

Anderson gritted his teeth as he began gingerly climbing down into the hole.

Geyer produced a small lamp and matches. "Ready?"

"Just send the fucking thing down to me. It smells like shit down here," Anderson barked.

When Anderson lit the lamp, it revealed a sewer far more ornate than anything Geyer had seen elsewhere in the world.

Anderson checked his diagram one more time. "It should be straight ahead. Wish me luck, Karl."

"Good luck, Anderson."

"Don't leave me down here to die," Anderson added then stepped into the shadows.

Geyer looked back toward the streets of Rome. No one took notice of a tourist leaning against the alley wall. For good measure, he patted the small pistol he tucked into his vest.

*Seven heads of the dragon.*

*Seven hills upon the earth.*

*Seven kings: Five who were, one who is, and one who will be.*

Back in Scotland, it didn't take the scholar Ross MacPherson long to find history books that described the tomb of the 10th Roman Emperor who followed Caesar Augustus. If Anderson found a corpse right under the noses of the Periphery, the Jesuits, and Eos, it meant they were very wrong about their theories.

If Anderson found an empty tomb, it meant Eos or the Church had already claimed one of the pieces to the End Times prophecy.

From below, he heard sloshing water. The ropes jerked, causing Geyer to clutch his chest in alarm. Still, none of the other tourists seemed to take note.

"Geyer?"

"I'm here."

"Thank God," Jamie Anderson said. "I worried I was going to be lost down here forever. Now help me up."

A few minutes later, the two leaned against the alley wall in front of the storm drain. Anderson was wet and reeked of filth. At first, all he could do is complain. Then his tone turned more reverential.

"So MacPherson was right?" Geyer asked.

"He was. I lost my bearings, but when I realized my mistake, I found it right where it was supposed to be."

"You found the hidden chamber?"

"There *used to be* a hidden chamber," Anderson emphasized. "But it has been cleared out. Even the names carved upon it were removed by hammer and chisel. Whoever took the body of Emperor Domitian wanted to make sure the world would forget about him."

*Whoever took the body…*

Geyer knew the answer was Eos.

Somewhere in the darkness, the same enemy was hunting them.

# CHAPTER 11



TARANTO, ITALY

1852

*My head hurts,* William Drummond Stewart thought in the dark chamber. *I think I'm going to be sick.* He found the edge of a stone sarcophagus and leaned against it to release the pressure on his tired legs. A few feet ahead, Karl Geyer continued his incessant question about the local guide's personal life. *Why didn't we stay together? I miss the others. I should have Professor Morgan with me.*

His beautiful but boring Texan guarded the women back at the *Mina* and Jamie Anderson, who refused to visit another ancient burial site, stayed back as well. Karl Geyer stood in the glow of Ross MacPherson's lantern.

A rush of saliva filled Stewart's mouth, followed by dizziness. He put his hands on his knees for balance, and then, in a sudden explosion that filled his nostrils, Stewart vomited on the stone floor, creating an impressive splash that extended several feet. Suddenly, his annoyance at the others was releived as well.

"Are you okay?" Geyer asked.

*Isn't it obvious? At least that shut Geyer up for a second.*

He heard MacPherson and the other guide returning, but a second wave of vomit—more through the nostrils—the worst— spewed before he could answer Geyer. By the time he cleared the mucus from his mouth, the others were standing at his side.

"Should we go back?" Geyer asked.

"Nonsense," Stewart said, clearing his throat. "I'm all pins and needles in anticipation of seeing what lies ahead."

In truth, he'd vomited in fear. His belly had been twisted up all morning because he feared another failure.

"Come, Lord Stewart," young Ross MacPherson said to him. "There's something up here that will certainly cheer you up." The defrocked priest stood just outside of the pool of vomit.

"Of course," Stewart muttered. "Show me what you found."

"The church is built atop the foundation of the old mausoleum," MacPherson said as he led them back to the area he'd been studying. "You were right about the Flavian family not being traditional Romans. They were indeed outsiders who served the Julian Dynasty right up to the Year of the Four Emperors. Back in Rome, we searched the ruins of Domitian's palace, but his home was always here in Taranto. This was the private mausoleum for his family."

"So I take it you found his corpse," Stewart asked bitterly.

MacPherson chuckled and smugly said, "Not exactly."

Stewart followed him deeper into the structure. On the streets of Taranto, the building had been a simple church, but underground, its footprint was much larger. Stewart stepped through the thick foundation wall into an area meticulously shaped—and quite empty.

MacPherson rushed over to the wall. He stood in a space where a sarcophagus could have been kept. "At one time, this was sealed," MacPherson began by pointing. "This was likely sealed with secured metal doors, much more security than a typical burial site. Whoever was buried here was meant to stay here for perpetuity. You can see where the hinges once connected to the walls as well as the pock marks from the chisels or whatever they used to get the seal off."

"A sealed vault?" Stewart asked, suddenly feeling better. "A resting place fit for a king."

"The other chamber was most likely used for aunts, uncles, cousins, etc, but this vault was specially made to make sure common folks did not have access. It's more like a treasure vault than a tomb, to be honest."

Each of them took a moment to step inside of the small space and look around. It was another dead end, yet Stewart felt uplifted by the discovery.

MacPherson continued, "They've stolen everything of value, but I believe, based on the way this room was constructed, that this was more than just a mausoleum—it was a place of worship."

"What kind of worship?" Stewart asked.

MacPherson only beckoned him closer. "In reading the Roman biographies about Domitian, the chronicles spoke about his macabre dinner parties being so funereal that his guests worried about being scared to death. Instead of worshiping the Roman gods of old, Domitian chose instead to worship an obscure deity—a god with four heads."

MacPherson's finger did not lift from the wall, and Stewart leaned in closer. Sure enough, the carved relief showed a mutated human with four heads. *Macabre indeed.*

The defrocked priest removed his finger to rush to the other side. "A chisel destroyed the names upon each alcove."

"Vandalism?"

"Oh, no, this was methodical or else all the other macabre art would've been destroyed also."

"So you think Domitian was kept in one of those four alcoves?"

"No," MacPherson said, stepping to the center. "I think Domitian's body was brought from Rome and placed here in the center of the chamber. You can see the outline upon the floor where his sarcophagus was likely kept. I think this was a place of worship before his death. After his death, he was sealed up with the others."

"What about those spaces on either wall from Domitian?"

"Imagine all four sarcophagi placed in the four corner alcoves of this chamber. At the center...that is where they placed Domitian, and in front and behind him are two reserved spaces that remained empty." He paused. "Have you done the math?"

*Seven spaces for seven kings.*

"But it's empty," Geyer noted the obvious. "So is that good for us or bad?"

Stewart patted MacPherson on the shoulder. "This is good, Karl. Even though it was emptied long ago, it means at one point, five of the bodies were gathered together."

"The kings from our list?"

"Yes, Karl," Stewart said with a groan. "Is it possible that Domitian had already found the five kings that existed before him?"

MacPherson shook his head. "Obviously, the corpse of the First King hadn't been found yet, which is why I think the space is made for his body. Emperor Domitian had the power and might of the Roman Empire at his disposal, so if he knew whom to look for, he certainly could have sent his agents out looking. But we don't know if he found one or all four, do we?"

"If he worshipped a god with four heads, I think he likely found them," Stewart insisted.

"Which kings?" Geyer asked.

Stewart turned to MacPherson and nodded.

"We don't know if our list matches the same figures that Eos searches for," MacPherson argued.

"But it is possible for the Romans to have access to the names from our list, isn't it?"

"In theory, yes."

"Which names?" Geyer insisted.

"Go ahead and tell him."

"We believe that the Sons of Darkness, as they were called by our friend in Rome, include Antiochus Epiphanes, Alexander the Great, Ramses the Great, and the legendary King Nimrod of ancient Babylon."

Karl seemed satisfied by the answer. *Is that why Nicollet chose him? To be the annoying vetter of theories?*

"How did Domitian manage to find the Four Heads?" Stewart asked.

MacPherson rubbed his receding hairline for inspiration and then a smile flashed on his face. "By 95 AD, the Roman Empire extended into Egypt and Greece and had access to Mesopotamia. The Flavians were servants of the Julian dynasty—until chaos allowed them to step up. I would assume that before Vespasian seized power, he had this shrine built here in Taranto. Then the stars aligned for the family: father, brother, and Domitian all rose to power. Why would you worship Roman gods when the gods of your forefathers guided you to power?"

MacPherson knelt down to inspect the outline of the center sarcophagus. "Even though Domitian was an outsider, he strengthened the Roman Empire. Historians say it never ran so efficiently, and because of this, it began to expand. One of his greatest feats was the temporary conquest of a large island in the Atlantic."

"Atlantis?" Stewart asked too quickly. Even in finding the chamber empty, its existence inspired him.

MacPherson scoffed and laughed. Then remembering his position, he grew solemn. "No, my Lord, I was speaking of Brittania. He did what few rulers have ever done—he conquered Scotland. It didn't last, but then again, neither did Domitian. He killed his own assassin and died childless, which allowed Rome to create a new dynasty. Rome had no love for this man and palaces he built in his own name were quickly claimed. I'm sure his loyal servants had no other choice than to bring his corpse here, where it could be kept safe."

"Safe? Apparently not," Geyer chuckled. "So where did they take Domitian's body?"

"I wish Professor Morgan were here," MacPherson suddenly said. Back in Scotland, they were theological rivals since Morgan was an expert in northern mythology. "He'd know the answer better than I."

"Morgan?" Stewart asked, thinking of the other expedition. *Alas, I wish they were all with us.* Apparently, he wasn't the only one thinking fondly of the others.

MacPherson stood. "After Domitian died in 96 AD, the Roman Empire slowly began to crumble yet still managed to hold on for another few centuries. In the cruel winter of 487, two enemies descended on Rome, forever ending the Ancient Roman Empire as we knew it. A barbarian named Odoacer swept into Italy, conquering the city of Rome before making the city of Ravenna his new capital city. This barbarian didn't last long. Another enemy of Rome, Theodoric the Great, stole the whole of Italy away from Odoacer, who withdrew to his stronghold in Ravenna. At a banquet meant to celebrate the defeat of the Roman Empire, Theodoric slew Odaocer and claimed all of Italy, including this mausoleum, as his property."

*My belief in Father MacPherson is paying off. He's a wonder.* "So who is this Theodoric fellow?"

"That's the curious part. Before we departed Murthly, Professor Morgan and I had a poignant conversation about a…family. At first, that family came out of the north with sudden and wild ambition. About the time the Flavian family was likely gathering the four kings together, this northern family began a generational conquest, and with each generation, as the power of Rome lessened, their power grew."

"What are you talking about?" Stewart demanded.

"The Goths. They came out of a small village in Sweden and invaded Europe. By the 4th century, they divided up into two separate branches: Visigoths and Ostrogoths. While the Visigoths sacked Rome in 410, the Ostrogoths of Theodoric finished the job. It seems Domitian's invasion of Scotland woke the sleeping giant."

"Goths?" Geyer also voiced the word.

"Goths," MacPherson repeated. "This mausoleum was not plundered. It was carefully extracted and carried away."

*Carried away? So my theory is true. The bodies are being carefully preserved.* "I take it they didn't carry it to Scotland?"

"Not that I've heard, Lord Stewart," MacPherson took in good humor.

"Is our quest at an end?" Geyer mocked. "Or do you have an inkling where they might've taken Domitian's corpse?"

Once again, MacPherson measured his words. "I wish I had Professor Morgan to make this a bit clearer, but I have a pretty good idea where to go next: Ravenna, the stronghold of the Goths."

"And how far is Ravenna?" Stewart asked.

"You're in luck. It's just a few days' travel up the coast of Italy from here."

# CHAPTER 12



Jamie Anderson understood monsters. He'd spent his entire life being stared at for being a dwarf. Despite his maintained ebony hair, his manicured flesh, and his unnecessarily expensive clothing, strangers either chuckled or gasped at him. Chuckles didn't bother him as much as the expressions of fear. Having been part of the Napoleonic War, he didn't give two shits any more about trying to change perceptions, but he still felt the eyes.

*Stewart was a fool to bring me with him. I stick out like a sore thumb.*

He certainly didn't have any fear. Now middle-aged, he walked with an ebony walking stick with a sharp blade hidden in the hilt. Any unwanted attention could be handled, but for good measure, the young Texan walked beside him.

Frank Penny wasn't large like Antoine Clement, but he was blessed with quickness and agility, something Anderson severely lacked.

And six-shooters.

Walking down the street with six-shooters at his side in a large leather holster and belt buckle almost the size of Anderson's head, Penny drew as much attention as a dwarf. The young man kept his mouth shut and followed orders. The two had never met until the young Texan showed up with Clement. The discipline at his age was disconcerting.

A step ahead, the former priest Ross MacPherson continued to second guess Anderson by looking at a wrinkled paper filled with paper marks. Even though MacPherson had lost his place in the world due to a tryst with a rich woman, his academic ego remained unharmed. "It should be two more blocks."

*It's three blocks ahead and on the left.*

Whether arranging dinner or travel, Anderson preferred to take Penny with him. When Anderson began a conversation, and exotic Penny stood quietly with his vacant eyes, folks listened to him, sensing the respect the armed escort gave him. Standing beside MacPherson turned him into some sort of odd parasite.

*Rich men traveling with a dwarf? Folks will eventually recognize the Fool of Murthly.*

Long ago, he played the part of the fool, but his years at Murthly gave him skills beyond pleasuring the maids and curious female guests. With Lord Stewart away for so many years, he managed the estate. From financing to organizing, Anderson spent his days behind a desk, giving instructions. For this reason, Stewart insisted he come on the trip. Aside from managing the funding for the expedition, Anderson also arranged all transportation.

While the married couples enjoyed their evening together, Stewart's team of investigators visited all the places written down on MacPherson's paper.

"Perhaps it's another block," Anderson offered after MacPherson almost spun himself dizzy trying to understand his error.

*We should've brought Professor Morgan with us instead of sending him west with Clement,* Anderson decided. Whereas MacPherson believed himself to be an expert in all matters under Heaven, Morgan spent his academic career chasing down a fairly epic legend—Eos.

After Joseph Nicollet's death, the Auguste Edouart portrait arrived, sending Stewart into a frenzy that brought Corey Morgan into their lives. The more alcohol the two consumed as they stared up from the couch at the silhouette of Nicollet, the stranger the theories became.

Neither asked Anderson his thoughts.

Yet he listened and remembered details.

Professor Morgan excitedly read from an Icelandic poetry book about an epic battle between the Goths and Attila the Hun deep in modern day Romania. "How would that tale end up in Iceland if

the Goths didn't maintain a connection to their Nordic homeland?"

While Anderson mixed drinks for the two, they concocted theories that connected survivors of the Genesis flood to the colony of Atlantis and survivors of the Atlantis cataclysm to the colony of Boreas. The People of the Northwind stayed to themselves for a millennia or more until something woke the sleeping bear from its slumber. Morgan speculated it was the expanding Roman Empire or Christianity while Stewart argued it was King Solomon and his quest for the Philosopher's Stone. Regardless, the Boreans became the Goths, and the Goths conquered Rome and took the stolen loot to the Shrine of Wuoth in Ravenna, which Anderson now sought.

"It's not going to look like Stonehenge," Anderson teased. "These people probably busted up any shrine to make foundations for the houses we're looking at now."

MacPherson put his hands on his hips. "There's a church over there. Let's check it out."

"The Shrine of Wuoth isn't going to be a church," Anderson insisted.

Penny gave him no help, so they followed MacPherson. They found a basilica with a tall belltower—all built in recent years. If Ravenna had once been a Gothic stronghold, then it would still be considered sacred by its contemporary adherents—the Order of Eos. For this reason, Stewart didn't show his face, leaving the inspection to his men.

"This church is only a few hundred years old," Anderson noted.

"Of course," MacPherson began, "when Gaston de Foix and the French invaded Ravenna, they likely leveled everything in sight during the siege. You remember what that historian said about the Battle of Ravenna?"

*Fuck…you…*

Anderson remembered the story from earlier in the morning. The local historian told them all about the 1512 Battle of Ravenna but mainly focused on the omen of the Monster of Ravenna. Three centuries later, the disgusting details about a deformed child remained long after details about the Goth invaders had faded away. The citizens of Ravenna believed the Apocalypse was at hand after a monster worthy of being Satan's child was born. With a horn on its forehead, wings, clawed feet, and a third eye, the deformed child was viewed as a bad omen and a sign of God's wrath. Shortly after, the French marched on Ravenna, leveling the town despite a fierce defense by the local Italians. All the while the local historian told the tale, he stared at Jamie Anderson.

"Over here, look, it's a hidden plaza," MacPherson said.

"It's private property," Anderson insisted as MacPherson walked around the left side of the church's front plaza and through a slight opening that led to a wooded plaza. From the streets, it was shielded, but slipping between the church and the new apartment buildings, they found a specimen of old Ravenna.

The trees, while towering and massive, had likely regrown in the past three centuries as well, but the reason nothing had been built in the space was obvious.

"It's like a shorter version of StoneHenge, isn't it?" MacPherson asked smugly.

*Fortune smiles on the fools,* Anderson decided about MacPherson's luck.

"Is this what we were looking for?" Frank Penny finally spoke.

"Yes, my dear boy, I believe it is," Anderson admitted. After insults and a wild goose chase, Anderson's mood finally improved when he realized MacPherson really did know what he was doing.

"What do you think?" MacPherson asked before he rushed ahead to inspect the geographical oddity.

Among the benches, herb gardens, and cascading trees, seven boulders rose in the garden, each buried up to its neck, leaving only table sized platforms in the hidden yard. Once, before the church and apartments were built around it, the massive boulders would have likely given any man, Christian or Pagan, pause. MacPherson had found a book on Gothic myths and legends, which told of a shrine to their god. Although the original name was lost to modernized translations of Odin or Jupiter, the title for the shrine, Wuoth, inspired Stewart once MacPherson translated it: *Raging Ghostly Host.*

Anderson immediately knew Stewart's interpretation. While Odin was famous for sending out his Valkyries to gather the slain

heroes from the battlefield to bring to Valhalla, his hall of the dead, Stewart and Morgan had found a unique variation of the legend that fit the purposes of Eos—collecting seven kings.

"I'm glad my French forefathers pillaged this damnable place," Anderson answered bitterly. "Between the Monster of Ravenna and this Shrine of Wuoth, the Goths deserved to be driven out."

"So you agree that this once was the Shrine of Wuoth?" MacPherson asked.

"I do," Anderson said. "Do you happen to know where the Goths went from here?"

MacPherson shook his head. "If the Goths really did sack Rome and Taranto in order to carry away the sacred treasure known as Wuoth, it's all gone. Whether it was the French in 1512 or someone else a thousand years earlier, there's nothing left in Ravenna to find. This will devastate Lord Stewart."

"We've reached a dead end," Penny said, looking around the closed plaza.

Anderson couldn't tell if the pun was accidental, but he laughed just the same. "You boys don't know Lord Stewart as well as I know him. The man is independently wealthy and unable to live a sedentary life. All this means is more paperwork for me as I prepare for the next stage of our journey."

"But we don't know where the Goths went after their defeat in 1512."

"It matters not," Anderson insisted and began the long walk back to the others. "Lord Stewart has seven names and seven destinations on that list of his. We might've reached a dead end with Emperor Domitian, but there are other names to investigate."

# CHAPTER 13



Lady Christina Battersby Drummond-Stewart woke hours before she intended to. First, she had to frantically find the waste basket to control the spew of two bottles worth of debauchery. Despite the basket almost tipping over during her second heaving torment of vomit, she kept her cabin floor clean.

Next, she had to deal with the cause of her early awakening—a throbbing leg muscle. She'd angered it just by rolling over quickly in bed, and now, it was fully awake. Just below her hip, on the inside of her right thigh, the tendon throbbed like a second heartbeat. If she kept her knees together—which had certainly not been the case last night—the pain wasn't so bad, but swinging her leg out made her see spots.

*This certainly won't do.*

Rising from bed and taking shuffling steps, she dealt with the mistakes of the previous night, including the scattered pillows and sheets from the other side of the bed.

As she prepared to step out of the cabin into the upper decks of the yacht, she tried to remember who she'd taken as a lover the previous night.

She'd gotten quite drunk after they arrived in port at Thessaloniki, and with so many fine eating and drinking establishments right off the docks, she'd gotten carried away.

Lord Stewart had immediately gotten to planning the itinerary for the latest port. Like a king holding court, he sent his knights scurrying back and forth into the city. After holding court for a few hours, he'd gone to bed early in preparation for a long day of travel ahead.

*It wasn't my husband who slept in my bed.*

For breakfast, she didn't need to be glamorous, but it still took a while to be presentable as befitting a lady. When she was finally suitable, she hobbled to the doorway, took a deep breath to prepare herself for the pain, and then walked as normally as she could down the hall of the yacht, up the stairs, and to the dining room.

*What time is it?*

Although she could smell breakfast, several of the tables had been cleared, which meant she was one of the last ones to wake. She turned to one of the servants and said, "Coffee, please."

*Oh, how I need coffee.*

She was on her second cup when Jamie Anderson entered the dining room. He gave a malicious grin upon seeing her.

*He knows.*

"May I join you for breakfast?"

"Only if you don't speak. I have a terrible headache."

"Yes, quite understandable. I'll meditate on the day's tasks until you need conversation."

*It wasn't him.* Sir Jamie had been sent with Sir Frank into the city, stealing away the handsome Texan for the evening. *So it wasn't Mr. Penny either.*

"Where is everybody?" she finally asked.

Jamie took several moments to study her before finally answering her. "Lord Stewart, Mr. Geyer, Father MacPherson, and Mr. Penny have all booked passage for a tour of ancient Pella."

All she needed to do was furl her brow for him to continue speaking. After thirty years of living under the same roof as Anderson, they knew each other better than husband and wife.

Anderson explained. "Pella is the home of Alexander the Great, one of the…kings of yore we're so interested in learning about. Lord Stewart is simply being thorough, for Alexander the Great has been a subject of curiosity for centuries, and more curious scholars than we have already been here. It should be a quick and safe trip."

The young dark-haired waitress with the dimples and slender hips took their breakfast order. Since leaving Ravenna, she'd learned most of the crew on *The Mina*. But suddenly, she couldn't even remember the poor girl's name. "What's so interesting about Alexander the Great that made my husband come all this way."

"Alexander the Great was a genius."

"Ah, now I understand."

For a decade after reaching puberty, the young lordling looked for adventure in beautiful bodies or faces. One of these adventures left her with their son George. As a servant in the Stewart household, she never dreamed of keeping him to herself. Even though he shocked Scottish society by marrying the peasant girl, he quickly chased after new adventures. Later in life, Lord Stewart looked for mysterious enigmas like Antoine Clement. His most recent phase had been intellectuals—professors, priests, and scientists—who could share the unknown with him.

Anderson continued, "Alexander the Great was more than just a genius, though. We're here because Alexander seemed prescient enough to be able to tie the past to the future. Alexander was fascinated by Ramses the Great, Nimrod, and the nameless kings of old, which motivated him to leave Macedonia to go out and conquer these mighty empires just so he could have a firsthand look at their secrets."

"He's the one from the Bible?" she asked. Father MacPherson had told her about Alexander the Great during the passage to Greece.

"Yes, while many scholars feel the Book of Daniel is revisionist history, if it was indeed an authentic prophecy, then there is no doubt that Alexander the Great was the fulfillment of prophecy."

"Mmm hmm," she vocalized despite the details boring her. *Was my lover Father MacPherson?* Christina tried to place where he'd been the previous night. She'd flirted with him plenty, but even though he lost his priestly collar, he remained aloof to her efforts—if not even insulted by them. It would have taken a lot of alcohol to seduce him, and he was either sitting at the table with her husband or running into town on missions. "And what are they trying to learn?"

"A few things. Despite reaching a dead end with Emperor Domitian, your husband feels emboldened about his beliefs for the five kings. First, they're going to confirm a few possible burial sites. The mystery of Alexander's resting place and his great golden sarcophagus has baffled treasure hunters for centuries now, and Lord Stewart is only going to places that have already been written about, but who knows? Perhaps they'll stumble across a hidden passage. Miracles happen."

*Like the miracle of a woman my age finding a lover.*

"They're hoping to find clues to understand the motivations of Alexander the Great. It appears as if our boy-genius general swept through ancient Bablylon, Israel, and Egypt with occult ideas in his head, but once he dominated these kingdoms, he didn't go home—he set his sights on the east."

*Please, no trips to the Orient.* She knew the dangers that motived their hasty trip yet she missed home. The waitress brought their breakfast, and for a few moments, they both grew silent. Realizing the conversation had stalled, she asked, "What's in the east?"

"That's what your husband wants to understand. Alexander took his army on a legendary invasion all the way to India."

"Please tell me we're not going to India!"

Anderson chuckled. "No, I'll be spending the rest of the day with the captain of the yacht making plans to sail to Egypt."

The captain's face came into mind. He, too, was middle-aged, although completely bald. He was lean and witty. *No, not him.* Although they flirted over dinner, the captain immediately departed the ship to deal with the needs of the yacht. "Good," she finally answered, adding, "Why did Alexander travel to India?"

Anderson never ceased to impress her. Like herself, he'd begun as a servant, and despite foul behavior and language from time to time, he proved to be organized and could remember details verbatim. "India wasn't his destination. He thought it would be the path of least resistance. He tried to pass through a northern route to the Himalayan Mountains, the infamous Gates of the Magogoli. Both weather and renegade tribes stopped him, so he took his mighty army to the south. If his men hadn't mutinied, his plans had been to travel through the Punjab region to find a holy mountain called the Navel of the Universe."

*Navel?*

Christina gasped, remembering the waiter. The young man had been delivering their supper meal to the table when she'd turned and placed her forearm into his crotch. Laughter ensued, and for the next two hours, he became the subject of teasing—and her flirtation. *Did I end up sleeping with him?* "And why was Alexander looking for this navel?"

"Ah, you know. He wanted to understand the secrets of the universe, just like William. Powerful men like to know who's holding their strings. For Alexander, he followed the stories of an early tribe of man finding enlightenment there."

"What kind of enlightenment?" she asked, remembering how the men had escorted her from the table at the restaurant. Too much wine required a steady hand, but the docks had been slippery, and her flat-bottomed shoe had slid out awkwardly to the side, creating a painful "pop" in her groin muscle. After she collapsed onto the ground, she sat there awaiting help.

"I've only heard them talk about these legends," Anderson hedged. "I don't know if I have the details right."

"I doubt many of the details will make sense to me, but tell me anyway until my mind is clear. I need a distraction from my present condition."

"Of course," he grinned playfully. "When you overlay all these legends, the basic narrative is that there once was an old kingdom ruled by a powerful man. This Great Sorcerer learned of his fate through some oracle of old, but instead of accepting it, he rejected it and went to war with the Creator."

"God?"

"Some see it that way. His fate was to be part of the world's destruction, so he learned as much truth and magic as a human can learn during a life, and when death finally came for him, he did something no other human has done: he trapped his own soul."

"Why?"

"Again, the overlapping of legends and lore describe a spiritual river that brings souls to the realm of the dead, but his soul did not make the journey. He used his magic to keep it from descending, and thus, he's caught in limbo between life and death—and the prophecy involving the end of the world is also caught in limbo.

These kings we seek…they are the ones your husband knows of because they are part of our history, but this Sorcerer King—no one knows where to find him after the legendary destruction of the Old Kingdom. Are you familiar with the tale of Pandora?"

"Of course, it's where all you men place your misogyny." A gentleman with white gloves had helped her up with a smile and a mischievous glint in his eye. When Christina fell down onto the deck, her cleavage almost came spilling out, and as she lifted her hand to her helper, she noted he'd looked down at her breasts.

"While Pandora is a Greek telling of the tale, there are other tales that mention how a young woman, a survivor of this great disaster, brought with her wisdom from the Old Kingdom. She intended her writing to be a guide for future generations—a way to avoid leading the world into another disaster. She gathered all knowledge of the Old Kingdom into a document known as the Pithos, so that after her death, her children would know what to avoid. Instead, her words did the opposite, leading evil men to seek the ancient places of the old world."

"Ah, let me guess—the Navel of the Universe."

"Apparently, in a hidden cave at this mountain, there are black stones upon which the code of the universe is written."

"Code of the Universe?"

"Everything that has happened, is happening, or will happen is written down in stone, including the designs of each and every creature. If you destroy these black stones, you destroy the future."

"Or the past," Christian mocked.

Anderson nodded knowingly. "Using the Pithos, Pandora's evil children began to scour the world seeking the answers. They found a few relics to affirm her story, but it was her own words that undid her cautionary tale. Even though the world is different from the Old Kingdom, her description of the stars allowed her children to know the line upon which the Old Kingdom aligned with our current world. The world is a big place, but it's getting smaller and smaller thanks to new inventions, and our enemies are racing toward oblivion."

"I don't understand. Are we trying to stop these prophecies?"

Jamie Anderson slid his juice aside and signaled the waiter. "Could I get a little gin?"

"Make that two," Christina added. "My heart breaks for poor Pandora. In the Greek version, she's just a curious idiot. In your version, she's simply trying to protect her children, only to do the opposite. I feel I'm doing the same thing on this trip. William still fascinates me. He was a wonder to me when I was a young woman, and even now, he's still a wonder to me. But I know I bore him. I know I don't interest him. I know deep down he sees me as a peasant."

"I know he still sees me as a whimpering dwarf, what of it? We're with him, aren't we?"

"Yes, but I'm afraid I've messed things up just like Pandora."

"You're referencing the bosun?" Anderson asked with raised eyebrows.

*Bosom!* The handsome young man that had rushed from the yacht had been the ship's bosun. Unlike the wait staff, the bosun had been a mystery to her still. He'd been working with his deck crew on repairs for the boat when they were called over to help Lady Stewart back to the ship. She'd gone on and on about his title, and after his grin at her bosom, she took things too far.

When the gin arrived, she slammed hers back in one sip. "We've never been truly husband and wife. Even before I gave him George, he was never mine and I was never his, but on this trip, I wanted to make him mine, but he only has room in his heart for a ghost now."

*Jean Nicholas Nicollet—the only one to deny him.*

"Strangely enough, I was hoping this trip would prove *my* worth to him, yet off he goes with his others while I sit here with the women. Some hero I am."

"Can we get rid of him?"

"Lord Stewart?"

"No, the bosun. I don't want to see his face lest I remember what I did last night." *Oh, but he was so handsome and young.* "Can you remove him from the ship?"

Jamie Anderson took a drink of his gin. Aside from his misshapen ears and a slightly beaked nose, he had a perfect face, freshly shaved. His expressive brow, kind eyes, and broad smile would have made for the face of Lancelot. Only he didn't have a diminutive body. "Removing him from the yacht could prove a little difficult. Before we left, each member of the crew signed on for a one-year tour, with pay bonuses dependent on numerous levels of secrecy. Even though none of them know what we're doing or where we're going, they know it's clandestine and dangerous. Removing him from the crew would create a security risk."

"You wouldn't have him killed, would you?" she asked with concern.

Fortunately, Anderson had a hearty, earnest laugh at the suggestion. "No, but I also couldn't send him home. I'd have to send him to some private location for the duration of the contract, but he could put us in danger if he didn't follow instructions."

"Oh, please, don't bother." Unlike William, she didn't want to keep her former lovers around as trophies. "It's not like it's the first time I committed adultery; I just didn't want him to think it was something that it wasn't."

"I'll speak with him and explain matters. A small bonus might help him ignore you for the rest of the trip."

"Could you?"

"Consider it dealt with."

With the matter of the injured groin muscle and mystery of her lover solved, Christina turned to her remaining breakfast for a few minutes before revisiting the unresolved matter. "So which side of the matter are we on? Are we trying to stop this prophecy from happening? Or are we serving the prophecy?"

Jamie lifted his empty gin glass. He waited to answer her until it had been refilled and half-emptied. "Apparently, we were on the verge of taking hold of the prophecy a decade ago before Nicollet asked this same question. He claimed to know the location of the Great Sorcerer's tomb and the tool needed to wake him, but this philosophical question stayed his hand." Anderson took a swig of the gin. "Do you remember Lord Stewart's trip to the Holy Lands?"

*How could I forget? He set me aside for his Cree lover.* She nodded.

"He tried to find answers for Nicollet, and discovered the lore explaining why Eos searched for the Great Sorcerer. On the other side of the coin, the Church also knew about the prophecy; some factions wanted to claim it and others wanted to destroy it."

"But isn't the prophecy tied to the Antichrist?"

Jamie raised an eyebrow. "Do you see why Nicollet delayed? Once Clement is done dealing with our enemies, he will ascertain what Nicollet found, securing it if necessary. Our mission is similar, while we're learning about the legacy of these kings, we will take hold of the prophecy so that our enemies don't do something foolish."

"Well, this conversation alone is far more interesting than anything that happened back at Murthly." Christina scoffed. "Please, distract me. Find something, anything to get my mind off of current matters."

Jamie looked past the yacht, to the city that was waking. "The city was one of the first cities to become Christian. The Apostle Paul wrote two epistles to the people of Thessaloniki."

"That's not what I need, Jamie. Not after last night."

"I'm not one for religion, either. Okay. Well," Anderson finished his gin. "Ah, I have one. The city is named after Alexander the Great's sister, Thessalonike, which I can tell from your expression, does not interest you," Anderson chuckled. "But let me tell you a bit of dirt about his sister. Alexander's father had several wives, so the palace likely had as much drama and intrigue as an Italian yacht."

Jamie winked at her eye roll.

"Alexander the Great's best friend and general, Cassander, ended up marrying Princess Thessalonike, but soon, both Cassander and the Macedonians began to question Alexander's loyalty to his homeland, so much so, that his own family began to plot against him, and after his return from India, he was poisoned. By whom? No one knows, but it is believed that his brother-in-law Cassander not only benefited but also did his best to destroy many of the occult projects started by Alexander."

"So Cassander was trying to prevent it from falling into the wrong hands. Like us?"

"I suppose that is true. There is a legend that after her brother's death, Thessolonike was transformed into a Mermaid, and when she approached a ship, she would inquire about her brother, asking "Is Alexander the Great alive?" If the crew answered in the affirmative, she would swim away, but if they answered in the negative, she would transform into a gorgon and turn the ship and crewmen to stone."

"I'm not sure what to make of that story."

"If she does make an appearance on our passage to Egypt, at least now you know what to say." Jamie Anderson winked and rose.

"Thank you, Jamie. Thank you for today."

THE END OF PART TWO

# PART THREE
## THE NORTH SEA

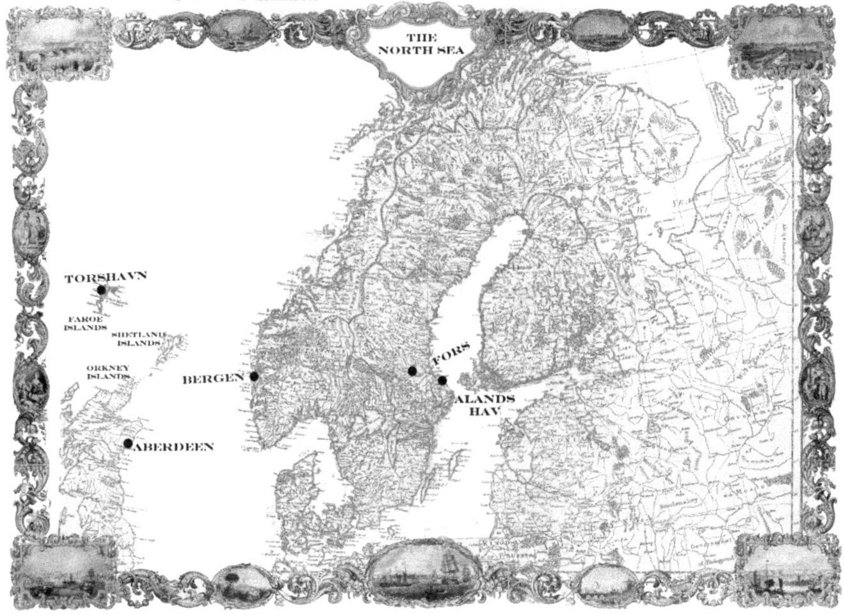

# PART THREE

# CHAPTER 14

ABERDEEN, SCOTLAND

1 8 5 2

Antoine Clement watched from the deck of the *Steamship Argyle* as its sister ship headed south from the port of Aberdeen. So far, Stewart's plan had gone off without a hitch but seeing his friend departing for the Mediterrannean filled him with deep sadness, which in turn, fueled his rage for even being in the situation.

In his life, the Canadian Cree had seen enough ships to not be overly impressed by the current vessel. The *Argyle* was powered by a single steam engine. The 100 foot, sleek vessel still had two thin masts on both sides of the twenty foot tall smokestack, yet it didn't rise more than twenty feet from the waterline. Like Stewart's vessel, it was enough ship to jump from port to port along the North Sea but not to cross the Atlantic.

Stewart's ship was still a dot on the horizon when Professor Morgan stepped out onto the aft deck and stood beside Clement. Once again, Stewart had managed to entangle a man of talent into his mad quest. Morgan spread both hands upon the railing and squinted at the horizon.

*Be safe, old friend,* Clement thought as he pulled his eyes away from Stewart.

"Lord Erskine's cabin has been readied. Perhaps his valet should see if he has any other needs," Professor Morgan said with a dimpled grin at their ruse.

*Lord Erskine.* While Morgan had the arrogance to play the part of a nobleman, Sergeant Cairns looked the part, and after four decades of servitude, he'd earned the role of a lifetime. Clement didn't mind taking orders from Cairns. "It was a long night," Clement answered. "Lord Erskine just needs his rest."

Both teams departed under the cover of darkness, and in three small rowboats, they'd snuck away via the Tay River before getting a small vessel to bring them up the coast from Perth to the larger port of Aberdeen. Stewart had sold his own private yacht to "rent" two ships out of Aberdeen. Each party had enough funds to improvise the rest of the mission.

"I suppose we could all use some rest after that dramatic departure from Murthly Castle. Do you really think the castle was being watched by spies from the Order of Eos?"

Clement nodded. "They'd paid a few of the locals to watch the comings and goings of the castle. So while they watched the front gates, we went out the back door."

"MacPherson told me that you traveled with Stewart to the Holy Lands."

"I did," Clement admitted. "It was 1839. Nicollet returned to the frontier with Geyer to meet with Chief Wahanantan while Stewart and I went to visit ancient Israel."

"Fascinating. What did you see?"

"Dust and stone."

Morgan laughed. "I suppose you would see a lot of dust and stone."

"A lot of stuff about King Solomon."

"Ah. Of course. He's a pivotal figure in the Bible as well as Masonic lore."

"Templar Knights. He talked a lot about them."

"Of course, the Templar Knights fueled the Great Crusades. Their name comes from the Knights of the Temple of Solomon. Legend has it that the entire conflict was invented so that they had an excuse to gain access to the old Temple. The old Norse and Norman families had an itch to scratch, and after visiting the old ruins, they turned their attention westward. That's ironic. Stewart explored the West and then turned his attention to the Middle East. Life truly is a cycle. What else did you see during this tour?"

"You'd have to ask Stewart about all those names and places. All I know is that it convinced him to listen to Nicollet…and here we are."

"I'm sorry about what happened to your father."

"He was an old man who didn't deserve to die like that."

"And you're heading back to America to get revenge on the men who killed him?"

"Yep."

"Stewart tells me the Order of Eos is thriving in America."

"Apparently, but some of them won't be thriving much longer."

"Ah, yes. You have a connection to a branch of the Sinclair family."

Clement shrugged. "I grew up with Sinclairs. It doesn't matter which Sinclair is responsible for the death of my father. I'll kill them all if I have to."

"I hope you know that I'm not coming with to help you kill anyone."

"I'll handle the killing. If I do it right, I won't have to kill too many. My father taught me how to hunt elk. Do you know what an elk is?"

"Large deer."

"They roam in great herds, like the Sinclairs. The chaos of the movement can almost be overwhelming, so, like the wolf, a sniper watches for one to step away from the pack. The one who runs alone becomes the target. It was the same thing for Mexicans during the war. Any Sinclair who steps away from the pack will be who I kill."

Morgan scoffed, "I think I understand."

The history professor stood silent for several minutes, a smug grin on his face that had Clement asking, "If you can't kill, then why are you coming with us?"

Professor Morgan took a moment to respond. "Curiosity. I lost my position at the last two universities for "spurious thinking," which is a way of saying I refused to accept the orthodox view. I found historians are trained to research but their publications must support the most widely accepted conclusions. Deviate from the norm and find yourself on the outside looking in."

"I don't follow."

"I was fired for disagreeing with historical facts."

"What the People believe is true."

"Excuse me?"

"It's a Chippewa saying."

"But you are…"

"Cree, a northern neighbor of the Chippewa. In my childhood, I spent quite a bit of time trading with the Chippewa. It's why I went ahead of Nicollet to Fort Snelling. The Chippewa saying asks 'what makes a fact a fact?' History often is what is agreed upon isn't it?"

"Exactly my point. I dared to suggest that Christopher Columbus was *not* the first to discover North America, and for my sins, I've been cast out by reputable universities. A few years ago, I visited Murthly Castle to see the library that once belonged to William Drummond of Logiealmond. Stewart allowed it, and after I lost my position, he offered his patronage in researching his own family, and of course, the Order of Eos."

"So you're familiar with our enemy," Clement politely offered a chance for Morgan to show off.

"Oh yes. It is a mythos as rich as ancient Norse mythology, which is where I first discovered it. Eos—the illustrious *Men of the Dawn*. In Norse mythology, four sons survive the great cataclysm known as Ragnarok. The Order of Eos believes it is descended from a godly bloodline, and buried deep in the earth, their gods wait to return and restore their place. It is a blurred line between mythology and history. I know Stewart has become a religious man. Are you a religious man?"

Clement, chewing on the inside of his mouth for a moment, answered, "I am a vile man, and whoever's version about the Creator is correct, I deserve his punishment. I think Stewart believes in redemption, which is why he sails first to Rome."

Nicollet had come and gone from his life like Halley's Comet, and now Stewart vanished from sight also. Without a word to Morgan, Clement returned to his cabin.

102

# CHAPTER 15



The next day, *Steamship Argyle* made port in Inverness. When viewing the busy dock, Lewis Cairns saw danger in each and every face. The faster they left, the better for the mission.

After several quiet minutes alone, Professor Morgan and Antoine Clement joined him at the deck railing as the crewmen secured the lines. *So much for being secretive and discreet.*

"How long will we be docked?" Professor Morgan asked.

"Just for a few hours," Cairns said. "We had to leave Aberdeen so quickly that our captain didn't have enough fuel or supplies to get us to Bergen."

"Which is where we'll be securing transportation across the Atlantic," Morgan repeated the plan.

"Exactly. Spontaneity was the key to our great escape from Murthly Castle. No one knew we were leaving; no one knew where we were going. If our enemies happen to figure out that we left by ship, they'd have to do some amazing detective work to know which ship and its destination."

"Then why are you nervous?" Morgan asked.

"We're still in Scotland," Cairns admitted. "Anything is possible. It'd take days for a good investigator to find out we hopped on a small ship at Dundee and then separated at Aberdeen. But a lucky investigator could have figured things out faster. So none of us are stepping off the ship."

"Absolutely, Lord Erskine," Morgan answered. The Professor seemed to be testing the boundaries of their relationship. While Stewart spoke highly of his loyalty and intelligence, Morgan also had a reputation for being arrogant.

"We're still in Scotland," Cairns repeated. "I'm still Sergeant Cairns, you're still Professor Morgan, and he's still Stewart's Indian friend. The invented title is only to be used when we're in foreign countries."

Cairns had known Clement longer than Morgan and glanced over to make sure he took no offense. Despite being a quiet man, Clement had a prickly nature and could easily be offended. From what Stewart had told him, Clement could kill a man without ever raising his voice.

"Sergeant Cairns," Morgan repeated. "I've known you for a couple of years now, and in all that time, I never knew you were a military man. I knew you were in charge of estate security, but, um, is that how you came into the service of Lord Stewart?"

"We served together in the 15th King's Hussars during the Waterloo campaign, which is why I worry about being recognized by one of the soldiers that served under us. After the war, I went into security. For my part, I investigated the death of his aunt."

"Ah, and that's when Joseph Nicollet entered the picture."

"Stewart met Nicollet in St. Louis," Clement gruffly added.

"Yes," Cairns said. "But it's where we learned the name Nicollet and how he'd been shown the map before Lady Drummond's death. That is when I learned all about the Order of Eos and those crazy prophecies and those cursed maps."

"Yes, the maps. So the Abbaron Map was in the possession of Solomon Delhut and the Al Marrakk Map was in the possession of Joel Poinsett."

"And we allowed Delhut to live in exchange for information about Nicollet's murderer," Clement added.

"Yes, the Delhuts and Sinclairs are both familiar names in the Eos legends," Morgan said. "And by allowing Delhut to live, he hired assassins to hunt down the men who threatened his life and walked away with the ancient Eos map."

"That's correct," Cairns said. He'd wanted to take in the view but instead found himself yapping away with the curious professor.

"You'll have to forgive me. A week ago, I was reading in the Murthly Library and now here I am in Inverness about to embark on a bizarre revenge tour. I'm just trying to understand my role in this venture."

"I heard Lord Stewart explain it to you in front of the whole group."

"Yes, yes, the ancient king in the ancient kingdom who created the Philosopher's Stone. I understand his theories, but what is my role in this expedition."

"You're our expert on the Order of Eos."

"After I kill the men responsible," Clement added, "we'll return to find the Stone."

"And that's where we'll need your expertise."

"I see," Morgan said. "I'm sure it'll be quite an adventure. But if Clement is in charge of revenge, and you're responsible for securing the relic, then it seems to me that I'm in charge of fact-finding."

*What is he thinking?* "Yes, that is a safe assumption."

"And spontaneity is key to this mission."

"It is. We'll secure new passage in Bergen and then the crew of the *Argyle* will have no idea where we went next. Likewise, Lord Stewart won't likely leave ship until he reaches Italy."

"Yes, I'm the one who suggested Bergen to him, but if we're also on a fact-finding mission to understand the Order of Eos better, perhaps I could propose a modification to our mission."

Cairns' glare was joined by an icy stare from Clement.

"If spontaneity is as important as my research into Eos, then let's stop by the Orkney Islands on our way to Bergen."

"If you give a good reason," Cairns insisted.

"The Sinclair family comes from the Orkney Islands. If we are about to hunt Canadian Sinclairs, it might help us to learn a bit more about our enemy."

"It's on the way?" Cairns clarified.

Professor Morgan nodded. "He wants to kill Sinclairs; I want to learn more about the Order of Eos."

"How long will you need?"

"A day or two at the most. A walk through a few cemeteries should be enough."

Cairns nodded. "Once the ship is resupplied, I'll update the captain about our new destination. It shouldn't hurt to make port for a day."

# CHAPTER 16

THE ORKNEY ISLANDS

1852

Corey Morgan checked his watch, then his satchell, and then his wooden box which had a few sandwiches prepared by the *Argyle's* cook. Lord Erskine and his valet—Cairns and Clement—stood upon the top deck as the crew secured the private vessel in the small, northfacing harbor.

He looked up to Lord Erskine and gave a friendly wave of appreciation for his fact-finding mission. It was true that nobody outside of family and a few scholars from Edinburgh could recognize him, but even so, a cabin boy named Harry stood at his side to accompany him on the brief expedition.

True to their reputation, the Orkney Islands were barren and drab with few trees in sight. If the islands were compared to a four leaf clover, the port of Kirkwall was right in the middle of the four leaves. Unlike Aberdeen, only a few other steam ships docked amongst smaller fishing vessels.

"Ready for an adventure, Harry?" Morgan asked.

"It's better than cleaning Lord Erskine's cabin."

*The lie is already taking root.* For his part, Corey Morgan played a novelist who was working on a narrative about the Vikings. Harry played the part of his son.

Once on the docks, Morgan learned where he could hire a driver, and in under ten minutes, the three were in a simple wagon climbing the hill that lead out of town.

"How long again will it take to get to the Ring of Brodgar?"

"It's good weather today," the driver added. "My girls will get you there in about an hour and a half."

"Dad?" Harry asked coyly. "What are the Rings of Brodgar?"

"They're often called the Stonehenge of the Orkneys. They are an ancient stone circle, and no one really knows who built them or when they were set up."

"What do they do?" Harry asked.

"They don't do anything. Many believe they might've been used for astronomical observations while others think they were once used for human sacrifice." He turned to the driver. "Do you get many travelers wanting to see them?"

"I reckon its one of the most popular reasons for any traveler to get off the ship. I bring folks out to it quite often during the summer."

There were several sheep farms along the main road, and the terrain continued to be sprawling green fields dotted by the occasional rock outcropping.

"You can see Loch of Stenness at the bottom of the hill. It's a shame they don't have a bridge or causeway connecting to the other side of the lake. We'll have to go all the way around the lake to reach the Ring."

"Have you lived on the Orkney Islands your whole life?"

"Oh, yes. My father has Norwegian and Scottish roots, but my mother's side comes from the ancient Picts."

"I've been told I have some Pictish blood as well."

"What are Picts, dad?"

"They were the remnants of an Iron Age tribe that painted themselves. Unfortunately, my book is going to feature the Viking Era. Say, you wouldn't happen to have any churches or cemetaries along the way?"

"There's a small church at Dounby, which is where we turn to reach the west side of the lake. But there is large cemetary near StoneyHill Castle overlooking the lake. I've heard tell that some of those gravestones date back a thousand years. Mostly Sinclairs."

"Sinclairs? I found a story that talked about Prince Henry Sinclair traveling to North America."

"I believe the folks who live in StoneyHill Castle are descendants of his. To my families, they are new blood. I think he came out of—oh, I forget the name of the town."

"Caithness?"

"No…Rosslyn. At that time, the Norwegians held the Orkney Islands and gave it to their Scottish ally."

"If it's no trouble, I'd very much love to visit."

"There's another road that'll still head toward Dounby. It'll just add ten minutes onto our trip."

The ruse had worked.

A few minutes later, Professor Morgan walked among the open fields overlooking the eastern shore of the inland lake. While the distant castle had a stone fence surrounding it, the cemetery had no such precautions, which allowed him access to the gravestones. The driver waited back on the road.

Across the narrow channel, Morgan could see the monoliths of the Ring of Brodgar, which explained why the Sinclair castle faced it. The cemetary was closer to the water's edge built along the gentle slope.

"Sir, may I be excused to relieve myself?" Harry asked politely. "I'd feel wrong relieving myself on sacred ground."

"Run along."

The boy ran down hill to a ravine filled with brush where he could get some privacy.

Suddenly horsemen came riding in hard from StoneyHill Castle. Even from a distance he could see rifles drawn on the driver. Then two riders charged down the hill and galloped between the gravestones.

"State your business."

"My apologies. My name is Scott Cauldhame, I'm a writer doing research into ancient Norse families."

"So you say," one gunman said.

"You're coming with us and we'll get to the bottom of this."

"I mean no offense! I was going to visit the Rings of Brodgar when my driver mentioned this old graveyard."

"Those are our kin you're standing on."

"We'll sort this all out up at the house and find the truth of the matter."

Nothing else was said. The driver had dismounted the wagon and was also being led by gun point to a barn outside of the stone fence. By the time Morgan entered the barn, the driver was already telling them all about who he was what his business was. The gunmen seemed to accept his story easily and then turned to Morgan.

"And what's his story?"

"Where'd you get him?"

"What's he doing here?"

The driver repeated the lie, which to him was the truth.

"And what gives you the right to bring a stranger into our private cemetary?"

Again the driver repeated the whole scene but ended with, "he was the one who asked about churches and cemetaries."

"What's your interest in our family?"

Then all eyes were upon Morgan. While he repeated the lie about being a writer, he remembered Harry. The boy obviously would've seen and heard the abduction, so the longer the story took, the better his chances were of getting back to the ship before the gunman learned about the "son." The trip had been about eight miles, so if the boy ran as hard as he could, he could be there in under a half-hour if he kept off the road. So Morgan quickly shifted to his interest in the Ring of Brodgar.

"Research?" One of the gruff-looking men repeated. "I don't like the sound of that at all."

"He's written down a dozen or more names in his notebook."

A third man actually started to eat the food intended for lunch.

"Tell us more about this book of yours."

The question allowed Morgan to improvise for a time. He spoke honestly about his childhood obsession with Viking culture and then broke into a tale about Vikings seeking a lost continent that would be America. The longer he spoke, the less afraid he became. All four men were rough and tumble but seemed to be earnest men whose role involved protecting the Sinclair estate at StoneyHill Castle.

"I know I should have gone up to the front door and explained myself. My driver simply followed my orders. I'll leave, go right back to the ship, and be out of your hair immediately."

Then the gunmen began to have private conversations.

"You can go outside and wait," one said to the driver. "We know your name and where you're from. If this fellow checks out, we'll send you both on your way. If not, we'll send you on your way."

The men chuckled and Morgan felt fear return.

Once the driver left, a new question made him fear even more. "Tell us about the ship you came in on."

*What have I done?*

Unlike the story about being a writer, this one quickly fell apart when he was pressed for more details, and showing nervousness was like the smell of blood to a hungry wolfpack.

"This isn't adding up. Are you believing this?"

"I'm not. Should I go fetch Mr. Mowatt?"

"I don't think it'll take long to get the truth out of him."

"I'll get the rope."

Despite his pleas, Morgan found himself being bound by the wrists and ankles and then stretched out like like the Vitruvian Man between a couple of beams in the barn.

"The problem we're having, Mr. Cauldhame, is that our Lord and Lady received correspondance a few weeks ago calling for heightened security and caution in the days to come. Then suddenly, out of the blue, you show up poking around our cemetary claiming to be a writer. So we need to understand more about where you came from and how you got here."

Morgan tried again to calm himself, but he could see the men preparing instruments of torture, which in a functioning barn, were plentiful. In the middle of explaining his visits to other Norse settlements near Edinburgh, the barn door flew open.

Shouldering his Manton hunting rifle, Clement found the furthest man in the room and shot him squarely in the chest. He tossed the rifle to the ground and quickly found his pistol strapped to his chest. Still advancing, he spotted the second furthest man and shot through the man's outstretched fingers to his lower neck.

With a twelve inch Bowie knife, Clement charged like an enraged bull buffalo at the closest man, piercing his torso with repeated punches before racing after the final victim. The fourth man had begun to run, but Clement rotated the knife in his fingers

and sent the heavy blade into the man's back, knocking him to the ground. Clement pounced and finished him off.

Professor Morgan wet his trousers as the knife suddenly rose and grew closer to him.

"Who else saw you?" Antoine asked. "Was it just these four? They held you for two hours. Did anybody else come or go?"

"J-j-just the driver," Morgan answered.

"You don't have to worry about him either. Did they take anything that can identify you?"

Professor Morgan shook his head and Clement cut him free.

"Hurry, they likely heard the shots from the castle."

Following Clement out the door, he saw that Harry had replaced the driver in the seat of the wagon.

# CHAPTER 17



Antoine Clement ignored the approaching coastline. Instead, he turned away. He walked to the stern of the private yacht and spent a few minutes staring into the gray of the Baltic Sea.

When Professor Morgan joined him, Antoine put both hands upon the railing so as not to strangle the man to death. Fortunately, the idiot kept his mouth shut for several minutes, the best sort of apology he could hope for, given the situation.

*He's likely stolen my chance at revenge.*

Over the past 1,100 miles, Clement refused to speak to the man and chose instead to sharpen his big skinning knife at the bow of the boat. For the past several days, Professor Morgan wisely kept his distance, but now, with land appearing on both sides of the yacht, the Professor braved proximity, even with the big knife strapped to Antoine's belt. "Remind me again why are we traveling east instead of west?"

The professor exhaled, his breath shaken either by fear or the cold. "Sixteen miles is all that separates Sweden and Finland. That island ahead of us is Alands Hav, the channel marking the separation from the Baltic Sea and the Gulf of Bothnia. With the element of surprise lost, we're embracing spontaneity and changing our destination—but only a short delay."

*He thinks I am just a dumb brute.* "Yes, I agreed with Cairns about the plan. Remind me why we are approaching Sweden."

"I figured before returning to Bergen, we'd take a slight detour to explore an old legend involving Sweden. It matters, in the grand scheme of things."

Antoine noticed a bit of dark crust lodged in his cuticles—dried blood.

*Perhaps Stewart was wrong about redemption.*

*A tiger can't change its stripes.*

Since he was a boy, Antoine had a talent: killing things. As a hunter, he had no rivals. Beginning with rabbits and squirrels and later with bison and elk, his ability to stalk his prey was topped only by his marksmanship. From his childhood at Hudson Bay to his adult years on the plains and in the Rocky Mountains, his skill at doling out death was done well. For that reason, Lord William Drummond Stewart hired him as a guide. If Antoine had no peer in North America, Stewart had few rivals as a European hunter. As soldier and hunter, Stewart's reputation preceded him, and their competitive rivalry turned into something unexpected. Antoine dedicated himself to Lord Stewart, and for a few short years, their competitive relationship thrived—until Nicollet.

Although Nicollet wanted nothing to do with a physical, intimate relationship, Stewart nevertheless fell madly in love with the little French scientist. At first, religion became a roadblock to the relationship, but Stewart accepted the challenge, getting baptized in St. Louis with Nicollet as his sponsor. Later, Stewart and Clement went on a trip to the Holy Lands to investigate Nicollet's theories on the origin of the Philosopher's Stone, but even alone with Stewart on the far side of the world, the burning fascination Stewart had once shown him had turned to other obsessions.

*Am I doomed to be a killer—and to die alone?*

Antoine flicked the dried blood from his cuticle.

Even after 1,100 miles of nautical travel, Clement still felt as if they were being followed. Cairns paid the captain and crew handsomely for the detour, especially after Harry returned to the ship wide-eyed. If anything of the murders were connected to them, heading directly to Bergen could've been a mistake. Professor Morgan was right; no one would expect them to go to Sweden. "What's in Sweden?"

Professor Morgan swallowed hard, a sign of nervousness. "Somewhere on the Mediterranean, our friends are meeting with an ancient organization known as the Periphery. I like the thought of a secret society guiding and watching over God's chosen people, but that also means that the Order of Eos is equally real. My focus is learning about our enemy. I know you want vengeance for the wrongs done to you, and I am here to support that, but Lord Stewart also tasked me with researching our enemy."

"My enemy waits for my blade in Canada," Clement insisted.

Morgan cleared his throat to boldly answer, "Your blade only cuts the grains from a single stalk of wheat, but the roots of your enemy go deep into the earth. We're in Sweden to understand the origins of our enemy. You've seen the portrait, haven't you?"

*The portrait.* Even dead, Nicollet continued to keep the attention of Lord Stewart. Even after finding vengeance, the portrait of Nicollet haunted Lord Stewart, sending him into a new manic frenzy. "The Island of Atlantis? Is that it beside us? Did we come to Sweden to find the lost island?" Clement mocked.

Morgan withheld any reaction, clearly still afraid. "The mythology of Atlantis—including tales of Hyperborea and Thule—describe survivors of the great cataclysm. A tall, light-skinned race whose blood was mixed with the gods searched for a new home. Many of the tales say the survivors went far to the east, searching for a sacred mountain that brought the world into creation; other tales say the survivors settled in the north."

"Ah, Sweden."

"There are many tribes and nations in the north, mind you, so it is like searching for a needle in a haystack, but when a family becomes a nation and later becomes an empire, that family is worthy of study."

"The Sinclair family?" Antoine asked bitterly, thinking of the terrible event that transpired days earlier. *I kicked the hornets nest.*

The pall of the event hung over them and still stuck in his cuticles.

"No," Professor Morgan answered. "The Sinclair family only gained prominence in the past few centuries. The family we are seeking gave birth to the Goths. Most historians believe the Goths began with King Berig, who came across the Baltic Sea to settle

and conquer Germany, but my theory is that following the destruction of their island home, the fair-skinned survivors settled Sweden, possibly as early as 2,000 BC, where they kept to themselves for centuries. Their stories became the origins of what we now know as Norse mythology. Tucked away for centuries in the north, they held to their old religion for generations until foreigners came knocking on their door."

*Like us.* "The Romans?"

"Likely. The Goths emerged around that time. With their isolation at an end, the Goths suddenly became active with an interest that drove them to wage war with Rome. Do you know where the Goth invaders finally settled?"

Clement felt his jaw tighten. *Just tell me.* He didn't want to play games with Morgan. He shook his head slightly.

"The Goths ended up destroying the Roman Empire before settling in the Transylvania region in what is now known as the country of Wallachia and—"

*How can he just rattle off facts after what happened?* "I've given thought to cutting out your tongue and feeding it to the dogs," Clement interrupted.

"I don't know how else to apologize," Professor Morgan said between staggered breaths.

"You *dare* speak to me about wheat and roots and the history of our enemy after pulling a stunt like you did back at Orkney."

Morgan shifted his weight away from Clement.

Now, standing at the back railing of the yacht, Clement flicked away at the last bit of blood shed in Orkney. "We're at war with the Order of Eos, especially the Sinclair family. You and I are both soldiers for Lord Stewart, but I outrank you in all matters. Your curiosity almost ruined our mission. I'm returning to America for vengeance, and *if* those men back in Orkney had found out who you were and why you were there—which they would have—the rats would have run back down into the cellar. I'm going to cut someone's heart out and eat it while it still beats for killing my father; anything Stewart wants from you is secondary, is that understood?"

Professor Morgan nodded.

*He's a fool but not a coward.* "Come with me, there is something I need to give you," Antoine said, leading back to the cabins of the *Argyle*. Each cabin was modest except for the false Lord's cabin, and Clement's floor had a chest large enough to be a coffin. He unlocked it and flipped open the lid.

Inside, he had a small arsenal of weapons, ranging from rifles and pistols to knives and bayonets. Once, he'd allowed Stewart's affection to clothe him, but in recent years, all of Stewart's affections turned into the finest weapons that could be acquired.

"Take it." Antoine handed Morgan a Colt Paterson revolver and a sheathed knife he'd acquired in the Mexican War. "These served me well."

Morgan acted as if Clement had handed him a human spleen.

"Two shots per man," Clement insisted. "It can kill three men if the trigger doesn't get stuck. And tuck this knife in your boot if there's more than three men."

Morgan wheezed. "I'm sorry."

"Don't apologize. We're at war, but before you say or do anything during our stop in Sweden, I want you to explain it to me first. From now on, you advise, and I'll act. Understood?"

Morgan nodded.

"Say it."

"I'll advise, and you'll act."

"Good, now tell me more about what we're going to find in Sweden."

# CHAPTER 18



Vaktar Forsberg bridled his team of North Swedish horses to the wagon and petted their muscular flanks as he passed. Unlike his normal routine of bringing a wagon full of milk canisters into town, today the wagon held a treasure.

Leif Forsberg, his father, stood with hands on hips as Vaktar finished preparing the wagon for the trip. While milking cows allowed the family to trade for other goods in the village on a daily basis, the other Forsberg trade was woodworking, and after a long winter, Leif and his three sons produced another masterpiece. Leif tucked the canvas tarp around it and violently shoved and pushed to make sure his sons had indeed secured the load. "You're a man now; I expect you to succeed all on your own."

Vaktar nodded. *Is this the final test for me?*

Grinning their well wishes, his younger brothers gathered beside their father.

Vaktar had been there when each of the horses came into the world as greasy foals, and now his future depended on their maturity as well. "Aska, Blixt, let's go."

The horses listened despite not being commanded by Leif, and the rig began its descent down to the river.

The Forsberg family lived on a wooded hill between the villages of Fors, Lund, and Avesta. At the bottom of the hill, the pines had been cleared centuries ago for grazing pastures, but the slopes of the hill still remained untouched old forest. Any tree upon the property was cherished for its workmanship, making each as valuable as the prized horses or dairy cows.

A man with an ax or saw, Leif had taught his sons, should be shot on sight. Vaktar never had to kill a pine poacher, but he did have to shoulder his rifle to warn trespassers.

Today, Vaktar descended the hill to Avesta. On the southwestern corner of the property, he passed the origin of the family namesake—the waterfalls. The land wasn't mountainous, by any stretch, but the large hill, with a circumference of three miles, collected enough snowfall to send rapids to the river, which cut through the sediment at the base of the hill to create a deep gorge.

The most treacherous part of his journey into Avesta was passing over the pine bridge. Hitting it crooked meant shifting the weight of the wagon and tipping his cargo into the flooded gorge. He slowed the horses on approach, just to square the wagon, and then lashed to increase the speed so that the wagon bounced— instead of catching—over the first beam. With enough speed, the wheels kept spinning and he was safely on the other side.

The town of Avesta was three miles from the gorge, built upon the Dalaven River, which began deep in the center of Sweden and ended at the Gulf of Bothnia. It once had been a thriving forge, providing the area with copper and iron. Now for Vaktar, it provided a far more valuable resource—a possible bride.

The trip to town alone meant not only earning his father's trust as a man but also that the sixteen-year-old boy could search for a bride. If he couldn't find one in Avesta, he'd have to search elsewhere in the world.

*The world is full of beautiful women.*

Unfortunately, Vaktar lost his front teeth in a fist fight with some boys from the village of Lund, rendering him unwilling to smile. He did twice the work as his brothers, knowing that his freckled face and red hair (and missing teeth) could be overlooked if he were as strong as an ox. At just sixteen, he boasted the barrel chest and broad shoulders of a forty-year-old man rather than a teenager.

No girls lined the streets of the town, so he kept his eyes on the road and led the team to the far northwestern side of town, where

the road met the bridge. Just before the bridge, he turned, taking a narrow street down to a factory parking lot.

There, the mayor of Avesta waited with a crew of several men, including a dark skinned giant from a foreign land. Vaktar and his three brothers had managed to load the wagon themselves, but the mayor had almost ten men waiting. It made Vaktar slightly nervous.

He'd beaten those boys from Lund despite being outnumbered, but these were adult men who waited for him.

As Vaktar set the brakes on the wagon, the group separated into two small groups, with the mayor and his sons taking a few steps away from the others.

"Ah, Forsberg, the prize has arrived."

Vaktar climbed off the seat of the wagon and began untying the canopy tarp. The mayor's sons helped and soon Vaktar was able to pull the tarp free, revealing the treasure.

"Lord Erskine, come see, come see. This should interest you."

The fat lord with his bushy white goatee and layered clothing came waddling over to the wagon. The dark-skinned foreigner and a black-bearded man followed. In the distance, two men stood at the pier, watching the proceedings.

Vaktar began undoing the heavy straps while the mayor gloated about his purchase.

"Speaking of living history, let me show you my beautiful new byrding."

"Is this a Viking longboat?" the bearded man asked, translating.

The locals laughed. "Viking? In a way, I suppose. We're river rats around here. Centuries ago, our craftsmen designed a boat that could not only be taken over the rocks and rapids of our Swedish rivers but could also cut through the big waves of the open sea. The Forsberg family is famous for their craftsmanship. Even though the days of the Goth and Viking are now ancient history, they still make a longship every three years. I happened to be the highest bidder for this beauty. It's only ceremonial, but it's still beautiful, isn't it?"

Lord Erskine said something in English, which Vaktar didn't understand well. The young translator with the black beard, however, spoke Swedish with a peculiar accent. "It looks very authentic."

"This isn't a replica," the mayor continued. "The Forsbergs have been making boats throughout recorded history. Before Avesta had a copper forge, we were famous for making these ships. They are virtually indestructible. If you're sincerely investigating Viking history, as you put it, you should begin and end with the Forsberg family."

Suddenly, all eyes were on Vaktar, who wished to be back home.

"Our journey is to find the Cnoyen family," the translator explained. "Lord Erskine's relatives are descendants of this fellow named Cnoyen." He looked down to his notebook correcting himself by stating, "Cnoyen of Dalaven."

The mayor and his sons began talking to each other. "We find it strange that anyone would claim to belong to the river rather than a town. There are not any families by the name Cnoyen. The name sounds Dutch."

The Lord and his men talked. As they conferred, they kept referencing a book, but Vaktar studied the dark-skinned man, who was unlike any man he'd ever met. From the details of his face, skin, and hair, Vaktar made an assumption: *He's a native from America.*

Finally, the bearded translator had a response. "Yes, you are correct. The fellow we seek was a Dutch priest by the name of Jacob Cnoyen. After visiting with King Magnus, this astronomer priest returned with men of his western expedition to their home in Dalaven. My apologies for the misreading."

"I know this story," the mayor declared and then put his hand on Vaktar's shoulder. "The lost men who found a northern passage. Twenty years gone, only to return as weathered old men. The men of the expedition were certainly Swedes."

The translator put his finger in the book then nodded. "Yes, yes, it does say Goths and Northmen were on the journey. How do you know this?"

"Leif Forsberg told me the story while sitting at his great stone chimney," the mayor bragged. "Our greatest export, beyond copper and ships, is the Forsberg men. They are all great explorers.

They travel out into the world and rarely come back. But when they do come back, they return with tales, and occasionally priests."

"Are you saying this boy can attest to the tale written in this book?"

Vaktar shifted uncomfortably.

"I'm only saying I've heard this story before," the mayor added. "I'm not even sure if Vaktar knows this story."

Vaktar knew the story. Neighbors would schedule seasonal visits with his storytelling father, bringing their children for hours of stories. As a result, Vaktar had heard countless stories of countless Forsbergs and their travels to distant lands. "I know it."

Everyone grew smiles.

"What are the odds, Lord Erskine?" the mayor posed. "I told you my village had a rich history. You should stay for a few more days and we can tell you more."

Lord Erskine nodded then had a private conversation with his traveling companions. The bearded translator kept eyeing Vaktar, which made him a bit uncomfortable. Finally, the translator asked him directly, "We'd love to speak directly with your father about his storytelling."

Vaktar looked to the mayor for help, but clearly, he was concerned with only bringing his prized vessel to his house—a trophy of his wealth. "It's a few miles north of here."

The men conferred before the translator spoke. "We'll leave some of our men here with our little steamship, but we'd very much like to travel back to your father and speak with him."

*Shit.* Vaktar thought the hardest part of his day was going to be delivering the longship to town. It was a test of manhood to steer the wagon along the safest path to town, but now, his manhood was being tested by his judgment.

*Are these men friends or foes?*

# CHAPTER 19

RUNEFIELD

1 8 5 2

*A bunch of bloody pagans*, Cairns thought as they toured the rocky hill above the farmhouse. *There is probably a shallow grave waiting for the three of us.*

Trailing behind them, Antoine Clement walked beside the Forsberg boy. Professor Morgan passed information between his host and himself. Leif Forsberg was a true Viking, and Cairns wondered if a skilled killer like Clement could contend with the brute.

Meanwhile Cairns felt like a transparent fraud. The entire Forsberg family eyed him suspiciously as if suspecting that under his fancy clothes he was a fat soldier named Lewis Cairns. It was easier being Sergeant Cairns, who took orders and kept to himself, than it was playing the part of a Scottish Lord, seeking to understand his family heritage.

*If this family turns out to belong to the Order of Eos, will Clement kill them all?*

It was looking more likely by the minute.

After an evening of warm hospitality, where Mrs. Forsberg tried to stuff as much food into them as humanly possible, Leif Forsberg woke them the next morning with the promise of a wondrous tour.

"These are runestones," Morgan finally declared like a child at Christmas, taking a moment to explain to him. "They chronicle important events—like a book written upon stone."

*Why do they give me chills?* "What are we doing out here, Morgan?"

"Patience. I owe Stewart my findings, and I'll give it to him when we return."

"You'd better not be putting us in danger again."

"Danger? From overfeeding? These are just simple farmers."

Yet seeing the runestones and their blood red lettering, Cairns wasn't so sure.

Leif Forsberg finally stopped talking, patting the top of the stone.

Morgan explained: The Forsberg family had a tradition that went back over a thousand yards. The eldest Forsberg son did not inherit, as most cultures followed, but instead, they were sent out into the world as explorers. Viking was not a nationality but instead a verb—to adventure. The woodworking skill passed down from father to son ended up with a firstborn Forsberg son in possession of a longboat that could take a dozen of his friends out into the world.

Initially, the "river rats" in the family would take their longships up and down the Dalalven River for a summer. Then, it became a competition to see how far one could get and make it back before the river iced up. The fun adventure eventually became ingrained, fueling what would first become the Goth invasion of the European continent and later the infamous Viking raiders of later centuries.

"If a firstborn son returned from his adventures, a runestone would be made to chronicle the journey," Morgan explained. "Most times, the firstborn son was never seen again, and tales would be told around the fireplace of imagined heroism. Every once in a while, a son would come back."

Cairns listened earnestly even if the details were being absorbed by Morgan.

Leif Forsberg stopped in front of one of the stones, which rose from the ground to meet his chest. He put a hand on it as if it were a prize cow.

"We know what the history books say about Christopher Columbus, but this stone tells another narrative. You're not the

first Scottish Lord to come up the Dalalven River looking for hardy sailors."

*They are connected to Eos,* Cairns decided, suddenly worrying about a trap. *What has Morgan done?*

Leif seemed to sense he'd made a misstep. "Forsbergs are simple men, but in our hearts, we yearn for adventure, especially adventure on the open sea. When such an opportunity comes, it matters not who asks—we send."

Professor Morgan finished translating and then knelt down to inspect the stone. "Most scholars believe the Cnoyen account is a myth. This stone is archeological proof."

"What does it prove?" Cairns asked.

"In 1349, King Magnus sent a rescue expedition to colonies *west* of Greenland."

"But west of Greenland is Canada."

"Exactly. Empires have been trying to make legal claims to North America in recent years, but combined with the written records and this rune stone, it would appear as if King Magnus beat Columbus by 150 years."

*If only Stewart were here to witness all of this. I can only trust that Morgan is taking good notes.*

Leif Forsberg shifted to point out a few features of the stone. "By the time this stone was carved, Forsbergs were Christian, but that did not matter to some of the families who worshiped the Old Gods. Our reputation as skilled sailors and longboat craftsmen was as strong then as it is now, and another Scottish Lord came looking for men to travel distant rivers in the west."

"I don't see the name of the Scottish Lord."

"No, this rune stone is meant to honor our Forsberg ancestor, not the man who hired him. The man who hired him was the Lord of the Orkney Islands."

*Sinclair. Damn it all, this is another bloody ambush,* he looked to Clement, who was always tense and ready for anything. Morgan would be no use and was caught up in the moment.

"Arne Forsberg left in 1342, no older than my son is today. He crossed the Atlantic, following the path from the Faroe Islands, Iceland, and Greenland, but from there, he pressed westward until he found the continent we now call America. He helped establish a

colony there, and then returned to Greenland to let the others know what they'd found. After visiting the Greenland colony, Arne returned across the North Atlantic until he reached the shores of Norway, but he was delayed when the Black Death reached Bergen. Five years passed before he could return."

"You're speaking of the Knutson Expedition," Morgan added. "There are church records from the Archdiocese of Nidaros in Bergen that claimed the Christian colonists in Greenland were enslaved and sent westward."

*It's the reason we were originally going directly to Bergen. Morgan found another piece of the old puzzle.*

"The rumors were true. The Scottish Lord grew impatient and swept up from his southern colony into Greenland, taking the Christian colonists prisoner, forcing them to man the ships that he took into the unknown. Bishop Bardson was tasked with finding the survivors, so he turned to my ancestor, Arne, to lead the rescue mission. Twenty-two years after young Arne floated down the Dalavan River, he returned from the New World with a friend, Father Cnoyen, the Dutch astronomer."

"That is quite a tale," Cairns admitted once Morgan finished translating Leif's response.

"Oh, this hill is filled with such tales. We could spend several winters telling such stories."

For the next two hours, Leif bragged about his family heritage through Professor Morgan, with Cairns feigning curiosity as the Scottish Lord Erskine. Since investigating the death of Lady Drummond decades earlier, Cairns understood the present day web of secret societies that wrapped up his friend Stewart, but he never understood their history. It chilled him to be facing such an enemy as the Order of Eos, even if Antoine Clement showed no reaction at all.

He wanted confirmation, though.

"So on the second expedition to America, Arne Forsberg was pitted *against* the Scottish Lord who'd originally hired him," Cairns stated. *This family isn't part of Eos…it was used and left for dead by Eos.*

"As I said, my family does not care for politics or religion as much as we crave adventure. A firstborn son has a duty to explore, while the second son has a duty to learn the history and trade of the Forsberg legacy."

"So *you* are a second son?"

"I am. My older brother Dagmar left home twenty years ago, and we have no idea if he is alive or dead. It was his intention to travel west, but instead of a longship, he took a steamship to America."

"So your son Vaktar…it is his destiny to leave home also?"

"Now that he is a man, yes. If he is ready this summer, he could take a horse, a pair of oxen, and go find his way in the world."

"What if he was to come with us?" Morgan asked.

"Excuse me," Cairns snapped to Morgan. "We're not just adopting a child."

"He's stronger than me," Morgan remarked, "and you've heard the family story. It's in their blood."

"He's sixteen," and then Morgan explained more to the Forsbergs.

"I'm a man," Vaktar insisted. "It would be my honor."

"You don't even know where we're going," Cairns argued. "I've seen too many wide-eyed boys die in my life, and I'm not going to be responsible for any more."

"Where are you going?" Leif Forsberg asked.

Morgan had found validation for the old Cnoyen legend in the runes, so Cairns first looked to Morgan and then to Clement. "What do you think?"

Clement cleared his throat. "Two astronomers? Two Forsbergs? Two Sinclairs? My French friend would call this Divine Providence. He looked for signs and omens to guide him. I didn't understand why we needed to come to this place, but now I understand. I think the boy could be an asset."

Having been a young man from a poor family, Cairns' only choice had been to join the military. He'd seen too many fathers cast away their boys to war. And adventure to America was a much easier pill to swallow. Cairns turned back to the father. "It is our intention to research this story about the Cnoyen Account, which means we'll travel to Bergen, Norway and then the Faroe Islands before searching for this 'lost colony' in America. Blood

has already been shed since we began, and it will most certainly be shed again."

Morgan explained this to Leif Forsberg, who then turned to his son. When the boy smiled a toothless grin, Cairns knew Vaktar was coming. Cairns could stomach men dying in war, but he dreaded putting the young man in harm's way.

And danger waited for them in America.

# CHAPTER 20

B E R G E N ,   N O R W A Y

1 8 5 2

Professor Corey Morgan felt the hairs stand up on the back of his neck, so he paused at the edge of an alleyway. *I'm being followed.*

The city of Bergen, Norway was built in the heart of fjord country, which meant the hills were steep and the port was deep. A network of channels protected the city and harbor from the open waters of the Atlantic Ocean, which is what made it the heart of late Viking history. Centuries after the raiders last sailed, Bergen still functioned as a major seaport yet the atmosphere remained warm and inviting. Brightly colored three-story homes, yellow and red mostly, stacked along the steep face of the fjord, making countless neighborhoods visible from the water's edge.

*If I mess up again, the halfbreed will kill me himself.*

Images of blood spurting from the Orkney men had filled his nightmares in the past few weeks, but the horrible wounds did not terrify him as much as the cold eyes of the man who took five lives without hesitation. Morgan killed those men with his recklessness, yet now he endangered the mission once again.

"The odds are in our favor," he'd insisted to the others when they arrived in Bergen. "Even if they knew we were departing from Bergen, they would've been looked for us weeks ago. Either way, we have the element of surprise."

Neither Cairns nor Clement mustered an argument against his proposal to do a little researching before departing for America.

Even if by some preposterous omniscient insight their identities had been discerned, the next step could not be guessed, nor could the port be guessed. *A million to one odds*, Morgan told himself. *Don't be such a coward.*

Morgan kept walking but remained vigilent

If he hollered, he wondered if Clement and Erskine would hear him back at the port, only a few blocks away. He felt his nose running into his mustache, so he wiped it with his sleeve, and while he gathered his senses, he cleaned his wire-rimmed glasses with the other sleeve.

His satchel was strapped over his head and neck to avoid pickpockets, and his hand found its way into his jacket, where he held the hilt of the short knife. With his right hand, he would clutch his satchel, and with his left, he would punch the knife into any possible thief.

Strangely, the streets of Bergen hid any criminal element from sight, and with a deep breath, Morgan continued walking.

Mariakirken, one of the oldest structures in the port city, guided him with its two towers of gray and white until he finally stood in front of the fenced yard.

Originally, there had been twelve churches built during the reign of King Olaf the Peaceful, who ruled Norway when St. Mary's Church was dedicated in 1070. Wars, fires, and plagues changed the city of Bergen since those days, but the beautiful church had been built to stand the test of time.

Morgan boldly walked up to the front door and found it locked. *So much for that idea.*

Morgan looked back to see if anyone on the streets took note.

They didn't. The few who were shopping or in the market continued as they were.

So he walked around to the side of the church, where big wooden doors with ornate iron hinges appeared to ward away any unwanted visitors. Surprisingly, the side doors were unlocked.

"Hello," he called out. As a scholar in Old Norse language and literature, he'd studied all the Scandinavian languages in order to help with his translation of the old tales. So in Norwegian, he asked, "Is anyone here?"

"Yes, hello!" a man's voice pleasantly called out.

A moment later, he stood toe to toe with the local Lutheran pastor, who introduced himself as Reverend Nils Krogstadt. For everyone's sake, Morgan introduced himself as Professor Cauldhame. Unlike Lord Stewart, he'd grown up poor, but as a scholar in the modern world, he knew education was his path away from tending sheep.

"I'm attempting a family genealogy, and from what my mother told me, her great-grandmother came from Bergen. Do you happen to have baptismal records of your parishioners tucked away someplace?"

Reverend Krogstadt did and brought him into the basement of the stark church where stone, wood, and a bit of stained glass reflected the cold northern climates.

"While I can show you the records, I can't help you navigate them. I'm working on writing the sermon for Sunday. If you come back tomorrow, the fellow who organizes our records could help you. I only officiate."

"I can tell this fellow is an orderly person just from the way these shelves are organized. Having been to several churches between here and Scotland, I can tell you that his system is very impressive."

"Which is why you should come back tomorrow."

"Oh, I can assure you that I wouldn't leave a stitch out of order. I have too much respect for the work he has done. I've done this a few times in other churches. I'll fetch you when I'm finished, and I can show you how I've left things exactly as I've found them."

"It seems a reasonable compromise," Reverend Krogstadt admitted. "I'll be down to check on you shortly."

With that, Professor Morgan began a trip back through time.

Five hundred years earlier, Mariakirken stood above Bergen's port, overlooking the comings and goings of commerce. Much of Europe was the same then as it was now. England, France, Russia, Denmark, Norway, and Sweden held similar borders while countries such as Germany, Castile, and Naples remained independent. Scotland, having won its independence, also stood alone.

Three centuries after the classic Viking era ended, King Magnus ruled both Norway and Sweden as regent for young King Kaakon. Bishop Ivar Bardson replaced Bishop Arni in 1347 as the leader of the Archdiocese of Nidaros, which covered the territories of Oslo, Bergen, Stavanger, Hamar, Orkney, and Iceland. Bishop Bardson should have governed over only the spiritual concerns of his territory, but after just a few short years, the Black Death crept over Europe and forced him into a different kind of leadership role.

Morgan had already researched the era of the Black Death. In a span of eight years, almost 200 million Europeans died from Bubonic plague. For Bergen, it arrived in 1349. In the middle of this chaos, a call for help was sounded on the edges of the known world.

A Christian colony in Greenland reported "raiders" stealing away half of their population for a westward expedition.

*The Order of Eos.*

Professor Morgan knew the ancient enemy better than Antoine Clement did, which is why Stewart wanted him to be part of Clement's revenge tour. At the time of the Black Death, Scotland was an independent nation. It had not been easy for Scotland. Under the leadership of Robert the Bruce, Scotland found itself at war with England. For his part, Bruce was excommunicated from the Catholic Church for murdering his rival in the Chapel of Greyfriars. When the warrant came for the arrest of all the Knights Templar on Friday the 13th, 1307, Scotland turned a blind eye. While Grandmaster Jacques DeMolay burned at the stake and the infamous Templar fleet vanished from LaRochelle, surviving Templars found Scotland a place of sanctuary. The price for sanctuary: fighting in its civil war. Aided by the influx of former Templar Knights, Robert the Bruce won Scottish independence at the Battle of Bannockburn in 1314.

In Orkney, the Sinclair family rose to power during this time, but Morgan found no mention of the Scots in the church records, which made sense. Yet he pictured a covert mission to colonize America, and unable to build upon early success because of the Black Death in Europe, the leaders of the Sinclair colony had to find workers elsewhere. From what Morgan had gleaned from his previous research, the Sinclair colonists raided Greenland around 1342. The Greenland surviving colonists needed help from Bishop Bardson.

The hero of the rescue operation was a local Bergen man.

Päl Knutson was a lawman from nearby Hordaland. He was sent by King Magnus to deal with the issue in Greenland.

*Sent to crush the Order of Eos,* Morgan realized. *Now Clement plays the part of Knutson.*

Greenland had a secret history. Following the "Little Ice Age" that began in the 1600s, Greenland remained almost uninhabitable, yet from the final years of the Viking era to the Black Death era, Greenland lived up to its name and became a fertile colony on the edge of the known world.

After discovering the *Book of Icelanders* and the *Saga of Eric the Red*, Morgan attempted to build upon his reputation as a Norse expert by writing about the era. He quickly lost his funding, his job, and his reputation. The world did not want to hear about a Sinclair expedition to America a century before Columbus. As much as he wanted to attribute jealousy or ignorance, he suspected what William Drummond Stewart later confirmed—the Order of Eos wanted to control the narrative.

Unlike his surprising discovery in Sweden, Mariakirken had no records of Knutson's death or any accounts if he ever returned. With civilization reeling from the Black Death, it seems the world forgot all about the conflict happening across the Atlantic.

*But no mention of the Danish astronomer Jacob Cnoyen.*

*Even so, this confirms part of the Cnoyen account as well as the tale of Arne Forsberg.*

Morgan finished his notes, packed up, and walked up to where Reverend Krogstadt was huddled over his sermon notes. "I thank you for your time. Good day."

"Did you find your ancestors?"

"Yes, yes, I thank you for your time." He found a spring in his step as he walked back down the hill. Soon, they would cross the Atlantic for North America, which would allow him to visit the places where Knutson once traveled.

*Hold on…*

His footsteps had an echo, and when he paused, he heard two steps followed by a hurried scramble.

He turned but saw nothing.

The specter of Eos loomed over everything.

His first priority remained his satchel. Defending his life came second.

The docks were five blocks away, so as long as the satchel wasn't ripped from his possession, he figured he could cause enough ruckus to get the attention of others. Even so, he found the hilt of the knife Clement had given him.

This time, instead of stopping or turning, he let his eyes scan for danger.

In the reflection of store windows, he saw the figure following him.

He thought about running, but by the time he weighed the decision, he heard the figure jogging toward him.

His fingers readied themselves on the hilt.

He felt a strong hand on his shoulder, which held the satchel. He slipped the knife from his pocket but had to cross his body while spinning to do anything with it.

A strong arm crashed down onto his left forearm, sending the blade clattering to the ground. As he turned to face his attacker, Morgan stepped backward and tripped on his own feet, falling onto his backside with enough force that his head recoiled also.

"Du är inte den vassaste kniven i lådan," the attacker muttered in Swedish.

Morgan knew the voice and meaning: *You are not the sharpest knife in the drawer.*

White fangs and a pink tongue grinned back at him, and Vaktar Forsberg extended a hand.

Morgan adjusted his eskew glasses and accepted the hand. "Apparently, I'm not. I thought you were a robber."

"Lord Erskine wanted me to follow you. I've been watching you since you stepped off the docks."

"You followed me to the church?"

"I even went down into the basement to watch you read. He wanted to test how much of a sneak I could be. How did I do?"

"Well enough," Morgan admitted but withheld any more praise due to his wounded pride.

"He also sent me to protect you, and now I understand why you need protection," the Swede teased.

Finally comfortable, Morgan walked with Forsberg the last few blocks to find Clement and Cairns waiting.

"Did you find what you were looking for?" Cairns asked.

"I almost stabbed the boy," Morgan protested to Clement and Cairns.

When Vaktar quietly shook his head in disagreement, the others laughed.

"I found reinforcement but not the evidence I'd hoped for," Morgan answered about his investigation into the Cnoyen Account. "What about you?"

"The *USS Volga* is returning to America tomorrow morning," Cairns said. "On the way, we'll be stopping at the Faroe Islands to pick up a load of Salmon bound for Boston. Any thoughts on Boston?"

"Not Montreal?" he asked, assuming they'd setout from the frontier via the Great Lakes. Then he remembered his occult history and smiled. *Boston will do nicely.*

# CHAPTER 21



Three hundred miles off the coast of Norway, the Faroe Islands serve as the midpoint between Europe and Iceland. With rugged terrain, few if any trees, and a tundra climate, the eighteen islands that formed "The Islands of Sheep" were an important territory during the Viking Era, but in recent years, the islands became part of the Danish Kingdom, despite the fact that Scotland was only 200 miles south.

Clement noted that like Bergen's homes, the houses of Tinganes were brightly painted to contrast with the stark environment. Without trees, the steep roofs were green to give the settlement a warm, friendly atmosphere for approaching ships.

"Nordic enough for you?" Antoine Clement asked Professor Morgan. The professor seemed to have found his backbone again and now dared to look Clement in the eyes when speaking.

"Yes, I'm curious to learn a bit more about Faroese history during our stop. The study of culture and heritage is so fascinating."

*Heritage.* Clement nodded. He'd learned several cultures in the past two decades, and after his father's murder, the word meant much more to him now.

Back in 1831, Antoine Clement wintered in the Black Hills in Lakota territory. His skills as a hunter and marksmen were known on the plains, and local Blackfoot Lakota invited him to spend the winter with them to hunt elk, deer, and bison. Isolated by the prairie to the east and the Rocky Mountains to the west, the Blackfoot Lakota had only a few encounters with the White Man, whom

Clement warned them about. During that winter, the Blackfoot Elders gave him a young bride, and by spring, he fathered a daughter named Little Star. When the snows melted, Clement, promising to return in the fall with goods and wealth, left his family behind.

Instead, he found alcohol and lost everything.

From newspapers purchased in Bergen, Clement learned that the wild west had all but been tamed. Both Wisconsin and Minnesota territories were open for settlement, and colonies of Scandinavians were taking advantage of geography similar to their homes. The *U.S.S. Volga* stuffed its hold with Scandinavian staples and cabins full of emigrants bound for Boston. Unlike the desperate Irish, the Scandinavians left for improved opportunity and economic standing with plans of purchasing farms and homesteads in the Great Lake region.

When Clement left Minnesota in 1837, only a few houses belonging to men like Sibley and Faribault existed in the territory where Chief Flat Nose, Sleepy Eyes, and Wahanantan ruled as monarchs.

*Is it all gone?* Clement wondered of the tribes of the frontier. *Whatever became of my young bride and daughter? Is my family and heritage lost?* He put his sourness away for a practical question. "Is there any connection to the Order of Eos I should be aware of?" Clement asked as the wooden-hulled sidewheel steamer pulled into the port.

"On the contrary, the Faroese likely despise the Scots, especially the Sinclairs."

Clement smirked. "How fortune."

"Yes, Lord Erskine could've booked passage on several ships going to various locations in America, but Divine Providence put us on the *Volga*."

*Divine Providence,* the words resonated within Clement. He hadn't known religion until he met Nicollet. God didn't exist in the violent hunting camps along Hudson Bay, and even in the serene Blackfoot Lakota camp at the base of Bear Mountain, it remained an abstract concept for Clement. Nicollet, however, pointed out God to him during their expedition to the headwaters of the Mississippi River. With a wink and a grin, each coincidence and stroke of good luck was seen as affirmation. *Divine Providence.*

*Is this more of the same?* Clement wondered and turned to Morgan for clarification. "So why do the Faroese despise the Sinclairs?"

Morgan lit up. "You *do* understand my theory about the Cnoyen Account."

"Eight survivors came out of North America after being lost for twenty years. Yes."

"The eight survivors found a way back home in 1364 and then all but vanished from history, until I found the Forsberg rune. It's difficult to speculate how the news was received by either the Church or by the Order of Eos. I do know what happened a generation later."

"Here in the Faroe Islands?"

Morgan shrugged. "No, first the Sinclair family rose to power. Henry Sinclair was born in 1345, a generation after Scottish Independence. Through marriage, he became the Jarl of Orkney and the Baron of Roslyn. By 1379, he became Admiral of the Scottish fleet."

"And this is *after* you believe Eos sent colonists to America," Clement clarified.

"Yes. When Cnoyen returned in 1364, the Sinclair family learned their colonization plan had failed. With his newfound might, Admiral Sinclair invaded the Faroe Islands in 1391."

"Revenge," Clement noted.

"Indeed. It's what I thought too, but the more I pondered the idea, as we followed the same course, the more I realized what Admiral Sinclair needed."

"And what did he need?"

"An eyewitness. Cnoyen fled with Forsberg deep into Sweden for a good reason, didn't he? He was being hunted by Admiral Sinclair. The invasion of the Faroe Islands served little political or commercial purpose, but if he was searching for information about the American colony—"

"It could allow him to return."

"At the Sinclair family chapel at Rosslyn, there are references to a trip made by his son, Henry Sinclair II, who, following the Faroe Island invasion, traveled to America in 1398, if the tale can be believed."

"A search and rescue mission."

"Yes. In 1401, the English invaded the Orkney Islands, killing Admiral Sinclair and ending all opportunities for Sinclairs. The rest is ancient history…"

Antoine Clement shook his head at how convoluted the Sinclair story had become since meeting Professor Morgan. It was no wonder Stewart put the two of them together.

"Is there something you'd like to share?" Morgan asked.

"Heritage does matter," Clement agreed, thinking of the Sinclairs he knew as a boy.

"The sins of the father, as they say."

"Yes, the sins of the father," Clement agreed. "My father was a brute. He taught me how to kill, and I spent my childhood trying to be as tough as he was. He was a Cajun from Louisiana, and when he learned how much money could be made in trapping, he went up the Mississippi, trapping as he went. Eventually, he found himself in a management position, which brought him all the way to Hudson Bay. There, he married my mother, a Cree woman. When she died, my father couldn't be burdened with raising a child, so he sent me to my aunt, also a Cree woman. At Oxford House, I was raised beside other white children, my cousins apparently, who were all named Sinclair."

Morgan gasped. "Wait, does that mean…"

Clement nodded. "It's why Stewart gave you to me. Someone at Oxford House knew where my father, Antoine Clement, moved after leaving Hudson Bay. They gave the address to my father's killer. When we reach America, I'll find out which Sinclair gave the order if I have to kill each and every last one of them."

# CHAPTER 22



Sofus Nielson had missed his previous chances. *I'm not going to miss my opportunity this time.* Despite his discomfort, he hid amongst wet anchor ropes that secured the transatlantic steamship to the docks. From his narrow vantage point, he watched the passengers disembark and spread out into the town for shopping and dining.

He'd seen the routine his entire life, but this time was different. *Today, everything changes.*

He set his rifle down and grabbed the small chest also hidden among the ropes. Already waiting on the docks were crates of dried salmon to be loaded into the cargo hold. He slipped the steel knife from its sheath and pried at the corner of the closest salmon crate. Finally, the nails gave way enough for him to use his hands to open the lid.

He turned, waited, watched to see if he'd been spotted.

He tossed several filets of salmon aside to make room for his wooden chest and then used the hilt to pound the nails back into place.

Content, he crept back to his hiding place.

His rifle was important to him as his right hand. At sixteen, he was as tall as a man but was thin and lanky. He'd never be able to win a physical fight, so he needed the weapon in the days ahead. He carefully removed the rifle strap from the rear clasp, wrapped it around his torso, and then tightly resecured it so that it rested across his back.

*Now, I just have to wait for the right time.*

The Port of Torshavn was the most exciting part of Nielson's existence, and it was only an artificial pier. He'd grown to hate his home. From the long winter days to the windy summer days, he couldn't bear another year. Almost half of the population of the islands lived near the port, leeching off the visitors each day.

He didn't want to be a cook.

He didn't want to work at the docks.

And he didn't want to risk his life fishing each day.

He was one of six boys, and only his older brother Matthias could inherit the family farm, not that Sofus wanted it.

*It's now or never.*

Sofus flexed his fingers, shaking them vigorously to bring as much blood to them as he could. Then, with no one watching him, he inverted like a monkey in the African jungle. He held onto the thick rope and locked his ankles around it, flexing like a caterpillar as he risked the dangerous passage over the water between the dock and the ship.

*Damn it.*

Once he reached the metal of the ship, his rifle tip clanked loudly against the hull, and he froze. Hugging the rope even tighter, he maneuvered a slight spin until his right hand could clasp the opening in the side of the ship. Only a few inches around the rope existed, but he'd studied the situation prior to attempting it, and using the side of the ship for leverage, he shakily stood upon the rope like a circus performer.

Once standing, he could reach the edge of the ship railing and…

His wiry arms were not very strong, but luckily, he didn't weigh much either, and he found just enough strength to lift himself up and over the railing.

Now aboard the *USS Volga*, his schemes took him no further.

Now he had to improvise.

He scooted over to the life rafts, unstrapped his rifle, and tucked it next to the oars. Only if the ship sunk would someone find his prize.

*Now, act like you belong.*

He took out the piece of paper he'd found the previous week—a boarding pass.

A passenger dropped it in the market, and he snatched it up and kept it. Granted, it was for a previous ship, a previous day, and another cruise line, but from the docks, he'd studied how passengers used the piece of paper to get their bearings.

Like a confused passenger, he glanced down at the paper as he walked to the stairs. Inside the passenger level, he knew better than to simply claim a room. Instead he found a public restroom and locked himself inside.

There he remained, unchallenged, for the next several hours.

At the ship's horn sounding, he knew it was safe for him to step out for a minute. When ships left port, passengers traditionally gathered along the railing to wave goodbye to passengers.

Sofus Nielson stood at the railing and waved goodbye to his home.

*I can't believe this actually worked.*

It was a brazen move for a stowaway, to be sure, but he did it with confidence and a smile. The ship was loaded with passengers from Europe, and after confirming there were no Faroese travelers, he had an opportunity to rub elbows with the real passengers. He moved positions several times along the rail as the big ship slowly maneuvered from the docks. One family traveled with a young teenager daughter, and he flashed his dimpled grin before approaching her.

"Hello, I'm Sofus. I'm bound for Boston."

"We're *all* bound for Boston," she answered dismissively.

"And after, I'm heading to the Great Lakes." *To see if the stories are true.* "What about you?"

"We're going to a place called Cleveland. My father builds railroads."

"Ah, my father catches fish. If you ever visit the Minnesota territory, ask for Sofus Nielson. I'll have the grandest farm in the area."

He left her with a nod.

He made small talk with a few other passengers and then vanished.

142

TWO DAYS LATER, he emerged from his hiding place, acting like he belonged. In truth, he was starving but he found a copy of James Fennimore Cooper's *The Pathfinder* in the lounge and Natty Bumppo became his traveling companion. First he fell in love with the damsel Mabel Dunhum, who spoke with the same voice as Miss Cleveland, and later he fell in love with the inland sea named Lake Ontario.

He pictured himself, hunting rifle in hand, guiding maidens across the wilderness.

Some days, he sat at a table not even reading but instead flipping pages as he listened to the other passengers talk. His favorites quickly became Lord Erskine, his valet Antoine, and Professor Morgan. The professor never shut up about Norse legends, which intrigued Sofus. Life on the Faroe Islands shut down for the winter, and tales were told that had been handed down through the generations. Hearing new tales made the passage, and his hunger, entirely tolerable.

One evening, Professor Morgan explained his theory on why the Vikings first focused on traveling east up rivers like the Volga, Rhine, and Danube, and in later centuries, westward to Iceland, Greenland, and Vinland. "If the theories about the "Lost Continent" are true, whether you subscribe to Atlantis, Thule, or Hyperborea as a name, then this Norse bloodline didn't *evolve* into great sailors—they *began* as great sailors. The random nature of invasion seemed to be more akin to searching than conquering. So what were they searching for?"

*Lost treasure!* Sofus surmised, hoping his theory was true.

The men retired to their cabins, still discussing theories, with Lord Erskine and Professor Morgan talking so loudly that Sofus could hear them debating as he passed. It so excited him that he slipped out of one of his six hiding places—this time the life jacket closet—to sit down in the hallway, book in hand, to read by the light of the hallway and evesdrop.

The men were now talking about Baghdad and Jerusalem, which Sofus knew as the heart of the Holy Lands.

"What if King Solomon found the 'secret knowledge' from antiquity? It seems obvious he had the means and interest,"

Professor Morgan said. "Once news reached the shores of Scandinavia, courtesy of the Romans, they woke with a motivation to acquire what had been lost."

"Or stolen from them," Erskine suggested.

"Look at the evolution of the Viking into European kings. They came out of the Fjords and left their descendants in each royal family. Look at the Normans and Rollo. Later families pushed for the Great Crusade. What if the Crusaders found something in Jerusalem?"

"The Templar treasure?" Lord Erskine asked.

"Think of it, Lewis, what made the Northmen do an about face? They found something in Solomon's treasure vault that led them to seek America."

*Lewis?* Sofus had listened enough in public to know the name Lord Wesley Erskine and his valet Antoine Clement, who slept in the next cabin. Professor Morgan was speaking to only one man. *A secret identity? So who is he? And what is he hiding?*

From the creak on the floorboard, he could tell the men stood, so rather than using his "I'm just reading" trick, he retreated.

When he rounded the corner, however, another stood in his way.

At first, Sofus grinned.

Then a strong hand took hold of his shirt.

He tried to squirm but only managed to pull the intruder out of the darkness. He noticed the boy's red hair moments before a strong fist smashed into his face.

And everything went black.

END OF PART THREE

# PART FOUR

## EGYPT

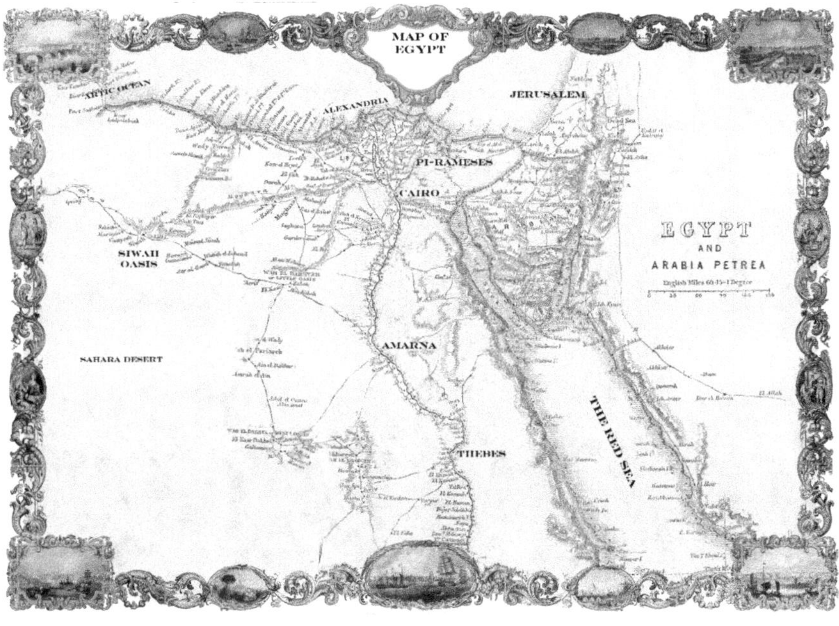

# PART FOUR

# CHAPTER 23



Pyotr Petrov reached the heart of the Ottoman Empire at Istanbul. He rode a ship like a common passenger, even though he was a servant of an invisible empire. As the travelers all disembarked, he kept his papers ready to show the port authorities that he was indeed a citizen of the empire.

At his side, he had his travel bag, which included weapons he'd originally intended to use to kill Lord William Drummond Stewart, who'd vanished into the wind. If the port authority officers got curious, he'd give them the name to make all interest vanish.

"Where are you coming from?" the officer asked.

"Scotland. I was vacationing," Petrov coldly lied.

After Stewart snuck sway from Murthly Castle in the dead of the night, it took Petrov several days to learn that they'd gone north to the port of Aberdeen. While he paid enough to the port workers to learn one of the ships was the Volga, not even money could give him an answer as to where they were going.

The answer was noted. The port authority officer didn't seem too interested in him. He jotted down the information without a reaction. "Where are you going?"

"I'm heading home."

"Varna?"

"No sir, that's where I disembark. I live in a little village a few days walk from Varna."

Again, this seemed to satisfy the officer.

It pained him to be heading home.

Vendita had a network of agents and assassins all over the world, and after spending months trying to kill Stewart, it was now time for another to try. If he was lucky, Lady Columbia would find a new purpose for him.

*I'm heading home…without my prize.*

# CHAPTER 24



*Should I smother him in his sleep?* Emma Geyer sighed loudly, removed the pillow that covered her own face, and turned to her snoring husband. From Karl's throat came noises that sounded like demonic possession or a bull in heat.

Instead of smothering him, she wacked him with the pillow.

Karl grunted, rolled onto his side, and farted loudly.

Emma had enough.

She wore her Italian lingerie, almost as fresh as the day she purchased it. She'd given her husband a few days to rest on their crossing of the Mediterranean, but neither rest nor lingerie helped him find his libido. She found a plush velvet robe hanging on the back of the bathroom door, slid her painted toes into fluffy slippers, and stepped out into the narrow hallway.

At both ends of the narrow hall, the windows showed a pitch black sky; morning was still hours away. Two glass doors sheltered the cabins from the drafty sea air, and in the corner of the front doorway, two large ornamental chairs guarded the exit. Emma climbed into the chair, pulling her feet up onto it to be covered by her velvet robe. She leaned her blonde head against the wall, a hard substitute for her pillow yet a silent reprieve from her husband.

*Maybe the rumors about Karl are true.*

Emma's mother had warned about the difference in their age, but the adventurous botanist captured her heart. The first year of marriage had been passionate, but like one of his plants, Karl needed the entirety of nature to spread his roots, and putting him in a pot seemingly sucked the life out of him by the day.

*Or maybe it's just me.*

Listening to Karl talk with Lord Stewart, Mr. Anderson, and Mr. MacPherson made her feel incredibly stupid. She didn't understand the significance of any of the people or places, yet Karl's face lit up for the first time in years. For that reason, she felt justified in encouraging the adventure. Yet she also felt jealous of the men stealing Karl's attention.

A cabin door opened just enough so that the light from the hallway became a dark crease in the doorframe. Embarrassed, Emma remained still as stone.

The head that came out belonged to Jamie Anderson, the dwarf. *The sweet-tongued fool of Murthly.* His advances had been relentless and at first upset her, but in recent weeks, she found humor in his foul innuendos, and her laughter only encouraged him more. She hoped Karl might become jealous.

Jamie returned again, this time sticking his entire torso into the hallway to look up and down the hall before he stepped out and began walking toward her.

Emma felt her heart pause, but Anderson kept his eyes on the nearby cabin doors, and once he reached his cabin, he gently opened the door and slipped inside. A moment later, the other door also closed.

*Lady Stewart!*

Christina Battersby had been a commoner just like Emma, but trysts with the second son of Lord Stewart resulted in an unexpected pregnancy. Yet instead of another bastard, William Drummond Stewart claimed the boy, George, as his heir and even had the audacity to marry Christina. From what Emma had gleaned, Lord and Lady Stewart were not a traditional husband and wife, which was why each had their own cabin.

*But sleeping with Anderson?*

At first, she felt jealousy, believing the dwarf had his attention focused solely on her. Emma tried to picture Lady Stewart with him, and then him with herself, and the mental images both disgusted and titillated her, and soon, thoughts of sleep vanished.

*Oh, well. No one cares if I sleep all day. I'm the true fool on this ship.*

She stood and stepped out into the cool sea air.

She gasped when she saw dots of light marking the horizon.

*That's Egypt.*

The dots were still several miles away, but they meant getting off the ship for an adventure.

Emma needed desperately to get off the ship and find some open space and new scenery.

"Trouble sleeping?"

Emma flinched upon hearing the male voice. She turned, expecting to see a crewman or even the kindly captain, but instead saw a mummy. "My apologies. I didn't see you sitting there, Lord Stewart."

Lord William Drummond Stewart sat on a lounge chair a few feet back from the prow of the boat. He was wrapped in quilts, with a steaming beverage on a smaller table at his side. "I couldn't sleep either. Have a seat."

If it had been any other man, she would have politely declined, but from the rumors about his sexual preferences, she knew she had nothing to fear from Stewart—the man loved men. He offered one of his quilts, which helped with the cool air. He was already dressed under his cocoon of blankets.

"Thank you, Lord Stewart. I worried about seasickness but instead I am plagued with snoring." *Do I tell him about Anderson and his wife? Does he care?*

"Ah…having spent time on the frontier with men like Jim Bridger, Thomas Fitzpatrick, Robert Campbell, and Ben Bonneville, I understand the cacophony of snoring and how it contrasts a serene location. I don't remember Karl snoring."

"They say that snoring increases as a man gains…in age."

Stewart smirked. "The kitchen prepared some coffee. Would you like some also?"

"That would be nice."

Stewart raised his cup to be seen by the ship's wheelhouse. A moment later, a door opened.

Emma studied the enigmatic man as he watched the coffee being brought out. In his mid-fifties, Stewart was still a handsome man. Although his ebony hair had deeply receded, it still grew as thick as his bushy eyebrows. After years of wearing a distinctive

mustache, Stewart was now clean shaven and meticulously groomed. He looked every part a nobleman. His eyes, in turn, studied her as a fresh cup of coffee was poured.

"Is that the northern coast of Africa in the distance?"

"It is. We'll make port in the ancient city of Alexandria by midmorning." He took a sip of coffee. "Are you familiar with the city?"

"I know it once had a great library," she remembered and quickly added, "And a lighthouse?"

"Indeed, it had both, but both are long gone."

"Karl told me about them. He says we are going on a tour of the Nile River."

"Ah, yes, after the boys and I go on a trip through the desert. We've arranged for tours of the Great Pyramid, the Sphinx, and other wonders of the Delta while we are away at the Siwa Oasis."

She felt herself deflate a bit. "How long will you boys be gone?"

"A few weeks. We'll be traveling upon a caravan of camels."

*Once again, they're stealing Karl away from me.* "What's so special about this oasis?"

Stewart hesitated, and for a moment, she expected a condescending answer until he replied, "We're searching for a tomb."

"I hear Egypt has plenty," she teased.

"Yes, well, we are searching for one special tomb. Those lights in the distance—that is the city of Alexandria, named after the Greek warlord Alexander the Great. The men who worshipped him, both in life and death, built the lighthouse and library to honor him as one of the seven "Savior Gods" of mankind. The lighthouse allowed an eternal dawn to exist and..." Stewart suddenly withdrew into his own thoughts.

*He knows I'm too stupid to understand any of this.* "But why Siwa?" Emma pressed in order to put him at ease.

Stewart grinned, his perfectly white teeth visible in the lowlight. He patted her raised knee. Both shifted to get a better view of the coast off the bow. "Yes, I skipped that part, didn't I? After Alexander the Great was murdered, his followers protected the body of their fallen king. They carried him from Babylon all the way to a secret desert location."

"It's not so secret if my husband knows where to find it," Emma joked.

"I suppose not, and for the better part of three centuries, Alexander's wishes to be buried at Siwa were ignored, and his magnificent sarcophagus was kept on public display in Memphis and later in Alexandria. Roman Emperors visited the tomb, which one day vanished, never to be seen again."

*Karl used to speak with such enthusiasm about the American frontier.* "And you think it was taken by his followers to this oasis?"

"MacPherson and I are in agreement. The Siwa Oasis is two hundred miles into the deep desert, which makes it one of the most isolated places on Earth. I know if I wanted secrecy and to honor a man I viewed as a god, it's where I would have brought him."

"Will it be dangerous?"

"If I'm right…yes."

Emma felt her exhalation shake, from both fear and the cold. *I wanted an adventure to stir something in him so that he might give me a child. I don't want him to die.*

"It might surprise you, but Karl knows how to handle himself in dangerous situations. He's stood in the presence of the great chiefs of the prairie and climbed the Rocky Mountains. He'll do fine."

Emma concentrated on her coffee rather than asking what she wanted to ask: *did you once sleep with my husband?*

"Are you enjoying our shared adventure?" Stewart finally broke the silence.

"I'm just floating along for the ride," Emma said. "I'm not sure where we're going or why we're going, but it certainly is better than staying in the greenhouse back in Dresden. The fresh air is lovely."

"When we return from the oasis, your husband will be able to tell you more about why we are doing this." His stomach growled loudly and both chuckled at the obvious sound. "Would you like the cooks to prepare an early breakfast?"

"I would, but I should change into something more appropriate first."

"Yes, go change, and I'll speak to the cooks. It's going to be a busy day once we reach Alexandria."

Lord Stewart rose, extended his hand, and helped her rise to her feet. She wore the quilt like a royal robe all the way back down to her cabin, where Karl still snored. She wanted to jump on the bed, wake him, and demand answers, but she didn't want to agitate him and push him further away.

Hearing about the coming multi-week journey into the deep desert, she let him rest and quietly dressed for the pre-dawn meal.

When she entered the small dining room, it wasn't Lord Stewart who greeted her but instead Lady Stewart.

Emma struggled to clear her throat. She looked around for Lord Stewart. *Does she know that I know?*

"Good morning," Christina said, lifting her tiny cup. "Come join me."

*This feels like an interrogation coming.* Except for a few hours in Rome, she hadn't spent any one-on-one time with Lady Stewart. Even though Lady Stewart had once been a commoner, she'd spent decades living in the lap of luxury, and rich people were usually quite mean.

"We're going to be traveling companions. Young Mr. Penny is going to be our escort while the others go on a trip into the desert. What are your impressions of Frank?"

*What am I supposed to say?* "I like his accent," Emma said as the waiter began to dote on her needs.

"Yes, my husband finds such a menagerie of friends. Do you think he is handsome?"

"I…I'm not sure if—"

"Such a devoted bride. I think he is handsome. I'm not sure if he fancies an old woman like myself. We'll soon find out. Care to make a wager between the two of us?"

*Is she suggesting the two of us try to seduce him?* "I don't understand."

"You're right. There's probably a reason why my husband has chosen Frank to be our escort. Frank the pistoleer. Do you want to know my theory? I think my husband fancies him because young Mr. Penny reminds him of himself when he was thirty years younger."

Frank Penny had a massive mustache for his age, which he waxed into sharp little horns that extended past his profile. "I never knew Lord Stewart when he was younger."

"Be thankful of that," she said and chuckled. "A pretty flower like you would have been an irresistible challenge to him."

*I wish I was back in Germany. I don't want to become her one day.* "Oh, well, I don't know what to say."

"Take it as a compliment. My husband was once a moth drawn to the flame of beauty. Do you understand my meaning?"

*She's talking about Lord Stewart loving men.* "I think so."

"Alas, he's a changed man now. Just as he was obsessed with his loins as a young man, now he is obsessed with antiquity. He stays up all hours of the night reading. When we were young, we once had common interests, but now…"

Lady Stewart looked sad and all her cruelty dissipated. *I need to show her the positives.* "You still share the career of your son, George. I've heard the two of you talking about him."

"Yes, he is now a soldier just like his father once was. For years, Georgie was my only companion, but now, I seek friendship. I hope you and I can become friends."

"I look forward to our great Egyptian tour," Emma said, even though she wasn't sure where she'd be taken. While danger lurked out in the desert, Emma faced her own challenges staying with Lady Stewart.

# CHAPTER 25



William Drummond Stewart would've shed a tear—if he hadn't been so dehydrated. Ahead of them, the Siwa Oasis opened up like an infected green wound in the belly of the Sahara. Compared to the endless sea of beige dunes, the trees and water seemed like a painting had been set against the backdrop of the desert.

Surrounding him, his Bedouin escorts spoke in relaxed syllables, knowing their water supply would be replenished soon. Karl Geyer was already sucking down water from his canteen. Jamie Anderson and Ross MacPherson gazed in wonder at the glorious sight.

Stewart introduced their destination in a cracked voice, "They say that Alexander the Great followed birds when he crossed the desert. The Egyptians refused to take the foreigners to the sacred Temple of Amun, so he told them that he was Zeus-Ammun reborn. After finding it on his own, he claimed the title of Pharaoh."

Karl Geyer wiped his double-chin to say, "This place reminds me of Mni Wakan."

"Pardon?" MacPherson asked.

The botanist caught his breath and explained. "On our final expedition together, Joseph Nicollet and I traveled out onto the Great Plains, where we found a large lake in a depression similar to this. Granted, it was surrounded by prairie instead of dunes, but it was also formed in a sunken depression. It was there that we met with wise Chief Wahanatan."

*I'm not the only one who wishes to still be in the company of Nicollet,* Stewart observed.

Like himself, Geyer had fallen under the spell of the wide-eyed dreamer Nicollet. Under each rock and behind each tree, a magical world waited to be explored. "I wonder what Nicollet would think of a place such as this."

"He'd be scaling the cliffs like a mountain goat," Geyer said, smiling for the first time in days. "Or shaking hands with the locals, hoping a few hugs and smiles could help him gain access to the elusive Tomb of Alexander."

"What should we expect from the locals, Lord Stewart?" MacPherson asked with apprehension. Away from Rome and Greece, MacPherson lost his confidence.

"The locals should be Siwi Berbers, who are conservative and religious. Geography has isolated them, but they have a fondness for Bedouin women, which is why we brought the maidens with us. Before Islam, the Siwi had a scandalous reputation of allowing homosexual marriage. Can you imagine such a place on earth?"

"Sounds like one of your Rocky Mountain Rendezvous," Geyer quipped coldly.

"I'm too old to imagine such things any more," Stewart said matter-of-factly. *I am no longer the man I was before I met Nicollet.* "Ross, you and Jamie know what to do when we get down there?"

"With a change of clothing, I'll look properly Bedouin."

"MacPherson I doubt you'll fool anybody with me coming along," Anderson added. "Must we be so public with our arrival?"

"If this remains an ancient stronghold for the Order of Eos, I know how to speak the code. With no way to verify our intent, they'll either open their arms or stall."

"And if there's nothing here?"

"Well, we all have a nice tan."

"Tan! I'm blistered and red as a lobster," Geyer protested.

"We only need one victory to win the war," Stewart reminded them. *If we find one corpse, we gain a great bargaining chip. With or without a sarcophagus, I'll learn if the tales of Alexander's tomb are true.*

FOR THE NEXT three days, Stewart lavished gifts and stories on the local elders. He and Karl told their tales of life on the far side of the world while Anderson and MacPherson all but vanished from sight. When they weren't eating, the two Europeans were given tours of all the notable sights, including the lake, the ancient fortress of Shali Ghadi, Cleopatra's Bath, the Mountain of the Dead, and the remaining wall of what once was the Temple of Amun.

This time together also allowed Stewart and Geyer time to heal their fractured relationship.

Once, they had both competed for the attention of Joseph Nicollet.

For Stewart, his relationship began when he abducted the scientist with the intention of torturing and killing him following the mysterious murder of his aunt, Lady Margaret Drummond. Nicollet's impressionable mind had memorized the details of the family's prized heirloom, the Al Marrakk Map, and once he reached America, the astronomer attempted to unlock its secrets. When Nicollet's innocence became obvious, the two men began to exchange secrets about the map and its subject. In a matter of weeks, Nicollet absorbed a lifetime of knowledge acquired by Stewart, but a relationship was never reciprocated. In fact, the unexpected took place, with Nicollet bringing him to the baptism fountain to be rededicated to the Lord.

At first, Stewart thought baptism was all a tease, a game. Yet Nicollet proved to be genuinely devout. Just like St. Anthony the Eremite, Nicollet saw himself as a righteous monk on a quest against the forces of darkness in the world.

A few years later, Karl Andreas Geyer pursued the French gentleman for intellectual reasons. Geyer joined Nicollet in St. Louis in 1838, accompanying him on three expeditions into the Dakota Territory. With the botanist at his side, Nicollet found the Lost Kingdom described by King Solomon.

In the end, neither could hold the bright gaze of Nicollet's focus.

Like a master chess player, Nicollet placed his pawns across the board for his final expedition. Nicollet remained in the public spotlight in Washington and Philadelphia while his apprentice John C. Fremont drew the eyes of Eos to the far west. His Jesuit friend, Peter DeSmet, began an expedition up the Missouri River, and for good measure, Stewart joined with Karl Geyer to travel together to the headwaters of the Mississippi River.

The two were bound for a Rocky Mountain Rendezvous near Yellowstone when news reached them of Nicollet's death. Stewart reacted with fury while Geyer emotionally crumbled.

"Emma thinks you and I were lovers," Stewart mused as the sun began to set on the Siwa Oasis.

"Should that surprise you? From what I've heard, you rogered anything in sight. I was a bachelor well into my thirties, after all, and I spent two years with you at Murthly Castle before returning home."

Stewart laughed heartily. "She does have a point. For me, everything changed after Nicollet."

"You loved him?"

Stewart scoffed, began to shake his head dismissively, and finally nodded. "Ah, but it was so much different. He believed in all of this," Stewart said, gesturing to the Siwa Oasis. "To him, God wasn't found in a dusty old book but out in the world. Nicollet saw His face in the stars, and on earth, he saw blue mud as proof that it was all real." Stewart looked around to ensure privacy. "Do you want to know my fear?"

"Damnation?"

"For fuck's sake." Stewart cruelly laughed. "We're all sinners. From sexual deviance behind a stable to butchery during war, I've checked off each and every sin on the 10 Commandments. Nicollet tried to convince me of God's enduring love, but how can I prove myself worthy to God when I couldn't even be worthy to Nicollet?"

"Is that why we're both here in the desert? To impress the spectre of Nicollet?"

Stewart paused before revealing his fear. "I refused to go to Lake Manitou because I'm afraid of what I'll discover in that cave Nicollet found."

"You think it's all a fairy tale?"

"No, just the opposite—I worry I'll find God in that cave. I was relieved back in Rome when we didn't find the Tomb of Domitian. Even though it is part of recorded history, it's easier for me to go on living while believing the story is all myth and legend. Now, here at Siwa Oasis, I look for the Tomb of Alexander the Great, but I worry what will happen if we do find it."

"You're afraid of myth becoming reality," Geyer surmised. "Is that why you were baptized back in St. Louis? God became too real?"

"I suppose. A man tried to shoot me in the face believing I was Nicollet. After that, and with all the things Nicollet convinced me of, the reality of Heaven and Hell shook me to my core. It was more than my…dallying. My material gluttony alone was enough to doom me to the fires of Hell, yet Nicollet walked me down to that Cathedral and convinced me I could become…what? One of God's mad men? And here I am."

"Here we are," Geyer said. "I'm not a religious man either, but as a good Lutheran, I learned my catechism lessons all the same. Take two of the Bible's most famous patriarchs: King David and King Solomon. By all accounts, David was plagued by his sexual desires, from Bathsheba to the love of Jonathan. He was a terrible husband, a terrible father, but when God needed him to strike down Goliath or fight a battle with the Philistines, David rose to the occasion. On the other hand, King Solomon was born with a silver spoon, raised in the light of God, and given wisdom greater than any other man, but by the end of his life, he was following the pagan gods of his concubines."

"So am I David or Solomon in your metaphor?" Stewart joked, bringing laughter from Geyer.

"Here we are, you and I, fighting against the darkness. Together, we will slay Goliath."

"I drink to your optimism," Stewart said.

LATER THAT EVENING, just as the flames turned to embers, Ross MacPherson and Jamie Anderson returned. Karl sat up in his chair in anticipation, but Stewart could not muster up any energy. He'd devoted himself so much to the chase that he had little

energy for triumph or defeat. Yet Nicollet had given him the mantle of leadership, so he leaned forward and put his elbows on his knees."Welcome back, gentleman. I was beginning to worry. How was your private tour of the Temple of Amun?"

"Tight," Jamie Anderson muttered. "And quite fruitless."

Stewart sighed and raised an eyebrow to Geyer. "That's a pity."

"However," Ross MacPherson said, rubbing his beard and revealing a grin. "We found something quite interesting at the Mountain of the Dead. You'd better pack your belongings. I'll tell you about it once we're safely away from this place.

# CHAPTER 26


P I - R A M E S S E S ,   E G Y P T

1 8 5 2

Jamie Anderson once believed his life had been saved for a glorious purpose, but today, his life was horse shit. He sat for a moment, craning his neck in the darkness for the long crawl back to the surface. Finally alone, he took a moment to rest and reflect.

First, he thought back to another exciting yet fruitless discovery back at the Siwa Oasis. Like everything in the open Saraha desert, Siwa was subject to mighty sandstorms, and even though it was built upon the top of a hill, the wind had filled the halls and tombs with sand. It was a necropolis for the Ptolemaic rulers visiting the legendary oasis, which meant that instead of dead Egyptians, it held Greek and Roman bodies. He and MacPherson thought they'd hit the jackpot with Gebel al Mawta, the Mountain of the Dead. The first day, a quick scouting of the Temple of Amun told them all they needed—it'd been plundered long ago. Alexander the Great's hidden sarcophagus was obviously not anywhere near the ruined temple.

He didn't find Alexander the Great, but he and MacPherson did find an ironic clue—Domitian had once been at the Siwa Oasis. At the center of the Gebel al Mawta complex, its largest vault belonged to a Roman historian named Quentis the Elder, who died after arriving at the Siwa Oasis. Having studied everything he could find about Domitian, MacPherson almost hyperventilated about the name. To the bewilderment of Ross

MacPherson, the lowly historian was given a tomb worthy of an Emperor.

"Explain to me again who is Quentis the Elder?" Anderson had asked back in Siwa. MacPherson argued that Quentis the Elder had likely found Alexander the Great's lost sarcophagus, and as a reward, Emperor Domitian rewarded his departed servant with an inexplicably grand tomb and then looted the place—likely taking Alexander with him back to the Shrine of Wuoth in Ravenna.

*Ultimately, another dead end,* Anderson reflected.

Next, he pondered his newest predicament: finding himself alone under countless tons of cut stone blocks. All the way from the Siwa Oasis, Lord Stewart and Mr. MacPherson spoke in excited syllables of the "treasure city" of Ramses the Great, who was known to the Greeks and Romans as Ozymadias.

They'd found Pi-Ramesses back in the lush delta where they briefly reunited with the women and Penny before visiting a "site of interest and convenience," as Stewart put it. There'd been nothing interesting or convenient about place. For Anderson, it meant crawling into the "gopher holes" of the tombs to see what they held. Once again, he fruitlessly climbed into the barren womb of the earth searching for fortune or glory.

*It's actually an ingenious design,* he thought, looking up at the stone ceiling.

Unlike the Mountain of the Dead, Pi-Ramesses had been built beside the Nile River in the lush Delta. Historians talked of it being a "northern" capital for Ramses the Great as he staged invasions into Hittite territory. Biblical scholars wrote of it as the reason for Hebrew slaves to be working in the Land of Goshen. Regardless, it shared one similarity to the Mountain of the Dead— it had been buried. Unlike sandstorms, floods buried the entire city with silt, and when the Nile shifted banks afterwards, the city fell to ruin and abandonment.

Yet Lord Stewart and Mr. MacPherson had a theory. *Which turned out to be a pretty shitty theory,* Anderson decided as he continued to crawl out of a space no full-sized man could crawl.

Behind him, he'd found his way down to the bottom of the buried structure. Once at the surface before flood or sandstorm buried it, the large building, mostly intact, had been recently discovered and had been untouched for almost three thousand years. Sixty feet below the surface, Jamie did not find a golden sarcophagus—he found a stable. The hidden alcoves described by local boys who'd bravely found the tunnel of air pockets left by settling silt turned out to be a series of cisterns for the famed cavalry of the evil Pharaoh.

*Even the horses took a shit in style.*

*And then there's me.*

Jamie Anderson could almost see the bright lights of the surface. Even though he'd been born a dwarf, now in his forties, he was strong and healthy, quite capable of the rigorous trip. Like the literary hero Quasimodo from *The Hunchback of Notre Dame,* Jamie's first brush with death happened as an infant. Even though his mother abandoned him, he was taken in by the wealthy family of Field Marshal Michel Ney, who during a visit home, decided to take the dwarf with him. The reason: "I've had too many good servants killed because they refuse to duck."

For the next three years, he learned the meaning of bravery from his adopted father, but at the end, in the Battle of Waterloo, Anderson found a new savior—Captain William Drummond Stewart, the enemy who spared his life and, later, brought him back to Murthly Castle.

*Fucking Stewart,* Anderson thought as he neared the surface and the Egyptian sun. *I've simply traded one madman for another.*

Back at the surface, Lord Stewart, Karl Geyer, and Ross MacPherson, all dressed like Bedouins, waited with hands on knees as Anderson climbed out of the hole.

"Did you find it?" Geyer asked.

Stewart handed him a drink of water. Despite being his Lord, Stewart had been a much kinder master than Field Marshal Ney and far more benevolent than Pharoah Ramses the Great was to the men who created the complex. He told the men what he thought of their theories, and while they traveled back to the Nile where the women waited, the big question was "What now?"

"Perhaps he's still under one of those pyramids," Anderson mused as he ate and drank his fill as the hired help treated him like a lord. *If I die on this expedition, will Stewart give me a grand tomb like Quentis the Elder?*

"The pyramids predate Ramses by almost a thousand years," MacPherson protested.

"He knows that Ross," Stewart defended. "Jamie is only pulling your leg, as they say."

Anderson winked. "I took private lessons right beside Thomas and Archibald," he said in reference to the other Stewart boys.

"So what is your theory, Jamie?" MacPherson asked.

"I'm not a religious scholar like you, but I do know that the 18th Dynasty had nothing to do with the north. Following the Hyksos Invasion, their capital city was in Thebes, hundreds of miles upstream from here."

"See." Stewart grinned. "Told you not to judge a book by its cover."

Anderson nodded. "I wouldn't have climbed into that hole if I didn't think your theory was sound, MacPherson. But it was based on a whole lotta 'if's. If Ozymandias was the Pharaoh of the Exodus…if Pi-Ramesses was indeed dedicated to his dead firstborn daughter, Bint-Anath…if Bint-Anath was a reference to the Canaanite goddess…if Anath was a reference to Semiramis. It sounded good before I climbed into that hole. Now your theory is shit."

"Perhaps Thebes?" MacPherson pondered.

*These men won't stop until they're dead—or I'm dead.* Under the shade of the covered cart, Anderson felt more like himself. "Lady Stewart seems to enjoy the Nile," Anderson added. "I don't think she would mind another few weeks."

"Of course not," Stewart muttered. "I've all but bankrupted Murthly to pay for our tour. She'd better be enjoying herself."

*Apparently, vast wealth only takes a fellow so far. Even though this expedition is a literal pain in my ass, I can't return empty-handed.*

"I apologize for my ignorance," Geyer began ignoring Stewart's comment, "but I thought Thebes was in Greece, first referenced as the cursed home of Oedipus and later as the restored city by Cassander, whom we feel killed Alexander the Great. Is there a connection between Greece and Egypt?"

"Connections," Anderson mocked. "These two could explain how that camel is King Arthur's heir if you gave them enough time. I don't know about the names, but I do know that while the

Giza region has been stripped of all value, the isolation of Thebes has at least thwarted tomb raiders. Now that Champollion has cracked the code of hieroglyphics, it's only a matter of time before scientists and linguists discern the rest."

"And will we find anything besides fossilized horse shit?" Geyer asked.

Anderson chuckled. "I expect to find plenty. But how will we tell Ramses the Great from any other corpse?"

"He was a King of Egypt. His tomb will be clearly marked," MacPherson protested.

*Both Emperor Domitian and Alexander the Great went through great efforts to hide their tombs. Will Ramses the Great be the same way?* Jamie Anderson shook his head. "I think they counted on you saying that."

# CHAPTER 27



Thebes did not impress Frank Penny. *It doesn't feel like the Bible. Feels more like El Paso.* Sure, it was hot, but most deserts were hot. Instead of the Rio Grande, the Nile River shimmered in the valley below.

Plus, everything was kinda backwards.

The Nile River flowed north, which was backwards, and the Valley of the Kings was on the western shore with a large mountainous bluff behind it. Back in El Paso, they came from the eastern shore with a large mountainous bluff at their backs.

*But still, pretty much the same.* Frank knew he was too stupid to offer any help to these learned men, so he did the only thing he could do—he stood guard.

With the sun finally setting, he decided it was time to take a hike. He hated the layout of the valley. It was steep, rocky, and without a tree or plant in sight. It was perfect for an ambush, which could happen from any of the countless ravines. Despite the difficulty, he aimed for the highest peak. His Wellington cowboy boots had little cushion for climbing, but they shielded his shins from snakebites and his feet from sand and gravel. Unlike the others, he refused to dress like a Bedouin, proudly wearing his black cavalry hat, his short gold jacket from his time with the California Lancers, and two holsters on each hip. His pants had red tassels up the seam, which the men in his company believed helped diffuse the heat of the sun.

Penny had his doubts about the effectiveness of the tassels.

*Huh*, Frank paused once he reached the top of the bluff. Instead of finding a peak, he found an almost perfectly flat roof to the valley, where the Nile once trickled before erosion cut away the entire valley.

Looking down at the dots that were the hired guides and the horses, he paced around the ruins, which were built right into the side of the cliffs, allowing all three men to walk right in. Lord Stewart, the arrogant dwarf, and the pretentious priest—they were all condescending assholes, in his view, but his father had been right about the grandness of the adventure.

Since leaving Scotland, Penny had been tasked with protecting the women. Both were beautiful for their age, but it was insulting work for a man of his experience. Although he was getting paid handsomely, his father had made the trip sound quite deadly. Adventures meant dangerous encounters and fights, but so far, it'd been mostly historical tours.

He walked to the eastern side of the bluff and was pleased to locate the Nile River just a couple miles below. He squinted to see if he could spot the ship, but the ripple of the river made it impossible to see such detail.

*It's good to see the world*, Penny decided. *One day I'll be fat and old like my father, but at least I'll have stories to tell.*

Frank Nicollet Penny never knew Joseph Nicollet nor had he ever met William Drummond Stewart when he received a letter from the Scottish Lord. Penny's father had studied astronomy in Philadelphia and met Joseph Nicollet in Baltimore. The two became fast friends. Duty soon took his father to Allen's Landing, which eventually became the city of Houston, where Frank was born in the sovereign nation of Texas. When war broke out in 1846, Penny was just a teenager, but thanks to his successful father, he had enough wealth to buy the finest horses and weapons to defend his young country.

After two years of war, he returned to Houston a changed man. Lord Stewart's reward for finding his old friend, Antoine Clement, turned into a well-paying security job, which led him to the bluff overlooking the Valley of the Kings and the Nile River valley.

As night approached, Frank sat down, cross-legged, and watched the torches marking the entrance to the tombs.

With this little adventure lasting only the evening, the crew of the yacht were given the task of protecting the women while the men were away. Penny was glad to finally be going with them again, even if he didn't quite understand the purpose.

Lady Drummond tried to paraphrase what they were doing: "Seeking redemption from the Lord." So they'd first gone to Rome and now to Egypt, looking for the tomb of Biblical villains. In concept, it sounded exciting, but now he wished he'd returned with Clement to hunt down the men who killed Antoine Sr. and Thomas Stewart.

Even though the city of Thebes sat on the eastern bank of the Nile, it wasn't a modern city yet, leaving the canopy of stars almost unaltered.

*Strange how the stars look exactly the same as in Texas.*

The Padre, which Frank called the defrocked Catholic priest Ross MacPherson, tried to give him lessons in astronomy, which produced no better understanding than they had for his father. He did remember the talk about the Big Dipper though, and how the seven stars represented the seven kings that would lead to the Antichrist.

*That part I remember.*

A horse whinny caught his ear. He leaned forward hoping he was mistaken, but having ridden cavalry for two years, he understood the sounds of horses. It wasn't the sound made by a stationary horse either. It was the sound made by a horse running at full speed.

The galloping followed, a thunder of hooves indicating several horses.

Frank Penny stood, locating the noise to the east.

At first, his heart leapt, thinking of the women on the anchored yacht, but anchored in the Nile, horses could not reach them.

The riders also did not follow the public road leading to the monument, which meant they avoided the Egyptian police of King Abbas. *Thieves robbing thieves meant the police would offer no help.*

Even in the darkness, Penny soon spotted the movement. They rode along the base of the bluff, past the Temple of Hatshepsut, to flank his group from the rear.

*Do I fire a warning shot?*

Darkness protected them, and the shot would only escalate the situation if misread. Instead Penny began a hasty retreat down the bluff.

For a few minutes, the riders vanished entirely, and all Frank could hear was his own breathing and footsteps.

Then all at once, the storm of hooves came bursting over the flattened part of the hill to the southeast of the cave. The Bedouin guides sounded the alarm, and for some inexplicable reason, three more torches were lit.

*Have we been set up?*

*Is it an inside job?*

Those answers were given when the attackers unsheathed their swords.

*Oh heck, these fellas aren't messin' round.*

Penny continued his scramble down the hill.

The Bedouins and bandits began shouting at each other in a foreign language, but Penny understood the tone and tension.

They were outmanned ten to two, from what he could tell, with the other men somewhere still inside the cave. When a third Bedouin came running out—giving away the position of Lord Stewart—the lead bandit slashed hard, dropping the hired guide to the ground in bloody screams. The other two Bedouins dropped to the ground in submission.

Frank continued to scramble down the hill.

Lord Stewart emerged from the cave shouting.

Luckily, the entrance to the tomb was inaccessible from horseback, which kept him safe from immediate attack.

Penny still hadn't been spotted.

He paused, identifying a new path to the ground. The 10 armed hadir began to dismount, with the leader still atop his horse with his bloodied sword.

*Sorry about this,* Frank said, taking aim at the beautiful Arabian.

The first of his twelve bullets smashed into the horse just below its ear, all but killing the magnificent beast immediately. The horse fell onto its side and trapped the rider under its weight.

Penny continued his descent into the dark valley.

With lightning bolts in each hand, his snarl, elongated mustachio, and broad brimmed hat turned him into a death-dealing *jinn*—scattering the bandits.

Stewart joined the slaughter, but only in self-defense.

Those bandits that turned made for easy targets, and Frank squeezed off a single round into each back. He'd seen revolvers explode in the hands of overly anxious users during the Mexican War, so he alternated between his left and right hand.

One of the bandits stepped forward, sword drawn, unafraid to die.

*Come & get it!*

With his left hand, he hit the man squarely in the chest and with his more accurate right hand, he ripped a bullet into the man's face. The sword clattered to the ground.

Another bandit also turned to attack.

His right hand clicked an empty chamber. His left hand fired a stray shot.

Suddenly, the swordsman was a few steps away.

Frank threw the empty right pistol into the face of the attacker, knocking him off kilter. Penny stepped into the attack, squeezing off a final shot with his left hand into the man's belly while grabbing the sword arm with his right. Using the attacker's momentum, he spun the man around and to the ground. Frank unsheathed his Bowie knife and slammed it into the man's torso, keeping a knee on his back as Death did the rest.

During a march from El Paso to Chihuahua, his unit practiced reloading their pistols on horseback, so now, it took him just a few seconds to get six more bullets into the hot chambers. Rising, he pulled the Bowie knife from the man's back to arm his left hand, and Frank Penny advanced.

Stewart had dropped two men, leaving the last two for Frank.

*My father didn't lie about Stewart's abilities.*

He rushed forward, knowing that a shot under twenty paces was pretty reliable. It took four of the six bullets to end the fight.

He scanned the darkness, but aside from the sounds of dying men, he saw no more threats.

Karl Geyer, the Padre, and the Dwarf also emerged from the tomb entrance, armed but terrified.

*Eight men killed*, if he included the broken-legged leader under his dead horse. *Not bad.*

His snarl turned into a smile as he tipped his hat to his benefactor Stewart, who'd killed the other two. "My father always said a Penny is worth ninety-nine other men."

# CHAPTER 28

A M A R N A   E G Y P T

1 8 5 2

William Drummond Stewart stepped out onto the deck of the yacht to see Frank Penny warming his face in the morning sun. *The boy is a bloody imbecile,* William Drummund Stewart decided. *A smiling psychopath with a ridiculous mustache.*

In contrast, Stewart felt like an old man. For the first time in over two decades, Stewart had shared his bed with Christina. When they returned to the yacht from the bloodbath back at Thebes, the others had to pull him off of young Penny or else he might've killed him. An hour later, he was weeping privately in the lap of Lady Stewart as she consoled him over the trauma of killing two men.

Now Stewart watched Frank Penny stand on the deck of the yacht, fully dressed in his ridiculous California Lancer outfit, going on as if nothing had happened. Penny spent the next few minutes adding wax to the tips of his mustache. The preening routine could go on for another hour, if watched, as he'd clean his pistols or his boots next.

*Antoine only killed when needed.*

*Frank Penny seems to enjoy it.*

Stewart walked around to the other side of the boat to avoid him and found Ross MacPherson already standing at the bow of the yacht.

Stewart stepped up beside him and joined his gaze on the eastern shore.

After a few minutes of silence, MacPherson asked, "Do you know what this place is?"

"I honestly don't care any more." He felt like apologizing to Nicollet and returning home in defeat. The yacht continued its ignominious retreat down the Nile River, not having stopped day or night for tourism. They slowed as they passed by cities and would then bring the yacht back to full speed as they fled the scene of the crime.

MacPherson shrugged. "Should we talk about Mr. Penny instead?"

Stewart, MacPherson, Anderson, and Geyer had been inside the tomb complex when the shooting began. By the time they understood what was happening, bodies littered the ground.

Stewart didn't want to think about Thebes or Penny. "So tell me about this place."

MacPherson's dour expression softened. "Amarna? Scholarship is divided, and in recent years, it has only gotten worse. The palatial ruins you see once belonged to Pharaoh Akhenaten and Queen Nefertiti. In the long history of the Egyptian dynasties, Ahkenaten is viewed as a heretic."

*A new candidate at this late hour?* "Are you changing your mind about Ramses the Great as one of the seven kings?"

"Not at all. Let me explain. Some scholars view Ahkenaten as the man who invented God. His insistence on monotheism in a culture that celebrated a pantheon of gods was beyond revolutionary, but as the heir to the throne, he had all the power and might to do what he wanted, which is why he moved his new capital two hundred miles downstream from Thebes."

"And what are your views of Ahkenaten?"

MacPherson measured a thought for several moments before saying, "He's the adoptive father of Moses."

*An interesting thought. I can't imagine the theological discussions Nicollet and MacPherson would have had around the campfire.* "And Queen Nefertiti is—"

"Pharaoh's daughter, in a manner of speaking. She's the one who 'drew' Moses from the water as a miracle after not being able

174

to give her husband a male heir. For a few years, Moses was a solution to the problem, that is until Moses refused to marry one of his Egyptian 'sisters' and another step-mother gave birth to Tutankhamun. Shortly after, enemies poisoned the great heretic Ahkenaten, but I believe his push into monotheism was influenced by his adopted son, Moses."

Stewart could still picture the young hadir staring down the pistol barrel right before he fired. "Well, thank you for the share, but how does that solve our Ramses problem?"

"It doesn't," MacPherson said flatly.

The two men stood silent at the nose of the yacht.

Months earlier, when Antoine Clement insisted on getting revenge on the men who killed his father, Stewart had no choice but to let his trusted right hand man depart for America while he himself went east to better understand the men who killed his brother, Thomas. After stopping in Rome, Stewart earnestly believed he was acting as an agent of light against the darkness, but after seeing Penny slaughter the attackers, he lost all conviction.

*Antoine never would have killed all of those men so dispassionately.*

Back at the Valley of the Kings, Stewart, Geyer, and MacPherson managed to roll the horse off the survivor, a man named Kaled El-Shahawy. He was neither Order of Eos nor some other shadowy secret society—he was local law enforcement. He'd heard stories of Bedouin nomads plundering one of the tombs and went rushing in to defend the historical site from plunder. El-Shahawy thought he was an agent of justice.

Had El-Shahawy known Stewart had official paperwork tucked into his chest pockets, the situation might've been diffused.

"Aw heck," Penny had said afterwards. "They came at our guides with swords drawn. My apologies, gentlemen."

And then Penny shot the survivor in the head, leaving them no choice but to flee. Stewart knew his hired guides would be wanted men, and the longer they remained fugitives, the better odds he and the others had of getting out of Egypt alive.

Jamie Anderson came out onto the deck next, moving to Stewart's side.

"How is Christina? Did you explain things to her?" Stewart asked. Anderson had showed up in Christina's room during

Stewart's private breakdown, and having known them since they were all young, the dwarf joined Christina in consoling Stewart about the murders and failures.

"Yes, I told her what happened and how we must now flee Egypt to avoid being beheaded as murdering infidels," Anderson answered. "She took that part in stride; however, she's quite upset about George."

*Our son?* "George? How in the world did she—" Stewart knew a letter had not come from their son. No one knew where they were. "Why is she worried about George?"

Anderson rolled his eyes. "I told her what happened to our wild Texan, and it made her weep. She attributed it to his time in the Mexican War and that he buried the effects of experienced trauma. She thinks Georgie will be changed by his time in the military as well."

"Rubbish. Neither of us turned into cold blooded killers after the Napoleonic Wars. I'm half tempted to tie up young Mr. Penny with a note confessing his crimes."

"I could get some paper."

Stewart scoffed at the sarcasm and smiled. "I owed his father a favor for finding Antoine after the Mexican War, and he sent back his son. I should have known it was a poisoned pill."

"The lad didn't know what was happening. For all he knew, he was saving our lives. Besides, it was another dead end."

Jamie Anderson was right—about both claims.

The terrible day had begun with a terrible discovery: the tomb of Ramses the Great had been empty for countless centuries.

During the private tour, the guides informed them that the tombs had been plundered. Ironically, another of Nicollet's friends, Egyptologist Jean-Francois Champollion, had explored the entire complex a few decades earlier. Even after spending the morning exploring all of the nooks and crannies, it became clear that even though Ramses the Great's body had once rested there, the corpse had been moved long, long ago.

"I had a dream just a few minutes ago," Jamie Anderson said to break the silence.

"Please," Stewart said, "I don't want to hear any lurid tales."

"Oh, this isn't a lurid tale. I had a dream that I was brave Odysseus, and that I'd entered the underworld and was swarmed by the dead."

"Makes sense considering what you'd found in that cache of bodies," Stewart said in reference to the second location the bribed guide had taken them.

"Yes, I was surrounded by all of these mummified corpses, and then one of them began speaking to me. He called out, 'My friend, my friend, how did you escape from the wicked sea nymph,' which is a reference to Calypso, I suppose. The corpse was disgusting, but I recognized one unique detail: the red hair."

"An Irish mummy?" MacPherson offered.

Anderson laughed. "No, my dream stayed within the pages of the Odyssey. It was King Menelaus of Sparta, who in the tales, was noted for his red hair. It's how the son Telemachus recognized his father's war buddy. The House of Tantalus, including Agamemnon and Menelaus, was noted for its red hair."

"What's your point, Anderson?" Stewart asked.

"I think it was all of the Thebes vs. Thebes discussion we had earlier. You remember? Anyway, sometimes my brain sorts things out while I'm sleeping. Homer wrote *The Iliad* and *The Odyssey* in the 8th Century BC, but the story of the Trojan War went back even further to strangely line up with—"

"Ramses," MacPherson anticipated.

Anderson grinned. "Ponder this for a minute…after the end of the Trojan War, the Greeks are set to return home from Troy when…kaboom! The biggest naval disaster ever recorded, courtesy of the Sea God Poseidon. Meanwhile in Minoa, around the same time, kaboom! The city blows up, leaving a volcanic crater now known as Santorini. Meanwhile in Egypt, kaboom! A foreign horde arrives to end the dynasty known by Joseph and Jacob and later to begin a new dynasty that culminates in Ramses the Great. The Bible describes "sea people" invading and settling in the region. In my dream, it wasn't a dark haired Egyptian who greeted me; it was Menelaus the red-headed Greek."

"What's your point exactly?" Stewart asked.

"Yes, what is my point?" Anderson scratched his head, still playing the fool to lighten the mood. "Oh yes! I've studied the

lineage of Alexander the Great. Most famously, he's the son of Phillip of Macedon, who claimed to be a descendent of Hercules. But it is Alexander's mother Olympias whose line is truly fascinating. Her lineage comes from Achilles, specifically from Neoptolemus, who ended up siring children who had connections to Menalaus, Agamemnon, and even Priam the King of Troy. The Curse of Tantalus passed through a thousand years of Greek history until it blossomed with Alexander the Great."

"For a small man you have rather large thoughts," Stewart teased.

"Of course! A cursed bloodline—is that your point?" MacPherson clarified.

"It was a strange dream, for sure, but I woke feeling as if it meant something. Tell me, priest, the kings we seek…is there any connection among them all?"

MacPherson hesitated, which intrigued Stewart and had him prompting, "Do tell."

MacPherson winced in hesitation. "It's mostly New Testament references, but there is a phrase: Son of Perdition. It is used in connection with the Antichrist, but in other places, it is used as a plural phrase: Sons of Perdition."

"St. John wrote about there being 'many antichrists,'" Stewart added.

"Exactly, so it does give me pause that there could be a similar concept to Anderson's Curse of Tantalus theory."

"I have my own theory," Anderson boasted. "Very nice."

"Yes, so with our seven kings…are they just random villains or is there a connection?" MacPherson asked.

"The Order of Eos is based entirely on heritage and bloodlines," Stewart added. "Granted, it's not a monarchy, or else I might be a villain, also. What do you think, Ross?"

"I think the biggest problem is that too much time has passed to honestly know. Say Nimrod ruled approximately in the year 2000 BC. Ramses the Great ruled in the year 1300 BC. Alexander the Great ruled in 300 BC. Hundreds of years passed between each. The bloodline theory has problems."

After reaching a breaking point last night, Stewart felt a spark rekindling within him. "What about Antiochus Epiphanes and Domitian? Could a cursed bloodline apply to either of them?"

MacPherson pondered with a knowing nod. "Most scholars in the Catholic Church interpret the Book of Daniel as empire giving way to empire, but I haven't seen support for a biological connection between all of them."

"The Sons of Perdition?" Stewart repeated to savor the theory.

"Or Anderson's redhead theory," MacPherson finished.

"Well, it was a strange dream," Anderson said and shrugged. "The mummies we found just before the shooting began were redheads, which is atypical of most Egyptians."

"So you think there was a Greek strain?" MacPherson asked.

"The tale says that Menelaus was stuck in Egypt for several years before speaking to a shapeshifting, ancient god. History records the Hyksos people ruling Egypt as foreigners for four generations—and then they vanish."

"I thought they migrated to Canaan," Stewart offered.

"Good point," MacPherson added. "Which is why Anderson might be onto something. Ramses the Great was an anomaly. His grandfather was a servant of the 18th Dynasty, not a member of the royal family. They married into the royal houses. Once Ramses came to power, he worshiped death gods like Seth and named his daughter Bint-Anath, a clear reference to the Canaanite goddess."

"Who's Bint-Anath?" Jamie Anderson asked.

MacPherson answered, "A renaming of Semiramis, the self-titled Queen of Heaven, who ruled Babel with her incestuous lover Ninus, or Nimrod, as he's called in the Bible."

Just hearing the back-and-forth between Anderson and MacPherson lifted Stewart's mood. It reminded him of the nights they'd brainstormed the list of villains who fit the ancient prophecy.

"So Ramses the Great is not only genetically different from other Egyptians, he's also spiritually different in his worship style," Anderson reviewed. "Is this not the same pattern for Alexander the Great?"

"He had a spiritual curiosity, didn't he? From seeking Solomon's Temple to finding the Temple of Amun, he did walk in

the shadows. Don't forget that he also attacked Persia, which is built upon the foundations of Nimrod's Babylon. It makes you wonder why he was willing to lose everything to invade the Himalayas. Why did he need to take his army so far away?"

Jamie Anderson stared down Stewart for a moment before answering. "Lord William Drummond Stewart has endless private wealth. Look at how far he's willing to go for a private obsession. Alexander the Great had the wealth of an ever-expanding empire at his disposal. If he managed to conquer Tyre, Jerusalem, and Egypt, do you really think a trip up the Nile would be too much for him? Of course not."

"You're right," MacPherson admitted. "Alexander the Great left no stone unturned. Historians viewed Darius and Persia as a regional rival, the empire that killed his father, but if there was a reason for conquering ancient Bablylon, no one would have been able to withstand his will. His history of seeking omens, prophecies, and lineage makes you wonder why he focused on Egypt."

"Remember," Anderson said. "Ramses the Great had a spiritual connection to ancient Babylon with his rekindled worship of Anath."

Stewart was too tired to join in the conversation, but he vetted the idea in his mind. *Beyond a cursed bloodline, there could be a connection between the private religions of these men. This is why the Order of Eos seeks them also.*

"Nimrod was a great builder and his son became the nation of Egypt. Egypt's own folklore tells of the legendary builder Imhotep. If Alexander the Great went to find the body of Nimrod, but couldn't find it, it makes sense to seek it in Egypt."

*It's what I would do,* Stewart admitted. He cleared his throat to join the discussion. "Let's say that Alexander the Great had more than just Frank Penny as a conquering army. What would he have done if he could have stayed as long as he wanted?"

The men pondered as Egypt passed by the deck of the ship.

"I think Anderson's dream was quite profound. How can you tell apart an underworld full of dead corpses? How would Ramses stand out?" MacPherson theorized aloud. "Ramses the Elder was a hired servant with biology unique from the 18th Dynasty.

Intermarriage with the dark haired Thebans created a family tree of darker skinned heirs, but for a few generations, the red hair would help identify the line."

"Both Eos and the ancient Egyptians believed their ancient kings would somehow rise from the dead, so they went through great lengths to protect the bodies. So I ask you this: why would the Egyptians bother identifying tombs?"

After a few moments of silence, MacPherson answered, "I believe their culture believes in the power of the name, which is why Champollian was able to find the name in the empty tomb."

"But why was the tomb empty?" Stewart pressed. Neither answered, so he rephrased his question. "If you knew men were going to try to destroy or steal the body, what would you do?"

"They'd preserve and hide the body elsewhere," MacPherson offered. "And let the tomb preserve the written name."

Anderson offered, "There is no way to tell a thousand year old shepherd from a thousand year old king without a note. Any of those corpses we found in the cache could have been Ramses."

MacPherson built on the theory. "If the tomb was empty, people would ask questions. Look at what we did when we found an empty tomb, right? We gave up. But if you leave a body and a note identifying the corpse, folks would have no other choice than to accept it."

"So you're saying back in Thebes, there's a decoy with a note?" Stewart asked.

"Better than that," MacPherson added. "The Shrine of Wutoch had four places of honor. Whether his men or Alexander's men came to Thebes, Domitian believed he'd found all four corpses. Yet Anderson's dream about the talking redhead could mean—"

"The Order of Eos has a shepherd's corpse," Stewart grinned. "Our mission was to find any of the seven kings and keep Eos from unlocking their prophecy. It makes me smile to think they might've failed centuries ago."

"Since we cannot go back to Thebes, I am determined to search for the tomb of Antiochus Epiphanes. Perhaps we'll find another of Anderson's redheaded mummies."

"A curious dream, isn't it?" Anderson countered.

Suddenly, the failure at Thebes didn't sting as much. "I've been giving thoughts to the Goths who sacked Rome and hauled away the loot of the nation. If we do not find the tomb of Antiochus Epiphanes at our next step, perhaps it is time to look closer at what became of the Goths. But first, we need to get the hell out of Egypt."

"Agreed," MacPherson said.

"I could not agree more," Anderson added.

Stewart patted the two on the shoulder, and then Frank Penny came around the corner whistling blissfully. *Perhaps one day I'll forgive him, but not today.*

# CHAPTER 29

V A R N A ,   B U L G A R I A

1 8 5 2

Pyotr Petrov stood on the pier leading to the lighthouse that jutted into the busy port, hoping for redemption. Steamships, sailing vessels, and fishing boats came and went. *The perfect location for a covert meeting,* Petrov decided.

One small fishing boat made a direct line from the northern city to the spot where he waited at the third lamp from the end of the pier. The nose of the boat touched and a man leapt to shore. The figure struggled for balance as he ascended the rocky slope but once he reached the top of the pier, he brushed himself off, straightened his back, and casually strolled in Petrov's direction.

"Good evening," the dark-skinned man said in English but with a strange accent. "The stars are lovely tonight."

"Indeed," Petrov agreed according to script. "I've been studying the lovely constellation Aquila. Do you know it?"

Aquila was the code word. In ancient mythology, aquila was the Eagle who carried Zeus's thunderbolts. As a servant of Lady Columbia, Petrov and others were her thunderbolts.

"It's a pleasure to meet you, Mr. Petrov," the man said. "I am Koot Bessant, an ally of Lady Columbia. I've recently come from Zamora Castle to make arrangements for the coming days. Things are moving quickly now, and war will soon come to the region."

*War? Her grasp now extends to nations.*

The port of Varna rested between two mighty nations: Russia and the Ottoman Empire. Petrov understood how Vendita existed beyond the flags of either nation. "What about my mission? Obviously, if she sent you, she's heard my requests."

"Unfortunately, the failure of your previous mission only managed to send the target into hiding, and for the time being, other matters must take priority. However, it yielded an unexpected opportunity. The Grandmasters of the Order of Eos have also gone into hiding."

After spending a few moments with Bessant, Petrov finally understood the origin of the accent and facial features: India. "Why would Eos flee?"

"Lady Columbia's desire to avenge the men who killed her mentor failed, and the men we targeted not only survived but also wrongly ascribed the act to Eos."

*Lord Stewart didn't just hide—he lashed out.*

Bessant handed Petrov a folder of profiles, "Your new assignment will be targetting the leadership of the Order of Eos. Like cockroaches, they've gone underground, but if history repeats itself, we know where they will hide. You will be stationed at Bagras Castle. Since we do not know with certainly, the documents describe the current leaders within Eos."

"I understand, and I will execute my duty faithfully, but why would any leaders of Eos come so far east? There are certainly—"

"In the coming days, there will be great political upheaval that will threaten some of the old Eos strongholds. They face danger at home, and soon their ancient stronghold will soon be in the center of war between mighty nations. Lady Columbia believes the leadership will show interest in old strongholds that once served them in the past. You are to take any of these Eos assets alive."

*To what end, I wonder.* This time, he didn't ask the question. Even if he sat and waited for a year, it was a way to get back in the good graces of Lady Columbia.

*This time, I will not fail her.*

THE END OF PART FOUR

# PART FIVE
## NEW ENGLAND

# CHAPTER 30



The city of Detroit had become a boomtown. Each morning, Solomon Delhut looked out his windows. On the opposite bank of the Detroit River, the city became more and more an eyesore. Knowing he'd have a busy day ahead of him across the river, he took his time savoring his coffee.

The house was quiet as only himself and Esther now lived there. His daughter Emily had married a businessman, and Pierre was sent to a private school in Albany in preparation for running the family empire. Granted, there was the household staff, but they didn't enter the house until it was time to prepare breakfast. The hired security patrolled the perimeter of the island. Thus, for a few more minutes, Solomon could be alone with his thoughts.

He remembered the face of the scarred Indian—the only face without verified identity—who'd been called Jim.

For a few years, his enemies had been true to their word. Solomon survived the intended massacre of his family by acting weak, and when William Drummond Stewart and Antoine Clement left, they fulfilled their oaths by hunting down the men responsible for the deaths of his French cousin, Berenger, as well as Joseph Nicollet.

Yet the home invasion left Solomon Delhut a changed man.

He now had a plan.

Crushing his enemies was an afterthought. Yes, he gave the names of the attackers to his more powerful friends, those who were also members of the Order of Eos, but revenge did not burn in his heart. He felt lucky to be alive.

Cowering to the intruders had saved his family, but it also made him even more curious about his family legacy. He'd personally surrendered his ancient map, which, although no longer necessary, still burned in his gut. The other map—*the Al Marrakk map*—had never been in his possession. He'd purchased it from Lady Margaret Drummond through his agent Gerard Berenger, but both died in the July Revolution and the map ended up in the hands of his enemies. Thanks to the soft hearts of his abductors, he managed to get some manner of revenge when Joel Poinsett "died suddenly" from Tuberculosis at his home in South Carolina.

His map—*the Abbaron Map*—had been in the family for generations. From what he could discern, the map had been given to Ettienne Delhut by Mrs. Pierre-Charles LeSueur in exchange for enough wealth to relocate her family to Louisiana to be with her LeMoyne cousins. Having studied the map for years, he knew the legend behind it.

If the tale was to be believed, wise King Solomon hired a large expedition (ships, sailors, navigators, soldiers, engineers, and miners) to search the world for the Philosopher's Stone. Solomon gave the leader of the venture, a Hebrew named Abbaron, his completed research in the form of the *Al Marrakk Map*. Both maps were thousands of years old now, but both had been made within a few years of each other. King Solomon's *Al Marrakk Map*, which Lady Drummond tried to sell, used stars as references for the expedition. The Abbaron Map, ugly and crude, was drawn after the explorers traveled deep into the heart of an unknown continent. The survivors tried to describe the place "where the water flows in all directions" noted by its "blue earth."

For thousands of years, the map of a failed expedition remained in a vault until the Knights of the Temple of Solomon discovered it buried beneath the ruins of the temple in Jerusalem. In 1188 at the Splitting of the Elm, one ancient map was given to the Order of Eos and the other was given to the Priory of Ormus.

While the Order of Eos kept their map secure for the next few centuries, the Priory of Ormus ended up losing the *Abbaron Map* to the Jesuits in 1605 during the chaos of the Gunpowder Plot. A century later, the Order of Eos lost the *Al Marrakk Map* when Edward Drummond, later known as the pirate Blackbeard, stole it from the Templar guardians and brought it back to Scotland, where it remained in Logiealmond for another century.

*But what good did the maps do anybody?*

Joseph Nicollet saw the *Al Marrakk Map* before it was stolen by Joel Poinsett, and he went right to the heart of the Minnesota territory, which he called Undine, the Blue Woman, to the place where "water flows in all directions." He didn't find anything.

Rumors insisted that the Philosopher's Stone had been lost near Bermuda, tossed into the sea by a spiteful Pierre-Charles LeSueur.

The blue ormus, or vitriol, left behind in southern Minnesota, had almost entirely been washed away or removed.

The Sinclairs insisted that Nicollet and LeSueur had either lied or been wrong, and they modified the legends to match the Missouri River, meaning the resting place of the Philosopher's Stone is hidden deep in the tributaries of the Rocky Mountains.

*But where was Nicollet planning to travel next before he died?* Delhut wondered.

No one could explain it to him, although Eos investigators insisted that if Nicollet had lived, he was heading out into the Rockies to join up with his allies: DeSmet, Stewart, Geyer, Clement, and Fremont.

While everyone else focused westward, Solomon focused on the early expeditions of Nicollet. Even though the Chippewa still held the north, and the Dakota still held the south, their strength was diminished: the State of Minnesota was opening to settlement, thanks to treaties. With a shell company in Albany, Solomon Delhut planned to buy up the land north of Little Falls where Nicollet and his Chippewa guide Chagobay found blue earth at a place haunted by a water spirit.

*Once I take possession of the land, I'll have all the time I need to privately explore my theories.* Nicollet had scoured the haystack for him and had shown him where the needle should be found. Now all he needed to do was do a little digging.

Having finished his coffee, Solomon Delhut stood up and walked downstairs. Outside, his staff prepared for his departure.

He ate breakfast with his wife, chatted with the house staff about the news, and met the carriage driver for his short trip to Detroit.

Belle Island had once been the home of the Anishinaabe people on their westward migration referred to as the Seven Fires. After leaving the shores of the Atlantic, the Anishinaabe followed prophecy and providence to Montreal Island and Niagara Falls before a young hunter found the sacred Megis shells that identified the third stopping place, Waawiyegaama, or Round Lake. Round Lake later became known as Lake St. Clair, the village became known as Detroit, and the island became known as Belle Island. Fur traders understood the strategic location between two Great Lakes and civilization took root long after the Anishinaabe inhabited Minnesota.

*My son shall have a bridge*, Solomon mused as he waited in the carriage for the ferry. The others teased him about his remote home, but more than ever, he loved the symbolism of living on one of the seven islands. While the rest of Waawiyagaama turned into urban sprawl, Belle Island remained wooded.

The past quickly met the future at his offices of North Star Roads. He'd left Montreal two decades earlier to expand his father's lumber empire, but in the city of Detroit, he discovered that while he could make money building the "corduroy roads" of logs, a more permanent solution was needed. Detroit needed metal, and with its place at the crossroads of the Great Lakes, he privately began to invest in the acquisition and distribution of metal along the Great Lakes corridor. His chain link fence business was a boom for the citizens of the growing city, and with the west opening up, rumors of vast sources of metal along the shores of Lake Superior would hopefully transform North Star Roads into a business empire.

The men waiting in his office, however, were not any of his business partners from any of his budding enterprises.

Duncan Dobie, Callum Gunn, and Lachlan Morrison sat, chatting pleasantly, upon the couches as Solomon Delhut walked up to them. *Loyal Eos men.*

"Welcome, Gentlemen, I hope I haven't kept you waiting."

"We arrived last night," Callum Gunn explained, "and we didn't want to bother you so late. Dobie and I were just conversing about the land purchases in Mahkahta County."

"Yes, Sibley has assured us that we'll be first in line," Solomon bragged. "Now that Wisconsin has achieved statehood, the Minnesota territory is still in the process of being organized, but our interests will supercede all other claims."

"Mahkahta?" Morrison repeated. Seeing Lachlan Morrison sent a chill down his spine. That man had a reputation as an enforcer, a killer, unlike the two Albany businessmen who joined him.

"Mahkahta is a Sioux word for Blue Earth. From what we've gleaned from Joseph Nicollet's four expeditions, his initial interest was near the headwaters of the Mississippi River. Apparently, he visited a place called Spirit Lake were there was strange blue vitriol found near a cave."

"Ah," Morrison feigned understanding. The other two waited patiently for Morrison to say anything else. Even though Gunn and Dobie had a higher financial status, they understood Morrison's place within the ranks of Eos. "What about our interest in the headwaters of the Missouri?"

Delhut nodded. "Certainly a possibility."

"Mahkahta County?" Morrison repeated. "Perhaps a bit too assuming? I understand why we're purchasing land, but should we be calling it that?"

"It's just another Native word."

Morrison sighed with disdain.

"What's the matter?"

Clearly, only Morrison knew the answer, and he took his time thinking about it. "Four men are dead in the Orkney Islands—all Sinclairs

"Shit. Stewart?"

"Likely. He and his entire entourage vanished a few days before it happened. We're not as concerned about Stewart as we are about those affiliated with Joel Poinsett."

"Poinsett? We didn't have anything to do with his death."

"You gave Stewart information that led to him, and those who supported Poinsett wanted retribution, which led to Stewart and

Clement's names being distributed amongst guilds that specialize in assassination."

"Some guild! Apparently they failed."

"Yes, but the death of Joel Poinsett has not only woken the sleeping bear but has also given it the fresh taste of blood. Your name has been distributed within the same guilds," Morrison explained.

"Me?"

Morrison looked down at a piece of paper. "Solomon Delhut. William Sinclair. Eduard Terront. Notice any connections?"

All three Grandmasters. With Stewart and the others, it'd been mindless vengeance over the death of Nicollet, but Vendita meant to exterminate the entire order. "Does this have to do with—"

Morrison nodded. "So it has been decided that the three of you are about to go on an unexpected, extended holiday until we can get to the bottom of it. I'll be traveling with you to make sure you properly vanish. Mr. Gunn will oversee your business affairs here in Detroit, and Mr. Dobie will make sure your plans for Mahkahta County in Minnesota continue as you desire. Most likely, you'll be back within a month."

*A month!*

The immediate anger Solomon Delhut felt turned to an icy chill as he thought about the scarred Indian holding a blade to his son Pierre.

*If it's war they want, it's war they'll get.* Yet he knew for now, he'd need to disappear.

# CHAPTER 31

B O S T O N ,   M A S S A C H U S E T T S

1 8 5 3

For the better part of three months, Lewis Cairns played the part of Lord Wesley Erskine. Having arrived in winter, the five travelers lingered in a rented house outside of Boston while waiting for spring weather.  After weeks of living off of Stewart's money, today they finally emerged from hiding.

Cairns waited patiently for his valet and the two footmen to finish transferring his luggage from house to coach. Beside him, his guide previewed the itinerary, but there were too many names and too many obscure connections for him to follow. He'd seen pompous noblemen just stand and nod, so he did the same thing in his role of Lord Erskine. Now even the locals doted on him. Forty years earlier, at the Battle of Waterloo, he expected to die any second, so the idea of living to be an old man, pampered by others, put a smile on his face.

"You can wait inside of the front carriage," Antoine Clement told him with a meek gesture. "We'll finish loading the luggage and the three of us will ride there."

"Of course," Cairns said. Professor Morgan continued talking in his ear as they stepped into the carriage.

Despite playing the part of haughty Lord Erskine, Lewis was frightened. He knew the names of the men associated with the Order of Eos, and after two hundred years in North America, they'd all taken root and thrived—finding independence from any royal family or government in Europe. Stewart's suggestion to use a false identity now made sense upon arriving in America.

Now Lewis mostly feared for his friend William, yet their relationship began with open hatred. William Drummond Stewart's wealth gave him military command, but the men belonged to Sergeant Cairns, who did everything he could to privately belittle the boy in charge. Although only a few years Stewart's senior, Lewis mocked Stewart to the men and challenged him when making decisions—only to find out the man was made of steel. During war, his view of Stewart changed. Not only was he right most of the time but he also had good luck.

He watched the Vaktar and Sofus help Clement with the luggage as they prepared for the next stage of the journey. At Clement's insistance, he gave the Sinclairs the last of the winter months to return to their home. Having given the mission proper time, they now continued with the revenge plan.

"We're loaded, sir," Antoine Clement announced with enthusiasm in his voice. Professor Morgon, however, looked nervous and reluctant. Back in Scandinavia, Professor Morgan had been allowed his research trip, but now the real men would take the reins.

The rest of the day consisted of playing the part of Erskine at the Hotel Pelham. After unpacking the luggage, Cairns collapsed onto his big bed while the others made plans for the weeklong stay in Boston to prepare for the next stage of the journey.

Following his nap, Cairns walked to the window to look out upon the city. For America, it was considered an old town, but compared to the cities of Europe, everything about Boston looked fresh and new. Below him, the busy streets of Boylston and Tremont allowed Professor Morgan, Antoine Clement, and the boys to come and go with little notice, but he had to remain visible at all times.

*Which is fine by me.*

He rotated his servants. At breakfast, Professor Morgan was at his side. After lunch, either Nielson or Forsberg sat with him in the smoking room while he read various newspapers. Although Clement offered other solutions, they decided to keep Sofus Nielson as a hired footman rather than risk him sharing details about what he'd learned during the crossing of the Atlantic. For supper, Antoine Clement would put on his eight-button jacket and stiff collared dress shirt and hung at his elbow as fellow travelers shared stories with Lord Erskine.

William Drummond Stewart's plan required patience and allowed Cairns to live in the lap of luxury as they created a false narrative for whoever watched them.

While waiting for spring, Cairns created a list—the leadership for the Order of Eos. Clement explained the roles played by the Sinclairs, Solomon Delhut, and Eduard Terront while Morgan explained the historical details of the families. Cairns knew why William Drummond Stewart had been denied membership. Drinking, hunting, whoring, gambling, bragging—these traits made the young nobleman too risky to be privy to the secrets of the ancient society, but Stewart's exotic uncle trusted him enough to leave his guard down.

Spurned by Eos, Stewart spent the summer after the Waterloo Campaign scouring the library at Logiealmond. It didn't take him long to discover that Eos was searching for a treasure lost on the continent of North America. Following the death of his aunt, Eos took back most of their relics from the Drummond family, but not before Lady Margaret tried to sell a map to an interested buyer from North America.

That was when Sergeant Cairns joined the story. What began as a simple murder investigation led to an investigation of two names: Jean Nicholas Nicollet and Gerard Berenger. While the astronomy professor proved to be a dead end—Lady Margaret met him only to drive up the price—the merchant Berenger had connections to several secret societies. Just days into the murder investigation of Lady Drummond, the July Revolution shook France. Suddenly, rioters with connections to the Illuminati, Carbonari, and countless Masonic Lodges flooded Paris. In the chaos, Berenger was murdered and Nicollet vanished.

Cairns reported all of this to Stewart, who then took it upon himself to go to North America to see if there were any truth in the old legends involving the Philosopher's Stone.

Several years later, Stewart returned with Antoine Clement and many answers. Lady Margaret ironically bound Nicollet and Stewart together for a common cause, but the bold scientist died before his grand plan could be completed.

Now, Sergeant Lewis Cairns prepared to repay Captain Stewart for the extra four decades of life he'd been given. The plan was three-fold. For Professor Morgan, it was investigating Eos in order to discern fact and fiction. For Antoine Clement, it was vengeance against the men who had his father killed. For Cairns, it was to find Nicollet's remaining allies on the frontier and then extract the Philosopher's Stone.

*But first…vengeance for Clement and Thomas.*

To do that, he had to put away the character of Lord Erskine after parading him around Boston for a full week. He changed out of his expensive clothes back to the simple clothing more suited for clandestine work.

Soon the others assembled in his room for the moment.

"Professor Morgan will stay here with the boys," Clement explained. "Our passage to Hudson Bay won't depart for another week, which will allow us enough time to complete the side-mission."

"I take it I'll be under the weather for the next few days?" Cairns asked, already knowing the plans for the first of three assassinations.

"You'll be bedridden by a stomach flu. The boys will fetch soups and basic remedies while Professor Morgan will linger in the lobby to avoid catching it," Clement added.

"It's not a short trip to Nova Scotia," Cairns added. "Are you sure you found reliable passage there and back again?"

"It's reliable but not glamorous. There's a fishing ship that hauls Halifax mackerel to Boston and then fills up with Boston cod to be transported back to England. It makes the trek every two days without fail. That gives us two days there, two days to scout, and two days to return—right on schedule to depart."

"That'll do," Cairns answered. "Are you sure about this? Once we begin, we go all the way."

"I'm prepared to go all the way. Are you?"

LATER THAT NIGHT, Lewis Cairns slipped out of Lord Wesley Erkine's window to meet Antoine Clement in the alley. From

there, they passed through the dark streets until they found their way to the docks. By the time the sun rose, Cairns looked back to see Boston in distant Massachusetts Bay.

Clement was more surly than normal. Had they been able to come directly to Boston from Scotland, they would've had the element of surprise. Like with hunting, when the prey was spooked, it took time before it returned and relaxed. Clement assumed the trip to Nova Scotia would be fruitless. So Cairns found a quiet corner of the steamer to properly clean his rifle and reflect on the men he was about to help Clement kill.

Numerous men played a part in the murder of Antoine Clement Sr., but Magnus Sinclair's name was at the top of the list. Cairns knew the biography by heart. Descended from a line of Sinclairs that traced their way back to those on the Orkney Islands, the Canadian Sinclairs took root two centuries ago, surviving wars involving the Micmac, Acadians, French, British, and Americans to call "New Scotland" their home.

TWO DAYS LATER, they stepped off the mackerel ship and onto the shore of Nova Scotia.

After studying Nova Scotia for so long, Cairns found it almost disappointing. The pines were pleasant; the shores were scenic; the air was inviting. Halifax was filled with regular-looking gents who went about their business with a friendly nod. Rather than finding a ride, the men vanished into the woods to walk the thirty miles in isolation. By evening, they hid in the trees overlooking the Sinclair estate.

Both Cairns and Clement had looking glasses to watch the mansion with their ready rifles at their side. The three story stone mansion had four rooms with windows on the top floor, another, four rooms with seven windows on the main floor, and another four windows and doors on the ground level. None of them lit up at supper.

*The house is empty.*

Antoine Clement seethed though his face remained passive as always. Cairns noticed how Clement held onto his breath as he thought, releasing it in angry bursts.

"I see something," Clement finally said.

"What? Where?" Cairns asked, putting his own looking glass down to see where Clement focused.

"On the island."

The estate of Magnus Sinclair sat near the shore of Mahone Bay, which connected directly to the open Atlantic Ocean. Several acres of pines had been felled to create lush green yards and to also open the shoreline to the view of the beautiful island behind it. On the island, Cairns saw two lanterns and a campfire.

"This is all Sinclair property," Clement insisted. "If they somehow knew we were coming, they might have fled to the island for protection."

"Or else they're on vacation and it's a couple of local boys out exploring."

"Go check the house," Clement ordered. "I'll watch from here. I'll cover you and keep an eye on those lights on the island. If you don't find anything, we're going to the island."

Cairns left the cover of the woods, hunched slightly, and approached the dark house. All the windows remained open without curtains drawn. His head pivoted, knowing that open windows would allow light to be seen if thieves risked a light.

*Someone could be watching me right now.*

He peeked and poked around the windows, his rifle strapped to his back and his revolver now in hand. The doors were locked and around the perimeter of the house, everything was tucked away and in order.

*Sinclair is gone,* Cairns decided, but he knew there'd be plenty of opportunity to kill their enemies on the next stage of the journey. Once he got around to the bay side of the house, he could see the lanterns much better. No more than two hundred yards separated the shore from the island, and in the woods of the island, the lanterns continued to move away from the campfire.

On the edge of the water, he saw a boat. *Clement might be right.*

A figure moved in the shadows of the campfire, and Cairns flinched so hard he almost squeezed the trigger. Luckily, he didn't. Clement came around the corner, pointing to the near shore.

"There are several small boats tied up in the little bay," he said, referencing the bottom of the hill. "We're going to get some answers."

# CHAPTER 32



Antoine Clement held his rifle as if reuniting with an old lover. His Manton rifle had been given to him by Stewart years earlier during an expedition. From its silver sight at the end of the barrel to the brass embossed plate at the hilt, he knew every inch of the gun. Back at Murthly Castle, he'd reunited with her, firing off enough rounds to adjust accuracy, but it'd been months since that moment.

He pointed the silver sight at the campfire, letting the glow of the fire turn his aim to a shadowy frame. The first shot was the most important. He needed to give Cairns a fighting chance by taking out the first target. Beside Clement, another lover waited should Cairns fail. His brand new Sharps rifle had been another gift from Stewart. Although the new silver rifle proved more accurate at the shooting range, he didn't trust it when it mattered most.

The lantern began returning to the camp.

Looking side-eye, he could see the figures approaching while his rifle remained pointed at the kill zone. Near the fire, the two targets would be almost blind to the darkness while Clement could clearly see their figures in the glow of the fire and lantern.

If Cairns did his part, he'd be hiding behind the big oak tree to confront the two. Once the signal was given, Clement would fire.

*Oak trees.*

The island was indeed strange. While walking from the port at Halifax to Mahone Bay, Clement saw the composition of the forest and fauna, but instead of pine trees, old oak trees—a species he'd not seen during the forty miles they traveled by foot—covered the island.

*"To make it easier to spot from sea,"* Morgan had explained back in Boston.

A hundred islands surrounded this stretch of Nova Scotia shore, and from a distance, it looked no different than the others, but up close, the difference was obvious.

*Bloody hell…*

The two figures that appeared at the campfire were boys.

Sensing a trap, Clement immediately looked over his shoulder.

The small oak forest remained silent.

He turned back to the boys. *Trespassers?*

The campsite was littered with luxury items reminiscent of how Joseph Nicollet camped during the 1836 expedition to the Mississippi River headwaters—more personal items than survival items.

*No, this is the campsite of boys and not security guards.*

*But who are these boys?*

Clement kept his rifle sights on the boy on the edge of the camp. The rowboat meant the boys still had an umbilical cord to the world, but the design of the camp indicated they'd been staying there for quite a while.

*Were they abandoned or did they choose to stay?*

Like the clueless boy in his aim, Clement had spent plenty of time abandoned by his father. For months at a time, his father would vanish into the Canadian wilderness, only to walk into camp like a mythical hero. Raised by grandmothers, wives, and daughters, he grew to idolize the great hairy beasts (especially his father) who would appear for a few days a year to rut and tell tales. Between these random sightings, young Antoine honed his hunting skills until he proved his worth to leave camp—and he never looked back.

Cairns boldly stepped into a camp in much the same way his father had done: with two pistols drawn. He spoke softly enough that neither boy so much as flinched when he appeared. He towered over them as they had just taken a seat.

*Give the signal, Lewis. These people killed my father.*

Cairns kept yapping, and soon the boys began yapping right back. They sat on their hands at Cairns command, and the wide-eyed boys nodded and spoke with enthusiasm at each and every question.

*Damn it! We're here for slaughter not small talk.*

Clement felt the curve of his finger touch the cold metal of the trigger as he debated taking the first shot.

During his two decades on the frontier, he'd taken thousands of lives. His killing habits worked right up the food chain: small animals around camp; the Hudson Bay polar bear that impressed his father; the countless deer, elk, and bison on the frontier; enemies that threatened Stewart's hunting party; and any Mexican soldier within range of his rifle. *Why not add two more to the heap?*

Cairns stepped between Clement and the boys—on purpose.

Clement lowered the hammer on the Manton and then pulled the shoulder strap around his neck as he stood. He picked up the Sharps and did the same, crisscrossing the rifles to rest squarely on his back. His fingers found his hunting knife.

Out of the darkness he advanced, taking heavy, confident strides just like that polar bear that planned on a juicy meal. First, Lewis Cairns grew wide-eyed and stepped back in alarm. Then the boys saw him and cowered even closer to the ground.

When Clement took hold of the nearest by the hair, a bleat of terror came from the boy's throat, which would be ended by the edge of—

A boot struck Clement in the left hip, sending him and the boy toppling to the ground. The hunting knife struck the ground, twisting in his fingers as his forearm took the brunt of the fall. By the time Clement found the blade, Cairns had pointed a pistol in his face.

"We're not killing children," the former sergeant snapped. "Is this how your sorry tale of revenge ends?"

*The old bear still has a bit of growl in him.* Clement's fingers tightened on the hilt of the knife and he reached for the boy again.

Cairns' thumb moved to pull the hammer back. "Don't test me."

Strangely enough, Cairns' left hand remained pointed at the other boy, who still sat on his hands in submission. The right pistol did not waiver.

*How many men did Cairns kill in the war?* Clement knew the story of the Battle of Hougoumont from Stewart's repeated tellings, and aside from knowing the Scotsman's role, he never pictured the sergeant's role in the bloodbath.

*Fuck!* Clement let go of the knife hilt and raised his hand in submission.

"Scoot away from the poor kid," Cairns insisted, gesturing with his cocked pistol.

"These boys are not the innocent lambs you believe them to be," Clement said, feeling the shoulder straps choking him until he rose to his knees. He brushed himself off.

"Only time will tell, but for now, I'll not have their blood on my hands—or yours."

Clement thought about how they'd spared Solomon Delhut because of the children, and because of that mercy, assassins learned their names. "Dammit all, why do you think we came all this way? Walk away if you don't have the stomach for it."

"I have no qualms shedding blood, and I'd leave your dead body right beside theirs if it suited my purpose, but then again, I'm not a bloodthirsty savage bent on revenge."

"Savage?" Clement repeated. *Does he want it to end here on this island?*

"Look at yourself!"

Clement let go of the boy's hair, but the child did not so much as move, whimpering with each breath. "If we let them live, matters will be even worse. Trust me. We should show them no mercy."

"How do you know they're not just a couple local boys seeking an adventure on the island?" Cairns asked. "Now sheath your blade and step back."

*Local boys?* Clement felt the fires of rage lessen and the sharp pain of morality pierce his mind. He picked up the blade and shoved it into its sheath. He raised both hands to show Cairns he'd forgiven the kick.

He rose slowly, his rifles clattering on his back. "My apologies."

"Now, are you going to show the restraint of a civilized human being?"

Clement nodded.

"Then as a reasonable human being, you understand these are not the men responsible for the death of your father."

"Yes."

"Before you came crashing in, we were having a very interesting conversation. Do you know what they were doing? Tell them, boys."

The two boys hesitated, glancing at each other. He saw then that neither had sprouted and were only perhaps boys of ten or eleven.

"Boys?"Cairns pressed.

The older boy answered. "We were searching for Captain Kidd's lost treasure."

"Treasure hunters," Cairns repeated, glancing at Clement. "So then I asked them if they were trespassing… What did you boys say? Are you trespassing?"

They both shook their heads.

"And why aren't you trespassing?"

The older boy answered again. "Because the island belongs to my uncle."

Cairns nodded. "And I then asked, 'Where's your uncle?' Do you know what he told me?"

*They're both Sinclairs. I know it.*

"He said that the whole family packed up for a vacation— unexpectedly. Grandma, the uncles, the cousins, all of them. So I asked why they were left behind, but that's about the time you came crashing in, frightening the boys. Now, why don't you go lean against a tree so the boys and I can finish our conversation."

*We tipped them off back at the Orkneys. If we'd raced across the Atlantic, we could have caught the entire clan unaware.* Clement stepped back, leaning into an oak tree.

"Okay boys, I think you can relax now. If you keep telling me the truth, I'll make sure my friend doesn't hurt you. By dawn, we'll be gone and all of this will seem like a bad dream." Cairns looked back at Clement, who ceased all hostility. "Why weren't you boys taken along on vacation? Were you bad?"

The elder shook his head. "No, we…William and I had piping Camp in Halifax in February, so we were taken in by a local family."

"You were going to learn to play the bagpipes?"

"Dad said the vacation was stupid, but Uncle Junior wanted the whole family to go, but there weren't any bagpipe instructors where they were going."

"And where did your family go?"

"Some island in Spain."

The younger boy corrected, "Madeira."

"See," Cairns noted, looking at Clement with fire in his old eyes, "These boys had nothing to do with your father's death." At Clement's scoff, Cairns continued, "My friend recently lost his father, and we were hunting the men who did it. I'm sure if something happened to your father, you'd want to do the same, wouldn't you?"

The boys nodded.

"My friend Roger and I are both from Halifax. We've been tracking these bandits for miles, and when we saw your fire, we thought it might be them, hiding from the law. What's your father's name? Perhaps we know him from Halifax."

"Magnus Sinclair. I'm Scott, and this is my brother William Henry."

*Son of a bitch*, Clement thought, thinking of the summers he spent hunting with Magnus Sinclair at Oxford House. *The little bastards even look like him.*

Suddenly, his fingers found their way back to his knife hilt, but then Cairns cleared his throat in a grunt, and Clement let go of the knife and walked back to the rowboat.

# CHAPTER 33



Professor Corey Morgan couldn't help but feel a bit disappointed. From the vague reference on Verazzano's map to the occult lore found in the Drummond library, he knew all about the infamous Newport Tower—the Viking tower.

As soon as he stepped out of the carriage, it seemed almost silly that the five of them had taken the sixty mile trip from Boston. While an impressive stack of stones, the Newport Tower was no taller than a generic windmill back in Scotland (although stripped of all functionality). It was a skeleton of stone that did not inspire awe.

Behind him, Sofus Nielson and Vaktar Forsberg jumped from the carriage followed by the gloomy Clement and Cairns. Cairns and Clement returned from Nova Scotia angrier than when they'd left, so Morgan knew an adventure would clear the air before getting back in a ship bound for Hudson Bay. *My investigation is the only thing keeping the peace right now.*

Forsberg and Nielson walked at Morgan's side for stories, which he indulged. "This might be one of the oldest structures in North America," Morgan explained as he walked quickly to the structure. A white picket fence surrounded the area to allow tourists to view but not to enter. "When explorer Giovanni Verrazzano passed through here, he spotted it from his ship and labeled it a 'Norman Tower,' which is why many of my colleagues believe it might have been built by the early Viking explorers."

Vaktar flashed a toothless grin at the notion.

"Why did they build it?" Nielson asked.

"If it indeed was built by the Vikings, it might have been used as a navigational landmark. If you're interested in exploration, a unique landmark like this, visible from the sea, allows you to know how far north or south you venture on the endless American coast."

"Who else besides the Vikings would have built it?" Sofus pressed.

Morgan turned to see Cairns and Clement standing behind him. "There's another theory involving a legendary explorer, Prince Henry Sinclair."

"Is that the same Prince Henry who kidnapped my ancestor?" Vaktar asked.

"Yes. If the story has merit, the Order of Eos used their ancient maps to travel to the lost continent in search of a lost treasure of unspeakable worth. To cross the Atlantic, they followed the routes known by the Nielson and Forsberg sailors of old. Once they reached the vast continent, neither their guides nor their maps were beneficial any more. Remember, at the time, no one knew the vastness of America, so creating a navigational landmark, here on this sheltered island, would have made sense. Some of my peers suggest that the strange design of this building was to make astronomical measurements in conjunction with the star maps they had in their possession. They knew the line upon which the treasure should be found, but they had no ability to get there without crossing the continent."

"We could break through those pickets," Clement offered. The boys nodded and grinned.

Morgan shook his head. "Oh, we already know where it points. Men have known for countless centuries the general line upon which the treasure would be found, thanks to Stewart's star maps." Morgan turned to Cairns. "Oak Island…it lies on what we know as the 44th degree latitude. In those days, they didn't know longitude or latitude, but the Norse sailors understood the stars and where they would rise on the horizon in any given season."

"That's why the island was razed and oak trees were planted," Cairns repeated the theory back to him.

"Yes, it would have been a starting point. The natives inhabiting Nova Scotia might've initially seen the Order of Eos men as gods, but once one bleeds or catches a cold and dies, the luster soon vanishes. My bet is the explorers went south because it was easier and warmer than staying in Nova Scotia. This tower was most likely built in the early days, both as a landmark and an astronomical center of almost religious purpose. The Order of Eos might don Christianity when it suits them, but their religious beliefs are old. Perhaps even older than the religion of the Vikings."

Nicollet had figured it out. The Men of the Dawn began their quest in the days of Atlantis, Thule, Hyperborea, and Noah's Flood.

"So why did you drag us here?" Clement snarled.

"I'm sorry for spoiling your chance at revenge," Morgan said, dodging the answer. "If I'd been more discreet back on Orkney Island, the man you seek—this Magnus Sinclair—well, your blade could have drank his blood. But see, that is the problem with the Order of Eos. They've spent generations dedicated to this legend. Unlike us, they are patient and cautious."

"Get on with it," Clement huffed. "What's the point of this stupid tower?"

"It's a monument to the Order of Eos. A tower built along the eastern shore—welcoming the dawn each day. Yet just like Oak Island, they gave it up centuries ago to continue the quest westward."

"If they gave up Oak Island, why did we find a couple stray Sinclairs still lingering around?" Cairns asked. "They had a mansion built across from the island."

"Trust me, they've moved on. They simply honor their heritage, which is why the entire family moved back to their old stronghold on Madeira Island—an old Templar stronghold."

"Professor," Clement snarled, still clearly upset at not getting to slaughter the two Sinclair boys he found, "why did those boys talk about finding Captain Kidd's treasure on Oak Island if Eos gave up on it centuries ago?"

Clement tried to bully him, but Morgan had met plenty of academic bullies in school, so he didn't give the brute a quick answer. "If being born into the Eos family tree is worthy of death, then William Drummond Stewart deserved death. Imagine what would have happened if you killed him with the same notion you wanted to kill those boys," Morgan countered. Cairns raised his eyebrows and Clement lowered his head in submission. "The Drummond library was fascinating, even if the Order of Eos denied William membership. He wasn't the only wild second son in the family. More than a century ago, the Drummond family took root in the New World, in another island—the Bahamas. A second son by the name of Edward Drummond, later known as the pirate Blackbeard, became the mad dog for the Order of Eos, but not before another famous pirate made a name for himself."

"Captain Kidd," Clement answered after getting his partial answer.

"Yes, while I am certain of Blackbeard's allegiance to the Order of Eos, bringing several of the lost Templar treasures back to his family in Scotland, the loyalty of Captain Kidd is quite puzzling. At first, it appeared he was hired by Eos allies, yet he acted against them. Ultimately, he ended up getting caught in Boston and sent to England where he was executed. Even after his death, however, his legend lived on. Despite a crowd of thousands in London seeing his execution, rumors grew that he rose from the grave to pilot a ghost ship that tormented the world for decades after this death. It is said he even paid a visit to Oak Island, where he plundered the buried treasure of his betrayers."

Nielson had been sponging it all up and asked, "Why did the two Sinclair boys think they were searching for Captain Kidd's treasure?"

Morgan studied the narrow windows and confirmed they were built to get astronomical reading rather than a view of the bay."If the legendary treasure of the Templar Knights had once been kept on Oak Island, it has long since been moved. In the 1300s, the Templar Knights were on the run even though they were supported by powerful renegade families like the Sinclairs. Nowhere in Europe would their treasure be safe, so it makes sense that the treasure would be moved to a secure location like remote Oak Island. By the early 1700s, between Captain Kidd and

Blackbeard, the security of the treasure was untenable and they likely emptied the vault."

"Or someone stole the treasure," Forsberg sagely muttered.

"Either way, the vault at Oak Island had served its purpose," Morgan explained. "Even so, it remains a monument to Eos, just like this tower is a relic of the past."

"What kind of treasure was it?" Sofus Nielson returned to Oak Island.

"The rumors vary: Spanish gold, secret documents, Templar relics, the Holy Grail, and even the lost Ark of the Covenant."

"What would the Ark of the Covenant be doing on this side of the globe?" Cairns asked skeptically.

"It might surprise you," Morgan answered. "From what I gleaned from the Drummond library, many of the relics go back to ancient times. But like I said, the great vault has been empty for more than a century now, which is why Eos abandoned it rather than leaving someone other than two boys to guard it."

Clement sighed loudly in frustration, looking to the stone tower for answers. "So now what? What is the point?"

"I've read all about this tower in my books, and there it stands—still. This tower fits the timeline and functionality as an astronomical tool. It confirms that Eos searched for something deep within the continent at the same latitude as this tower. I must admit that when we began this adventure together, the Order of Eos seemed as real to me as if I was searching for King Arthur's Holy Grail. After you let those Sinclair boys go, I couldn't travel to Oak Island, could I? If those two boys tell their story, and they will, the Order of Eos will know we were there."

"Eos already knew we were coming," Clement muttered.

"Yes, but now they know we've arrived, so this might've been my only chance to find some of the evidence that Prince Henry Sinclair was here a century before Christopher Columbus. Perhaps I'm a fool, but it seems as if the scholars are ignoring any Norse evidence, and who does that serve?"

"Are you saying the Order of Eos is shaping our history books?" Cairns scoffed. "You're blaming Eos scholars for getting fired from your position at the University?"

"Does this look like a windmill to you?" Morgan asked Cairns.

"I don't know what this is," Cairns answered gruffly.

"I do, and I needed you to see it before we continue onto the next phase of our adventure."

"Our next phase?" Cairns asked.

"My chance at revenge is over," Clement muttered.

"Perhaps, but perhaps there is another way you can claim revenge." *We could claim the Holy Grail before our enemies grab it, but are we seeking Lapis Exillis or Lapis Elixir?*

"How can I get revenge when the snakes have crawled down into their hole. Are we heading for Madeira Island?"

"Oh no," Morgan responded to Clement who grunted. "That would certainly be what they'd want. We'd be captured or killed quite easily there. My point is three fold. First, those boys do not know your identities do they? So the cover story of Lord Erskine looking to book travel for a hunting expedition to the west still works."

"Yes, but the only reason to go west is to kill Delhut, who obviously slithered into a hole like the Sinclairs ."

"You forget there are other reasons to go west, but you touched upon my second point—Madeira."

"You just said it'd be suicide to go there."

"Oh, it is, but the boys told us something about our enemy. From the Orkney Islands to Madeira, the Order of Eos honors its heritage, and once they learned of danger, they went home to places of safety. The Order of Eos is spread far and wide across America, but thanks to Nicollet, we know where they were heading, don't we? If word reaches those out on the frontier, where might they go? Home."

"Oxford House," Clement muttered.

"What's Oxford House?" Nielson asked boldly.

Cairns took measure of Clement before explaining. "Antoine grew up at a trading post on Hudson Bay called Oxford House." He then turned to Morgan. "If Magnus Sinclair left for Madeira, it's possible other Sinclairs were out on the frontier and might just now be returning home." He then turned to Clement. "You might still get your chance at revenge."

"So is there treasure at Oxford House?" Nielson blurted out again.

Morgan chuckled. "Not the Oak Island treasure, I'd assume." He pointed up to the narrow windows and then pointed his arm westward. "The earliest Eos explorers crossed the Atlantic and ran into a vast continent here. When they discovered an untamed wilderness due west, they likely changed tactics to find another way around the continent."

"They went north," Vaktar Forsberg answered knowingly.

"Yes, and so shall we." Morgan tousled the boy's hair and then herded them all back to the carriage. "Thanks to this tower, I know the line upon which the most sacred Eos treasure was expected to be found."

"What treasure is that?"

"Countless men have wandered out onto the frontier looking for signs of blue earth; they believed that vitriol would reveal the resting place of the original Philosopher's Stone."

"The Philosopher's Stone is at Oxford House?" Nielson asked with a grin.

"No, but those early Eos sailors would have had to get off of their ships and begin exploring by foot. If we don't find any Sinclairs at Oxford House, then we'll turn south and follow the line set by this tower.

"Hmmph," Clement grunted shaking his head. "Nicollet had it all figured out a decade ago. He fooled them all by preparing for another expedition farther west into the Rockies, but he'd already found a place where the earth bled blue. I already know where the tower pointed. I've been there. I'll take all of you there, but only after I make the earth bleed red."

"Then on the morrow, we sail for Oxford House, gentlemen," Morgan said, feeling his heart stirred by hope. "And we will find out if Nicollet found the resting place of the Philosopher's Stone."

THE END OF PART FIVE

# PART SIX
## THE OTTOMAN EMPIRE

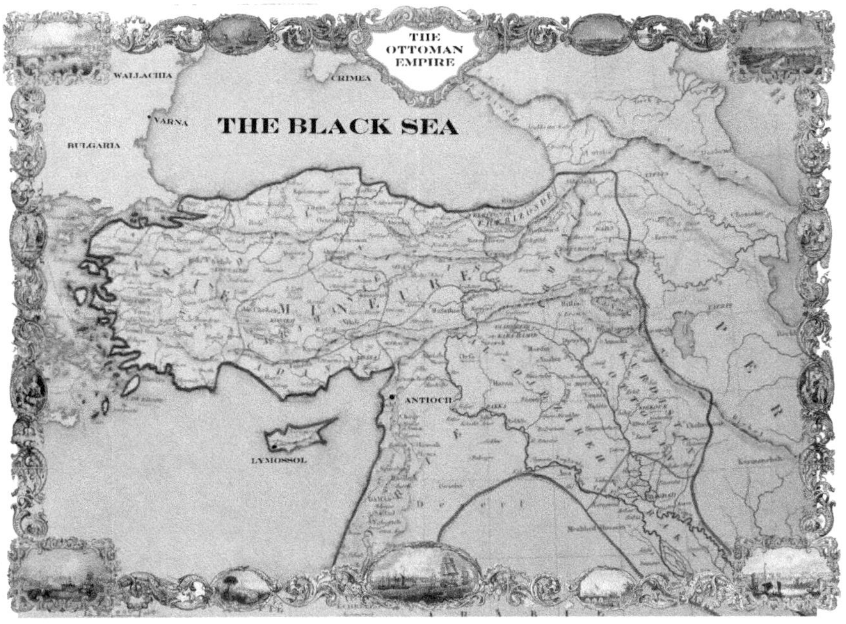

# PART SIX

# CHAPTER 34

ANTIOCH

1853

Christina Battersby Stewart refused to tour another ruin. While the men changed into their adventure clothing and clasped weapons to their belts, she found a nice spot on the top deck. *Today I'll do nothing but get drunk.*

William had tried to explain the significance of the stop and she'd purposefully yawned in the middle of his explanation.

He took the hint.

After fleeing Egypt, they cruised past the Holy Lands, and despite the significance of places like Bethlehem, Jerusalem, and the Sea of Galilee, her husband insistently pushed them along. The others didn't notice, but she knew the reason: Antoine Clement. Several years earlier, her husband brought his handsome pet back from America. The lords and ladies fawned over the exotic foreigner, but Stewart had plans for the two of them. After selling his maternal Drummond estate, Logiealmond, he took Clement on a tour of the Holy Lands, including Jerusalem and ancient Babylon stops.

The morning sun warmed the chill she felt in her heart.

"Can I get m'lady any breakfast?" a cabin boy asked.

"Just a drink, my dear. Something fruity with a little vodka," she responded.

She watched as William organized the men on the rear deck. Ross MacPherson checked his stuffed satchel with documents, Jamie Anderson stuffed his backpack with snacks and lunch, Frank Penny preened in his outfit, and Karl Geyer studied a map.

*Silly, silly boys.*

Her drink made the parade of masculinity more tolerable.

William came bounding up the stairs once everything was prepared for the day.

"We're ready," he said. "Are you sure you don't want to spend the day shopping in Antakya? It's the site of an ancient city, but you'd find all sorts of modern amenities."

Shopping meant having to choose between Frank Penny or Ross MacPherson as a chaperone. "No, thank you. It's a lovely summer day. I think I'll just enjoy the stillness."

William hesitated and pointed to the distant mountain range. "We're doing a tour of the ancient ruins, and by noon, we'll be up on that mountain. I'll wave."

"I'll be sure to wave back," she mocked, but then more sincerely added, "Do stay out of trouble."

"It's certainly a dead end, but we must be sure."

"Of course, how very scientific of you."

William took a step toward the rear deck but stopped. "What is that supposed to mean?"

"You're just being thorough," she said, knowing she'd cruelly brought up the memory of Nicollet. "I understand, and I'm not complaining."

"We'll likely lift anchor tonight. Are you sure you don't want to explore the city?"

"I'm taking a break, darling. Please let me just be alone for a day."

"We talked about this before leaving home."

At the time, it'd sounded like a grand adventure, but that was before the Texan made them wanted fugitives. Additionally, in recent ports, they learned that war was brewing between Russia and the Ottoman Empire, which threatened their plans as well as putting their son into harm's way. "Yes, yes, I know. I'm not being difficult. I just want some space."

Christina watched Lord Stewart march down the stairs. For his age, he was still incredibly attractive and fit, and it almost made her jealous that he was aging much better than she was. At 55, she diverged from voluptuous to frumpy. Even in a silk robe and sunbathing attire, she knew the cabin boys were no longer interested in a woman who should be a grandmother. She had the cleavage to catch their eyes, but as soon as they saw her varicose veins or the fold and rolls along her midsection, the game was over. Her wrinkles were hidden by makeup, and her deep red lipstick made her smile still sparkle, but Christina knew she'd grown old since she left. The letter she received at Tel-Aviv accelerated it.

Emma Geyer came bursting through the double doors with a breakfast plate in hand. Despite eating enough food to feed two people, Emma retained her youthful figure.

*Oh, you little bitch.*

In truth, it was hard to dislike Emma and the worst characteristic she'd displayed on the trip was being young.

"Good morning, Lady Stewart," she said from the nearby table. "Did you sleep well?"

*She knows how I slept: alone.*

As a former plaything of William Drummond Stewart, Christina knew what it felt like both to bask in the glory of his attention and then to have the clouds of his disinterest ruin everything. Jamie Anderson also understood this. Having watched Karl Geyer for several months, Christina saw how he, too, grew stronger just by being in proximity with the man. "I slept well enough, how about you?"

Emma smiled but didn't answer. "It's nice to be anchored. I still feel like I'm moving though." She turned and watched the men disappear into the crowd beyond the port. "So this is ancient Antioch?"

"Do you have any idea why we're here?"

Surprisingly, Emma nodded. "This was the capital city of Antiochus Epiphanes, the evil king mentioned in the book of Maccabees. Karl told me this "Mad King" was one of the worst villains in the Old Testament world."

"Karl told you. So why are we here?" Christina asked again, keeping a solemn face.

"Oh," Emma said to give herself enough time to chew the piece of ham she'd cut. "From what I understand, Antiochus not only persecuted the Jews but also fixated on conquering Egypt. Karl said the origins of a "line drawn in the sand" saying came

from his invasion of Egypt. Our men suspect that evil old Antiochus invaded Egypt for sinister purposes, if you understand my meaning."

*A fellow tomb raider.* Christina gave Emma a few more minutes to finish her slice of ham before asking it again a third time. "Yes, but why are *we* here?"

"I'm sorry," Emma said, sipping her tea. "I'm not sure I understand your meaning."

"It's a very simple question that has been bothering me for the past few days: why are *we* here?"

"Oh, you mean *us?*" Emma shrugged at Christina's nod. "I suppose we make it appear as if we're just wealthy tourists. A group of men might arouse suspicion, but a few married couples— it makes sense for some elite Europeans to be traveling together."

"Don't forget, Mrs. Geyer, that the men are also protecting us by bringing us on this expedition. Some faceless adversary could kill us or kidnap us." Christina scoffed at the notion. "I wonder where I stack up in the grand scheme of things. Of all of Lord Stewart's companions, where would I rank? As kidnapped prisoners, which would make him most vulnerable to an evil mastermind?"

"I suppose it would have to be you—his wife."

Christina scoffed again. "Come now. You might be young, but I know you're not stupid."

"Then his son and heir?"

"William George Drummond Stewart...my Georgie? That boy is certainly *my* Achilles heel, but I don't know if his father holds him in such high esteem. The two hardly know each other."

"He couldn't stop talking about him after our stop in Tel Aviv."

"Oh, that's just his nostalgia for military service. William's father forced him into military service, and Georgie joined because he wanted to impress his father. The more I doted on Georgie, the more he resented me. I fear I drove him into the military, and now he's been deployed to an active war zone. No...the loss of Georgie might break William's heart, but I don't think it would *take* his heart."

Emma seemed to understand the emotional toll of the Tel Aviv letter from Georgie.

*What of Antoine?* Christina continued her thought. While William still spoke glowingly about their years together out on the frontier, something had happened to them, which resulted in the two ending up on opposite sides of the globe.

"He seems to be quite fond of my husband," Emma said, an expression of worry coming over her face as she finished her breakfast.

"I don't think you need to worry," Christina playfully dismissed.

"I'm sorry for even suggesting it."

"Don't be sorry. The rumors about my husband are very real. He's taken most of his friends as lovers at one point or another, but that was when he was a young man. When he left for America, he was—a wild man, but then he met someone who changed him."

"Mr. Clement?"

"No, Antoine became a friend—a very good friend, in fact— but he was one of several mountain men who captured his heart. It was the strange little French scientist, Joseph Nicollet, who *changed* him. I don't know exactly know what happened, but—he got baptized! He returned from America with his Native-American lover at his side and a sudden interest in Christianity. And after Nicollet's death...I've never seen him so serious about matters beyond his own needs."

"Karl was very close with Nicollet also. Before he became traveling companions with your husband, he spent three years with Nicollet."

"Yes, but somehow Karl found his way through the heartbreak to marry you," Christina said bitterly. "While Lord Stewart is once again filled with bluster, his heart remains empty, and no young history professors, defrocked priests, or wild Texans seem to interest him any more. So I ask again: what are *we* doing here?"

"We're here to support our husbands."

Christina laughed so loudly it came across as rude, and she cupped her mouth to stifle her earnest reaction. *She meant it, too.*

"I'm sorry. I don't mean to be so flippant, but this question has sincerely plagued me since the incident in Thebes."

"Mr. Penny."

"Yes. I understand that Professor Nicollet died under suspicious circumstances, and shortly after, Antoine Clement senior and Thomas Stewart also died. Young Mr. Penny shot those men without hesitation, and his resolve made me question the nature of this quest we're on. We've been to Rome, Cairo, Thebes, the Holy Lands, and now Antioch—and our husbands are willing to kill or be killed for…what? I understand that Antoine Clement and the others went back to America for some sort of revenge, but we're not on the trail of revenge. Nor are we hiding in some discreet location. Why are we here, Emma?"

"I'll be sure to ask my husband when he returns," Emma said and then rose. "If you'll excuse me."

Christina looked away, far off to the mountain. Despite the brightness of the day, she felt a dark cloud creeping over her. She wished she could openly ask William about the real reason they were running all around the world, but she feared the truth behind his answer.

# CHAPTER 35



William Drummond Stewart grew frustrated with the tour and openly despaired his choices. *What am I doing here?* When removing his hat, his fingers felt the sweat in his thinning hair. He set it back on top of his head, choosing to be uncomfortable rather than looking like an old man. A large chunk of rubble offered itself to him, and he sat down with a loud sigh.

*There's no tomb up here.*

From the mountain, he could see the beauty of the city and the river below. One of the dots in the distance was the *Mina*. There was nary a shadow on top of the mountain, bereft of tree or temple. Stewart looked up to the cruel sun.

Jamie Anderson waddled over to join him upon the slab of broken stone. He, too, had been caught off guard by both the altitude and heat. The younger men—Frank Penny and Ross MacPherson—followed the local guides on the tour of the hundred square yard complex of nothingness. Karl Geyer guzzled water from his canteen an hour back on the tour and had just stopped. He waved at them to continue on but showed no intention of finishing the climb himself.

*Have I put too much strain on Karl? Anderson doesn't look much better either.*

"I don't know how much more of this I can take," Anderson blurted out honestly.

*Is he talking about the day…or the entire expedition?* "At least no one is charging at us with swords," Stewart said, thinking of Egypt again. The brief tour past the Holy Lands had been a symbolic reset after the disaster at the Valley of the Kings. There had been no purpose to it other than reflection. But now, back on the quest, another failure threatened to steal his motivation to continue.

"I have a confession to make," Jamie Anderson began and paused.

Stewart looked at him, perplexed by the sentimental tone. *Is this about Christina?* Back at Murthly Castle, secrets could be easily kept in the vast expanse of the estate, but stuck on a yacht, secrets were much harder to keep. "Do you?"

Anderson grinned and held up his canteen. "I filled it with wine this morning. I couldn't bear the thought of another tour of ruins. So I'm a little drunk and very, very thirsty. Could I beg you for a sip from your canteen?"

"Only if I can have a sip of your wine."

The two smiled and exchanged canteens.

Jamie drank so heartily that he had to wipe away the water came down both corners of his mouth with the back of his hand. "Thank you. I remember the first time you offered me a drink from your canteen."

"So do I," Stewart said, thinking of the Battle of Hougoumont.

"You'd just cut the head off my best friend in the world," Anderson remarked.

Stewart took his mouth away from the canteen and joked, "Did you poison the wine?"

"I could have killed you a long time ago if I'd wanted to. Looking back, I don't even remember his name now. I was a dwarf and he was a giant. It seemed like a natural pairing."

Stewart remembered. "I about shit my pants when that monster came through the door with an ax. He had his choice between me and my friend Terrance, and when your giant friend buried that ax into Terrance's shoulder, I had to act before he turned for me. I got a medal for taking that giant's head off."

"Chauvin!"

"Excuse me?"

"His name was Chauvin," Anderson clarified. "He was a bully because of his size. He wasn't even French—he was an American."

"I killed an American giant?"

"You did. What did he call himself? A Cajun. He was from the swamps of Louisiana, and when Napoleon rose to power, he thought it sounded like an adventure to hop on a ship and fight for his homeland, France. Nicholas Chauvin—what a lunatic! Do you know, if we'd taken that farmhouse that day, we would have taken Hougoumont, and Napoleon might've won the battle and won the whole bloody war. Instead, Chauvin chose to kill Terrance."

"I'm also glad Chauvin chose Terrance," Stewart admitted. "Shall we drink to dead friends?"

"To Chauvin!"

"To Terrance."

Stewart drank several gulps of wine. "When I first saw you, I thought you were a boy."

"I was a boy. Those bastards thought it would be funny to have a dwarf as the company drummer, so they dressed me up in uniform and treated me like a mascot of sorts. When I couldn't keep up, Chauvin would put me on his shoulders. I couldn't fire a gun, but I could show bravery. When it became obvious to the officers that the farmhouse was defended by only a few men, they picked Chauvin to finish things off, and I followed in his shadow right up to the moment you killed him. When that door shut me in, I expected my head to join his. Life is full of surprises."

"I'm glad I didn't let them kill you," Stewart said.

Ross MacPherson appeared, engaged in a detailed conversation with the local tour guide. There was lots of pointing and talking, but the tour had effectively come to an end.

"There's no tomb up here, is there?" Stewart asked.

"Did you really expect to find a tomb?"

"I did, honestly. I hoped, at least. Do you think I'm a fool for doing this?"

"Yes, but I also think there's sound logic in your 'Heads of the Beast' theory. If we'd found Nimrod, Ramses, Alexander, or Mr. Epiphanes, what would have been our next step?" Anderson asked.

"We'd keep them from our enemies," Stewart answered. "All we need is to steal one and the whole prophecy collapses."

"Perhaps that was already done for us—centuries ago. What if these kings of old are now just dust or ash? Why was it so important for you to find the corpses?"

Stewart sighed, looking across the way at the former priest. "You're not a religious man, are you?"

"Let's just say I'm still a little bitter about being born a dwarf."

Stewart grinned. "The 'Heads of the Beast' theory is based on the Book of Revelation, but there's another section of the Bible that seems to echo this same concept. I don't know it as well as MacPherson does, but the gist of it is that the prophet Daniel also wrote about the coming of the Antichrist. For him, three kings had already lived and died, leaving four to come in his future. Although Christian and Jewish scholars are divided, the beasts likely described Alexander the Great followed by Antiochus Epiphanes.

Stewart continued, "Most scholars believe both the Daniel prophecies and the Book of Revelation prophecies simply discuss the passage of time: one kingdom following another kingdom. It's a fine theory, but having studied my enemies, there is a very strong 'the dead shall rise' theme in their mythology. They seem to be seeking to unearth these buried kings. The same prophet, Daniel, gave us another strange prophecy about an evil man that caused old Nebuchadnezzar many restless nights. In his vision, the coming Antichrist was made up of several different parts."

"Hold on, you think the Antichrist is going to be like Frankenstein's Monster?"

"I don't have an explanation of how it would work, but when Daniel talks about this monster being pieced together with 'the seed of men' and then the Book of Revelation saying the Antichrist will be 'of' the previous seven kings, it makes me think the corpses are going to play a part in all of this."

Anderson scoffed. "So perhaps it is best that Antiochus Epiphanes' body no longer exists."

"You're right. If I found it in a chamber under my feet, what would I do with it? Am I doing all of this out of spite for what happened to my brother and friends? Do I want to stop the prophecy of the Antichrist if that also means stopping the return of Christ himself? How does humanity find its happy ending?"

"Hey, Father Ross!" Anderson shouted out loudly enough to halt the conversation he was having. "Come here. We have a question for you."

Ross MacPherson, Frank Penny, and the tour guides all joined them. MacPherson was the only one showing any enthusiasm after a long day. "What is it?"

"The Antichrist is the epitome of evil, right?"

"Yes."

"And from what I remember, he's going to bring death and destruction to the world, right?"

"Yes."

"So if I had a chance to shoot that bastard in the head—before he's taken over the entire world—I should take the shot, right?"

Stewart found enough humor in the proposed scenario to grin to himself, but he paid close attention to see how MacPherson answered.

"Not that it would do you any good," MacPherson offered. "There are many scholars who believe the Antichrist will in fact be wounded and killed but that he will be brought back to life to the astonishment of all."

"See?" Stewart turned to Anderson with a wink. "The undead shall rise." Then turning back to MacPherson, he asked. "So did you discover where Epiphanes' tomb is located?"

"Well, that's just it," MacPherson started, "this secret complex up in the mountains was never meant to hold the body of Antiochus Epiphanes; it was—how do I explain—a staging area for him."

"Staging?" Stewart pressed.

MacPherson looked down as if ashamed of what he was going to say. "I remember debating about Antiochus Epiphanes back in your library, and I argued that the man never did much to earn the nickname 'The Abomination of Desolation.' Yes, he desecrated the temple in Jerusalem, but who hadn't? I wondered what qualified this guy as being so evil to be one of the unholy seven. Well..." MacPherson turned to gesture at the smooth platform built atop a mountain peak. "This is where he waged war on Heaven."

"Waged war on Heaven?" Stewart scoffed.

"I'm not sure what that means exactly, but our local guide tells of a legend that the Mad King built this platform so that he could wage war against 'the host of heaven.' Instead of raising armies to battle the armies of mankind, he raised an evil army meant to battle the host of heaven, and here is where he waged war. Our guide says that Antiochus Epiphanes managed to capture some important angelic figure and kept his hostage for the better part of seven years, which is when Antiochus Epiphanes was killed by another angel, ending the siege on Heaven."

"Son of a bitch," Stewart muttered in surprise to the outlandish theory. Unlike the other epic historical names, Antiochus Epiphanes had the least historical impact, but a literal attack on heaven changed his perception. "Wild story—but no corpse?"

"Even his own people hated him," MacPherson continued, "So after his death and defeat, his loyal followers took the body and hid it so that his enemies could not desecrate it. There are no stories to follow up, unfortunately."

*Loyal followers? An old version of Eos.* "Well, gentlemen, at least you got to visit ancient Antioch," Stewart said and stood up. He waved to the river below even if he didn't know which speck on the river was the *Mina*. He turned to the path and saw Karl Geyer still waiting below. "We're heading back."

Karl Geyer gathered up his stuff and began walking back to the ship.

"Are we heading back to Scotland?" Anderson asked.

"Home?" Stewart scoffed. "Oh, no. I think I've got this all pieced together. I've been thinking about this since we visited the *Temple of the Four Heads*."

"Care to share?"

"I wish we had Professor Morgan with us," Stewart admitted, "But my gut is telling me that our path will follow the Goths."

# CHAPTER 36



Pyotr Petrov loved studying nature, which was filled with all types of killers. Whether hunting by day or night, land or water, animals adapted to their environments. A year ago, he hunted like a lizard, changing his appearance as he waited. Several months ago, he transformed his hunting style into that of a bird of prey, sweeping over the sky while keeping a sharp eye on the ground below. Today, he emulated the wolf tarantula indigenous to area.

Under the cover of darkness, the two-inch spider prowled around rocks, underbrush, or into trees—capable of killing reptile, insect, or mammal with its powerful bite. A few feet from where Petrov sat, he spotted the wolf tarantula in its hole—peering out at him the same way he peered out at the world. The past few nights, Pyotr had also prowled the night, gathering information about his wary prey. With a target in constant motion, he could not afford to waste energy chasing—so he found a burrow and waited.

The bait towered above the landscape in the distance. The castle now known as Bagras had a history that stretched back centuries. Although originally built by Arabs trying to withstand invading Muslims, a Byzantine emperor fortified it to protect the nearby city of Antioch. Centuries later, a new group of invaders— the Knights Templar—used it as a staging area. Knowing how the elites within the Order of Eos loved to study and celebrate their history, Petrov set his trap months ago and waited.

Like the Tarantula, Petrov hid during the day. He found several tall trees that shaded his hiding spot. He'd brought a few books about the Knights Templar with him to Antioch, but those he finished during his first few weeks of his vigil. Plus, after hunting for Scottish and French Templars in recent years, he already knew his prey.

Today, he read about the Assassins.

*The History of the Nizari Ismailis* told all about this legendary group of killers known as the Assassins. Petrov was on his third reading of the text and nibbled on dry bread and cheese as he reviewed their history. For two centuries, the infamous group terrified anyone who crossed them. Ironically, Pyotr Petrov was now labeled an assassin even though his mortal enemy originally used the word. The Assassins were from Egypt, Persia, and Syria and lived in fortified hills. Their *modus operandi* was to ingest hashish prior to killing their opponent, and then in packs, descend upon the victims in groups with knives. They caused a great deal of trouble and never feared death; any caught would gladly die because of being promised riches in the afterlife.

*Efficient but lacking skill.*

Petrov re-read the book to understand their exotic religious beliefs. Yes, they were considered Muslim, but they held unique beliefs that reminded Petrov of his Templar targets. Many of the modern day Order of Eos members were considered Christian although their beliefs were antithetical once properly understood. Apparently, the Assassins were known as the "Seveners" and believed that a messiah was coming to bring justice and peace to the world. The Mahdi, as they called this sacred prophet, would signal the arrival of "The Bringer of the Resurrection."

*Another corpse being brought back to life—what is it with these death fanatics?*

Petrov had been born into the Eastern Orthodox Church, so he knew all about resurrection. Choosing to worship the living rather than the dead or spiritual, he'd rejected these death religions. The Templars had their secret god—Baphomet, the infamous head they worshiped prior to the Catholic Church discovering the practice. Even after the bloodbath of Friday the 13th, worship of their dead deity continued. The Order of Eos still searched for their "seven" with hopes of a resurrection of a dead god.

*Caput Mortuum—Death's head. And what is the truth about the head?*

Petrov set his book beside his body and stretched out his legs. leaned back on his elbows, lifted his toes, stretched his legs and flexed his abdomen muscles in a silent workout. All the while, he kept an eye on the wolf tarantula looking out at him.

*The Assassins also wanted to resurrect a dead god. Is there a connection between the two stories?* The Assassin reign of terror was brought to an end by the Mongol Empire, who used determination and technology to uproot the impregnable mountain castles of the assassins. In the same way, he now uprooted Lady Columbia's enemies.

*Ah, what an assignment that would be! To assassinate the Assassins!*

Petrov took a sip of wine, just enough so that his beverage would last the day. Once dusk came, he would strengthen his body and then visit the river port to collect information about comings and goings of foreigners to the port. He led a lonely life as dedicated to his purpose as the priests and pawns of his enemies— if not more.

*Their gods are dead—my goddess lives and breaths.*

He'd studied the young mythology of his own belief system to know the name of his goddess did not belong to any specific human. Unlike the gods of Eos, Islam, or Christianity, the goddess Columbia did not exist two centuries ago let alone two thousand years ago. In fact, the term didn't come into existence until 1697 as a simple reference to Christopher Columbus—which was *not* why the name took root. Both Christianity and the sly masonic beliefs espoused by Eos had taken root in America—two forces sending humanity racing towards doom.

The defense of humanity took root in the writings of an anonymous woman known as CB. Her initials became vocalized as the word Columbia, and her brilliant manifesto on the defense of humanity from superstition and prophecy became popular with certain founding fathers who understood the opposition.

Petrov stared up at the setting sun, feeling its warmth upon his face, just like the newest iteration of Columbia once stared upon his face. Just like CB, she was just a woman, but she represented ideals that made her worthy of worship. For now, she held the torch of truth in a world of darkness, and when she died, the torch would be passed to another. The current Columbia, like himself, would not allow humanity to perish in a few generations.

*I'll lay down my life for a world that does not understand her.*

Petrov's meditative prayers were suddenly answered when a carriage came up the road to the castle. Most tourists arrived in the morning and flocked in gawking herds. Dusk meant an end to tours, yet this private carriage arrived an hour before dusk.

*Is it him?*

After putting on the brakes, the driver stayed put.

A local tour guide opened the carriage door, already talking as he gestured to the old Templar stronghold. A younger man in American garb stepped out next, a pistol at his side.

*Curious.*

And then his prey stepped out of the carriage. Dressed in wealth, the middle-aged man wore a hat to hide his face. He stretched his back for a few moments and then slid his hands in his pockets as he sent the tour into motion.

*Curiosity killed the cat.*

Since the failed assassination in Croatia and the massacre in Orkney, the wealthy rats had scattered to the wind, which was why Petrov evolved from a predatory hawk to a predatory spider. Even the most ardent fanatic had moments of doubt, and after leaving the protection of the nest, this fear meant a predictable habit— going to places that would affirm their shaken beliefs.

Pyotr Petrov knew he wasn't the only hired killer on earth. In fact, he knew Columbia had hired dozens of other assassins following the murder of her own mentor. The echoing waves of vengeance passed back and forth across the Atlantic. He'd taken the job in Croatia because of proximity to his home in Bulgaria, and then, in shame for his mistaken identity gaffe, he traveled to Scotland to set matters right. The enemies of Columbia had taken the hint, and instead of chasing them, he waited.

His patience now paid off.

He nodded to the wolf tarantula in its hole and rose from his hiding spot.

The local tour guide had already brought his prey inside, so Petrov circled around the perimeter of the castle so that he walked directly toward the parked carriage.

He stopped twenty paces from the bored driver. "We close the gates at dusk," Petrov repeated what the man already knew. The local maintenance crew often showed at dusk.

The driver only shrugged.

"Ah, a rich one?" he clarified.

The driver smirked and nodded.

As if he belonged, Petrov walked to the open door. He'd done the tour himself, just to see the draw. The fortress had once been a precious jewel in the Templar treasure trove, which is why he'd chosen the place as bait for his target.

Once inside the gate, Petrov stepped into an alcove where guards once sat for hours during their shifts.

*Today, I must be better than an Assassin. I must be a wolf tarantula.*

He unsheathed two small knives, holding each in his tight fist.

With eyes shut, he played the attack in his mind, rehearsing it in the shadows of the alcove.

The three men exited the fortress and passed by the shadow of the gate alcove without notice. They took several paces toward the carriage before Petrov followed.

The delicate dance of death began with the security guard. Sneaking up behind him, Petrov sank his blade into the right side of the guard's neck for leverage, then wrapped his left arm around the man, sunk the second blade into the man's chest and cradled him in an embrace. With his left arm holding the man steady, he punched repeatedly into the security guard's collarbone area causing an explosive spray of blood.

"Lachlan!" his prey gasped, wide-eyed.

Petrov left his right blade in the security guard's body, reaching down to the man's holster for the pistol. Shooting from the hip, he squeezed the trigger three times, hitting the tour guide twice.

He released the security guard's body, which presently dropped to the ground. He turned, revealing that he held a new knife in one hand and a pistol in the other. He raised the gun to his prey, but the alarmed target stepped backward, tripped on a rock, and fell backwards.

So Petrov aimed at the carriage driver and fired the last three shots at him, hitting him all three times.

Two hundred yards away, four local men walked up the road from Antioch. They stopped when they saw the slaughter from a distance. Turning back to the castle, Petrov only saw an empty doorway.

*How fortunate.*

He advanced on his stunned target. A cupful of blood came from a gash on the back of the man's head. The dazed man winced as his world spun but still tried to get to his feet.

Petrov advanced with the knife. He knelt down, prepared to sink four inches of steel into the man's throat. Instead, the man's eyes fluttered and his head fell back, drooping limply to the side.

*He knocked himself out. How fortunate!*

For good measure, he kicked the man in the side—to no effect or reaction.

*The grace of Columbia smiles upon me today.*

Taking his prey by the feet, he dragged him all the way back to the carriage. There, he found extra leather rein material, cut a few lengths, and bound his prey. He quickly returned to the bodyguard, gathering a few bullets from his gaudy holster.

He threw the driver out of the seat and unlocked the carriage brakes. He lashed the horses, sending them the opposite direction of Antioch toward his escape port on the western shore.

A mile from the castle, he halted the horses and put on the brakes. He hopped off the bloody seat, walked to the door, and flung it open as his prey still slept in blissful oblivion.

The sun was setting and darkness would offer its protection soon.

*Do I kill him or do I risk more?*

Taking hold of the man by the shirt, he lifted him up into a sitting position. He struck the man in the cheek twice, prompting a flutter in his eyes.

When the man opened them, Petrov leveled the barrel of the gun to touch his nose. "Tell me your name. Say it true, and you will likely be spared."

"Who are you?" the man muttered.

Petrov cocked back the hammer of the pistol. "Confirm it or I'll kill you now."

"Solomon Delhut."

Petrov opened the chamber of the pistol, just for safety, dropped the chambered bullets onto the ground. Then, with the butt of the pistol, he struck Solomon Delhut in the forehead just above the hairline—for good measure.

*Looks like the spider has caught a big fly.*

# CHAPTER 37

ANTIOCH

1853

Frank Penny prowled the upper deck of the yacht. While the crew of the Italian vessel also kept watch, they were all tasked with the preparation and maintenance of the ship, so their concern was always divided. Penny had nothing else to do but watch for danger.

To reach the city of Antakya, they'd gone up the Orontes River, which was a considerable challenge for a vessel meant to be on the open sea. With a mindset of defense, he didn't like where they'd anchored. When flooded, the Orontes River was wide enough for seven yachts to be parked side by side, but the river was not flooded. In fact, it was low enough that the channel would only support the width of two yachts, leaving the rest of the river a minefield of boulders. The bald captain of the *Mina* boasted the ability to drop them off downtown, which he did, putting the nose of the yacht right under the bridge.

Eyes now watched down from that bridge.

The unguarded eastern bank was also a concern for Penny; someone could come up and out of the brush in a matter of seconds. The wide western bank allowed for small vessels to approach and pull up right beside their parked yacht.

*I'll be glad when we leave this damn place.*

They were set to depart in the morning. Lord Stewart and the men had returned from their excursion into the eastern mountains—with no success. The crew whispered that they'd be plotting a course back to Ravenna.

*Have we reached a dead end?*

*And then back to Scotland, I wonder?*

Penny still didn't understand what they meant to accomplish at such exotic locations beyond hiding from the men who hunted them, but he enjoyed his role of providing security for a wealthy nobleman. He would have been content lurking in the woods of Murthly Estate and waiting for a stranger to appear. This trip had allowed him to see parts of the vast world he never would have seen, though.

Of course, he hadn't expected to kill people on the trip, and his actions at the Valley of the Kings still upset everyone. Even though they'd fled Egypt, they were still in the Ottoman Empire, and that meant law enforcement was also a concern. Good guys and bad guys hunted them, which is why Penny kept prowling the upper deck.

Along with the bridge and the riverbank, he kept an eye on other yachts. The bridge kept them from passing any further, but a hundred yards north, a pier had several dozen vessels, most of them a tenth the size of their big yacht. If he stooped low at the nose of the yacht, he could see the activity on the docks.

He stood at the bow and watched the pier for a few minutes.

Like at most riverfronts, the criminal element thrived in the shadows. With so many people on the yacht at all times, thieves chose the easy plunder of supplies rather than boarding the yachts with visible security guards.

One of the Italian crewmen stepped beside him and looked ahead at the distant pier. "Anchor ropes," he said.

"Excuse me?" Penny asked.

The Italian gestured with fingers, making a climbing motion. Then he pointed to the front anchor rope. "Anchor ropes."

*Ah, he's encountered plenty of thieves. They climb up the anchor ropes.* Armed with the new information, he left the bow to check the stern rope.

On the rear deck, Mrs. Geyer stood at the railing. "Hello, Mr. Penny."

"Is anything the matter?" he asked politely. Even though she was lovely, his father had taught him to respect married women, so he gave the two wives as little attention as required.

"I just needed some fresh air," she said. "All this travel becomes a bit much."

He nodded, taking the hint, and continued to the rear of the boat for more observation.

*Yep, if I were a thief, I'd have my friends pull up in the shadow of the propeller, send my smallest friend up that rope, and then have him drop stolen goods from the ship down to me.*

Luckily, nothing anchored behind the yacht.

Penny stayed there for a few minutes and then made a slow return along the starboard side. He mostly listened, knowing his ears served him better than his eyes in this the situation.

That was when he heard an American voice in the darkness.

"Delhut!" it shouted. "Help! Help! My name is Solomon Delhut!"

Curious, Penny rushed to the bow.

"Delhut," the shout repeated, and then, a silhouette moved on the bridge. At first, it looked like a man praying while he ran. *His hands are bound.*

A second figure appeared on the far western side of the bridge in pursuit of the bound man. He didn't look like local law.

*This doesn't look good.*

"Help me! I'm Solomon Delhut. I'm being kidnapped," the bound man shouted out again.

The second figure continued his pursuit and fired a warning shot in the air. While the shot startled the crowd around the bridge, it also brought a small yacht to life in the shadows beyond the bridge.

*Delhut is trying to get to that yacht.*

Pistol in his hand, Frank didn't have a plan.

Solomon Delhut continued moving, but when another warning shot rang out, Delhut threw himself over the railing and into the water.

*Better to risk drowning rather than getting shot in the back,* Penny decided.

With his hands bound, Delhut's body hit the water's surface like a hard slap to the cheek. He emerged, splashing and kicking in the water.

*He'll drown if he doesn't reach shallow water soon.*

The pursuer ran to the railing of the bridge, but Delhut's cries for help were quickly answered. Gunfire erupted from the smaller yacht parked beyond the bridge, pinning down the shooter.

"Amsukah! Amsukah!" the shooter barked out orders to the shadows, and from the distant shore, voices responded.

*The kidnapper's allies?* Penny wondered.

A small boat immediately launched from the starboard shore like a crocodile spotting a zebra in the river. The shooter ran to the place Delhut had jumped and also leapt into the water. By the time he surfaced, the small boat was there to pick him up.

*Neither man is giving up easily,* Penny noted.

No more than fifteen seconds had passed, and Delhut still was floundering in the water.

The crew of the *Mina* had noticed the commotion. Italian shouts filled the air, and a crewman appeared beside Penny at the bow. Penny pointed to the little boat and the fleeing victim. "Kidnappers…victim…friends of the victim," Penny identified Delhut, the small boat that'd picked up the shooter, and from under the bridge, the much larger vessel, perhaps a thirty foot steamship, puffing out smoke.

Lord Stewart came rushing to the bow also. "What is all this ruckus?"

"Some fellow just jumped off the bridge," Penny answered. "He said he was being kidnapped. Should we do something?"

"It's not our concern," Stewart said coldly. "Keep an eye out for danger. It could just be a distraction."

The small boat soon caught up to Delhut, who was hauled aboard in a move that almost overturned the ten foot vessel. Oars splashed frenetically.

*Looks like the kidnapper has recovered his victim,* Penny observed and looked back toward the shadows of the bridge.

A gunshot sounded from the smaller steamship.

"What's happening, Penny?" MacPherson asked upon joining the others at the rail.

"I'm not sure. I heard them shout out the name Delhut."

"Delhut?" Stewart repeated angrily, and then turning to the rest of the yacht, he yelled out loudly. "It's a trap! To arms! To arms!"

Stewart ran back to the cabins.

*But who should I shoot?*

The bald captain barked out more Italian phrases, and suddenly a flood of lights filled the river. Four men rowed with oars. In the bow, the kidnapper held Solomon Delhut around the neck with his left arm and a pistol with his right. By the time Stewart returned, the small boat was only twenty yards away from the side of the ship.

"Why aren't you shooting?" Stewart asked.

"I don't understand what's happening."

Stewart looked out. Both parties were fully illuminated in the darkness, and as Stewart looked down at the figure of Delhut, the kidnapper  flashed recognition of Lord Stewart.

*Oh shit!*

The kidnapper's pistol lifted.

Penny managed to shove Lord Stewart to the ground during the hail of bullets. Lord Stewart groaned, but he hadn't been hit by a bullet at least not that Penny could see.

"Stewart—"

Penny saw a seven-inch splinter of railing sticking from the collarbone of the Scottish nobleman. A garbled groan answered him.

Still they both rose from the railing, guns drawn, but the little rowboat had vanished into the darkness. The thirty-foot yacht was just turning downstream. On its deck, four men with guns scanned the same darkness for an understanding of the danger. Seeing the *Mind*'s deck, one of the men panicked and fired a shot.

Then unholy hell opened up.

At first, the four men on the smaller yacht had the advantage, and the bosun and a deckhand were hit. The earlier call "to arms" brought a dozen armed men to the scene, including Penny and Stewart, and when fire was returned, the four men were cut down in seconds.

Then silence returned to the river.

The bald captain appeared to check on his customer and noticed the large shard of wood stuck in Stewart's neck. He immediately tried to tend to his wealthy guest.

"We need to get the women away from here," Stewart said, clutching the splinter in the side of his neck. "Eos has found us."

"No," Penny said to both men in authority. *The kidnapper can't run very far. Plus, if these are Eos men, we need to find out what they know.* "They didn't know we were here. Something else has happened. Get a dinghy and board that yacht," he told the captain. "If there are any survivors, bring them on board and then burn the ship. I need ten minutes and then we need to leave."

Stewart answered. "We need to get the hell out of here before the authorities arrive."

"Ten minutes," Penny insisted. He slipped his revolvers back into the holster and latched them in. He ran over to the mooring line and climbed down the rope to the starboard shore.

If he were the kidnapper and had just been spotted, he would have turned right back toward the city rather than continue downstream, which meant the fleeing rowboat might be pulling onto the opposite shore at that very minute.

Penny ran toward the bridge.

Not only would it give him good vantage of the shadowy river, but it would also allow him to quickly cross and cut off the double-back. Alarmed locals gathered at the pier, but facing no external threat, they mostly congregated and pointed downstream toward the shooting, which had stopped.

Penny reached the midpoint of the bridge when his bootheels slid to a stop. A bloody man came stumbling toward him.

Instead of looking downstream, he stumbled toward the upstream side of the bridge where the small yacht had been parked.

*What are the odds? This fellow is obviously Delhut's ally.*

Penny unleashed a pistol and rushed to where the man caught himself along the bridge railing. "Are you okay mister?"

The man had several wounds to his torso and a horrific wound to his neck, which his fingers attempted to plug. "Are you an American?"

Penny nodded.

"There's been a kidnapping. They've taken—"

"Delhut?"

The man's eyes widened. "Yes! Yes. We need to—"

"Come, come," Penny said, putting an arm around the man to help him to the *Mina*. "We'll help you find him."

# CHAPTER 38



ABOARD THE MINA

1853

Emma Geyer wept. She knew she needed to say something, but considering all the chaos and turmoil of the past few days, she just couldn't find the words. No one had so much as bothered her the past two days, including her husband, who'd spent most of his waking hours in the dining room, just in a different capacity than normal.

Back on the open sea, her white enamel chamber pot had become her closest companion, and she found herself hugging it with her left arm.

*I'm not solving anything in here.*

She quickly tied her long blonde hair in a braid, washed her face, and slipped into a simple, modest dress for her dramatic plot twist.

Outside her cabin door, two of the maids were still cleansing the hall of blood stains created by her husband. Entering the dining room, she could not help but remember the horrors from a few nights earlier. As the *Mina* raced down the Orontes River, four bloody men had been placed on the tables. Despite being a botanist, her husband rolled up his sleeves to serve as the ship surgeon since the ship's doctor was only comfortable with tinctures and potions for illness. Lord Stewart's wound had been the least severe, yet upon removing the splinter, his neck wound produced enough blood to keep him woozy. Lady Stewart, upon seeing her husband so pale, became inconsolable as she wept in the corner.

The poor bosun died within an hour. A bullet entered his chest below his right nipple, filling his lung with blood. Emma held his hand as he quickly faded.

Her husband managed to pull the bullet lodged in the deckhand's shoulder, and by the following morning, he was sitting up drinking coffee.

The wounded stranger that Mr. Penny brought on board appeared to have died. He had several knife wounds, and after losing so much blood, he remained on the brink of death until almost supper the next day. Karl had managed to stitch up his wounds while the man was unconscious. That night, Lachlan Morrison miraculously came back to life, and by the next morning, the dining room had returned to its original function.

Emma sat alone as she ate breakfast.

Lord Stewart came in to dine next. At first, his eyes looked for other options, but seeing her alone, he nodded in resignation and joined her.

"How is the patient faring?" she asked.

"Morrison's talking. I think he understands the peril of his situation."

"I was referring to you, Lord Stewart?"

His hand went up to the blood-stained bandage wrapping his neck. "Ah, 'What wound ever did heal but by degrees.' I'll be fine."

She didn't recognize the quote. "If I understand correctly, we'll be making port in Cyprus today?" *And then my nausea might cease.*

"Limassol. It's a large port, so we should be able to be discreet. Our crimes in Egypt will be more concerning than what happened in Antioch. I doubt news outraced us to Cyprus."

"Unless the kidnapper lies in wait," she added.

Lord Stewart winced as if he'd never considered the idea, but the wince turned out to be focused on his neck. His fingers pressed the crimson bandage. "My priority is to keep everyone safe. Our docking will be discreet."

"Is Karl tending to Mr. Morrison? He was out of bed when I woke."

"Yes, his skills with a scalpel, scissors, and sutures have been wasted on plants all these years," Stewart answered, sounding impressed.

"What's going to happen when we reach port?"

Lord Stewart rolled his eyes. "That is all still being decided. Honestly, there is so much information being sorted out that I don't know what we'll do next. A lot will depend on what Lachlan Morrison tells us. But to do anything, we'll need supplies."

Emma swallowed hard and then took drink of water before saying, "Lord Stewart, there is something you must know. I think it might help you make a decision on how to proceed."

Stewart grinned mischievously. "Go on."

"I am quite sure that I am pregnant."

# CHAPTER 39

LIMASSOL, CYPRUS

1853

Lachlan Morrison sipped wine with his former enemies. Like real gentlemen, they all introduced themselves, but Morrison knew that behind the smiles were daggers, and if he didn't play his cards right, they'd dump his body in the sea. From the young Texan who carried his body back to the ship to the plump doctor who sewed him up, they all sat around him now for an interrogation that meant life or death.

*And I mean to live.*

"Explain to me what you were doing in Antioch," Lord Stewart demanded.

"We had orders to vanish. To disappear. Mr. Delhut saw it as an opportunity to vacation, so he sent his family on vacation, and with me as his personal guard, he decided he wanted to visit some of the ancient Templar castles still standing."

"Why Antioch?" Father MacPherson asked.

"Mr. Delhut's fascinated with Templar history. At one time, Bagras Castle was a staging point for the invasion of the Holy Lands during the Great Crusades. Mr. Delhut has keen interest in his family heritage."

"And while you were visiting Bagras Castle, you were attacked. Tell us more about your attacker."

Morrison remembered stepping through the alcove and the flash of daggers. Strangely, the knife wounds didn't hurt until the following day, which had allowed him to follow Delhut and the kidnapper back down to the port. "If you're looking for a name, you won't get one. I have no idea the name of the man who attacked me and kidnapped Mr. Delhut. But I can tell you why they wanted him dead—it's because of you."

"Me?" Lord Stewart asked.

"Your Drummond blood belongs to the Order of Eos even though your character kept you from attaining membership."

"My character?" Stewart angrily scoffed.

*Let's find out how badly he wants to kill me.* "My apologies. For while you are certainly not a poof, you are indeed a sodomite. While this behavior was practiced during the days of the Templars, it became an exclusionary quality in retrospect. Our order existed long before the Templars, but when we bestowed leadership on men such as yourself, and there was no heir produced, our good work crumbled. Surely, you are familiar with the Hermit? Lord Clair's bloodline was the strongest in the Order of Eos, yet he refused to sire a child, and when our enemies murdered him, he became a cautionary tale for new members."

"Oddly enough, I do have a son, and your accusations do not upset me. If this is your attempt at swallowing a poisoned pill to avoid giving up your secrets, you're mistaken," Stewart said with a smirk. "We saved your life for a reason. We only want an understanding."

"So does our enemy, it appears," Morrison admitted. "Why else would they bother abducting Delhut? I wonder if my failure will one day be a cautionary tale. For countless centuries, our quest has continued, barely noticed by the world. If it was noticed, we'd vanish for a generation and then resume. And then you and Joseph Nicollet began shouting about it for all the world to hear. It's no wonder you got him killed."

"No, no, no," Lord Stewart dismissed. "We know *who* killed Nicollet. We found the killer on our own accord."

"Oh, I know about your investigation and how it first led you to the home of Solomon Delhut, where you held a knife to the throats of his wife and children. Did you not think there would be consequences?" *I shouldn't have said that. I'm digging my own grave.*

Lord Stewart gestured with an open hand to the others. "Do you see? It's just as I told you. The Order of Eos put a bounty out

on us. I hope the kidnapper tortures Solomon Delhut slowly for what he did."

"For what?" Morrison repeated. "What do you think he did?"

"Don't be coy. We're speaking the truth tonight. Confess, and you might be spared."

Morrison shook his head. "You still don't understand what *you* did. We share a common enemy. I don't have names because they don't prance around in public like you do. They don't take positions of power like the Order of Eos does. We're being hunted by the same monster—the Vendita."

Stewart chuckled. "Is that title supposed to send shivers down my spine?"

*Stewart doesn't know. No wonder the Eos men in the Orkney Islands were targeted.* "I know you are not an ignorant man, but you're just a lucky man. Nicollet was a lucky man for a while, too, until Vendita finally caught up with him. Have your investigators not told you about the Vendita? Has your focus solely been on Eos?"

"I'm growing tired of this," Lord Stewart said to the others.

"Tell us about Vendita," Father MacPherson said. "The longer you talk, the longer you stay alive. Talk as if your life depends on it—which it does."

Morrison nodded in understanding, but in the back of his mind, he knew they'd also just bandaged him up. "Then let me explain: The Men of the Dawn predate Christianity and Judaism. We took root at the Dawn, and our branches grew strong in the sun, but one day, the great tree split in half when the fruit became too much to bear."

"That's a beautiful metaphor," Lord Stewart mocked. "The Splitting of the Elm at Gisors?"

*He knows his history.* Morrison nodded. "The Order of Eos continued, but the other branch twisted and changed—threatening all that we had done. At first, it called itself the Priory of Ormus, or the Priory of the Elm. When the Catholic Church arrested all known or suspected Templars in 1307, its branch almost withered while the Order of Eos survived and thrived. For a while, the Priory of Ormus grew strong and almost took hold of the prophecy—and then, it vanished overnight. For a century, nothing was heard of it."

"Is that why I've never heard of it?" Stewart asked.

"Then monarchies began to fall. Although the name Ormus had died, it took on many names to confuse us. Its adherents threw away names like Freemason, Illuminati, and Carbonari. Their purpose was clear though: Destroy the Catholic Church. Destroy the Monarchy. Destroy the Order of Eos. Only a man such as yourself, with such a great ego, would take things so personally. You and your friends are only collateral damage in this war."

"My brother died because of you bastards. My friend Joseph died. Antoine's father—"

*He's thinking about killing me as a scapegoat. My death will keep our secrets hidden, but can I count on Delhut dying without spilling his secrets?* Morrison quickly promised, "I can help you get revenge."

Lord Stewart chuckled at the desperate offer.

*Keep talking, like the priest said.* "Vendita,' as we call them, decentralizes their command, and they avoid passing down leadership through family lines. We didn't take them as a proper threat until recently, but now that they've crept out of the shadows, we're beginning to understand them better."

Stewart took the bait. "Go on."

"It is important to understand and study your enemy, wouldn't you say? Once you branded us your enemy, you immersed yourself into the history of the Order of Eos. You've been tracking down almost three thousand years of history in…what? Two decades? That's impressive. In the past two decades, we've been trying to understand Vendita. Once, when it was called Ormus, it was more fanatical than Eos. Then, in one generation, it changed. We wanted to understand *why* it changed. The answer surprised us: they learned when the world would end."

Stewart shook his head and added, "Only God in heaven knows the answer."

Morrison scoffed. "Oh, don't fool yourself. Your god has a plan and a very specific date in mind."

Father MacPherson leaned forward with interest. "So you acknowledge God the Father?"

"Of course we acknowledge the Creator. Do you know how far back the Order of Eos goes?"

"We do," Stewart answered. "I could have been a great Presider over the Order of Eos if I hadn't been denied. Did I feel spurned? Yes. In my anger, I read all about my uncle's secret society, so yes, I know how Eos goes past Freemasonry, the Templars, and even the Goths. I know why you see yourselves as the Men of the Dawn."

*Instead of a leader, Stewart turned into an enemy.* Morrison gathered himself. "Then you know why we took a solemn vow to avenge ourselves against the god that destroyed the Old Kingdom. Father MacPherson's god is a villain, and you are all clueless fools. We are in a race against time. We seek the secrets that will give humanity a victory in the war to come. If it is a battle between mankind and MacPherson's god, we know defeat and total destruction is inevitable. But if we can light the Sacred Fire and wake our ancient allies, then we can prevent the coming war."

"A race against time? How so?" Stewart asked.

*I can't do this alone. I need to convince them to join me in this fight.* "Didn't your friend Nicollet tell you? Surely, he understood."

"Why would Nicollet know?"

"The cosmic clock is ticking. MacPherson's god is not only a villain but also a symbolic villain. He sits back with a smile on his face each time the clock chimes the hour. The hour is late. We are approaching ten o'clock and destruction comes at midnight. It last chimed in 1835, and will again chime in 1911. Do I need to spell it out to you learn'd men?" The pain in his wounds made him a bit light-headed.

"2061," Stewart muttered low.

"I don't understand," MacPherson said.

"Halley's Comet is the clock. These lunatics believe the world will end in 2061," Stewart translated.

"Is this a case of the pot calling the kettle black?" Morrison asked. "The Jesuits have long suspected this, and so have the Periphery and other factions within the church. Which side did you ally yourselves with?" Father MacPherson opened his mouth to answer. "Ah, it makes no difference, does it? Our enemy—Vendita—calculated the date, and upon learning it, decided that the only way to save humanity was to keep the prophecy from happening."

"Seems like a fruitless gesture," MacPherson said. "Who can stand against the will of God?"

"Vendita has much of the knowledge once held by Eos, and with the kidnapping of Mr. Delhut, they could gain even more. Don't be so confident in prophecy, Father MacPherson. Take, for example, the many prophecies about the Christ. King Herod learned of one and massacred the entire town of Bethlehem. Imagine what Herod could have done if he'd learned about the details of the prophecy two hundred years in advance rather than the two days he had to act. That is what Vendita is doing. They know the prophecy from both sides—Eos and Christian. If they take away what is needed, they break the prophecy and stop the end of the world."

Father MacPherson scoffed. "Doubtful."

"I share your awe and fear for your god, which is why I view him as a villain. So I will speak in terms you understand. You know all of the Seals, Bowls, and Trumpets in your Book of Revelation, don't you?"

"I do."

"When the Fifth Trumpet sounds, what is given to the angel that comes from Heaven to Earth?"

"The Key to the Bottomless Pit."

"And tell your friends what the common interpretation of the Bottomless Pit is."

"It is an underworld of sorts, where the enemies of God are kept."

"Ah, like the souls of your Seven Kings," Morrison added. "Or in this case, the Destroyer, as he is so called by your scribes. Regardless of how you view this prophetic figure, it is a key moment in the End Times. Now imagine if Vendita possessed the key."

Morrison took a moment to sip his wine. His fingers went to the bandage where a knife had almost taken his life.

Stewart looked down at the table.

Geyer's focus changed to spots around the room.

The Texan had a mindless stare.

Father MacPherson, however, blinked, his mouth agape.

"The key is only a single item that Vendita could target. They reckon that if they destroy or possess the items mentioned in the prophecy, they will thwart the pending doom and rescue humanity from the yoke of the gods."

The room remained silent.

"You spoke to Mr. Delhut about this after you accused him of being involved in the death of Joseph Nicollet. What did he tell you about the key?"

"He hoped Nicollet could find the Philosopher's Stone."

"And the ancient maps? Why would he just give them to you?"

"We were being watched. Nicollet was being watched. He wanted us to lead Eos to what you couldn't find."

"There wasn't a uniform agreement on this plan. Some thought it foolish, others thought it bold. Either way, you helped us discover a shared enemy even if you weren't able to find the last pieces of the great puzzle. The best I can do is offer an apology for what happened to your brother and the others. Your instincts were right. Magnus Sinclair didn't like the attention any of you were receiving, but instead using Eos killers, he hired independent assassins to do his bidding, and Eos stepped right into a trap laid by the Vendita. Not only did they have your names but they also had the names of the men who hired them."

Morrison remembered the rage shown by Magnus Sinclair after Delhut told him what'd happened. After Joel Poinsett was killed by Stewart and the others, the order was given. Suddenly Vendita's assassins knew the identities of both parties.

"The Drummond family and the Morrison family were once close allies, so I have a proposal for you: help me rescue Solomon Delhut."

All the men reacted angrily as he expected—except for Stewart, who waited in silence until everyone else grew silent also. "What does Delhut know?"

"Too much, unfortunately. He's a modern man, like yourself, who had an almost unhealthy interest in the past. When we learned about the threat to our families, instead of simply going into hiding, he saw an opportunity to visit some of the historical sites once possessed by Eos, but even before we left, he knew the lore. How close did you come?"

"Close to what?"

"Finding the kings? That's why you were Antioch, right? Looking for the tomb of Antiochus Epiphanes. How close did you come to finding them?"

"We found dust."

Morrison scoffed. Just like Nicollet boldly went searching for the Philosopher's Stone, Stewart went boldly searching for the seven kings. *Delhut knows where the corpses are kept.* "I'm not a stupid man. I know I owe you my life, and that my life is still in your hands. Why would you let me live? I need to offer something of great value, don't I? That's why I need to know how close you came? I need to see what I can still offer you."

"You have nothing to offer. We've been to Rome, Taranto, Ravenna, Pella, Alexandria, Siwa Oasis, Valley of the Kings, and Heaven's Gate—dust."

*Impressive.* "What did you find in Ravenna?"

"We found the Shrine of Wuoth, enough to know we're on the path yet far from the end."

"It wasn't a trail you were supposed to follow. Who would have thought the Roman Empire was a bad investment? We lost the prized Shrine of Wuoth only to discover that our enemies were allies, like you and I. The problem with a generational quest is that branches splinter off. When the Roman empire was sacked by the Goths, all seemed lost, but in truth, it only exchanged hands. The Ostragoths are simply known as the Eastern Goths, but even more plainly, the east is the rising sun, the goddess Eos. They were the Men of the Dawn, an empire without borders that had come out of the north generations ago to claim the prophecy. They understood the importance of protecting the treasure from enemies, so they took it from Ravenna and hid it."

"And where did they take it?"

"That's what Solomon Delhut once asked. He was a true believer long before you broke into his house and threatened to murder his family. He rang the warning bell to wake the Order of Eos only to become a target of his enemy. I need your help to rescue him."

"Why shouldn't I let him die? Why should we not throw you overboard?"

"Instead of killing him, Vendita took him hostage, which means they will torture him until he gives them the answer. If Vendita finds the Shrine of Wuoth, the prophecies can be destroyed. My beliefs will be shattered. Your Christian beliefs will be shattered. We are allies, you and I."

"But you don't know where they took Delhut."

"True. They could be torturing him on some remote Greek island. If we knew for certain where Vendita was based, we'd wipe it off the face of the earth. I do know that if Delhut tells them about our secret stronghold, they will not kill him until they have confirmation. When they look for it, we will be waiting in ambush—that is my opportunity to rescue him."

"It seems a fair trade, but before I can agree to it, I need to know where we'd be going."

*The Ostrogoths were enemies until they weren't,* Morrison decided. *Perhaps Stewart is the same.* "They took the Shrine of Wuoth to one of the most remote places in the world. Its natural walls were built by the gods long ago. It has stood against kingdoms and armies for over a thousand years, and not even the mighty Ottoman Empire could conquer this little patch of land."

Morrison paused, seeing that all the men appeared to be hooked by this information. "The Goths called it the Castle of the Seven, but our enemies never knew the secrets of the castle. All they knew was that anyone who entered the woods never came back alive, and thus the region became known by the Latin word for woods—sylva. But no one knew what existed *beyond* the woods, so it became known as Transylvania."

## THE END OF PART SIX

# PART SEVEN
## CANADA

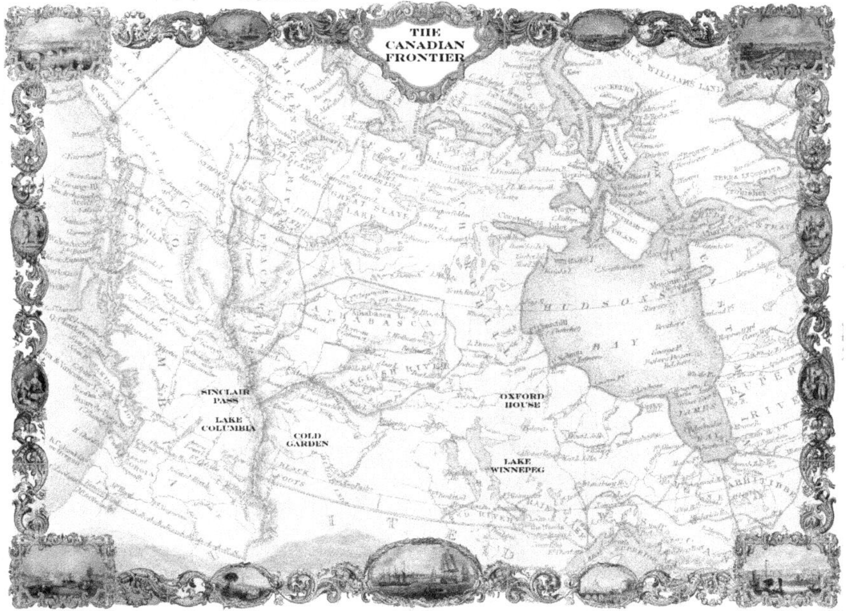

# PART SEVEN

# CHAPTER 40

OXFORD HOUSE

1853

For two centuries, the Hudson Bay Company had privately owned the land known to the local Cree as Manitou-wapow—or Manitoba. Although Henry Hudson is credited with discovering the massive interior bay that created a passageway into the northern interior of the American continent, the Cree who lived along the shores of Hudson Bay encountered numerous invaders from across the Atlantic Ocean. When the fur trade industry exploded, Hudson Bay quickly became a lucrative, albeit remote, way of avoiding the chaos of the Great Lakes waterway. For a short while, France and the LeMoyne family tried to capture the outpost in the Hudson Bay territory before turning their attention to the Gulf of Mexico and a southern passage up the Mississippi River.

After 1713 and the end of Queen Anne's War, England claimed the entire watershed of the Hudson Bay, which became known as Rupert's Land. For the century that followed, the Hudson Bay Company turned the region into a fur factory with posts at Rupert House, Moose Factory, Fort Albany, Fort Severn, York Factory, and Fort Churchill.

For Antoine Clement Senior, York Factory on the Nelson River offered the furtrader of French ancestry an opportunity to work sparsely populated rivers and lakes rather than the heavily populated Louisiana Territory. Clement Sr. supplied furs to the York Factory—a large, white wooden building—on a narrow peninsula between two rivers that emptied into Hudson: the

Nelson and the Hayes. The only reason the York Factory existed so far north was to process furs, and further up the river, smaller posts existed for the same purpose—to trade furs for supplies to survive in the rugged north. The farther up a river a fur trader went, the easier it was to find virgin territory ripe with beaver. Because of its remoteness, Clement Senior chose to make a home just north of Oxford Lake, which allowed him to bring his furs to posts on either the Hayes River or Nelson River. For a large man—which Clement Senior happened to be—a portage over land made it possible to earn money smaller men could not risk.

Thirty years after Antoine Clement Jr. left home, he returned to find only maggots feeding upon the corpse of his childhood. *What am I doing here?*

Like his father had done fifty years earlier, Antoine Clement Junior left his companions on the Nelson River to portage to Oxford Lake. The house where he'd been born had been toppled by forty years of cruel winters, but his destination had never been his childhood cabin. Setting his canoe down in the Carrot River, he paddled toward the closest town from his youth—Oxford House.

*I do this part alone,* Clement told himself as he steered toward the shore rather than to the docks of Oxford House. He'd heard rumors of what had happened, but seeing it with his own eyes finally made it real. In 1836, Antoine Clement Junior had arrived at Fort Snelling in the Minnesota territory to see the final years of the fur trade industry. Stewart sent him ahead of Joseph Nicollet to play the part of a simple but strong Metis, Brunia—a part he was born to play. Back in 1837, traders whispered about changing trends in New York City fashion and also a vanishing population of beavers. Now, Clement looked at the rotting corpse of the fur trade industry in Canada.

As a child, Antoine relished trips to Oxford House, where a season's worth of furs would be traded for precious goods. Shops of all sorts provided whatever traders needed, from dry goods to luxury items. Oxford House never grew into a city where people built streets full of houses, but at its height, it took hundreds of merchants to deal with the influx of commerce.

Even though Clement was a large man, he also knew how to be invisible, and with a whiskey bottle filled with water, he stumbled to the edge of town, choosing trees and alleys to assist in spying. Under his jacket, he had pistols and knives in case he needed to make an immediate kill, and he also had his rifles hidden along with his canoe, just in case. After four hours of stealth, Clement stepped into public view to wander into the town cemetery.

Even though he knew where his Cree mother was buried, he avoided going directly to her grave marker. He looked for the Sinclairs. Bill Sinclair came from the Kingdom of Great Britain a full generation before his father, and like Antoine Senior, Bill Sinclair married a local Cree woman. For the Cree, giving a daughter was meant to be a lifetime partnership between father and son-in-law, and for most marriages, it became exactly that. Bill Sinclair married Song-on-the-Water, the daughter of a Swampy Cree chieftain named Young-Man-Chief. With his Cree bride, he not only established a trade network with the local hunters but also sired fifteen children with her. Antoine's childhood was surrounded by young Sinclairs, and he toured the graveyard to see which ones remained his living enemy.

*There she is.*

*Hello, Mother.*

Antoine knelt down upon the grave of "Starlight" Clement. He didn't really remember her face very well, but he found pieces of her in the women he wooed between Hudson Bay and St. Louis. His father had been away when she died, and he and his brother Francois had to go to the neighbors to deal with the corpse in their house. Even after she was buried, their father didn't return to Antoine and Francois, so they spent a year at Oxford House.

Both the Clement boys and the Sinclair boys were Metis, but what separated them was the fact that the Clement brothers were viewed as wild heathens and the Sinclair boys were pampered city kids. It was a violent year living at Oxford House, and when their father did return, the boys refused to return to the town where the bullies lived.

*Now, I have returned with revenge in my heart.*

Antoine rose and continued down familiar roads until he stood in front of the Sinclair house, built on a hill overlooking the trade post.

A light was on.

The day was growing long, and he watched the house from a distance, but there was no traffic, no one going in and out.

*They've all fled to Madeira.*

*Why am I even here?*

A figure crossed in front of the kitchen window.

*It could be a servant.*

Antoine cocked his pistol, then placed it in his weaker left hand so that his right hand could later grip a knife. Knives were quiet, and he only planned on using the pistol if necessary.

Magnus, Thomas, and Jameson Sinclair were his greatest tormenters during that awful year following his mother's death—and he could remember their faces quite well. Junior Sinclair had already been a grown man working alongside his father at the trade post, and neither of them gave much thought to helping the motherless Clement boys.

*Would the blood of Thomas or Jameson atone for my father's death?* Antoine wondered as he approached the backsteps. *Am I looking to take a hostage? Will I have to torture them? Or their children?*

With this hilt of his knife, he pounded on the back door.

It opened a moment later, and an old woman stood in the doorway, as puzzled as he was. For the first time in three decades, Antoine Clement remembered what his mother looked like.

# CHAPTER 41



The old woman was not his mother. Although she had his mother's eyes, the woman standing in the doorway was easily in her eighties.

"I thought you were dead," Song-on-the-Water said, her hands on her wide hips. "Or are you a ghost that has come back to haunt my family?"

"You remember who I am?" Antoine asked.

"Of course I do," Song-on-the-Water answered. "You are the Brown-Giant, Brunia-Missabay—and you have returned to fulfill your destiny."

"I've only come to avenge my father."

"Hmph," the old woman voiced and turned away from the loaded pistol. "If you have come for vengeance, your father's blood is on my hands. Come, sit, eat, and I will explain."

Even though he'd hated the Sinclair boys, Song-on-the-Water had always been an honest woman. Song-on-the-Water walked by the table, pulled out a chair, and then turned to the kitchen. He sheathed his knife but switched his pistol to his dominant hand. He accepted her invitation to sit at the table, keeping the pistol ready should the old woman produce a weapon from the cupboards. A few moments later, she returned with bread and pork.

"You have your father's frame but your mother's face," Song-on-the-Water noted. "She was my brother's daughter, which makes us blood relatives. I remember when they brought you to my home after her death."

"So do I," Antoine said bitterly. "Where are your sons?"

"My sons are grown men who now protect their families."

Antoine reacted by taking a deep breath but he did not argue with the old woman, and instead, held his breath and bit his tongue.

Song-on-the-Water seemed to have noticed. "I did not know why they asked about you. 'Whatever happened to those boys we took in?' I knew your father took the family to St. Louis because he sent letters to me. When I learned about your father's death, I knew what my sons had done. Years ago, my husband showed up on his big ship, and my sons departed on other big ships. I am the only one who remains, for I refused to be part of their schemes any more."

"Who was it? Who asked about me?"

"Magnus. He came to collect the entire family, and in the chaos of stealing my grandchildren, I gave little thought to why he asked about the children of my niece."

"It was Magnus?" Antoine repeated and pictured his childhood bully. William and John Sinclair were grown men when Antoine was young, but Magnus, Thomas, and Jameson were of similar age. Several daughters gave the Sinclair family a small army to lord over the traders. Now they were all gone into hiding. "I need to understand. Who leads the family now that your husband is dead?"

"Junior runs the business, but Magnus leads it. He is one of three men from three families that came to our land. Can you forgive me for my part in your father's death?"

Antoine ignored the question. "What do they want? Why are they willing to kill others to get it?"

"The Men of the Dawn? They have been coming to our shores generations before I was given as a bride to one of them. Once, all they sought was a passageway, so we let them pass. Then they came as conquerors but only to control the land."

"What do they seek?" Antoine pressed, thinking of Joseph Nicollet and William Drummond Stewart's tales about the Philosopher's Stone and the history of the quest that went all the way back to the Holy Lands. "Explain it to me."

"As a boy, you were baptized with water and spirit into the Christian Church, and I also took a Christian name when I was baptized. Shouldn't everyone seek to understand the mysteries of life? My family teaches to keep an open mind and find truth in all things, which is why my people found truth in the stories from the other side of the world. One of those stories involves water. In the Christian Bible, it is told in the story of Noah. My people explained the story in another way.

"When the world was young, mankind served the Creator by tending to the creatures he'd placed in it, and for a while, there was harmony. Then came Wisakachak the Trickster, who brought chaos and turmoil to the world with his lies. He learned the secrets from Beaver and Muskrat, who were charged with containing the waters of the world with a great dam. Once evil Wisakachak learned their secrets, he trapped them and turned to destroy their work. He found a powerful stone and used it to break the dam, bringing a flood that buried the entire world. But the flood waters were so powerful that they trapped Wisakachak in his own mischief and freed Beaver and Muskrat. With the help of Raven, who flew over the floodwaters gathering survivors, Muskrat gathered trees into a great raft, and Beaver dove down to the depths to bring up soil to make a new earth."

Antoine remembered the tale from his childhood, but the campfire tale now took on new meaning in light of Nicollet's knowledge.

Song-on-the-Water looked down after telling the familiar story of the flood, but she was not done. "Wisakachak remains buried deep under the earth, but he is not forgotten. The Raven remembers him, and it is said that he still watches over the place where the Trickster is buried. The survivors that the Raven gathered onto the new earth also remembered Wisakachak and while the descendants of Beaver built a new world, the descendants of Muskrat searched their old friend, Wisakachak. Even though the Creator made Wisakachak his most powerful creation, he made sure that the Trickster was buried deep under the earth. Yet still—he is the source of water. Now do you understand the intent of my wicked Muskrat children?"

*This is what Stewart feared. Wisakachak is either another name for the Devil—or is the first of Stewart's seven kings. America: a lost continent with a lost king.* "And how do you know this?"

"Giving your daughters away in marriage does more than just rid yourself of an extra mouth to feed—it also allows your daughters to learn secrets. My husband was sent here to find a place where the water flows in all directions."

"They are seeking Wisakachak?"

"That is *our* name for the Trickster, not his. Although Magnus and Thomas gathered up all of my grandchildren to bring them back east to safety, Jameson did not return with him."

"Is Jameson here still?"

"Not long after your father took you and your brothers to St. Louis, my husband sent Jameson away. First, back to Scotland, and then, on a pilgrimage to the Holy Lands. When he returned home, the family's interest in the fur trade waned, and all of our focus turned to finding the headwaters of the great river known as the Missouri."

It took Antoine considerable focus not to laugh aloud or even smirk. *Nicollet's ruse worked.*

After men such as William Morrison, Henry Schoolcraft, and George Fanshaw eliminated the Mississippi River as the legendary river in the Philosopher's Stone lore, the Order of Eos immediately shifted its focus west—until chance brought Joseph Nicollet into the story. Having seen the ancient map, Nicollet followed in the footsteps of Eos. Once he drew their gaze, he developed a plan to confuse his enemies, and for his final years, he made plans for a final expedition up the Missouri River. Friends like Father Pierre-Jean DeSmet, John C. Fremont, William Drummond Stewart, and Karl Geyer lent their talents to the ruse. Nicollet's great distraction, however, came to a sudden end at a hotel back in Baltimore when an assassin poisoned him before he could join the others. Nicollet's friends took their vengeance—but the Order of Eos swallowed the bait even after Nicollet's death. "Where did Jameson go?"

"He took well over a hundred people with him, well-provisioned, in order to lay claim to the territory known as Oregon, where he planned to go deep into the Rocky Mountains."

*The source of many rivers—and a place where the Great Creator piled the mountains high upon the back of Wisakachak.*

"But that was a decade ago," she explained. "Jameson took the colonists in 1841. There are rumors that he returned to the Red River Colony for more men, but I have not seen him since he first left."

When Antoine left St. Louis, he also traveled up the Missouri River into the wild frontier, where he made a living as a guide and hunter. It was a thousand miles from his childhood home of Oxford Lake to the Canadian Rockies—and several hundred more to reach the other side of the Rockies and the shores of the Pacific. *It could take years to find him.* "Think…did any news return from Jameson to his brothers and sisters?"

"So I can help you kill my son?"

"Trust me, Song-on-the-Water, by stopping one man, I could save the lives of all your grandchildren and great-grandchildren."

"Does he really mean to wake Wisakachek from his slumber?" she asked. "When he returned from his trip, he brought something back with him—a strange stone carved before the days of the flood."

*Did he already acquire the Philosopher's Stone?* Antoine felt his heart leap in his chest. Years earlier, he'd taken Nicollet and Chagobay to a cave at Lake Manitou. If Nicollet hadn't died in 1843, he would have joined Taopi, Faribault, and the son of Sleepy Eye on a quest to return to Lake Manitou. *Is it too late? Has our plan been thwarted?* "Did you see this stone?"

"It was broken—a black slab, with strange writing upon it. Magnus claimed they were the words of an ancient prophecy and that they would guide Jameson to the right place. I've never seen such a thing. The stone was carved with such perfection and polished to such a fine sheen that it looked like a window opened into the dark night. The stone absorbed light without reflection— only the broken edges of it made it seem real. Do you know what it was?"

*No, but I'll be sure to speak of it with Professor Morgan.* Antoine shook his head. "Did any of the colonists return from this trip? Any of them?"

The old woman shook her head. "No, none of the colonists returned, but their guide did. You know him. You gave him his name when you were boys—Crooked Arm, of course now he is *Chief* Crooked Arm. You could speak to him—if you are foolish enough to risk it."

Antoine had risked confronting Crooked Arm once, and it almost cost him his life.

To find Jameson Sinclair and the mysterious black stone, it was a risk he had to take.

# CHAPTER 42



Professor Corey Morgan waited with the luggage and the boys. Somewhere—a few miles south of their camp along the Red River—Lord Erskine and Antoine were hiring men for a great hunting expedition across the northern prairie.

*Either that or they're murdering someone.*

Morgan knew the purpose of their journey to America, and he also understood why neither man trusted him to partake in the vengeance. Instead of a trunk full of weapons, he hauled a trunk full of books, texts, and notes.

*I am tasked with solving the mystery surrounding the Order of Eos—that is all.*

Vaktar Forsberg endlessly sharpened the knife Clement had given him. Sofus Nielson sat in a nest of three trunks, drawing upon a notebook with a pencil that was nearly to its nub.

*My research assistants,* Morgan scoffed. Both boys were armed with revolvers to help defend the luggage. The idea of arming untested boys had bothered him, but both had more combined grit in them than he had.

"How long will it take to get to the mountains?" Forsberg asked, putting away his blade. The hulking red-haired boy walked over to the shade of the camp and sat down beside Morgan, who knew what he wanted—more stories.

*At least they enjoy my tales.*

Morgan opened his vault, but only for a dash of realism. He found his Arrowsmith map of British North America with the

United States outlined in yellow, Mexico outlined in Green, and Canada outlined in pink. It'd been 10 years since J. Arrowsmith published the map, and most of the empty spaces had been filled all the way to the Pacific. He placed his finger at the southern end of Lake Winnipeg. "We are here. The river we traveled on, the Nelson, connected to Hudson Bay. From the bay to where we camp right now it was a trip of about seven hundred miles."

He looked up to see if the young brute was listening. "But that was by steamship. We're about to make the rest of the journey by horseback. The journey across the prairie will be another seven hundred miles, but once we reach the mountains, the difficulty increases."

Vaktar leaned closer, and Morgan winced a little bit as the boy's rampant body odor offended him.

"Do you think my Viking ancestors ever traveled this far inland?" Forsberg asked.

"I think it's possible but very unlikely."

"My ancestors made the trip," Sofus Nielson said matter-of-factly, bringing the conversation to a halt.

*He's either a jokester or a compulsive liar.*

Nielson's nose remained in his notebook for a few more moments before he looked up. When he noticed the staring, he asked defensively, "What?"

Sofus Nielson was older than Forsberg—perhaps by a couple years—but he still had a smooth baby face and thin arms and chest of a boy. "My forefathers traveled all over the world. My grandfather told me stories about it. We're descended from Thor."

"Thor had red hair," Forsberg challenged. "If anything, I'm a descendant of Thor."

Nielson shrugged, his eyes returning to his paper. "That's not the way my grandfather tells it. My family went out into the world to look for Jormungandr, the Midgard Serpent."

*Is he saying this just to impress me?* Morgan wondered.

Forsberg did not like Nielson stealing his thunder. "Thor died in the Ragnarok. How could you, of all people, be his descendant. He was a god."

Nielson would not be bullied. "In my language, our family name Nielson means 'Cloud Champion.' Who was the Norse god of thunder and lightning?"

"You're not a descendant of Thor."

"Tell him, Professor Morgan."

*Oh dear God, what have I created?* "Yes, Thor died in the Ragnarok in the act of killing Jormungandr, and even though the world was destroyed during this battle, there were a few survivors, including the two humans who hid in the tree and four lesser Norse gods, two sons of Odin as well as Modi and Magni, the sons of Thor."

"Are you telling me this scrawny thing is a descendant of Thor?" Forsberg asked jealously.

With a grin, Morgan shook his head. "I'm just saying that the tales allow for the bloodline of the gods to continue into our time."

For a minute, the unexpected dispute seemed resolved—until Nielson opened his mouth to say, "Except instead of going west, my ancestor went south from here. It was probably the Nielson River before it was changed to Nelson."

"What are you talking about?" Morgan asked, now interested.

"The story you've been telling Vaktar and the others—the one about Jacob Cnoyen—my forefathers were also on that expedition."

*The clever boy is just trying to get a rise out of Forsberg.* Since they found the stowaway on the Atlantic crossing, he'd grown bolder and bolder with his storytelling. "Was he? Who was he?"

"My forefather? He was just a nobody, like me, but in his blood, he was another Cloud Champion, making him a gifted sailor. He just happened to be at the wrong place at the wrong time when the Sinclair ship stopped for supplies. He was Tao Nielson—one of the eight survivors of the expedition who went deep into the heart of this continent."

*Too specific to be believable.* "He was part of the Cnoyen Expedition? Why is this the first time I've heard about it?"

"You never asked. Forsberg isn't the only one with old bloodlines."

"Tao Nielson?" Morgan repeated almost in a laugh. He'd been able to research all about Jacob Cnoyen, Ivar Bardson, and Pal

Knutson, but he'd never learned much about the crew. So he had no way of corroborating or disproving Nielson's tale.

"My grandfather told stories about the eight men who were abandoned for more than a decade."

"Did he? Who were they?"

"Well, there is Cnoyen of Berg, of course. I think there was a priest also—named Tveit. I don't remember if that is his first or last name. Forsberg's forebear was Mikils Forsberg, a giant of a man. Then there were the others: Drummond, Dobie, and Morrison."

"Drummond, Dobie, and Morrison? That's only seven survivors."

"Oh, I forgot Bjarni. Bjarni Olafson. He was with them, too. They were all part of the larger expedition of men sent by the King to go rescue the lost Greenlanders."

*He's heard this tale from me. Now he modifies it.* "What about Pal Knutson, the expedition leader, did you forget about him?"

"I didn't forget about him," Nielson said defensively. "He just didn't survive. I only know the names of the survivors—the ones who walked all the way back. A lot of them died."

"Probably got attacked by Natives," Vaktar offered, and then turned to Morgan. "Are we going to run into Natives on our trip into the west?"

"Clement is half Cree, and most of the tribes between here and the Rocky Mountains are Cree, so I wouldn't worry."

"They didn't get killed by Cree," Nielson added. "They ran into the Greenlanders, and a great battle took place, leaving only 8 survivors. Those were the men who found a way back home twenty years after they left."

This tidbit gave Morgan pause. According to the records he'd found, the royal court of Norway mentioned Pal Knutson leaving in 1354. If Knutson spent several years searching, and several years coming home, he would have returned in the 1370s—about the time Prince Henry Sinclair of the Orkney Islands began a revenge tour that led to his conquest of the Faroe Islands in 1391. "Your grandfather told you this story?"

Sofus nodded enthusiastically. "My forefather stood right where we are standing. I recognize it from my family tales."

"You recognize it? How?"

At this, Forsberg sighed with disdain, stepped away, and walked down to the river edge.

Nielson shrugged it off and answered, "From Greenland, they followed the same route we just took. They followed the coast until they entered Hudson Bay, following the shore until they could go no farther west. They left their big ships at the mouth of the Hudson Bay and the rest went by canoes up the Nelson River all the way to where we are now—Lake Winnipeg."

*Am I a fool who wants the story to be true?* "Hold on, how many men were on the expedition?"

"My forefather was part of the ship's crew, but…they didn't want to risk a mutiny, so they left ten men behind to guard the ship and took the sailors with so the ship didn't leave without them. There were thirty men total. Eight of them were experienced sailors from Gothland and the others were Northmen from Bergen and Faroe. The King and the Bishop first hired men from Gothland since they knew where to go. That's why there was a Forsberg on the trip."

*What would've pushed these men to journey so far inland? Is Nielson combining Forsberg's stories with the stories of the Newport Tower?* "And they found their way out here?"

Sofus nodded and rose, carrying his notepad with him. He'd made a map with a clearly defined Hudson Bay and Nelson River. "They left the big ship behind at Hudson Bay, and then, like the Vikings of old, they traveled upstream. From here, at Lake Winnipeg, they continued up a long river that flowed straight south until there was no more river. That's when the battle happened."

"Battle?"

Nielson's eyes grew wide as he nodded. "Just like us, they were men with old blood lines who knew all about the lost continent. But these men were not sent by Sinclair. These men were sent by the Church. It wasn't a rescue mission like you told it. It was a mission sent to stop them. They found the missing Greenlanders camped at the place where water flows in all directions, and they battled them until only 8 remained to tell the tale."

"What were the Greenlanders doing at this watershed encampment?"

"Most of them were thralls, taken from their home by the Order of Eos, but after so long, how could Knutson know who to trust? Both leaders were killed and the eight banded together to get home."

"And what was the Order of Eos doing at this watershed so far from the rest of the world?"

"It's like you said—they were searching for the survivors of the Ragnarok."

*He's making this all up as he goes. I just mentioned that to him a moment ago.* "Searching for survivors of the Ragnarok?"

"Yes, except it wasn't Modi, Magnir, Vidar, or Vali they were searching for; it was somebody far worse. They were searching for the King of Muspelheim himself—Surtr, the powerful fire giant. You know, the one who led the armies of evil and personally killed Frey. They were seeking him so that he could be freed from where he was buried alive."

*Is that what we're chasing after?*

*A buried god?*

*Surtr? Wisakachak? Manitou?*

"Instead of going west," Nielson concluded, tucking away his notebook, "we should be going south."

*Oh, we will, Sofus. Before this trip is over, we're going south.*

# CHAPTER 43

C O L D   G A R D E N

1 8 5 3

Vaktar Forsberg did as he was told. He quietly stood behind Antoine Clement, so close, in fact, that he could see dandruff on the man's deerskin collar. With each passing mile, Clement transformed from the solemn valet for Lord Erskine to a panther in human clothes.

Resting on one shoulder, Vaktar cradled the beautiful rifle at his chest. It was loaded and ready, which is why he kept his hands a distance from the trigger—as instructed.

Clement rested on his belly, his piercing eyes level with the top of the ridge and the sights of the other beautiful rifle.

*Which one is he going to pick?*

*Which one will die?*

Vaktar could only imagine what was happening on the other side of the ridge. Two days ago, the two set out from their camp at the Elbow River, where the others waited along with several guides they'd hired to assist with the trip across the Canadian prairie. With no permanent settlement or outpost for hundreds of miles, and the Rockies looming in the distance, Clement grabbed Vaktar and headed off for the foothills.

*Clement is no fool like Professor Morgan,* Forsberg decided, pleased to be in the company of the esteemed hunter.

When the rifle shot sounded, Vaktar flinched, but in the next heartbeat, he passed the rifle forward—just as instructed. By the time his hands reached for the third rifle lying beside him, Clement had taken aim and fired a second shot. His empty hands waited for

Vaktar to pass him the third rifle, and a moment later, the third shot rang out.

Then, Vaktar looked over the ridge.

Two dead mule deer were already on the ground as the herd stotted through the grass and away from the sound of danger. A third mule deer stumbled from the pack, tried to continue, and then fell to the ground.

*He got all three.*

Vaktar was smiling when Clement turned and gave him an approving nod. "Collect the rifles."

Vaktar's movements sounded like a battalion passing by; in contrast, Clement moved like a shadow. By the time Vaktar had everything collected, Clement was already halfway down the hill, knife in hand.

"When gutting a mule deer," Clement began and Vaktar absorbed each and every lesson. For the next hour, Clement taught Vaktar how to field dress the deer. Back in Dallaven, Vaktar believed he was a tough farm kid. Spending a few hours with Antoine Clement out on the frontier, however, showed him a human at his zenith of predatory skill.

*This journey should impress my forebearers.*

Later, as the others rose at their approach, he walked proudly in step with his towering mentor. Lord Erskine had hired a cook, two drivers, and four horseback rangers before leaving Winnipeg, and while they were all experienced men hardened by the Canadian environment, they also revered Antoine Clement.

*Let Nielson have the professor.*

Professor Morgan and Sofus Nielson sat at the campfire, just as they'd done during most of the crossing. Back in Dallaven, Vaktar felt as if Professor Morgan was a heavenly angel sent to pluck him from his dull existence. The tales of the Vikings seemed as remote as the tales of Thor and Loki, but then Professor Morgan showed up from out of nowhere not only to validate so many of the stories but also to then bring Vaktar under his wing on an old-fashioned adventure.

All that ended when Sofus Nielson forced himself into the narrative.

At first, Vaktar enjoyed his company. Both were of similar age and experience, and the two crossed the Atlantic in harmony. With each passing day, though, the tales grew bolder and the truth more far-fetched.

"Ah, the hunter has returned. Did you find game?" Professor Morgan asked.

Vaktar nodded.

Sofus held up another drawing from his notebook. "We've decided to name this camp Kald Gart."

*Cold Garden,* Vaktar translated the old Norse words that connected the three of them. *A fitting name.* The camp was made at a union of two rivers that flowed east out of the Rockies. Nielson's drawing showed the arrowhead as well as the area where they'd been hunting to the west.

"We got three mule deer," Vaktar declared, glancing down at the bloodstains.

Neither gave much of a reaction, and Vaktar walked past them so they could continue sharing silly stories.

A few yards away, Lord Erskine and the cook sat together at another fire. "How was the hunting?"

"We shot three mule deer. Mr. Clement is butchering them right now."

"That's excellent news," Lord Erskine answered with a smile. "That means we should have enough fresh meat to continue into the mountains. As scenic as this location is, I've tired of the sedentary life."

Vaktar didn't know how to answer, so he shrugged and continued to his tent.

He cleaned himself up with a rag and stripped off his heavy hunting jacket.

*It's sure been a good adventure.*

He and Sofus had both hoped to head south from Winnipeg. For Sofus, it was to prove the truth to his ridiculous tale about a 1300s trip to North America. For Vaktar, he wanted to reconnect with his Uncle Dagmar. Vaktar had just been a child when his uncle left Dallaven. This left the second brother, Vaktar's father, behind to tend to the property at Fors. In the dozen years since Dagmar left, the family received only two letters. The first told of

his safe arrival in America in 1836, and the second indicated his plans to travel up the Mississippi River for work in a new territory now called Minnesota. Having seen the expanse of North America, Vaktar now understood how poor his odds were of actually stumbling across his uncle.

A single pistol shot filled the air.

Its echo reverberated, and Vaktar was armed and ready before the sound stopped—only to be replaced by thunder.

The sky remained clear and the peaks of the distant mountains clearly defined. It wasn't thunder that rumbled.

*Hooves.*

Vaktar's heart fluttered when he saw a cloud of dust on the northern river. At first, he thought it might be a stampeding herd of buffalo or even a confused herd of mule deer but the splashes of color told him something entirely different: Indians.

Everyone began to arm themselves, including Sofus. Vaktar searched for Clement.

"Wagons!" someone shouted, and the small caravan began to tighten.

They'd encountered several bands of Indians as they passed through Canada, but the Assiniboine, Hidatsa, and Arikara came out of curiosity or for commerce—and in much smaller numbers. Now, fifty warriors rode at them in full gallop.

Three days after setting up camp, Vaktar finally understood Clement's skepticism about the defensive position of the camp. Even though the northern river was the larger of the two rivers that surrounded them, the horses barely slowed as they descended the banks and easily crossed the river atop a large sand bar.

*Antoine!*

Everyone but Clement had gathered behind the protection of the wagons. He had taken the mule deer down to the river to process the meat and he stood tall and alone as fifty warriors advanced toward him.

Curiously, Clement knelt down and continued processing the deer.

The riders divided, passing by him like a stone in the current.

"Calm yourselves men," Lord Erskine shouted out. "They'll kill all of us if we shoot first. Don't provoke them."

*He's right.* Vaktar watched as the warriors raced around the wagons, encircling the entire camp. None of them had weapons in hand.

"Cree," one of the drivers said. "The Rocky Mountain Cree."

"Is that good or bad?" Professor Morgan asked.

"It depends on who is leading them."

Antoine Clement stood back up, knife in hand. He quickly sheathed it and bent over to pick up a hindquarter leg of mule deer, which he lifted and set on his shoulder.

Three riders crossed the river slowly but did not veer around Clement. They came right up the bank and stood in front of him.

"Oh shit," a ranger muttered.

"What? What is it?" Morgan asked.

"It's Crooked Arm," the ranger said, readying his rifle.

"That's good," the cook muttered. "Crooked Arm is an ally. He's a Christian now. Methodist, I think. He took the name Abraham."

"I saw him kill three Blackfeet all by himself," a driver offered.

"No, you don't understand. The river in front of us is the Elbow River. It's his river. He claims all of this as his hunting ground," another said in a panic.

"But…" Vaktar found his voice amongst the men. "We were hunting south of the river."

"Quiet," one of the rangers muttered. "This could go sideways in a snap."

Strangely, Vaktar didn't feel the same fear the others did as they watched the situation unfold. The fierce warrior slid off his mount, followed by his two lieutenants. They stepped forward to face Clement.

"Shit, shit, shit," the eldest ranger muttered. "We're all going to die."

"Calm yourselves," Erskine commanded.

"What's going on?" a guide asked the elder ranger in a whisper.

"From what I've heard back at Winnipeg…Crooked Arm has only lost one fight in his entire life—to a Swampy Cree warrior named Brunia-Missabay, the Brown Giant. Clement is the man who gave him the name Crooked Arm."

Vaktar had every confidence that Clement could still beat Crooked Arm in single combat, but the group was outnumbered five to one. Their ranks were filled with boys and gentlemen while Crooked Arm brought warriors.

*Could Sofus kill five of them?* Vaktar wondered. *Could I even kill one?*

# CHAPTER 44

S I N C L A I R   P A S S

1 8 5 4

*Nicollet is laughing in his grave,* Antoine Clement thought to himself. Ahead of him, Chief Crooked Arm's scouts guided their horses through the narrow passage into the valley. His childhood friend and rival rode beside him. Back at Cold Garden, they'd traded the mules and wagons for the swift horses of the Cree. Behind him in the column, Lewis Cairns and Professor Morgan rode amongst the Cree warriors and the boys rode at the back.

Together, they'd traveled for 80 miles through the most rugged stretch of the Canadian Rockies, following a path that once only their ancestors knew. The days had been short and much of the journey had been in the cold shadow of the mountains, but now, sunlight met them at the spine of the turtle.

"You're not going to find them here," Chief Crooked Arm said to Clement about the Sinclairs. "The Shuswap live here."

"Are they your enemies?"

"No, but their resources are limited. They allowed the white men to camp here during the winter months before they continued to the ocean."

*And now it is known as Sinclair Pass. It's been claimed and put on the maps.* Jameson Sinclair, brother of Magnus Sinclair, led 121 pioneers from Oxford House across the Canadian prairie to race Nicollet to the headwaters of the Missouri River. Back in Washington DC, Nicollet found himself marooned without funding and his apprentice reassigned—allowing Sinclair's bold move to happen in 1841.

And Nicollet's bluff had worked.

John C. Fremont, Nicollet's apprentice, eventually found his way west without Nicollet. William Drummond Stewart also returned, going up the Missouri River. Nicollet's Jesuit ally, Pierre-Jean DeSmet, added to the subterfuge by traveling upstream as well. The Order of Eos took the bait hook, line, and sinker—shifting all its resources to the Canadian Rockies.

Had Nicollet lived, he would have swept back into northern Minnesota, collected the Philosopher's Stone, and vanished with the help of the Periphery. Unfortunately, an assassin poisoned Nicollet's drink, and all the grand schemes came crumbling down in the fall of 1843.

Yet Jameson Sinclair remained in the contested Oregon Territory. "So where is he now?"

"South," Crooked Arm answered. "He's still searching the mountains, singing his song, and hauling his stone with him wherever he goes."

*A stone? It must be the stone Song-on-the-Water mentioned.* "Tell me again about this stone."

"He kept it hidden from the other white people in the caravan. Only those in his inner circle knew about it. I knew because he brought me with him whenever he left camp, but he only saw me as an ignorant savage."

"Was it unnaturally smooth?" Antoine asked, gesturing with his hands to make a mental image the size of a cannon ball. "A white egg?"

Crooked Arm recoiled. He widened his arm to make the shape with his arms about two feet wide and three feet tall. "It was much larger than that. Only a man your size could carry it, and it was black, not white."

*Perhaps I can still serve Nicollet and Stewart by acquiring this strange stone.*

The sound of trotting hooves grew louder, and from the corner of his eye, Antoine saw Professor Morgan listening intently to the conversation. Morgan nodded as if apologizing and then cleared his throat to ask, "Was the stone cut by the hand of man?"

Crooked Arm hesitated. "Yes and no. It had edges and corners but it was also rough, as if it had been broken off from a larger piece of stone. The edges, though, were so perfect that I doubted that any tool of man could have cut it."

"It might surprise you what ancient man was capable of doing," Professor Morgan insisted. "Describe the color of the stone. You said it was black."

"Blacker than night, for at night, the stars dot the heavens, but when I looked upon the stone, it was like I was looking at a hole in the world. I could see the dust upon its surface, but beyond that, only black. Does that make sense?"

"It makes perfect sense," Morgan said with his crooked grin.

"So it's not Nicollet's stone, is it?" Clement clarified.

"No," Morgan scoffed. "It's neither the sacred Water Drum nor the White Egg of Wishwee. This is something entirely different, I believe." And then turning back to Crooked Arm, he asked. "Was their writing upon it?"

"Yes and no," Crooked Arm answered vaguely.

"Tell me about the writing," Morgan pressed.

Crooked Arm took a moment to measure his words. "The words were not letters but were strange shapes."

"Runes," Morgan added.

"But they were not painted upon the stone or cut into the stone," Crooked Arm added. "They were part of the stone like a fish frozen in the ice."

*It's all part of the big puzzle, but what is it's purpose?* "What are you thinking?" Antoine asked Morgan.

Professor Morgan reached under his hat to scratch his head and then tugged at his black beard. "I'm thinking all sorts of things. The most obvious answer is that Jameson Sinclair is in possession of an ancient Viking Rune Stone, one that was planted in the earth and then broken off at the base, but that doesn't explain the finer details, does it?"

*At least it's not the Philosopher's Stone,* Clement decided. *A purpose greater than revenge still awaits us.*

Morgan offered a theory. "Legend says that after Odin learned of the coming doom of Ragnarok, he sacrificed himself upon the great tree to learn the secrets of the universe. When he returned

from death, he possessed the secret knowledge of runes, which he gave to mankind. But it begs the question: what runes did Odin discover? Who created this runic language for Odin to learn?"

Professor Morgan winced as if in pain and shut up for a few minutes as the entire caravan came out of the shadows of the mountain and into the narrow, open valley.

"Ah," Morgan finally ended his pained pause. "If only I'd paid more attention to ancient histories that weren't based on the Norse. I once encountered a book on eastern religions and myths that told of black steles that held the plans for the universe. Or was it the Egyptian tale of Thoth, who wrote the universe into creation?"

"So Sinclair had a black rock?" Clement bluntly reviewed.

Crooked Arm smirked and nodded. "The Sinclair expedition camped ahead. I later took them all the way to the Pacific to a place they called Puget Sound."

"And what was waiting for them on the other side?"

"Nothing but the sea. Sinclair tried to explain it to me. He said that his British people were in a race to claim the land and if there were colonists living there, their claim was strengthened."

Professor Morgan continued the explanation. "The United States bought much of its territory from France in the Louisiana Purchase, but in the far west, Spain and Russia first tried to lay claim in the 1820s, but more recently, following the Mexican-American War, those two nations withdrew their claims. Britain, however, tried to argue that Rupert's Land extended as far south as the 42nd Parallel at the border of the Columbia River because of a treaty with Mexico. All that went to hell of course following the Mexican War, and the United States claimed everything to the 49th Parallel."

*Sinclair is stumbling around in the dark, searching for proof of his beliefs.* Antoine looked around the continental divide, remembering how Nicollet searched for another divide that led the Red River north and the Mississippi River south. This valley was narrow. "So this is our plan," Antoine started loudly and halted the column.

Lord Erskine and the others gathered around where he'd stopped. Once they were ready, Clement continued. "Instead of chasing after my enemy, I'm going to let him come to me. He thinks he killed me back in St. Louis, so when he learns I am alive, it will hurt his pride. Back at Oxford House, rumors have already begun to spread about me. We will grow new rumors here."

He turned to his blood brother Crooked Arm. "You said there is a southern passage back to Cold Garden didn't you?"

Crooked Arm nodded.

This pleased Clement. "On your way back to Cold Garden, I want you to tell everyone you meet how a wealthy Scottish Lord paid you a large sum of money to lead you to this place, where they are building a new colony."

"Will I see this large sum of money?"

"If I live, yes, I'll make sure of it. Do not search for Sinclair, but tell the mountain tribes that you saw the Brown Giant, Antoine Clement, in the party. Tell them I am a poor drunkard who lives in a cabin with a young boy."

Antoine nodded to Vakar Forsberg, who grinned a toothless grin.

"Now that I know the northern passage, I will meet you back at Cold Garden when this business is finished."

"What about us?" Lord Erskine asked.

"You will be part of the lie. Create an outpost right on the mouth of this river. Mr. Stewart will pay our hired men for their efforts. Trade openly with the Shuswap, but tell each of them about me. Warn them about me, in fact. I will build a cabin south of here, right on the river, leaving Jameson Sinclair no choice but to pass by it once he learns about my name being used in this valley."

"Just you and Forsberg? He'll catch you unaware one day. We didn't come all this way to let you fail."

"He will be cautious, and if he sees a dozen men, he'll run, knowing I've come for him, but if he shows up and sees me alone, he'll confront me. I want him to step into the trap. Vaktar will be the eyes in the back of my head, and Nielson will do the same for your camp. I'll let this bastard come to me. His black heart will lead him right into my trap."

# CHAPTER 45



Located at present day Astoria, Oregon, the delta of the Columbia River is nearly 3,000 miles due east of Oak Island, Nova Scotia on the opposite shore of the continent. During the Oregon Boundary Dispute, the United States claimed that Captain Robert Gray of Massachusetts sailed up the river in 1792 aboard his private ship *Columbia Rediviva* and thus negated the 1799 Russian claim and the 1807 British claim. War was averted, and Britain surrendered its rights even though the Columbia River began far to the north near Sinclair Pass.

Several hundred miles downstream and three hundred miles south by land, Jameson Sinclair ascended out of the Columbia River valley with his squad of explorers. He sang ancient words as he walked beside Abraham, his gray mule, who pulled a modified rickshaw that carried their dried food, some water, and the Odin stone.

The five men with him had long ago proven their worth, and they needed no explanation or justification for his strange behavior. They all fanned out a hundred yards ahead, behind, and beside him, rifles at their shoulder. Only Donald McBain remained close enough for a conversation, and his purpose was only to coax the mule along the path.

In his hands, Jameson Sinclair held a sketch of the area. For the better part of a millennium, his ancestors had explored along the 44th Parallel North even when it wasn't known by such terms. The ancient maps had told them how to calculate the angle based on stars at certain times during the year, and somewhere along the line, the lost kingdom of the original alchemist waited to be rediscovered. Beginning with France, Europe had been explored centuries ago to no avail, and now, after several hundred years, Sinclair had the honor of finishing the search of North America.

Upon finishing a verse from the ancient song, he said, "This is far enough." McBain immediately went about his duties. Soon there would be no more places left to search, and despair entered his heart because the quest might have all been a lie or misunderstanding. The other men all paused, taking a drink from their canteens while Sinclair prepared his offerings to the ancient gods.

Odin gave his life twice to begin the quest, so Jameson Sinclair did not grumble about the duty his family had given him. As the fifth son, he would not inherit the family business or even be a presider in Eos. He was a footsoldier, a priest. When Odin died the first time, he returned from death with secret knowledge—the runes. Even though the broken Odin Stone was only a piece of a much larger prophecy, it was proof the gods once existed.

*In the Ragnarok—*

Jameson Sinclair hesitated at the next verse of the ancient song. Sitting in the Rocky Mountains, he understood how mighty the war between the gods and the giants had once been. The world had been broken following the final death of Odin, and in the Oregon Territory, he sat upon one of its greatest wounds, a fissure in the earth where stone buckled up high into the air. The Christian texts told of a great flood four-thousand years earlier. Many other religions, including those of the local tribes in the Rockies, shared similar narratives. Modern scientists now assessed that the event happened much, much longer ago. *How long have the Men of the Dawn been searching?*

Sinclair continued the ritual and song, letting his offerings to the mountain merge with the air.

In the Ragnarok, the gods and the giants perished in battle, but four gods fought against the fire giant Surtr as the world buckled around them. Thanks to Odin, the humans were safely protected, but the four surviving gods were buried alive—somewhere on the planet. Ancient magic would be needed to wake the gods, and the most powerful tool had been buried along with the gods. His ancestors believed the ancient kingdom existed along the 44th parallel north, and the magical song written upon the black stone could awaken what has slept for countless years.

When the song ended, Jameson Sinclair lifted his eyes to the sky.

Nothing had happened.

Another failure.

The only difference today was that one of his men was walking up toward him.

"What's wrong?" Sinclair asked.

"I heard shooting in the valley below," his personal guard told him. "I think they're attacking our base camp."

Sinclair left cattle, supplies, and two dozen men, women, and children below at a primitive log cabin fort they'd built last fall. It was the only shelter north of Walla Walla.

"McBain," he said, turning to the youngest member of their party, "stay up here until things are settled. You know where to go if I'm killed."

Sinclair and his four riflemen hurried back down the valley back toward the Columbia River.

Once they reached a ridge overlooking the complex, he saw three-dozen natives around the perimeter of the shelter. "Who are they?" he asked. "The Cascades?"

His senior bodyguard shook his head. "The Cascades are allied with the Americans in this area. Those natives below are the Klickitats."

"Why would attack our camp?" another man asked quietly.

Sinclair suspected the answer. Even before he left Oxford House years earlier, he knew an old enemy had returned. *Could this attack be the Priory of Ormus wearing the mask of the Klickitats?* "How do we handle this?" he asked his senior body guard.

"If we start firing, we might be able to hit a few of them from this distance, but then they would scatter and harass us for days. They'd either burn us out or starve us out. They think we're down there."

"Trey left this morning for Fort Walla Walla," one of his men reminded him. "He might've heard the attack also and gone to get help."

"Or he was killed prior to the attack," Sinclair countered. "As long as the men in the cabin hold tight, they have the advantage. The Klickitats will run out of ammunition first."

"But then they'll turn to fire."

Jameson knew the log complex had been built with enough firing stations to repel such an attack. It would be a siege of attrition and ammunition.

Sinclair took measure of the situation and slipped behind a small outcrop. "We have an advantage being up here. They don't know about us, yet they have the place surrounded. Before we scatter them, we'll get to the bottom of this. We just need to wait until nightfall."

BY THE NEXT morning, four Klickitats were dead and one woke to consciousness, bound and gagged, in the little alcove of the ridge overlooking the siege. Having spent the better part of a decade in the Oregon Territory, he and his men had gotten to know the local Native tribes, who'd been pitted against each other during the border dispute between Britain and the United States. They knew the wave of Manifest Destiny had crashed against the shores of the Pacific, yet Sinclair knew this sudden act of violence had another motivation.

"Were you hired to attack this outpost?" he asked the bound Klickitat.

The prisoner nodded in affirmation.

"Were you hired by an American?"

His head shook.

"British?" Sinclair pressed.

Another head shake.

"Spanish?"

A third head shake.

*It's the Russians.* Once, the Priory of Ormus had been primarily English while the Order of Eos had been French, but over the past few centuries, both societies had spread into several other nationalities. Rumors of Ormus colluding within the Russian Empire now seemed believable.

"Something's happening below," one of his men called, taking his attention away from their prisoner.

From a hole in the ceiling, two riflemen appeared on the roof of the stockade and wiggled into position. After taking position, though, the roof riflemen waited.

*The men in the cabin are going to make a run for it. They don't even know we're up here.*

The Klickitats were also rattled, discovering their dead and missing. Grouping together, their perimeter suddenly became porous.

*Just wait, you fools,* he wanted to shout to the men trapped in the cabin.

But those inside of the stockage acted in desperation.

Two men with water buckets rushed out of the front door for the river. Either for fire defense or drinking, the need for water necessitated the risk. At first, the dash was quiet, unnoticed, but by the time the buckets were full, gunshots rang out. Bullets struck the ground around them as they ran back. The riflemen on the roof kept the Klickitats from running them down, but a hail of bullets followed them all the way to the door, where one of them fell out of the cabin. They managed to drag him back inside by his heels.

A knife was unsheathed, but Sinclair shook off the retribution. "The fools should have stayed put. The Klickitats now assume men snuck out of the cabin to kill their friends. We'll wait until nightfall and teach them the error of their ways. Until then, we'll interrogate our prisoner."

Jameson Sinclair knew the history of the Oregon territory, but he reviewed it all with Ormus in mind. Nikolai Rezanov claimed to be the first European to be born in the territory, and thus, his presence should have given Russia claim to the Oregon Territory as well as the Alaska Territory. Born along the Columbia River in 1818, Rezanov claimed his grandfather and father already built a permanent home and trading post by the time Captain Gray sailed up the river on behalf of the United States of America.

Even though his testimony was thrown away, Rezanov remained as the land changed ownership. By the time Sinclair and his colonists arrived in the 1840s, Nikolai had established a foothold in the area through trade and marriage, and his influence only grew in the past decade with an unexplained influx in wealth—which manifested itself now in the form of rifles.

*My brother Magnus was right about Ormus playing possum.*

*Rezanov has turned the Klickitats into puppets in order to stop me.*

That night, when the Klickitats descended on the stockage with torches, Sinclair's men descended on their illuminated targets with knives.

When morning came, a surprise waited for all three groups.

Led by Lieutenant Philip Sheridan, a group of soldiers came sweeping in unannounced to rout the Klickitats. In their company, Jameson Sinclair's nephew, Trey Sinclair guided the soldiers to the besieged outpost.

The Klickitat prisoner joined the dead before Jameson Sinclair descended the mountain.

The lieutenant and his sergeant turned and galloped in their direction as if chasing fleeing Klickitats. Sinclair waved at them to make matters clear. The lieutenant trotted up. "Mr. Sinclair?"

*Why would they be looking for me?*

He tensed, fearing a trap.

"Why are you fellows out here?"

"We were ranging north on the Columbia, near the border, when we were given a mission to go find Jameson Sinclair. Lucky for you, we were already heading this way."

"What was the message?" *If the Russian wants me killed, that message has been received.*

In the distance, the cavalry continued to hunt down the fleeing Klickitats, which interrupted the conversation.

The young soldier explained, "There's a situation up at the headwaters."

"The headwaters?" Sinclair said aloud, thinking of where he'd begun his exhaustive search of the territory. *Did I miss something?*

"A friend of a friend, it seems, wanted you to know that a man claiming to be Antoine Clement is building a trading post on Lake Columbia."

Sinclair felt himself grow flush. "Can you describe this man?"

"I was given a description. He's a half-breed. A mountain of a man. A drunkard with a young boy at his side."

*Clement lives?*

When the conflict ended, the cavalry met the survivors inside the cabin, who were hauling out their dead and wounded into the open yard. Sinclair remained a hundred yards from the dazed survivors. Only Trey Sinclair spotted his uncle, who rushed up the hill to greet him with a broad smile. "I thought they'd killed you," he said in reference to the man who'd been shot in the head during the water run.

*Perhaps they did.*

Jameson Sinclair stayed on the mountain slope, summoning Donald McBain, Trey Sinclair, and Lieutenant Sheridan to hear his plan.

The faceless body that had opened the door for the runners would be buried with his name. Trey and McBain both understood the reasons why Jameson Sinclair needed to die. The family was in danger, and to keep further harm from coming to it, he needed his enemies to believe he was dead. So the faceless body would be buried with his gravestone.

*First I will deal with this Russian Rezanov myself,* he decided. The dead in the camp needed their vengeance.

In the north, another enemy needed to be dealt with, and if word leaked out that Jameson Sinclair had perished, the half-breed would lower his guard and turn to the bottle.

*And then I will kill Antoine Clement.*

# CHAPTER 46



Antoine Clement heard about trouble to the south, but he maintained his careful vigil. He also heard the rumor about the death of Jameson Sinclair, but he ignored it. By the time summer ended, the matter would be over and he could return to his other promises.

Life on Lake Columbia had been the second favorite season in his life.

Even though Vaktar Forsberg had no idea what the rumors insinuated, the boy had become like a son to Antoine over the course of the summer. Hunting, fishing, trapping—the boy sponged it all up. Together, they maintained a precise routine. Forsberg departed before dawn to inspect traps, hunt, and fish. Playing the part of an aging drunk, Antoine purposefully let the boy do all the work while he lazily lingered around the cabin, ate breakfast, and drank coffee on the front porch.

Vaktar would disappear for hours, but not just for the obvious reasons. By noon, he'd meet with Sofus Nielson at the stream that fed Lake Columbia to pass on any information to Lord Erskine and the others. By supper, Vaktar would return to the cabin.

Being the bait for a trap left him plenty of time to think about his past.

After fixing supper for Vaktar, Antoine wished the boy a good night's sleep and pulled his chair out to the camp fire to sit out under the stars and think about Jameson Sinclair.

*There's no way he's dead. It's a ruse.* Of all the Sinclair boys back at Oxford House, Jameson had been the cruelest, meanest, and wildest. While Junior had been the calm elder, and Magnus had been the ringleader, Jameson became the enforcer. The older brothers turned him into a bully and then unleashed him upon the world. There had even been news of a funeral, but Antoine refused to believe it.

*No, he's out there.*

Looking up at the stars, Clement found the north star and remembered a promise. The promise had been made to a strange shaman who had not even been part of the tour. He and Stewart had traveled north of Jerusalem to the headwaters of the Jordan River to investigate a foreboding cave. It was after the tour when Clement found a need to privately relieve himself in the thick brush where he found the man sitting under a willow tree beside the little creek.

"I found you," the old man said.

Now, Antoine couldn't remember if the greeting had been in English, French, Cree, or another language he knew. The salutation cut to his core, and he found himself standing before the man, a servant to a new master.

"Who are you?" Clement countered.

"The comparison is blasphemous, but I am also a beginning and an end, an Alpha and an Omega, but only in a smaller part of the story. Come, step forward."

Strangely, Clement allowed himself a moment of vulnerability.

The old man reached up with one hand while clutching the willow with the other. His fingers touched Antoine's sweaty forehead and then inspected the damp tips of his fingers. "It is you, but you've changed. Promise me that you will return."

Clement didn't understand. "I'm on a vacation. I'll likely never return to this place, let alone your country."

"Look. Remember. Do you recognize this willow? Its roots reach far under the earth to a different river and a different cave. You stood upon the roof of his tomb. If you'd stretched out your hand, you could have held the weapon to destroy him and his foul magic."

"Who?"

With his thumb, the old man wiped away the sweat from his fingertips and then held his hand out. "You are the lost heir. Your blood, sweat, and tears can destroy him."

"Destroy who?" Clement had insisted loudly.

"His name is lost to us, for even his living heirs would not utter his name. When you look up at the stars, know that his star is the first of the seven, and from the loin of the beast will come the eighth. Promise me that you will return and claim your birthright."

"I promise," Antoine muttered before hurrying back to Lord Stewart.

He never told Lord Stewart about the surreal encounter.

But years afterwards, the promise to the shaman still haunted him, just like another failed promise to a woman had driven him to alcohol.

Now, he looked up at the constellation commonly known as the Big Dipper. Stewart told him all about the seven stars, including the one known as Merak, the loin of the beast.

*Is that your name? Is the Alchemist's name Merak?*

Clement doubted it. He'd heard other names for the constellation. The Anishinaabe guide Chagobay told a story of the Fisher Cat battling the sorcerer the Wintermaker. His first love, his beautiful young bride, had called it Tun Win, the Blue Woman.

*What does it matter?*

*Who cares about the name?*

Clement had broken his promises. He'd broken his promise about returning to Lake Manitou just as he'd broken his promise to return to his young bride—and his infant daughter.

Vaktar Forsberg ended the long night of broken dreams and promises.

"Did you ever sleep?" the boy asked after seeing him yawn and stretch outside the doorway of the cabin.

"I am haunted by bad memories."

The boy shrugged and began preparing himself for his day in the dim light of dawn.

*I need coffee,* Clement decided and rose from his chair. He loudly began rummaging around, searching for a burlap bag that held the coffee beans.

"I'll be off, then. Hopefully with some of those trout I saw gathering in the pool."

Clement nodded. *Yes, a trout and then a nap during the heat of the day.*

By the time he found the bag, Forsberg was a hundred yards away, rifle on one shoulder and fishing pole on the other.

With the bag in hand, Antoine went into the cabin to fetch the coffee grinder. The boy had enough sense to leave him alone when he was in a foul mood, but Antoine still felt badly that the boy hadn't even waited for breakfast.

*I'll make it up to him with supper.*

When Antoine stepped back into the doorway, a knife greeted him in the belly. He dropped both the grinder and bag of beans in order to grab the hilt before it left his body. He held it there, pinned against his rib just below his beating heart.

He looked up.

The face holding the knife was hidden, for in the distance, the light of dawn created a shadow on the man's face.

"You're looking quite well for a dead man," the shadow said.

*Jameson,* Antoine thought as he held the knife steady.

Eos had arrived.

# CHAPTER 47

LAKE COLUMBIA

1854

Vaktar Forsberg stopped when he realized he'd forgotten his fishing knife. He touched his right thigh to confirm its absence. He was already past the peak and descending the other side of the ridge where the little trout pool waited.

*Dammit.*

Turning back meant the fish would likely see his approach and make them wary, but without the knife, any fish he caught would spoil in the afternoon heat, forcing an early return also.

*Dammit.*

Uncle Dagmar had given him the blade when he was just a child, and for several years, he had to observe the blade under supervision before it finally became his property. The three inches of steel were nothing special, but the hilt had been carved into the shape of a trout with an open mouth. The darker wood of the scabbard had the five fins of a trout, and when sheathed together, it had been a toy as much as a tool.

At the top of the ridge, he could see the little trout pool on one side and their little cabin on the other—and horses.

He froze while he took in the scene. Six horses were tied together behind a little cut in the base of the ridge, hidden from the river floor but exposed from his angle. One man stood beside a strange looking cart.

*Where are the other men?*

Two figures came spilling out onto the ground in front of the cabin.

Vaktar descended in leaps and bounds like a mountain goat when he recognized Antoine as one of the men, but he skidded to a halt when he saw the back of a man also watching the scene.

Another lingered at the river's edge, watching the fight.

They came by night.

Vaktar put the fishing pole against a tree and slipped out of his shirt, setting it on a branch. With his rifle in hand, he quietly moved a dozen yards from where he'd left his shirt and laid on his belly. Cold stone and pine needles brought focus to his mind.

As Antoine rolled on the ground with his attacker, Vaktar put his crosshairs squarely in the center of the closest man's back.

He squeezed the trigger and brought death and thunder to the valley.

*Please be awake, Sofus. Please.*

As the shot echoed, he heard the grunt and stumble from his target, but he remained hidden behind the stone as he quickly reloaded. The first shot had not even finished echoing across the valley when a second shot rang out, the bullet whizzing through the air to strike a nearby tree.

*They killed my shirt,* Vaktar realized, swallowing hard before rolling out to expose himself. The smoke cloud gave him a target, but he rushed the shot and his bullet struck granite a foot to the left of the shooter.

Vaktar dropped his rifle and charged.

He didn't glance once at the nearby shooter but kept his focus on the first man. He knew he had only a handful of seconds to reach the body. At the last second, he did glance up, only to see the nearby shooter finish reloading and lifting the rifle to his shoulder.

Vaktar dove onto his belly with such force that he reminded himself of a boar hog. He'd knocked the wind out of his lungs and tried to ignore the horrifying drowning sensation as he crawled over the pooled blood to where his first kill had dropped his own rifle.

Touching the foreign rifle, he found his second wind, drawing it back into his lungs in a long, pained groan. The dead man's thigh erupted in a splash of blood as the nearby shooter on his right flank rushed his shot.

Knowing he had a moment, Vaktar put the muzzle next to the hair of the dead man's head. At a hundred yards, the shot was challenging, but the morning air was calm. Without knowing the rifle's sights, he aimed low, hoping a miss might ricochet into the man.

The shot struck the man in the center of his hips and dropped him to the ground with a cry of pain.

Two of the three men were advancing—one from the river and one from his left flank.

Blood on his chest, Vaktar left the foreign rifle to sprint as fast as he could to the Alamo. Antoine Clement had explained the significance of the rock depression that overlooked the cabin. He'd used it as a metaphor to explain how a handful of Texans had rallied inside of the stone fort to hold off thousands of Santa Anna's men for days while they waited for Sam Houston's nearby cavalry to arrive. Behind the safety of their stone walls, the men in the Alamo defeated Santa Anna and won the war simply by keeping their heads low and taking careful aim. Santa Anna was trapped between a rock and a hard place when Sam Houston's cavalry came rushing in on the third day of the siege, putting the entire Mexican army to the sword.

A shot fired and a bullet whizzed over his head, prompting Vaktar to zig and zag. Ten yards from the Alamo, Vaktar heard a second shot ring out, and he stumbled violently, somersaulting forward with such force that he almost knocked himself out when his chin struck the stone front of the sanctuary. He had enough sense to ignore the spots in his eyes and crawl forward the last few feet.

He rolled over the natural wall and dropped onto his side out of sight of the riflemen. He ripped off the tarp, opened the rifle case, and pulled out the Manton muzzlcloader.

*Which one do I choose next?*

The gap in the rock decided for him. He placed the muzzle between the two boulders, and in the narrow window, he saw the left flanker take a spot behind a tree. The river shooter had reached the cabin and hugged a wall while he searched the mountain for a shot.

But the man with the horses hadn't taken found a hiding spot yet and only cowered.

*He'll do.*

It was the farthest shot, but he had the trusty Manton, Clement's favorite. As he took careful aim, controlling his breath, Vaktar felt his heart pounding and pain seeping into his concentration. He grit his teeth and prepared the shot.

He squeezed the trigger.

He didn't even wait to see if he made the shot. He set aside the Manton and picked up the Sharps rifle from the case, but in doing so, he looked back to see a toe sitting in a pool of blood.

*Dammit.*

He ignored the pain.

Swift as a prairie dog, he rose for just a fraction of a second before ducking back down out of sight. Two bullets struck the rocks surrounding the Alamo.

In that glance, he saw all he needed. His bullet had hit the man and frightened the horses to such an extent that two broke their reins to follow the startled horse with the strange wagon on a gallop toward the open ground between the cabin and the river. The glance also told him the river watchman had taken aim beside the cabin while the left flanker began a charge up the hill.

Vaktar, knowing it could be his last, let out a breath,

He rolled to a center firing position, again putting the muzzle between two large boulders. He stared down another barrel, but the river watchmen had a blind shot.

Vaktar fired.

He heard footsteps and blindly thrust his hand into the rifle box a third time.

The man roared from behind him and Vaktar's fingers flinched as it touched the hilt of the pistol.

A shot fired, and the bullet bit Vaktar's left forearm and his fingers that still held the Sharps rifle went numb—but his right fingers found a tight grip on the pistol.

Vaktar spun the revolver and fired at the center of the shadow hovering above him. The man's weight descended, crushing him, and Vaktar felt the butt of the rifle strike him twice, but the second and third bullet discharged directly into the man's torso took the fight right out of him.

Even with three shots, the man didn't die immediately, but as the life leaked out of him, he also stopped trying to kill Vaktar, who managed to wiggle out from under the dying man.

Vaktar lifted his left arm to see a forearm bone come through the bullet hole and his left hand dangling limply.

Having chased down plenty of wounded elk, Vaktar remained calm and reminded himself that death would not come immediately. He pulled out his belt and tightened it at his bicep. His missing toe no longer concerned him.

For a moment, he aimed the pistol at the left flanker's head but thought better of it.

*I need these bullets.*

Vaktar stood up and looked around for a moment. In the distance, the horses continued running. He didn't see any men standing, so he rolled his body over the walls of the Alamo. He hopped mostly on one leg, keeping his balance with his good foot. A bullet had gone right through the toe of his boot, taking the two middle toes with it. He tried not to think of his mangled left arm.

At the bottom of the hill, beside the back wall of the cabin, he found the river watchman still alive. He lifted the pistol to the man's face but then lowered it and squeezed off a shot that struck him in the heart.

Around the corner, the first thing he saw was a human ear lying on the ground. Blood trails crisscrossed the spot where Clement had been staring up at the stars just a short time ago.

In front of the porch steps, Vaktar spotted his fishing knife, unsheathed and covered in blood.

The porch railing no longer existed, and the posts that remained were smeared with blood. The two bodies that had crashed into it were a few feet away—motionless.

Antoine Clement had a bloody forehead with a stream of blood running into his left eye and across the side of his nose. From his mouth, more blood covered his chin, his neck, and his chest, where he held a bloodied human head to his chest. At the center of his chest, a splintered shaft of railing post was shoved up under his ribs.

*Wait…that's not Clement's body.*

Stunned, Vaktar blinked again. Clement's powerful left arm wrapped around his attacker's neck, held in a vice by his right hand. For a moment, it looked as if the shard had been part of Clement's body but it was the attacker, lying in front of Clement, who had the post shoved into his chest.

Clement released his left hand, and the attacker rolled off him and onto the deck. Clement was covered in blood with multiple wounds. The most grievous produced bloody air bubbles.

Clement lifted his hand and, despite the blood in his mouth, muttered, "Behind you."

Vaktar turned to see the far right flanker, rifled raised, fifty yards from the cabin. Vaktar had hit him squarely, but like himself, the man pushed his body through the pain to face his foe.

A shot rang out.

It wasn't a miss.

But it also wasn't the flanker's gun that discharged.

The flanker fell face forward, revealing the blonde hair of Sofus Nielson standing with his own hunting rifle at the edge of the trees.

*Sam Houston has arrived*, Vaktar thought, and slid up against the stairs of the porch.

# CHAPTER 48



Professor Corey Morgan threw his blanket aside in frustration. *What is that racket?*

His fingers found the rifle beside his sleeping mat, and when he sat up, he couldn't locate the source of the noise. He'd camped alone, hoping to make the two day hike in one day. The previous night, he'd reached the bluff sandwiched between the three peaks, but the optical illusion of a human head changed with his new vantage point.

Now, he saw three distant choices, and thus, the cave spoken of by the local Shuswap tribe seemed impossible to determine.

*Perhaps I should name them after the Norns*, Morgan thought. In Norse mythology, the Norns were three maidens who not only tended to the Great Tree but also controlled the fates.

The crashing continued.

Morgan stood up, spying a spot in the valley leading to the Columbia River.

*What in the world is that?*

An exhausted horse was ascending the valley, and strapped to both sides, a two-pole gurney dragged behind it.

*Poor thing, you're heading the wrong direction.*

"Hello," Morgan called out softly. "Hey, hey, hey."

The horse took notice, trotted a few more paces, and then stopped.

Leaving behind his small camp, Morgan walked toward the frightened beast, making soft noises to avoid startling it. When he finally drew close, he saw blood splattered on the horse's flank and his heart sunk.

He immediately tried to free the pole cart from the side of the horse, but without a knife, its leather bands were difficult to deal with.

He walked back to the cargo area, which was made of burlap sacks, leather straps, and buckles, which his fingers quickly undid.

Inside he found the corner of a black stone.

Frantically, he pulled away more until he saw strange runes within the stone itself.

*Sweet Jesus, what is this?*

A gunshot echoed, causing him to flinch.

So too did the horse, and in a moment, it bolted ahead, taking the black stone with it.

Morgan began in pursuit, but when he heard the second gunshot, he stopped.

Standing at the base of the bluff, Sofus Nielson lowered the rifle he'd fired into the air. "Professor Morgan! We need you! Vaktar and Antoine are wounded badly. They're dying, Professor Morgan."

Professor Morgan looked back at the galloping horse up the slope. *I know where we're at. It won't go too much farther. I'll see what's the matter and come back for it later.*

THE END OF PART SEVEN

# PART EIGHT

## THE DANUBE RIVER

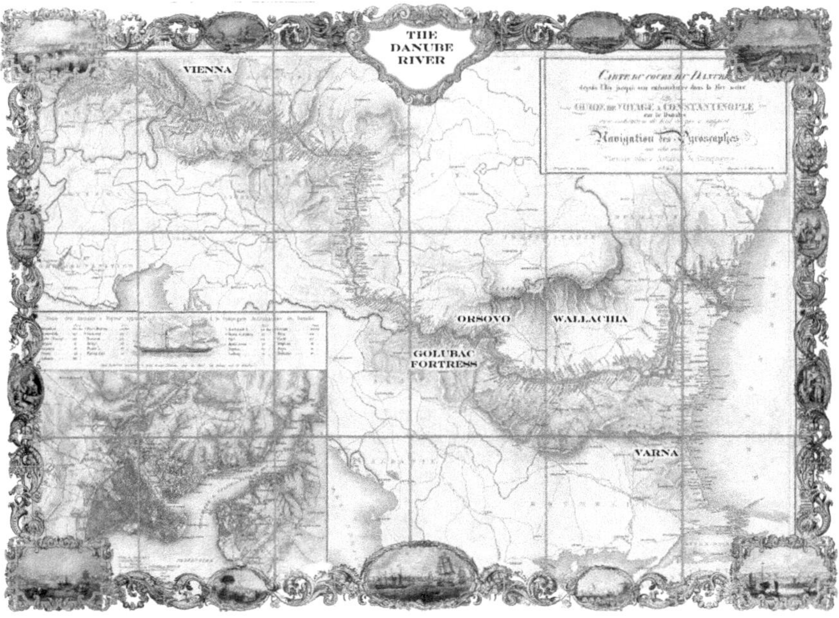

# CHAPTER 49



William Drummond Stewart woke early, slipping out of bed so as not to wake Christina. The sun had not yet come up, but enough light arrived to help him quietly dress without disturbing her.

After spending time in mansions, yachts, and palaces during his life, waking in a small cottage felt like the most secure fortress in all the world. He paused at Karl and Emma's room but then kept walking. He tip-toed down the hallway and stairs and walked to the front door. At the coat rack, he secured his pistol before slipping on his jacket and grabbing his bowler hat.

The cottage was one of a dozen small houses that lined the streets of upper Vienna on the edge of Schweizergarten, a large urban botanical garden on the edge of the city. Stewart flipped up the collar on his jacket to be as invisible as possible. His fingers brushed over the bristle of his shaved head before setting a hat atop his head. The hair of his beard had sprouted to over an inch—effectively transforming him into the image of his father.

*Not a bad place to hide from the world,* Stewart thought as he passed from the row of cheap cottages into the gardens. A college friend of Karl Geyer had taken stewardship of the park and was paid a modest wage to tend to its botanical needs. *Has this quest robbed Karl of his golden years? He could remain in such a place.*

Risking the odds of a miraculous encounter with someone who knew him, they'd chosen Vienna, Austria, as the safehouse for Emma and Christina. From all they learned from their hostage,

Lachlan Morrison, both Eos and the Vendita would likely target the women to get to the men if they dared return to Murthly Castle. The Swiss Garden was as secure and random as either man could come up with.

Hoping to calm his frayed nerves and anxiety, Stewart walked along the outside of the park. He'd spent the previous day writing his last will and testament since he was about to depart the following day down the Danube River and into the lion's den. As he walked, he could not help but think of his son. Two decades earlier, George had been born to a servant girl, Christina.

*Imagine how my life would have been different if I'd listened to my father.*

Thomas, his slain brother, would have become a Cardinal by now.

Nicollet would have arrived at St. Louis, run out of funding, and most likely would have been teaching at a St. Louis University still.

Antoine Clement would have returned from his visit to St. Louis to go back to his young wife and daughter out in the Black Hills. With Clement's French ancestry, he would have served as a guide and buffalo hunter.

*And me? If I'd listened to my father, I would have found myself the fat, arrogant Baron of Murthly Castle after marrying some noblewoman. Christina and George would have stayed servants.*

Instead, William Drummond Stewart fled Scotland for adventures on the American frontiers. George had been born a bastard, and even though Stewart later married Christina and legitimized his bastard son as heir, the boy had never truly been a son to him. George idolized him, but in the way a child idolized Achilles or Odysseus. Having heard tales of the Napoleonic War, George grew up wanting to be a soldier. By the time Stewart returned home from his odyssey, his son left home to begin a career in the military.

*Will my estate please him or curse him?*

Stewart paused, noticing a solitary figure sitting on the grass in the center of the park looking up at the heavens.

*Obviously, I'm not the only one who has things on his mind.*

He kept walking.

From the various newspapers he'd read between the port at Venice and the train ride to Vienna, he learned that his son's military unit, the 93rd Highlanders, were being sent to the region to deal with the growing threat of Russian aggression.

*Do I really believe in coincidence any more?*

Christina demanded that he write their son prior to his departure, but Stewart didn't want anything to be traced back to their temporary home in Vienna.

Stewart's hand went to his pistol inside of his jacket as a tingling sensation descended his spine. *I'm being watched.*

The man at the center of the park was watching him.

And then he saw the man reach for something.

Stewart glanced for cover, just in case.

The man raised a hand and waved.

Instead of reciprocating, Stewart looked to see if assassins were coming out of the woodwork.

"It's me, you fool," a familiar voice called out.

*Karl? What is he doing?*

"Come join me on the lawn," Geyer insisted, patting the grass.

Stewart crossed the lawn, standing over his friend. "Care to explain yourself?"

"I couldn't sleep."

"I know what you mean. Between the yacht and the train, I couldn't help but feel my mind still spinning with motion."

"No, it's not that. I was looking at this garden. I could have had a similar garden back in Germany if I'd stayed. Instead, I had the adventure of a lifetime. Twice. I don't know if I could go back to such a sedentary life. I've decided to accompany you down the Danube."

"But your child? The whole reason for coming here was so you could take care of Emma."

"We still have a few months, and even after that, the child will only be an infant who will only want its mother. If it's a boy, I'm going to name him Nicholas, after—"

"I can't take that away from you. I've wasted my life away from my son. I can't let you do the same. You'll grow to regret it."

"What I regret is that Nicollet died alone in that hotel in Baltimore. If I'd been with him, things would have been much

different. I can't do the same with you. I know you plan to hire men to accompany you, but I can't let you face this danger alone. I've written up my own will and testament. I have a spot for you to sign, if you'd be so kind."

Stewart took the paper and had to hold it against the pale light of the sky to read the dark letters. *Foster?* "You want me to adopt your son if you die? Now you're definitely staying here."

"Emma comes from wealth, but God forbid, if I should die in the days to come, I would not want him raised by her family. Let both of them come to Murthly Estate. Let little Nicholas become your ward."

*Has the old Karl finally returned?* "This is a pointless conversation. I'm getting on that boat later this morning, shaking your hand, and leaving you with the women here in Vienna."

"Sign. Please," Karl Andreas Geyer insisted.

It was good to have his old friend back, and Stewart signed.

# CHAPTER 50



Jamie Anderson watched the naval battle from atop the roof of the yacht. Below him, the passengers and crew of the *Mina* pressed against the railing.

*A battle of the gods.*

Since leaving Murthly Castle, Anderson had read all the stories about gods battling upon the earth only to leave a path of destruction behind. Now, he saw Thor's lightning bolts and the groan of the Midgard Serpent upon the waters of the Black Sea. The captain had doused the ship lights as he approached the battle, allowing those on the *Mina* to watch from a safe distance of five miles.

With Father MacPherson, Frank Penny, Lachlan Morrison, and several crew crowded along the observation deck, Anderson grew frustrated at his stature and improvised.

With the aid of his own looking glass, Anderson climbed to the highest platform, the yacht's roof, so he could see if the gods would smile on their venture.

The port of Varna was the largest port along the western shore of the Black Sea. After parting ways with Lord Stewart in Cyprus, Anderson took charge of the remaining expedition and the yacht, which traveled north through the Aegean Sea and the Bosphorus. At Istanbul, they were detained by the Ottoman Empire, which thoroughly terrified Anderson. The port authorities, however, were not looking for suspects from two unsolved murder sprees within its empire. No, they were preparing for a war with Russia.

*And it looks like the war had begun earlier than planned.*

In the flash of the cannons, Anderson could spot the flags flying from the two naval formations. The distinctive red flag with the white crescent and star made sense. Bulgaria had been part of the Ottoman Empire for the past few centuries. The white, blue, and red flag of Russia, however, should not have been present.

When they'd left Murthly Castle, Russia's border had been north of Moldavia, but now it possessed Moldavia, Transylvania, Wallachia, and Bulgaria—threatening the feasibility of their plans.

Had it not been for a clash of gods, they would have made port at Varna and then traveled another two hundred miles to the delta of the Danube River.

*They'll soon look to me for answers for our next step.*

The Russian fleet was losing badly. Ships exploded. Ships burned. Ships sunk.

Suddenly, daylight arrived in the orchestrated slide of lantern shutters.

*We got too close!*

Atop the cabin, he remained in the shadows as the flood lights came from behind the ship. A siren followed the flood of lights.

Shouts came from the ship that'd sneaked up on them from behind, with one phrase quite clear to Anderson, "Prepare to be boarded."

*An order in English? What does this mean?* To his left and his right, he saw other wolves prowling in the darkness. They were smaller, fast-moving ships that sailed in advance of a larger armada. A second navy had arrived at the Port of Varna.

*England has joined the Ottoman Empire in its war against Russia.*

Anderson peeked around the edge of the roof, careful so as not to fall ten feet to the deck below. A small boarding vessel with a dozen or so soldiers approached the side of the *Mina* with the larger cruiser ready to blast them out of the water.

*I wonder what Lachlan Morrison is thinking of this?*

Frank Penny stayed at the side of the prisoner, who despite his professions of common cause certainly could have caused trouble. For that reason, Anderson did not leave his concealed spot. Traveling with a dwarf certainly would have identified the yacht for concerned parties.

The boarding party, however, only had Russians on their mind. They stomped around the yacht, asked questions, and ended up in the command room speaking to the captain, who explained they were planning on traveling up the Danube River.

"That is not happening," the British officer explained. Anderson realized the plan to reunite with Stewart had fallen apart. Apparently, a squabble in Jerusalem led to the cries of Christian persecution by the Ottoman Empire, leading Russia to "come to the aid" of Christians in Crimea and the Danubian Principalities. Russian armies led by Mikhail Gorchakov and Ivan Paskevich seized the area while the Russian fleet caught the Ottoman Fleet at port. "Now it is our turn to surprise Russia."

The British officer explained how an alliance with Britain and France quickly turned the tide, destroying the Russian fleet and routing its ground forces. "The southern Danube will be an active war zone for the next few months. Best turn around now rather than become a casualty of war."

A few minutes after the boarding party left, the British fleet pressed forward to Varna.

Jamie Anderson climbed down from atop the roof and joined the others in the bridge. When he appeared, all conversations ended. "Explain to me again your theory about Vendita having ties to Russia," Anderson said to Lachlan Morrison.

Lachlan Morrison remained pale and weak following his attack. "It's certainly not an alliance with the Tsar, if that's what you're thinking. Vendita despises monarchies. Just like with the French Revolution, there is a revolutionary element within Russia seeking to overthrow the Tsar. I doubt the Tsar even knows the true danger of the threat, but Mr. Delhut is now far behind Russian lines where we can't reach him."

*I can't let Stewart arrive at the rendezvous all by himself.* "Penny, get the maps," Anderson ordered. Before the two vessels departed Cyprus, Morrison had given them enough details for them to make a plan. Stewart sailed up the Adriatic to bring the women to a safe location in Vienna, which would then allow them to come down the Danube River. From the Danube, they'd reunite at the natural lake where the Danube River narrowed, still a distance from the secret Eos stronghold.

A moment later, they all leaned forward to assess the situation.

"So you don't know where they have taken Mr. Delhut," Anderson assessed, "but you do have an idea where he'd be leading them—once he's tortured."

Lachlan Morrison looked fearful. His loyalty to Delhut was as strong as what Anderson felt for Stewart. "Maybe it's all coincidence, but if the agents of Vendita used Russian aggression to their advantage, it couldn't have come at a better time," Morrison admitted. "Following the collapse of the Roman Empire, Eos needed a new stronghold and the Carpathian Mountains were chosen due to remoteness. As has been the case for centuries, Russia swept through Moldavia and Wallachia, but they went around the region supported by the Order of Eos."

"Transylvania," Father MacPherson said, referencing the map.

"How tough is this Delhut fellow?" Frank Penny asked.

Morrison didn't answer and Anderson lifted his hands in incredulity at the Texan's question. *No one is tough under torture, you fool.*

So Penny commented, "We're in a race, it seems. The kidnapper only leads us by a week or so. It'll take them time to get him to their secret lair, torture Delhut, and then muster a force to go into Transylvania. Each day that Delhut endures torture gives us a day to catch up."

*Ah, we're still in a race to the rendezvous.* "Lord Stewart will be coming down the Danube, which is unfettered by war," Anderson said, pointing to the upper Danube and Vienna. "If we make port at Varna, we could travel by horse behind the current front lines and potentially get ahead of the kidnapper."

Lachlan Morrison nodded. "It's better than risking the lower Danube, but by horse, it'll take us two more weeks."

"Lord Stewart will likely get there before us," Father MacPherson added. "What will he find waiting for him at the rendezvous location?"

Morrison put his finger on the Danube River. "There's only one way to enter our stronghold, and a fortress guards the passage."

"The Iron Gates?" Anderson clarified, seeing the small identification along the Danube River.

"If the Roman Empire could not conquer it, what makes you think Lord Stewart will be able to get past. Get me to the Iron Gates, gentlemen, and I'll do the rest."

*What an arrogant bastard,* Anderson decided, but Morrison's confidence gave him confidence that at least the Russians wouldn't get there first.

*So it'll be a race across Bulgaria.* Anderson began explaining the details of the new route.

# CHAPTER 51



ZAMORA CASTLE, WALLACHIA

1854

Bound in shackles, Solomon Delhut's blindfold was removed by Pyotr Petrov once the carriage came to a halt. "Welcome to Zamora Castle," Petrov announced after keeping Delhut blind and ignorant for the past few weeks of travel.

Mountains filled the carriage window. Since his abduction, he'd tried to keep track of how many miles they'd traveled. Much of that time had been spent locked away below deck, but during transfers, Solomon tried to piece it all together. He knew they'd traveled north from Antioch by ship, and then by river, and finally by carriage. *Have they already found the Eos stronghold?* Solomon wondered, but he had never been there in person. So he asked, "Where in the world is Zamora Castle?"

Petrov's eyes narrowed. He could tell the young man finally felt comfortable. "Those are the Carpathian Mountains. We're on the eastern edge of old Transylvania."

Delhut despaired, knowing the Eos stronghold had been built in the wild mountains deep within the Carpathians.

Zamora Castle did not inspire any fear at all. If anything, it had a pleasant, welcoming air about it. Tall poplar trees, meticulously groomed, encircled the large parking lot, where almost a dozen other carriages were already parked. On the air, the scent of supper drifted out of the large doorways of the castle, which boasted clean, new brickwork. Most of the modern castle was ornamental wall and didn't offer much defense. It did have a three story watch tower with a squad of local Romanian guards manning it, but the castle reeked of wealth instead of power.

"We're not expected, so be on your best behavior until I can properly explain the situation," Pyotr Petrov leaned and whispered into Delhut's left ear.

*This will be where I die*, Solomon decided and knew if the opportunity presented itself, he'd take his life to avoid spilling any secrets he might hold—or to be used in bargaining.

If there'd been a chance to flee, it would have happened back in Antioch. No sooner did the small boat reach shore than three hired assassins joined Petrov, and in an hour, they were gone. By the time they reached the sea, Petrov had a platoon of help. When they reached another port at Bulgaria, Petrov became the commanding officer of almost two dozen men, although none of them were official military of any distinguished country. Now rugged men on horses surrounded the carriage, some still tense and ready and others dismounting to make introductions to the curious staff of the castle who appeared to greet them. Petrov left Solomon in the company of his killers while he walked up to the castle.

After a few minutes of conversation, Petrov returned with a smug smile. "The good news is that I've acquired a table for the feast tonight. Unfortunately, I won't be able to make proper introductions tonight. We're not the only unexpected guests."

The dining hall, with its vaulted two-story ceiling, held almost fifty Russian officers of varying rank, with the lower ranked officers near the door and the majors, colonels, and even two generals seated near the elevated stage area, where a long table faced the hall.

Petrov walked Solomon along the outer edge of the hall to a new table placed a few feet in front of a side door. The rest of the room was already feasting and drinking, and the servants placed table settings on it just as the pair reached it. With Russia at war with the Ottoman Empire and its English allies, it made sense why the English speaking prisoner remained in chains. The servants at Zamora Castle had bathed him and given him a change of clothing for the formal dinner. Since Solomon was still chained at the wrists, Petrov pulled the chair out so he could sit and then sat down beside him. "Quite the sight, isn't it?"

"What's happening here?" Solomon asked of the huge dining hall and assembling guests.

"Since I last visited, quite a bit. Russia sent an army of over 200,000 to steal the Danubian Provinces from Ottoman Control, believing the region to be ripe for the taking, which it was. A few years ago, there was a revolution in Hungary that gave Russia a taste for the wealth of the region, and with the decline of the Ottoman Empire, they decided to seize the lower Danube a few months ago. It didn't go well. What they didn't anticipate is that the western powers of France and England would back the Ottoman Empire. These jovial gentlemen dining here today are in full retreat after learning England and France have brought armies and navies into the Black Sea."

*English and French armies might allow me to find my way home*, Delhut realized as he found a ray of hope in his despair.

Delhut flinched when an unexpected figure appeared looming over his shoulder.

"My apologies, dear," a young woman said, placing a hand on his shoulder and pecking him on the cheek. She then leaned over to kiss Petrov on the lips in the familiar way of former lovers. "I'm so happy you've finally returned," she said.

"Lady Zenaida," Petrov said as if he didn't expect her, "you've returned as well."

"How could I be abroad when there is so much happening in the region. Who is your friend?" Even though the young woman spoke in English, she had a Russian accent.

Delhut looked over to Petrov, who shrugged. "You're with friends now. Introduce yourself."

Solomon knew he was in a pit of vipers but remained cordial nevertheless. "My name is Solomon Delhut, I'm a businessman from America." He then raised his cuffed hands and gave an apologetic shrug.

"He's also one of the Grandmasters for the Order of Eos," Petrov explained.

The young woman gasped with thrilled understanding, and then turned to Petrov with a respectful nod. "You've done *very* well. This is going to save hundreds of thousands of lives."

*They mean to torture me for specifics about the stronghold,* Delhut realized. *My death saves them a military invasion.*

"That's what went through my mind as I held a pistol to his head," Petrov said. "Imagine if I'd killed him as ordered."

"Oh, this is quite fortuitous," Zenaida clasped her hands and turned. "I'd like you to meet my companion, Koot Bessant, from Tibet."

"Yes, we met about a year ago during my last visit."

"Ah, yes, he was instructing Lady Columbia, wasn't he?" Zenaida said as Bessant nodded in confirmation. "After my visit to Wallachia, I plan to return with him to Tibet."

Petrov scoffed. "You've lived a thousand lives in two decades. When I last saw you, you were marrying that Russian fellow."

"He bored me. That marriage only lasted a few months before I met a delicious Hungarian opera singer who took me on a tour of the Mediterranean. Then I met—oh, Mr. Delhut, you'll like this part. In Egypt, I met an American named Albert. He quickly bored me also, but not before he brought me to America to meet some of the Indigenous shamans who spoke of something called the Seven Fires. Are you familiar with this prophecy, Mr. Delhut?"

Even on an empty stomach, Solomon felt as if he'd vomit. His forefathers had followed the Seven Fires migration of the Chippewa from Montreal to his current home in Detroit. It seemed his enemies knew as much about the lore as he did. He nodded as he tried to find words. "I live in Detroit, which was once home to the Chippewa people. I believe their legends tell of such a prophecy."

"I was only able to meet with those who remained in Nova Scotia. It was a rather disappointing experience, to be honest; unlike the Tibetans, who have practiced their religion unchanged for thousands of years, the poor shamans I met were like dogs beaten by the stick of Christianity. They certainly didn't know what to think of me."

*That's understandable,* Delhut thought as he studied the eccentric young woman.

"Can we join you for dessert?" Zenaida said to Petrov. "When I heard you'd returned, I couldn't wait to see you. Do you know what's happening here tonight?"

"Yes, I was briefed. I wanted our guest of honor to…witness it." Petrov continued to produce a dimpled smile but his eyes glanced to the doorway behind them. The Russian elites had drivers and escorts, but Zamora Castle conscripts provided the rest of the security, along with the killers brought by Petrov.

On the elevated stage, servants appeared and began to bring the desserts and fill the glasses with wine. Both Petrov and Zenaida turned their attention to the empty table. A servant brought the two generals from their smaller tables to the grand table on the stage.

"She's arrived," Zenaida said softly.

Delhut could tell from the way the servants buzzed around that a guest of great importance was waiting in the wings. He looked around to see the reason for the sudden energy. Even the two Russian generals seemed excited by the build-up.

A beautiful woman in a red, silk gown appeared, and when the generals rose, the rest of the room, including Zenaida and Petrov, also rose. Petrov tugged on Solomon's chains to get him to also stand. The woman glided over to the grand table, took a glass of wine, and lifted it high. The room grew silent.

"There is a reason why all things are as they are," the red woman began. "And I welcome you men into the house of my husband, Count Kouzenas. Let us drink to his memory and to the blood alliances that bring us together today. To Count Kouzenas."

The toast was made but Countess Kouzenas did not sit.

"Years before I met my husband, I was witness to another alliance. My father, a nobleman from nearby Transylvania, knew the importance of alliances, and on behalf of Czar Alexander, forged a political marriage with my mother, the Princess of Baku. Decades ago, this moment of alliance was forged to strengthen Russia. So let us drink another toast. To my father's ambitions."

The Russians appeared to be appreciative of their local hostess's sentiments.

Countess Kouzenas still did not sit.

"As a young girl of seven or eight, I was visiting my mother's home in Baku. My mother's people, a strange land of fire-worshippers, were superstitious. That was the day I met a man who changed my life forever. He was a tall, handsome modern man of science who understood that Baku was not special because of its fire-worshippers but because of its petroleum reserves, which could help make Russia a powerful nation—if it gave up its superstitious and antiquated ways."

Suddenly, Zenaida stood up from the table, raised her glass, and addressed the Countess with, "To my Lady Columbia!"

Delhut shivered as he felt a cold chill run down his spine, and beside him, Pyotr Petrov gave a cold look.

The Countess lowered her head in humility and gave a slight shake of her head. "You must excuse the enthusiasm of my friend."

Several men chuckled at the unexpected enthusiasm.

The Countess continued, "This night is not about me; it is about honoring the past, and honoring old alliances. My husband and father made alliances with Russia, and so, in your hour of need, these alliances have sheltered and fed your weary armies and have given you access to this castle. Alliances must be carefully cultivated since change does not happen all at once. In order to shape the future, careful pruning must be done, and that stranger who came to Baku years ago understood such things. Even though I was just a girl, I swore myself to him, for I knew *his* vision of the future was the only thing that could save humanity from itself. So I'd like to make a final toast. Another toast to honor old alliances. To Joel…Robert…Poinsett."

The Russian crowd, not knowing the name, did not give the third toast the same enthusiasm but finished the wine nevertheless.

*I'm already dead, aren't I?* Delhut knew the name of the man killed by Nicollet's allies and felt as if the guillotine had already dropped upon his neck.

The Countess, however, glided right past her place at the table and out the side door. No sooner had she stepped out than a line of waiters holding dessert trays streamed through the doors. They waited at each table to serve the final course.

Pytor Petrov cleared his throat, speaking in a soft voice to Zenaida. "Now you may make your toast."

"To my Lady Columbia, a light in the darkness!" Zenaida shouted with such fury that the soldiers recoiled in disgust.

The silver domes were removed from the dessert trays. Knives flashed. Blood sprayed. Chaos ensued.

*The wine was drugged,* Delhut realized when none of the officers moved swiftly enough to avoid their fate. None on their table had partaken. The slaughter was comprehensive and without mercy. Extra guards appeared at the doorways, preventing anyone from escaping. The few men who did not drink the wine rose, only to be struck down by riflemen from second floor alcoves.

Outside, cannons thundered.

The retreating Russian army had fallen into a deadly trap.

Petrov stood and pulled the chain to bring Delhut to his feet also. A wide-eyed Zenaida stood beside them, still holding her cup, a horrified grin on her face. Bessant still sat motionless at the table.

Petrov turned to one of the guards standing at the door. "She wants their hands taken to make her Anath garlands. See to it her wishes are fulfilled. We'll be traveling to the Raven's Nest immediately."

Then Petrov turned to Delhut. "Countess Simona is very excited to get to know you, but first, one more trip before you can rest."

# CHAPTER 52

GALUBAC FORTRESS

1854

The Danube River begins in a field near the German town of Donaueschingen. From the Black Forest to the Black Sea, it flows 1,500 miles through several countries at a rate that would take a leaf floating upon its surface less than two weeks to travel. For commerce and conquest, the Danube had obvious strategic value. One of the most distinctive regions of the river is known as the Iron Gates. The river flows through a narrow gorge between the modern countries of Serbia and Romania. Upon entering the gorge, the river is flanked for sixty miles by mountainous walls.

On the western entry to the gorge is Golubac Fortress. Beginning in the Roman era, the narrow entry point of the gorge developed from a settlement into a key defensive position. The ten-tower fortress is built upon the steep southern side of the gorge and has repelled over 120 attacks throughout its tumultuous history. During the Middle Ages, when the mighty Ottoman and Kingdom of Hungary battled, it was even fortified with a strong chain that stretched to the opposite shore to a rock known as Babakaj.

For William Drummond Stewart, the Golubac Fortress had another special significance—it guarded the gateway to a sacred vault. From the "Hat Tower," the tallest and oldest of the ten independent towers within the complex, Stewart could see his private yacht and recently hired Austrian brute squad docked a few hundred yards from the complex. Karl Andreas Geyer slowly and steadily climbed the narrow path leading to the tower, where Stewart had been alone for the better part of two hours.

While the fortress still had a looming presence on the still waters of the gathered Danube, an even larger hill loomed behind the rocky peninsula. *A modern artillery team could make quick work of this old girl.* For this reason, the Serbs left a few token military units, who readily accepted donations from touring aristocrats.

Looking north, Stewart could see Romania and the turbulent waters of the Iron Gorge. *Somewhere along that north shore is Morrison's road.* Prior to departing Cyprus, Morrison had given them the approximate location of the Eos stronghold, and then the men chose this location as a rendezvous. *Apparently, I arrived first. I hope all is well with the others.*

Huffing and puffing filled the air, drawing Stewart's attention. Geyer was red-faced and sweating. "What are you doing climbing all the way up here?"

"I found something very interesting," Geyer said and then had to catch his breath. "You'll like it. It's an old map." Geyer took another moment to catch his breath. "Hoo, that is a climb."

"If you're going to be chasing after a toddler soon, you're going to need to be in better shape."

Geyer rolled his eyes. "But imagine the stories I'll be able to tell in front of the fireplace."

"So what have you brought me?" Stewart asked, turning to confirm they were alone.

Geyer had something resembling a quiver strapped to his back. "The local historian and I had a nice conversation last night. I asked him to tell me about the history of Transylvania, and he shared some local lore. First, he connected the region to the Goths, and how not far north of the Iron Gates, a great war was fought between the Goths and the Huns. Even though the Goths faded into oblivion and the region became part of Hunnic Empire, he said there were pockets of Goth territory that never submitted. Of course, the rulers of these lands changed hands dozens of more times, but this area in eastern Transylvania remained a stronghold for the descendants of these Goth kings."

"Kings?"

Geyer nodded his head. "Of course, they used the term Voivod, which simply means commander, but what interested me is the fact that there were originally seven voivods in this remote Gothic region."

Stewart chuckled at the symbolic detail. "Of course. Why should this surprise me?"

"Oh, it gets better. These seven Voivod? They called their alliance the Order of the Dragon."

"Bloody hell," Stewart muttered. *Who needs Morrison? This place was easier to find than I expected.*

"Oh, and that's exactly what trespassing armies discovered. Curiously, these Gothic Transylvanians were funded by western foreigners, who helped finance the construction of their castles, but along with money, they sent out their builders—a secret guild of masons."

Stewart chuckled again, rubbing his gray beard. "Mmm…let me guess. Sometime around the 1100s?"

"Yes, the height of Templar power. All seven castles were constructed during this time in the most remote, rugged territory imaginable. The land held little wealth, few people, and limited resources, yet unimaginable funds went into these locations."

*A perfect fit,* Stewart decided. "The fortresses were meant to guard—not to conquer or advance power. It's why nations swept right around them."

"When I told my new friend where you were from, he said that it made sense."

"Why does it make sense?" Stewart recoiled.

"He said that for hundreds of years, young Englishmen would come down the Danube to Golubac, claiming they were skilled ballista men sent to guard castles in Transylvania. They would camp here until the Transylvanian escorts came to take them to their posts. For generation after generation, these young men would arrive but were never seen departing." Geyer took out the map, unrolling it.

On it, Stewart saw a medieval map on the Iron Gates gorge with the pool at Golubac at the western side and the Iron Gates at the eastern. Seven stars seemed to indicate the location of the seven castles belonging to the Order of the Dragon, which now

seemed obvious; it is as if the Carpathian Mountains were the spine of the great reptile. Stewart pointed onto the map. "This where Morrison meant to take us? It seems too much like a trap."

"I agree. Look here," Geyer said, putting his finger upon the northern shore of the Danube. It was a road that led into the heart of the Carpathian Mountains.

"That must be it. That must be Morrison's Road, and the Order of the Dragon is certainly controlled by Eos loyalists. How else do you explain the English ballista men?"

"What are Goths if not Old Saxons? Anglo-Saxons?" Geyer said. "If I were Eos and I had the bodies of five of the seven kings of Armageddon, I would invest all my money into the greatest treasure vault money could buy."

"Should we go take a peek at this mountain road?" Stewart offered. *Perhaps we'll intercept Delhut before he arrives.*

"Without Anderson and the others? They're sailing upstream at this minute."

"Unless Morrison betrayed them already. Or they ran into trouble. I don't care about saving Solomon Delhut as much as I care about finding the cache of kings. After all we've learned about Eos, I can't imagine a world where *their* prophecies come true."

"Neither can I. Our Austrian mercenaries are bored out of their minds. We could buy horses and explore a little. The map indicates it's no more than ten miles from here."

"With the chaos happening in the east with Russia, it might be our only opportunity to travel without drawing attention to ourselves. If we can find it without bringing Morrison, we could catch them ill-prepared. It might be our only chance to surprise them."

"It has the makings of another fireside tale, doesn't it?"
*Oh yes, Let's go see this Dragon.*

# CHAPTER 53



The shooting stopped. Even while asleep, Captain Stewart knew what it meant—an assault was coming—and dreams of an older trauma filled his mind.

A pile of dead friends were stacked in the corner—men missing pieces of skull after catching bullets while firing through the stone windows of the farm house. A few men remained at the windows firing at the French advancing from the south. Looking around the farm house, Stewart didn't even know most of the men. The Battle of Waterloo had been such chaos that fear drove them to band together to make the stand. Beyond the farmhouse walls, Napoleon waited to devour the world.

Stewart rushed down the stairs to the main floor, where more bloody men were stacked against the inner walls, dead or dying. Sergeant Lewis Cairns was one of them, and he had lost so much blood that he could no longer stand. Luckily, his eyes followed Captain Stewart from the stairs.

"Supplies coming in," a soldier shouted.

*No! It's a trap.*

Two doors opened.

The first was the north gate, which had been the place where the retreating English forces had supplied the valiant company who'd stayed at the stone farmhouse to hold off the entire French Army. With a provisioned sniper in the well tower, any French soldier who dared scale and drop over the wall was shot dead before taking three steps. A hundred dead Frenchmen revealed the accuracy of the sniper. Only four men manned the big cattle gate built into the stone wall. When it opened, a solitary wagon of ammunition from nearby Allied Ridge was rushed through—but it was too late. The French had sent a squad on a suicide mission.

At the same time the wall gate opened, the door of the farm house opened, and Stewart saw the horror of the French plan. A monster with an ax came around the corner, bellowing and charging through the void. Behind him, his squad followed, overwhelming the gatekeepers and rushing for the farm house.

The farmhouse door slammed shut, but a few seconds later, the ax head broke through the door.

And again.

And again.

When the entire door seemed about to come off of its frame, Stewart put his shoulder into the splintered pieces of the door.

This was when Stewart had a full head of hair and a mustache that tapered in little horns.

*My God, I was so strong back then,* Stewart reflected on the life-altering moment.

But it wasn't nearly enough to hold back the French giant.

The door suddenly exploded with fury, catching Stewart in the face, tossing him backwards and pinning him against the wall.

He heard roaring and screaming. The door had broken his nose, blinding him with blood and pain for those first few seconds. When he wiped away the blood from his eyes, the giant stood in the center of the room, taking limbs with each swing of his ax. French pistol men stood at his side, but half of the shots were fired into deadmen.

Between the door and the wall, a bayonet rested, and Stewart's fingers wrapped around the handle. With his shoulder, he shoved the door closed, placing his foot against the bottom.

The slam of the closing door caught the giant's attention, and when he turned, Stewart already had the sword in motion.

Now, when he looked at the giant's face, all he could see was Antoine Clement, even though that had not been the case back in 1815.

*Is that why I took notice of him?*

*Did Antoine remind me of the French giant?*

Back on the frontier, Stewart had almost gasped when he first witnessed the brutish hunter. Now his subconscious revealed the origin of his fixation on Clement.

This time, in his familiar dream of that fateful day during the Battle of Waterloo, the giant who looked like Clement muttered a final phrase before he died, "Sacre Bleu."

The giant's head came off with relative ease, just as it had done years earlier, but when it hit the ground, it rolled over to reveal a different face—a bearded face. The stranger still had Clement's eyes.

His nightmare of Hougoumont began to crumble into nonsense. While he still saw Jamie Anderson, the last of the surviving Frenchmen who'd entered the farmhouse cowering with his regimental flag, his nightmare of that day transformed when a second squad of figures appeared. A sinister man with a black hat adorned with raven wings held a pistol. A tall, wiry man with piercings, tattoos, and green hair stood beside the sinister man.

A chubby teenage girl, with white objects shoved into her ear canal stood with an open mouth and horrified eyes. With disgust in her eyes, she muttered to Captain Stewart, "You killed him. Now there is only one."

Another figure approached, a young woman obviously Indigenous but with mixed features of the Sioux and Chippewa. She stepped forward, kneeled down beside the beheaded corpse, and picked up the giant's head. As soon as she cradled it in her hands, it burst into flame, blinding Captain Stewart so that he had to look away.

*This isn't real, and it isn't memory.*

*Wake up!*

When Lord Stewart opened his eyes, the bright light of the flaming skull had transformed into the moon.

*It's night.*

*I'm an old man now.*

*I'm camping on the hill overlooking the village of Baile Herculane.*

Stewart's heavy breath caused Karl Andreas Geyer to roll over on his sleeping mat and fart loudly in the quiet night. Their brutes camped just a bit farther down the hill.

*Is this an omen that Clement is dead? What's happened on the other side of the world?* Stewart realized he might not ever learn, nor would Antoine learn of what happened to him if they failed.

An afternoon ride up the mountain pass had turned into a fifty-mile tour of the Carpathian Mountains, which were slightly smaller than the Rocky Mountains in America. The Carpathians were certainly beautiful, but in his imagination, he'd turned the secret stronghold of Eos into a landscape where evil dripped from the rotting trees. *I'm almost disappointed by it.*

As Lord Stewart sat up, his reality quickly came back to him as memories of his nightmare faded away. From the shore of the Danube River, they followed a small stream that was marked on Geyer's map. A village named Ravenesca drew them five miles up the path and a few more miles up the slopes of the Carpathians.

Having been to the Goth city of Ravenna, coincidence could not be overlooked. Either Morrison had been lying or they simply hadn't found the right location. Ravenesca did not hold a secret Eos vault filled with dead kings.

Fortunately, all was not lost, for the villagers had welcomed and fed them.

Instead of returning to the rendezvous location, Stewart, Geyer, and his Austrian team of hired mercenaries decided that with beautiful terrain and good weather, they would press forward to another castle on the map in the nearby village of Bania, a city built in a large valley between high mountains.

War, the villagers explained, had destroyed their Saxon castle centuries ago.

At that point, Geyer speculated that the looping path was only fifteen miles from another of the seven castles that gave Transylvania its Germanic nickname. Baile Herculane was only a short distance to the Iron Gates, where Jamie Anderson and the others would soon pass.

Now, waiting for the day to arrive, Stewart reviewed what he knew and tried to form a plan. To pass the time, he did pushups and squats to wake his body. When he lost patience at waiting alone and another Geyer fart, Stewart kicked him with the toe of his boot. "Let's get going. The sun will be up soon, and I want to return by noon."

"I was dreaming of Emma," Geyer complained with his eyes still closed.

"I was thinking about the name of this village," Stewart began when Geyer groaned and slowly woke up. "You're familiar with the legend of Hercules—the legendary demigod hero. I wonder if it could be a metaphor for one of our guys. A legendary hunter? Sounds like Nimrod, doesn't it? The fact that the locals had six statues in this remote corner of the world is a bit peculiar."

"You're reaching," Geyer said, rolling over. "Hercules is just Hercules. After the Romans defeated Burebista and conquered Dacia, they pissed out a couple statues here to mark their territory. Are you going to next suggest that Baile has a connection to the Canaanite god Baal?"

*A connection to Anath and Ramses.* "Does it?"

"No."

"The statues were interesting, though. Don't you think so?"

"I think I'd like to get some more sleep. It's still night. Go back to sleep."

*Disappointing.* After speaking with Lachlan Morrison, everything about Transylvania made sense, but since crossing the Danube, nothing about the rugged region gave indication that it was the secret abode of Darkness.

For a moment, he returned to his nightmare about the giant Frenchman, wondering what it meant—and then he heard a howl. Followed by another, closer.

Geyer sat up with a gasp. "You don't suppose that was a—"

"Wolf? Yes, I think it was."

A third howl brought the Austrian mercenaries to attention as well, and they began to load their weapons. Most of the howling came from the east—toward the rugged Carpathians. Then, a few howls came between the camp and the village below.

"Those bastards are surrounding us."

One of the Austrians fed the fire, another frantically loaded his weapon, and a third turned to Lord Stewart to say, "Climb the trees."

"I'm an experienced hunter," Stewart insisted.

"Then shoot from the trees. They're coming."

Geyer studied his rooted options and picked one with lower, thicker branches. Stewart found another, a younger tree with branches that would let him climb to safety. He rushed over to help Geyer into his perch when he saw the man struggling.

"I don't think I told you about the legends surrounding this region," Geyer said, breathing heavily as he found a place to stand in the crook of the old tree.

Stewart had to jump to reach his branch. Unlike Geyer, who wasted away on wine and cheese, Stewart was still robust for a fifty-year-old man. Once his fingers wrapped around a branch, his stomach muscles were able to pull his hips up until his feet wrapped around the tree branch, and like an opossum, he pulled himself up the tree.

Geyer often chatted nervously when afraid. "Herododus claimed that the people in this region were werewolves, men who were capable of shapeshifting at night. You don't suppose the villagers turned into wolves?"

Stewart ignored Geyer. The mercenaries began lighting branches, throwing them into the perimeter to expand the amount of light in the darkness. Suddenly, eyes appeared.

"Lycans, they were called," Geyer continued. "It's said that Burebista went into battle with a giant white wolf at his side. The locals are said to worship Zalmoxis, a man made into a god who lives in a cave. He wears no clothing or armor and it is said that no weapon can hurt him."

"I'd rather face a naked man than those damn wolves," Stewart said.

One of the mercenaries fired off a shot, and the sharp whine proved the wolves were not mythical beasts, but a moment after the wolf stopped whimpering, the interlopers doubled in volume.

*Hundreds of them.* "Climb! Quickly!" he shouted to the men below. Only one mercenary climbed a tree.

The others held their ground, but the wolves began to prod the perimeter. Staggered shots rang out, but emboldened by the size of their pack, the wolves risked a few to test their prey.

The attack came suddenly.

A throng of twenty wolves ran right through the center of the camp, ignoring the gunshots. They bull-rushed one of the

mercenaries, dragging him screaming into the darkness. Three men ran for the trees, but they'd no sooner turned their back on the wolves than they were grabbed by their dangling feet and pulled into the darkness.

With the scent of blood in the air, the attack grew more frenzied, and soon, the pack grew louder than the gunshots. One of the mercenaries managed to get into the tree, but all the others were cut off, swarmed, and killed.

Then the wolves tried to climb the trees.

Geyer was vulnerable, for the split in his tree was only ten-feet high, and with a running start, the wolves could jump into the crook. Whimpering, Geyer climbed higher, his arms and legs wrapped around the tree, but he left his former standing place open.

A wolf jumped into it, taking a moment to find its footing. It turned to see Geyer's foot just above and grabbed hold.

Stewart's shot hit the beast in the flank, but its teeth did not let go, and as it fled the tree, it tried to jerk Geyer along.

For a moment, the wolf hung suspended, but Geyer's grip held strong, and the wolf took only his shoe to the ground below.

*This is not how I wanted to die!*

For the next two hours, the wolves feasted on the hired Austrian mercenaries. When dawn arrived, the forms of two hundred wolves surrounded the camp. They eyed the tasty morsels in the tree, but then their ears perked and the entire pack turned toward the river valley.

*The villagers must've heard the shooting.*

Half of the wolfpack retreated. The other half rose and began a new hunt.

Thunderous gunfire erupted, followed by the sound of galloping horses. Those wolves who'd rushed toward the horses ran for the deep mountains at full pace.

In the dim light of dawn, Stewart saw the large shapes of mounted horses coming up the valley. Although outnumbered 4 to 1 by the wolves, the mounted cavalry had bayonets and pistols, decimating the wolves that remained.

The riders flowed right around the camp.

A second wave followed and slowed.

An officer took assessment of their bloody camp and the three survivors in the trees. Then he began barking out orders in Russian.

*Russian? Not exactly the rescue I'd prayed for.*

# CHAPTER 54

ORSOVA, ROMANIA

1 8 5 4

Eight miles south of Baile Herculane, Ross MacPherson could hear a battle raging up the river valley. The constant pop of rifle fire sounded at the break of dawn, and by noon cannon fire brought thunder to the clear sky. Behind him, the Danube River formed a large pool fed by the Cerna River at a place where the river bent back south and away from the Carpathian Mountains.

*We've arrived too late.*

Having found a pack of Austrian mercenaries waiting at the rendezvous point back at Golubac Fortress, Anderson took command of the small yacht, and they all ferried to the place where Stewart had headed. Upon landing at Orsova, Anderson and MacPherson went to the locals to find out what was happening while Penny guarded Morrison below deck.

The locals in Orsova said a small Russian army was cutting through the same pass for a surprise attack in an effort to regain its recently lost territories in Wallachia and Moldavia. The battle, therefore, was between local militia and the Russians. There'd been no word of another group transporting a man fitting the description of Delhut.

*So what has become of Lord Stewart?* MacPherson wondered as they returned to the small yacht. The answers remained up the road at Baile Herculane, where Stewart had last been seen alive.

"We need to be careful with what we tell Morrison," Anderson explained once they reached the dock. "He can't know how weak we are right now. We need him to remain our guide."

"What do we say about Lord Stewart?"

"I'm not sure yet, but I do know we can't hide the sound of battle echoing down from the mountains."

So they turned to their prisoner for insight.

Having recovered from his wounds, Lachlan Morrison had grown stronger by the day, which worried MacPherson. Now Morrison returned to a land held by Eos for centuries. To remind himself of the spiritual battle, MacPherson had taken to wearing his crucifix and black attire even though he was no longer a priest. Even though Morrison was personable, he remained a mortal and moral enemy, and for that reason, he remained chained since they knew not who had won the battle up at Baile Herculane. To keep Morrison in the dark, they pretended to have a plan much grander than it was.

Jamie Anderson began the bluff. "Lord Stewart's organizing the Austrian mercenaries, and he's tasked me with supplying the journey. Can you give me a rough idea on how many days I'm going to have to feed a hundred men on horses?"

Believing the bluff about the number of remaining mercenaries, Morrison scrunched his face in thought. "Do you have a map? While I know our destination, I don't know the miles."

Once it was produced, Morrison put his finger on the Iron Gates. "So we're here, and the Carpathian Mountains are the Dragon with Seven Heads."

"From the Book of Revelation?" MacPherson recoiled, having never head the title until now.

"Well, the Order of the Dragon is neither Catholic nor Christian, is it? There's a pass that circles the head of the Dragon, with Ravensca acting as the eyes for the body. About 10 miles up the eastern side of the pass, there is a crossroads. Your hundred men will be watched by the Order of Eos, and when the danger is assessed, word will be passed up and down the spine of the dragon by men who've served Eos most of their adult lives. If attack is warranted, there won't be much I can do to stop the carnage. I know this might sound like a trick, but a smaller force might stand a chance. It could be easily overlooked."

*Anderson's plan worked. Morrison believes we are much stronger than we are.* Father MacPherson nodded at Morrison's suggestion as if agreeing to it.

"And from this crossroads," Anderson said, putting his finger on Baile Herculane, "how far to the stronghold?"

"The Stronghold?" Morrison shook his head. "We're not going to the heart of the dragon. We're working together to rescue Solomon Delhut from Vendita. I'm taking you to one of the seven castles, where we will meet Eos loyalists. We'll need more than 100 men to deal with the rising power of Vendita."

MacPherson vetted the idea with Anderson. "Our primary goal was to rescue Solomon Delhut, but we don't know if he's dead or still a prisoner."

"If Vendita has learned the location of the Stronghold, they could be taking it by force right now."

"So our secondary goal is to stop Vendita isn't it?" MacPherson said aloud.

"Letting Morrison contact Eos could serve that end," Anderson admitted and then turned to Morrison. "How many men does Eos have in the area?"

Morrison shrugged. "Who can say? I know that over the past few centuries, there have been several attempts to take our castles, but the cost is too high for most governments. If Vendita has indeed turned Russia into a pawn, then this invasion could be an excuse to wipe out these Eos strongholds. If we can warn them, Eos will both help us protect the treasures and then we can rescue Solomon."

*But how will we find and rescue Lord Stewart?* MacPherson turned to Anderson and rolled his eyes at the complexity of the problem.

Anderson added, "If Vendita has a private Russian army pushing into the area, perhaps the English forces we saw at Varna will be arriving soon. Do we wait?"

This seemed to panic Morrison. "Ask your spiritual adviser. We need to protect the treasures, don't we?"

*Heretical bastard,* MacPherson thought but agreed with a nod. "We need to act swiftly. Vendita is a greater danger to humanity at this point than the Order of Eos."

Morrison guffawed at his answer. "You boys saved my life and helped get me here. I won't betray you when this is done. I might even let you see the treasures before I ship you home under threat of death if you ever leave that home again. If you're truly Godly men, you'll trust your Lord to bring his prophecy to fulfillment. I guess we'll see whose god is better at making promises."

MacPherson ignored the taunt. Morrison was indeed a snake that would bite them given the right opportunity. "So like us, Eos hires mercenaries to guard over these seven castles."

Morrison nodded. "It was decided generations ago that secrecy was paramount. Poor, desperate boys are sent in, given a castle, and then asked to defend it. It's a proven formula."

"What happens when they grow old?"

"They are given flocks to shepherd. The old men watch the pass, hills, valleys, and mountains."

"So Eos never hires locals?"

"They did once. It was nearly an abject failure. One of the local leaders, Vlad Dracul, ruled over one of the seven strongholds."

"Dracul? The Order of the Dragon?"

"Yes, unfortunately, our locally born hero got captured by an invading Hungarian army. They carried him and his family from Bran Castle to Castle Corvinus. Dracul broke, just like Solomon Delhut will break, and helped lead this Hungarian king into the Carpathian Mountains, where he fought against his former allies."

"The Order of the Dragon…these are all Eos men," MacPherson restated.

"Since the failure of Dracul, all seven castles have been manned by private mercenaries who have no families or local connections. In Dracul's days, the castles were manned by mostly Saxons. Fortunately for us, the Hungarian King Corvinus didn't care about our treasures. He only cared about strengthening his kingdom in advance of the Ottoman Empire's invasion. For two generations, the traitor Dracul and his son waged war on the remaining six Eos strongholds and the invading Ottomans before his reign of terror ended. Luckily, the Ottomans killed his son Dracula in battle, and

Eos gradually retook what was lost." Morrison paused, lifted his shackled hands, and took a drink from the glass sitting on the table. "For the past four centuries, Eos no longer utilizes local help. Mystery and tall tales now protect us better than any military force. The locals suspect dark deeds. Their imaginations have turned the Eos strongholds into the haunts of monsters."

"So Delhut, like Dracul, will be tortured to turn against Eos?" MacPherson rephrased.

Morrison nodded. "But unlike the Hungarians or Ottomans, I'd suspect that Vendita now has some sort of local boss in the area, most likely local born, who is using the Russian army to achieve what Dracul failed to do."

Anderson's brow wrinkled. "So when this Hungarian King Corvinus captured Dracul, why didn't he capture the treasure?"

"That's the way of Eos. This is why it's important that I inform any of castellans. You build a great vault, fortify it, and then bury the treasure in a remote place that no one would suspect. The Seven Castles are shields. When King Corvinus laid siege to Dracul's Castle Bran, all he managed to do was kill some Saxons and gain a hostage. Meanwhile, our other castellans unleashed their men and monsters into the mountains."

"Monsters?"

"Eos grows packs of wolves and whenever scouting parties stick their noses where they shouldn't, Eos unleashes them ahead of our hunters. Armies die by attrition and terror. It's a formula that has worked for centuries now."

*Well, that's all I needed to know. There's no way in Heaven or Hell I'm bringing Morrison any farther than Orsova until I find out what happened to Stewart.*

THE NEXT DAY, Ross MacPherson found himself approaching the remnants of a battlefield. The citizens of Baile Herculane were burying the dead and took little notice when a dozen men rode in from the south.

"Ask them what happened here," MacPherson said to Stewart's mercenary officer.

When he got his answer, he relayed it to MacPherson. "A Russian army came down the pass, hoping to reinforce Wallachia and Moldavia. A local army came sweeping in from behind to crush it."

*A local army? Does he mean Eos?* "Ask him what he means by local," MacPherson instructed.

This answer took much longer. "It was an army of Gypsies."

"Gypsies? Are you sure he used the word Gypsies?" MacPherson asked.

"Local Romani slaves who were liberated and then joined her army."

"Whose army?"

"He doesn't know her name. He knows she is a countess who fights for her people and *hates* the Russians. He called her the Lady of the Light."

*Columbia...*

*Vendita is already here.*

*We might be too late.*

Before MacPherson could explain his theory to the others, two riders emerged from town. One man MacPherson didn't know, dressed in the fashion of their Austrian mercenaries. The other fellow he knew just from his figure—Karl Andreas Geyer.

*Where is Stewart?*

"They took him," Geyer began as soon as he was close enough to be heard. "After the Russians cleared out all the wolves, they withdrew back to the battle. It lasted all day before the shooting stopped. Stewart refused to let me leave my place of safety, and he went down the hill for a better look. That's when I saw them capture him and bring him back to the north."

*And now Vendita has Lord Stewart along with Solomon Delhut.* MacPherson realized he'd now likely need Morrison in the days ahead.

THE END OF PART EIGHT

# PART NINE
## LAND OF THE BLUE WOMAN

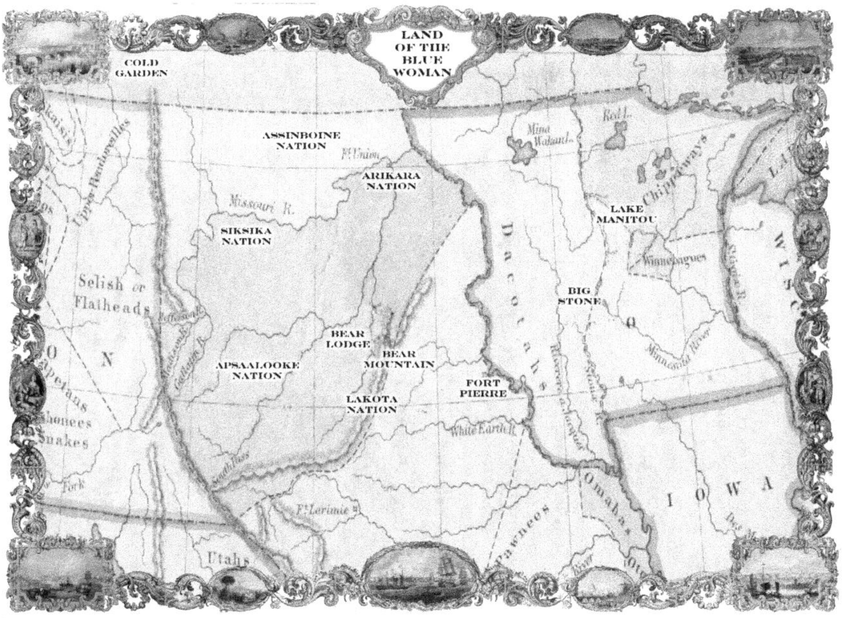

# PART NINE

# CHAPTER 55

C O L D   G A R D E N

1 8 5 4

Sofus Nielson could only watch them dying slowly. He'd wake each morning, hoping to see a change for the better, but each day, infection and decay stole a little bit more from them.

Waking at Cold Garden always brought optimism for the first few minutes of each day. With the mountains behind him to the west, his tent flap opened to the rising sun, which at dawn, illuminated miles of prairie ascending above the horizon.

Facing the same rising un, Professor Morgan sat outside.

"Good morning," Sofus greeted him. "Can I get you anything?"

Professor Morgan shook his head. He'd been serving as doctor for the infirm, a task that seemed to sap the last bit of strength—physically and emotionally—he had. Then he scoffed. "Go find me that stone."

Several days earlier, back at the Columbia River, Professor Morgan did all he could to just stop the bleeding. No sooner had he bandaged a wound than Chief Crooked Arm came riding in to warn that the Klickitat warriors were out in force and heading north. After spending months at Lake Columbia, they were packed and gone by the next day, traveling back through the narrow paths in the mountain to find relative safety back on the prairie. Sadly, Lord Erskine had also fallen ill, an ailment in his bowels. With none of them capable of riding, Crooked Arm left to go get his healers at his camp in the north, leaving them camped at the Bow River.

*Perhaps I can go search once the healers return.*

Responsibility kept the Professor at the side of his patients, but he told Sofus all about the black stone he'd seen carried by horse into the mountains. "Jameson Sinclair hauled it all the way out here for a purpose," he said after they left the carnage of the fight. "We must go back and find it."

Now, they camped a hundred miles on the wrong side of the mountains.

"I'll see what I can do," Sofus said and walked to the tents of the others. The Professor's dedication to his task was admirable, but Sofus worried more about the men.

Lord Erskine sounded the worst. For the past three days, he groaned and moaned for hours on end, stopping only to blast fecal matter onto the rocks outside his tent. He didn't even bother wearing pants, and when Sofus stepped into the tent, Lord Erksine had a blanket draped over his lower body.

"Let me get you some fresh water," Sofus said, "The more you drink, the sooner this will pass."

"The more I drink, the more I shit. In one end, out the other," Erksine bemused.

The cold fire had a kettle of boiled water, and Sofus refilled Erkine's small pitcher. "Get better soon. There are important decisions to be made."

Next, he visited the tent of Vaktar Forsberg, whom he expected to die soon.

Forsberg's lower left arm had darkened, and the veins in his upper arms were inflamed. Since yesterday, his eyes hadn't opened, and his body shivered.

*He doesn't deserve to die so young.* In hindsight, all the pettiness and rivalry between the two now seemed foolish. Vaktar had become like a brother to him. Sofus set a wet rag on his forehead and left to inspect Clement.

Despite the loss of blood and the severe stab wounds, Clement never lost consciousness. He had strength to only whisper, for if he tried speaking in a full voice, his lung wound brought horrible fits of coughing that ended up with him vomiting blood.

"Good morning. Good to see you're still with us."

"How's the boy?" Clement asked.

Sofus sighed at the familiar question. "He's holding on. It'll be a beautiful day. It might do him good to spend it in the sun."

The worst of Clement's wounds was the stab to his lung where Jameson Sinclair sunk his blade at the beginning of the fight. Fortunately, Clement had found Forsberg's filet knife on the edge of a nearby table, and the two mortal enemies pierced holes in each other until one submitted to the will of Death. During the melee, Clement managed to bite the ear off of Sinclair, and in turn, had his defensive arm stabbed four times. He had a sixth wound on his right side, which oozed blood slowly.

His mood, by contrast, remained almost jovial. "Any sign from Crooked Arm?"

"It's still early."

"Did I thank you for saving me?"

"I didn't save you," Sofus claimed. But he had saved Forsberg. Even though Clement had broken the neck of Jameson Sinclair, the final gunman would have killed Forsberg and Clement. "Forsberg saved you."

"I made a promise," Clement began but stopped with a cough.

"Save your strength. Rest for a few more days, and then we'll worry about your promise."

When delirious or dreaming, Clement would mutter bits and pieces about his broken promise, so Sofus understood the seriousness of his vow.

After visiting everyone, he walked back to Professor Morgan. "I'm going to take a horse and see if I can do a little hunting," he said and untied the steed. Before leaving he called out to the Professor, "I'll keep an eye out for your black stone."

The tattered expedition camped two days from the mountains, but along the river and the foothills, game was plentiful, and Chief Crooked Arm left them with plenty of ammunition as well as horses, including one with a travois.

Sofus still didn't like riding, so he led the horse on a new path.

He watched for animals drinking along the river. Today, a pair of large geese lingered in some foliage along the edge of the river, which gave him time to get his rifle ready. When he took the shot, one of the geese flapped its wings erratically, but like Forsberg and Clement, it simply refused to die and flapped off another ten yards.

*Oh, it stopped.*

Sofus followed leisurely, making sure he brought the horse with him, but when he reached the place, the goose had vanished.

*Just my luck.*

He walked into the brush a bit, stumbling at a place where the bank fell away. He almost fell forward into the water but caught himself on a large stone.

*Well, this is curious.*

For a brief moment, he thought he'd stumbled across the black stone seen by Professor Morgan. His foot rested on a stone that looked like it'd almost been carved or cut, if not for the rough edges on one end and a vein of whiter stone clinging to it like fat on a juicy steak.

*Bedrock?*

The river certainly could have smoothed the surface, and flooding could have snapped it off cleanly. The more he looked, the more the rectangle proved to be flawed with grooves and imperfections.

*It could make a nice headstone,* Sofus grimly observed.

It took all of his might, but he managed to haul it up the bank and secure it to the travois. They still had plenty of dried goods, so today, his trophy brought him back early.

*Professor Morgan will think I've found his black stone,* Sofus grinned at his unintentional prank.

A half mile from camp, Sofus stopped the horse.

*Trouble!*

Chief Crooked Arm had left four of his best warriors to stay with them until he returned, and all four men, as well as Professor Morgan, stood armed.

A group of thirty riders stopped in a cluster just in front of the camp.

One of them dismounted and stepped forward.

The burly white man wore the black robes of a Jesuit Missionary.

*Whether friend or foe, I hope he can help heal my friends.*

342

# CHAPTER 56

C O L D   G A R D E N

1 8 5 4

Lewis Cairns rose from bed feeling significantly better than the previous day and thought, *It looks like I live to fight another day.* The medicine given to him by the Jesuit had done the trick. When he dressed, though, he did not dress in the clothes of Lord Wesley Erskine since the ruse was over and Clement had gotten his revenge. Today, he dressed in the clothes of Sergeant Lewis Cairns.

Cairns stepped outside to the cool air of autumn.

The thirty Arikara escorts were camped along the Bow River still, and sitting at the center of the throng, Father Pierre-Jean DeSmet rose and walked over.

From the adjacent tent, Professor Morgan and young Nielson also stood, advancing to him. *They'll look to me for leadership now. How long have I been ill?*

"We managed to save the boy's foot, but the arm had to be removed at the elbow," DeSmet said. "With the infection cut away, the boy is already doing better. Clement, however, survives only by the grace of God."

Cairns extended his hand, and a strong meaty hand shook it tightly. "Lewis Cairns."

DeSmet turned to Morgan with a wry smile. "I was under the impression you were a Scottish Lord."

"Your medicine saved my life. I owe you an honest accounting."

"An honest accounting?" DeSmet scoffed. "Do you know who I am?"

"The boy told me your name last night, but I've known the name of DeSmet for several years now."

"Yes, I am your ally. I've been your ally since before Stewart's family heirloom was stolen and even before Nicollet decided to come to America. I know about the secret war that rages, and I am here to give the Indigenous people a voice in the madness. Even while I'm out here on the *edge* of the frontier, I receive correspondence from the other side of the world. Before I found you, I knew that Lord Stewart had traveled to Rome and how his other companions were traveling west. Your presence on the frontier comes as no surprise."

"Well then, it's an honor to meet you."

DeSmet gave no reaction to the flattery. "Let us go speak with Clement. He should know all that has happened since you parted ways with Stewart."

Cairns turned to young Sofus, "Give us some time to talk privately. Go check on Vaktar."

Nielson begrudgingly followed orders.

Cairns could smell death as soon as the tent opened. Clement was cradled in blankets in a state of undress, allowing his wounds to be tended. Despite the size and strength of the brute, it was clear one of his wounds had become infected. A Bible already sat beside his bed along with other items belonging to the priest.

Clement looked first at DeSmet before smiling in surprise at Cairns. "Ah, good, now we can continue this adventure," he said.

*I hope his vengeance was worth his life,* Cairns thought sadly.

"First, let me provide information about your companions traveling in the East," DeSmet said. Beginning with an account of Stewart's visit to Rome, DeSmet gave a vague accounting of the travels around the Mediterranean, but after last being seen near Antioch, not even DeSmet's network of agents knew where they'd gone.

"We've kicked the hornet's nest," Clement said when DeSmet finished. "We were so hell-bent on revenge and justice for Nicollet, that we didn't think of the consequences. While Eos and the Sinclair family certainly had a part, we didn't understand the influence of one sickly American politician. We should have let tuberculosis kill Poinsett."

"Vendita," DeSmet started, "in Italian, it means *transfer*, which is what happened after Minister Poinsett's death. Power transferred to others within the clandestine organization. The Catholic Church believes Vendita is much different than Eos, and as their name implies, they plan on infesting their enemies so that control can be transferred. Their influence on the Russian government, for example, is already being manifested. Russian agents in the Oregon Territory were already hunting for both Eos and your party. They've already infested Washington with their politics and have even set their sights upon the Catholic Church. We believe their plan has been at work for more than a century, so even Poinsett was only a disciple of their philosophy."

"What do they want?" Cairns asked.

"Strangely, they believe Christ will return but oppose the idea. At the heart of their tenet is the idea that our world is coming to an end in the year 2061, and the only way to fight it is to eradicate the prophecies within mankind."

"They want the map," Clement answered.

"Oh no, it is more than that. Destroying the relics of old certainly helps them, but they want to destroy the system. If they can destroy the Catholic Church, for example, they believe they can free mankind from the impending doom. This philosophy, however, extends to other adherents of the prophecy, which is why they are determined to wipe out the Oceti Sakowin, the Anishinaabe, and any other Indigenous people who do not give up the old ways and accept their modern philosophy."

"So you're not so much an evangelizer as a guardian," Cairns surmised aloud.

The tent flap lifted a bit, and the blonde head of Sofus Nielson peeked in. Behind him stood a very pale Vaktar Forsberg, who advanced with the help of a crutch under his right armpit. His foot was wrapped in a clean bandage, a sign the wound to his toes had healed. His left arm was also bandaged at the elbow, also without seepage. Taking off the boy's forearm and hand had saved his life.

"I'm ready to travel when you are," Forsberg said to Clement, who grinned at the suggestion.

"It seems as if I am the only one holding us back," Clement said, smiling through his pain. "My recent brush with death has only motivated me to remember a promise I made long ago. I mean to fulfill this promise, too, with the help of my friends."

Cairns looked around the room. They all understood that Clement was dying and that no known doctor could stop the infection from claiming his life. Denying him would take away all the fight remaining in him. "What do you need, Clement? Tell us how we can help."

"Bring me home," Clement said. "I need to see it one last time."

*Oxford House? We were just at Hudson Bay?*

"To your father's home near St. Louis?" DeSmet asked.

Clement shook his head. "No, I made a promise to her before any of this madness began. Bring me to *her* home. Mato Paha."

# CHAPTER 57

M A T O   T A P I L A

1 8 5 4

Chief Thunderface began tossing around his bedding in desperation. *Where is my knife? I need to show them I can still protect my people.*

Finally, the blade tumbled out of his bedding.

He snatched it up, strapping it to his waist as his wife looked on with frightened eyes. She held his youngest son, a toddler of two. "Don't worry. We will overwhelm these trespassers. I only need to wet my blade to keep the younger men in their place. I won't do anything foolish."

"Perhaps this would be a good time for a younger man to lead the attack," his wife pleaded. "What else do you have to prove?"

*I owe this to my people. I promised them a miracle and have only fed them ash.* Thunderface felt his heart racing and took a deep breath to calm himself. "Today, I'll make our sons proud."

Chief Thunderface focused on his weak knee, and as soon as he tossed open his teepee door, he grit his teeth through the pain, making the young hunter Charging Bear run to keep up with him. His nephew, Standing Buffalo, held his horse while a few dozen warriors waited to be led.

*Perhaps I should let Standing Buffalo lead this attack and then support him as chief. If I fail, someone from Standing Rock or Bear Mountain will rightly claim leadership of the Sihasapa.* Yet it wasn't the ways of the past, and with so much change happening, dying in combat might be better than the alternative.

A bolt of pain shot through his leg as he climbed his horse. He fought the pain and the spots in his eyes for a few minutes before turning to his nephew. "Did you find your father?"

"No, he's already gone to the Black Hills."

Sharing the field with his brother-in-law, Grey Heron, would have helped matters. Information provided by two teenage hunters ws all he had. For all he knew, he could be going into a trap. Thankfully, he had his nephew, along with three dozen warriors, beside him. "Crawler?"

The other young hunter came jogging up to his chief, who ordered, "Take one of my horses and ride to Thunder Rock. Tell them we are facing trespassers and then bring others with in case we fail. You know the pass they are traveling near?"

"Antelope Ridge."

"Find us there," Thunderface said, and then turned to Charging Bear who stood waiting. "You'll be able to lead us back to where you saw them?"

Charging Bear smiled, knowing he'd pleased his chief. "I will."

TWO HOURS LATER, they reached Antelope Ridge to prepare the ambush. As the elder strategist, he and his younger officers dismounted and climbed to the top of the ridge. Young Charging Bear, his smile no longer seen, came with them.

For countless generations, his band, the Five Lodges, had been given guardianship of the most sacred places to the Seven Council Fire nation. The other tribes all knew that the land between Bear Lodge and Bear Mountain belonged to the Blackfoot Lakota. While their closest neighbors, the Siksika, Cheyenne, and Apsaalooke, knew trespassing would bring about the wrath of the entire Oceti Sakowin, their western neighbors also knew the "Sioux" had weakened considerably in the past generation, especially the Dakota in the east. *Perhaps they are only testing my resolve.*

Charging Bear, lying down on his belly beside Thunderface, pointed off in the distance. "There they are. I told you. It looks like they've broken camp already."

*And are heading right into our trap.*

At the base of Antelope Ridge, his gathered riders were ready to flood in from both sides while the snipers prepared to fire down on them from the rocks. Unlike the frenzied sneak attacks of the Cheyenne or Crow, the trespassers were not in a hurry, a sign they'd been traveling for quite a long time.

He studied the horses first, but what he saw only added to the confusion. Arikara ponies mixed with Cree horses. While the Arikara were from the upper Missouri River, the Cree belonged hundreds of miles to the north.

In addition to the strange horses, he saw the distinctive clothing of white men. Several white men, in fact. He all but gasped when he saw the black robes of a Jesuit priest.

*Is it a sign? A message?* "Hold. Tell our riders to hold."

He blinked his eyes, hoping to get a little more clarity.

The entire party of thirty riders stopped, but not a man dismounted. Then two riders, one on a white horse and the other being the Jesuit, separated from the group, advancing almost half-a-mile before stopping at the base of the ridge. Traces of red covered the white horse's flanks.

*But is it blood or writing?*

The odds of his men defeating a group of thirty armed riders were terrible. While his Blackfoot warriors might've held the element of surprise, the trespassers clearly knew they were being watched and the price of victory would be too high. With a scowl, Thunderface looked at Charging Bear, who gave an apologetic grin, a slight shrug, and then looked down in shame.

*My hunters were spotted.*

"Stay here," he said to Standing Buffalo, not wanting to risk the life of his nephew if this was indeed a trap. "I will go speak with the man."

Thunderface took hold of Charging Bear by his thin arm, pulling him along.

*This won't be a pleasant walk,* he thought, as he stood atop the ridge and began his descent. For most of the rocky passage, he used Charging Bear as a crutch whenever his bad knee gave out and kept a hand on the boy's shoulder.

The man upon the horse had a familiar look. He dressed like a white man but had the appearance of a Cree or Metis. The white horse was marked with red paint, a characteristic often used by the Five Lodges.

"I am Father Pierre-Jean DeSmet, known also as The Great Black Skirt. I am seeking entry into the territory of the Blackfoot Lakota. This is a sign of my friendship."

The Jesuit lifted a small object above his head.

For the next ten yards, Thunderface ignored it, trying to remember how he knew the other figure. While still on the slope of the ridge, yet within arrow range, he finally recognized the turtle-rattle once given to the Great Sorcerer, Joseph Nicollet.

A flood of memories and emotions filled him. He remembered hearing the tales of the man who'd brought the serpent star. After countless months of searching for the man, he remembered Nicollet finding *him* upon the eastern prairie. But a decade had passed since the joyous meeting.

Thunderface looked to the throng of thirty, hoping to see the colorful vest of the Great Sorcerer. "Has the Great Sorcerer returned?"

"No, but we are friends of Nicollet, and we have come in his stead."

"I know you," Thunderface said to the slouched over rider. It was then he realized the the markings upon the horse were not just writing but also blood.

"I am Antoine Clement, Brunia Missabay, the Brown Giant. I made a promise years ago, and I am here to fulfill that promise."

And then the Brown Giant fell from his horse.

# CHAPTER 58



For two days, the body of Antoine Clement was left on a wooden scaffold so that his spirit could find its way to the afterlife. Having spent time with the Lakota, Father Pierre-Jean DeSmet understood the significance of the ritual, and after giving Clement's body to his grieving widow, knew he'd be able to perform a Christian burial afterwards.

Clement lived another two days after he'd fallen from his horse, allowing time for his estranged wife and daughter to find him before he passed.

"How could we forget him?" Thunderface had said outside of Clement's teepee while White Feather and her daughter Little Star sat at Clement's side. "He was bigger than my men, stronger than my men, and braver than my men. Of all the women in our tribe, White Feather was the most beautiful but also the most aloof. Her family descends from the Spirit Lodge of the Five Lodges. Many thought she would never take a husband, but when she saw the Brown Giant, she gave him the challenge of carrying a buffalo skull to the top of Bear Lodge, which he did. Within a year, they had a daughter and Clement was hunting beside my men. When news came that white men were willing to trade goods for guides, Clement promised White Feather he'd return the following season, but he never did—until today."

*He'd gone to St. Louis and found a new love—alcohol.*

Prior to his death, Clement marked his white horse with drawings of his journey from Bear Mountain to St. Louis and then around the world. Both aging chiefs, Grey Heron and Thunderface, wept when telling stories of Clement and Joseph Nicollet. DeSmet carefully pressed them about the significance of calling Nicollet the "Great Sorcerer." Having also traveled with Nicollet, DeSmet understood most of the reasons, including the arrival of Halley's Comet. As they sat around the fire for Clement's final hours, the old chiefs told their tales about the Serpent Star and the legend of the Wishwee, the Star Man.

Grey Heron's son Ohanzee fervently believed the tales told by the elders of the Spirit Lodge and departed immediately to go face the shape-shifting Unktehi known as No Soul. Shortly after, a traveling holy man visited the Black Hills, claiming to have met the Wishwee in distant St. Louis, which shook the hearts of White Feather and all who knew the Brown Giant, who'd followed his destiny to the distant city. When the shaman said the Wishwee was indeed in the company of a Brown Giant, the entire nation believed the stars were aligning for some cataclysmic change. For this reason, Thunderface gathered up his people and traveled hundreds of miles in search of the Great Sorcerer Nicollet. When they found him, White Feather's heart broke when she learned her Brown Giant had traveled to the far side of the world.

White Feather and Clement's daughter, Little Star, grew up hearing about her father's exploits from the two years he was with them, as well as myths about his life at Hudson Bay, the Rockies, Minnesota, and his travels around the world. Mother and daughter devoted themselves to the legacy of Clement, and at Bear Mountain, on the edge of the Black Hills, they began a life of prayer and contemplation; White Feather never chose another husband.

"The people of the Five Lodges," Thunderface explained, "are different than the other bands and tribes of the Seven Council Fires. Their beliefs are much older. They guided our people to this land—a land which we now guard. White Feather is part of the Spirit Lodge, those who keep the ancient knowledge about death. The other four lodges represent the earth, the sky, water, and fire. Our holy men, like you, still worship the Creator, but our stark differences have made it apparent that both cultures have lost pieces of the story. While my people remember the old ways of the

Creator, your people carried stories of the new ways of the Creator. I took my youngest son to the Holy Man Renville, who baptized him with the name Adam, and since then, I've tried to teach him our legends, especially the old ones."

DeSmet revisited his grief of losing Nicollet and suffered at the fresh loss of Clement. His traveling companions also took the loss hard, so the stay the Bear Mountain allowed them time to emotionally heal.

After two days of mourning, White Feather and Little Star came out of their teepee. White Feather had cut off her hair, a tribute to her fallen husband. Little Star, a maiden nearing the age of twenty, had severed the tip of her little finger and had placed a dozen wooden pegs through the flesh of her forearms. Her face was blackened with dried blood.

She was the most horrifying and beautiful creature DeSmet had ever beheld.

"His spirit has passed on," White Feather said to DeSmet. "You may now have his body."

Her Blackfoot family gathered around her and her daughter, leaving the other mourners to tend to Clement's body. Crooked Arm and his lieutenant remained in the company of Stewart's band of madmen. *The Serpent Star lit a fire that is still burning.*

The toothless redheaded Forsberg boy cried almost as hard as Clement's family. Just a short time ago, the boy had been on death's doorway himself, but after removal of his putrid arm, the boy had grown stronger by the day.

With the help of Chief Thunderface, Clement was brought seventy miles from Bear Lodge to Bear Mountain, where his wife and daughter camped. Unlike the stump-shaped Bear Lodge, Bear Mountain did resemble the hunched back of a great bear, sleeping along on the eastern edge of the Black Hills. The people of the Spirit Lodge camped at the base of the solitary butte.

And it was there they buried Antoine Clement—Brunia Missabay, the Brown Giant.

The dozen men spent hours rolling away boulders at the base of the mountain, and they placed his body in the alcove, covering it with dirt before returning the boulders.

"Clement told me about seeing the pyramids," Professor Morgan said after DeSmet finished his Roman Catholic prayers. "Now he has a tomb that rivals even the Great Pyramid."

A short distance away, the Lakota drums sounded and a chorus of voices filled the air. Five figures—Chief Thunderface, his son Adam, old Chief Grey Heron, White Feather, and Little Star—returned from the camp to join their guests.

"Several promises were made," White Feather said once she stood close enough to the group. "But only one promise was kept. I thank you for bringing him back to me, but now we must speak about what comes next."

Neither the professor nor the false lord seemed ready to take the mantle of leadership, and soon, all eyes were on DeSmet, so he humbly explained, "I only recently joined these men."

"Part of what you said is true," White Feather answered, "but your black robe has been part of this story for generations. Let us sit and talk about what happens next."

DeSmet already knew what needed to happen. He'd bring the four weary travelers to Fort Pierre and send them home on a steamship down the Missouri River to St. Louis.

"Before my husband died," White Feather began, "he told me about the enemy that struck him down and another promise he'd made. I will stay here and mourn, but his daughter will go with you to finish the journey."

DeSmet shook his head as he translated her statement to the others. "Clement came for revenge on the men who killed his father, and his revenge has taken his life. The journey is over."

"No, the journey continues. Wishwee made a promise generations ago to come back," White Feather said.

DeSmet didn't understand the word she used. *Star Man? Is she referencing Nicollet the astronomer?* Little Star's Lakota name translated as Wichapi, and the word she used sounded similar to the word. "What is Wishwee?"

"The Serpent Star marked his arrival," White Feather said. "He is the one who found the weapon to defeat the evil shapeshifter No Soul. Wishwee is the only one who could wield it, but he left to seek the council of Black Robes. He promised to return with Black Robes at his side. You are the fulfillment of that promise.

You will take his daughter with you so that his destiny can be fulfilled."

DeSmet learned the Lakota language several years ago, but White Feather's isolated Blackfoot variations confused him. "Are you speaking of the Great Sorcerer, the one we call Nicollet?"

White Feather lifted a hand to point to the elder chieftains. "They wrongly believed Nicollet was sent back to us to serve as the Wishwee, but the Serpent Star did not summon Nicollet, it summoned Antoine Clement."

For a moment, DeSmet almost argued against her confused details. Yes, Clement was in St. Louis when Halley's comet appeared. DeSmet also remembered how Clement took the name Brunia and went ahead to Fort Snelling. When Nicollet arrived, Clement was part of the expedition that went to the headwaters of the Mississippi.

"If he had lived, my husband would have returned to Wanagiyata to battle No Soul."

Again, DeSmet struggled to understand her dialect. "I don't understand Wanagiyata. What is this place?"

White Feather repeated. "It is a lake we call 'Place of Souls.'"

"Wanagiyata? Lake of Souls?" DeSmet clarified.

Professor Morgan cleared his throat. "Clement traveled with Nicollet to a place the Chippewa called Lake Manitou, or Spirit Lake. He told me about it. Once he got his revenge, it's where he planned to go next."

"Nicollet planned to map the upper Missouri River," DeSmet insisted.

Lewis Cairns found his voice. "You were part of a ruse, Father DeSmet. Fremont, Geyer, and Stewart all were part of an elaborate bluff."

"A bluff? Do you mean that Nicollet never planned on mapping the upper Missouri River? Why did Eos send its servants to the Great Divide then?"

"To race Nicollet," Cairns said. "His enemies in Washington made it impossible for Nicollet to fund his plan, but they believed he'd tipped his hand. You were kept in the dark because of your Jesuit loyalties, but your actions helped convince our enemies.

While Fremont, Geyer, and Stewart were far out west, Nicollet was planning to return to Lake Manitou."

"Yes, Wanagiyata, the Place of Souls," White Feather insisted, seeing her support grow among the others.

DeSmet almost smiled thinking of how Nicollet had fooled so many. DeSmet even gave misleading information to his superiors in Rome. *He was several moves ahead of us.* Yet the details again confused him. "No, I don't understand. Nicollet never found anything. He was stopped by Pillagers. Why do you think Nicollet was the only one who could wield the weapon to kill No Soul?"

"I've told you already. The Serpent Star did not summon Nicollet. It summoned Antoine Clement. Clement had the blood of Wishwee flowing in his veins—not Nicollet. Wishwee is the one who made the promise generations ago—not Nicollet."

*Clement? The ogre was a mongrel. What is she talking about? Nicollet was almost a Holy Man.*

*Think…what is the Wishwee?*

*Did he woo her with lies? Did she believe he was someone he wasn't? The man did take on the persona of different names for different people.*

"Did Clement tell you this story?" DeSmet pressed.

White Feather shook her head. "No, I told it to him. It was a love story about the daughter of a mighty Dakota chief and a foreigner, a white man. In those days, the Serpent Star also appeared—a sign that he was the Wishwee, the one who would defeat No Soul by wielding the White Egg. Despite the danger posed to her, she took him deep into the Land of the Blue Woman, into the Haunted Valley, where the earth bled blue. Wenonah showed him his destiny, but before he could act upon it, fate tore these two lovers apart. He was taken back east, and her vengeful father sent her far to the west to live here at Bear Mountain. By the time these two lovers found each other again, both were married, but he proved she was right all along when he unearthed the sacred egg of creation, wielding it for all the people to see. That was when he made the promise to her—to me—to us—that he would return one day with the Black Robes at his side to fight the evil shapeshifter No Soul and to rip him from his cave."

*It can't be. She's speaking of Pierre-Charles LeSueur.*

DeSmet knew the legacy of the Jesuits. He knew how in the early days of exploration, the Jesuits sent their brightest and best to follow the mysterious Seven Fires Migration of the Anishinaabe into the west in search of the Seventh Stopping Place—a lake with a turtle-shaped island.

He knew how the mighty Sioux empire—the Seven Council Fires—repelled both the Anishinaabe and the French for generations. But a series of disasters led France to the French Revolution, which almost destroyed the Jesuit Order. DeSmet been sent back after a generation to "make assessments."

Because of Joseph Nicollet, DeSmet also knew the legacy of two men who came to the Frontier in 1682—a year Halley's Comet appeared to the world. Baron Lahontan's records of his travels were spurious at best. The other account baffled later explorers, who went looking for a copper mine that didn't exist.

*Pierre-Charles LeSueur was the Wishwee?*

DeSmet felt light-headed. LeSueur had been out to the frontier in the 1680s, returned to France with samples of blue earth, and then traveled up the Mississippi River with a mining expedition deep into the heart of Sioux territory. *But LeSueur died in Cuba.*

Yet LeSueur, like Clement, was a giant of a man.

*No, that can't be.*

Antoine Clement senior—a Frenchman from a family of fur-traders, had left the Louisiana territory for better opportunities on the Hudson Bay.

*Dear God, LeSueur had children with Marguerite LeSueur. She settled with her LeMoyne cousins in the new territory, remaining there even after her first husband died. She remarried—Nicholas Chauvin.*

DeSmet didn't need to see the full family tree to know the truth: LeSueur's blood flowed through the generations to fulfill the promise he made to Wenonah.

Little Star—Wichapi—Wishwee.

# CHAPTER 59



Sofus Nielson hopped from rocky patch to rocky patch, pretending they were sheets of ice floating on a spring river current. In reality, the field of stone was exposed bedrock that peeked out of the prairie where the retreating glaciers had carved out two waterways: the Red River and the Minnesota River.

Down the hill, the camp had been set along the shore of the narrow lake. A few miles north, they crossed a stream that Professor Morgan claimed was the headwaters of two rivers, but it was only a flooded ditch to Sofus. After leaving the Black Hills, they'd crossed the Missouri River north of Fort Pierre.

*Now that was a river!*

Unsaddling the horses, they had used log rafts to cross and let the horses swim in the muddy waters. Once they crossed, Chief Thunderface brought a few horses to trade for a wagon, which allowed Forsberg, supplies, and even Professor Morgan's prized slab of stone to be carried across the prairies. Another Indian chief, Waneta, recently joined them, guiding them to the crossing place of the two rivers.

All told, they had more men now than when they'd arrived in America.

Yesterday, the Dakota warriors gathered at the exposed stone to say their prayers, and Sofus was forbidden by the Jesuit Priest from bothering them due to his curiousity.

Today, though, they all hunted and fished in preparation for the final leg of the journey, leaving the granite playground to him.

After so many weeks of seeing grass, this majestic patch of stone that formed the walls of the river valley, was breathtaking.

The Jesuit, the Professor, the Lord, and three Chiefs sat together down by the lake making plans for their incursion into Minnesota.

Even though he was told numerous times to mind his business, Sofus gathered it was going to be dangerous.

But it involved some sort of treasure.

Clement's daughter, Little Star, walked beside Vaktar Forsberg up the hill.

*I wonder if I'm in trouble?*

No one from the camp seemed to be looking up at him—a good sign.

Nor did Forsberg and Wichapi seem to be in a rush.

With the help of Father DeSmet, Forsberg spent the past few weeks trying to tell Little Star about her fallen father Antoine.

Wichapi was beautiful. Sofus couldn't deny his feelings for her, even though she was foreign to him. She had her father's eyes and his height, yet the jet black hair of her mother's people. Even though she was dressed in deerskin and beads, she walked as if she were royalty.

Sofus looked at his toes once they neared.

"Father DeSmet told me he thinks he knows where my Uncle Dagmar is living," Vaktar said to him once they were close.

"How does he know that?" Sofus asked.

"The river in front of you," Forsberg pointed with his stub. "It flows for ten days downstream before it reaches a bigger river called the Mississippi. He said a Catholic priest has a church there, and one of the parishioners is named Forsberg. It must be my uncle. I'll show him what happened to me."

"Are you going to visit him?" Sofus asked, suddenly fearful of losing his traveling companion.

"I'm not sure where we're going after this. They're down there right now trying to figure that out. Once we get to Lake Manitou, we're going to have enemies all around us. Chief Crooked Arm wants us to withdraw west and then return home through Hudson Bay."

"Do you remember that story I told you," Sofus began, thinking of Hudson Bay.

Forsberg frowned. "Your ancestors did not travel to America five hundred years ago."

"Sure they did," Sofus defended. While he couldn't be sure of matching the names to the real places, he'd heard the tales told dozens of times back home. *Why does everybody doubt me?* "I was thinking that this is most likely the place where they camped. Professor Morgan said that because of the Ice Age, the rivers were bigger back then. I bet the water came all the way up to these rocks. If that's the case, I bet they simply paddled up in their Viking ships and anchored here. I bet they were looking for the same place we are seeking—Lake Manitou."

"Your ancestors weren't Vikings. You're just saying that to make me mad. I can still kick your ass. I'll shove my stump into your nose."

*Can't both of our family stories be true?* "I'm only repeating what I was told."

"You're making this up," Vaktar insisted.

Sofus became distracted by the solemn beauty of Wichapi, whose forehead wrinkled as she listen to them speak. "Can she understand us?"

Vaktar shook his head. "They've been pretty cut off—where she lives. They've had hardly any white men, even Vikings like you, visit them."

*A magic egg? I wonder if it connects to the Professor's Black Stone?* "Why do you think she's coming with us? What's going to happen when we get there?"

Vaktar shrugged.

"Does she have a husband?" Sofus pressed.

"I don't know. I don't think so. I think she's like a nun or something."

*He wasn't acting like she was a nun.* "Oh shut up. You're just saying that because you're sweet on her."

"Am not."

"Are too. You're always talking to her."

"I'm just trying to explain to her a bit about her father."

Sofus deflated a bit and remembered his grief. "Clement? What's so special about him? I mean, besides the obvious."

"The way Professor Morgan talks, they think he's some long lost hero. Do you know the King Arthur stories about a hidden king?"

Sofus shook his head.

"You're a Christian, right?"

Sofus nodded.

"Okay, then it's like when the Bablyonians conquered Jerusalem and killed the King of Israel, and then, six hundred years later, Jesus showed up as the lost heir. Apparently, Clement is like that."

"Clement is related to Jesus?" Forsberg let fly with his good arm, striking Sofus so hard in the chest that it echoed like a drum. In hindsight, Sofus realized he'd spoken too quickly. "Ow, that hurt."

Wichapi smiled, making the act hurt even more.

Forsberg stayed in place, his eyes at his feet as if he also regretted the act. "Father DeSmet wanted to talk to you. Don't lie to a priest, okay?"

*I'm not lying.*

Then Forsberg quickly added, "DeSmet wants to hear about your story."

"He does?" Sofus felt his spirits lift.

Forsberg looked him in the eye and nodded, the closest he'd ever come to believing him. His brow narrowed before he asked, "Do you know a fellow named Abbaron? Or Kokebi?"

Sofus shook his head.

"Well, DeSmet and Morgan were talking about these two guys, and when DeSmet heard about your tall tales, he wanted to hear you tell it yourself."

"Fine, like I said, I'm only repeating what I was told."

Both Sofus and Vaktar turned to walk back to camp, stopping after a few steps to see why Wichapi hadn't moved.

"Chippewa," she muttered, looking east.

Sofus put his hand to his brow, and he saw the three tan horses galloping toward them. Then he saw three Indigenous riders. Finally, he saw their bows.

"Get her back to the others," Sofus said, scrambling down his rock to where he'd left his canteen and pistol.

"Give me that pistol," Forsberg demanded.

"No, get her out of here. I'll hold them off."

"Fire off a shot to get the others."

"There are three of them, and I've only got six bullets. Get her to safety, and then I'll fire off the shot."

Forsberg took her by the arm, hobbling as he ran on his wounded foot. Wichapi looked back at Sofus with concern.

*That's right, I'll protect you.* Sofus took a few steps toward the charging horses, who grew larger with each heartbeat. He glanced back, knowing the riders would reach Forsberg and Wichapi before the camp even knew what was happening.

He fired a shot in the air and the charging horses slowed.

But only to fire their arrows.

Two flew over his head, but a third struck him squarely in the chest.

Strangely, its impact was no worse than Forsberg's punch a few moments earlier.

*They mean to kill me.*

Sofus lowered his pistol, took aim, and squeezed the trigger. A red splotch appeared on the flank of the horse, which lurched and bucked, tossing its rider.

One rider charged forward, notching another arrow. He was bouncing so badly that Sofus fired off two misses. The arrow came right at him, striking him in the thigh. This one hurt.

But the rider was almost on him. Luckily, the rider was now a larger target, and Sofus's fourth shot struck the rider in his lower throat. He dropped his bow to clutch at his mortal wound.

The third rider, who'd stopped, now saw the peril the boy posed, and turned his tan pony. Sofus missed the fifth shot but hit the rider squarely in the back, yet somehow, the man managed to keep riding.

*Look at that,* Sofus thought when he viewed the arrow sticking out of this sternum. He could see the thread of the arrowhead where it tied onto the shaft. Except for a bit of blood that oozed, it still didn't bother him much.

Chief Waneta's riders were already on horseback and charging up the hill. *I think I got them all, though.*

The Chippewa who'd shot him with two arrows was dying on the ground. The other was trapped under his fallen horse, and the third was growing smaller by the moment.

*Well, this will impress Wichapi.*

The Dakota horsemen rode around the rocks to pursue the wounded rider. Others hopped off their horses to deal with the two wounded.

In the distance, Father DeSmet took Wichapi into the protection of the camp while Professor Morgan ran up the hill where Sofus stood alone.

"One of them shot me with an arrow, but it doesn't even hurt," Sofus called out, pointing to the arrow protruding from his chest. He looked down to see blood dampening his pants. *Now that one hurts.* It'd pierced the flesh just above his knee.

*Great, now I'm going to have a limp, too.*

Professor Morgan was out of breath by the time he reached the edge of the granite stones. He looked to the bloody Chippewa a few feet away as well as the one being pulled out from under his horse by Waneta's Dakota.

"I think I got—" Sofus said before a cough cut him short. He felt a bit of dampness on his chin and touched it to see blood.

*Did I bite my tongue in all the excitement?*

Professor Morgan's eyes grew wide as he climbed up the rock.

"It's just stuck in my breastbone. It doesn't even hurt, see?" Sofus wiggled the shaft of the arrow then pulled it out. It did leave a jolt of pain, and he gasped at its sharpness. When he did so, a strange sucking noise came out of his chest.

*Oh no,* Sofus thought and then his world began to fill with dark spots and more blood dripping down his chin.

# CHAPTER 60



To distract his grief, Professor Corey Morgan studied Nicollet's 1843 *Map of the Hydrographical Basin of the Upper Mississippi River,* which Father DeSmet had given him. His copy was one of thousands made by the federal government in anticipation of the settlement of the region. In the east, Henry Hastings Sibley had quickly organized military expansion to Fort Snelling and then swindled the Dakota to sell millions of acres for pennies an acre, with special consideration for the "half-breeds" already living in the territory. Sibley's recent "Traverse des Sioux" treaty meant the Dakota would be forced onto reservations along the Minnesota River and taught how to farm.

*It was a lie.*

From what Morgan could tell, none of Thunderface's Lakota or Waneta's Dakota understood what the sale of land meant nor would they become farmers. Already, according to DeSmet, the white population around the "stone fort" swelled, and politicians and businessmen intended to begin organized settlement as soon as 1855.

*Any mysteries left undiscovered by Nicollet will soon be plowed over by pioneers new to this land.*

Yet far to the west, the land remained much the same as Nicollet had seen it—open prairie. After leaving Big Stone, they passed by Ta Kara Lake and then stayed on the ridge Nicollet had drawn onto his map. None of these lakes were named, but Morgan understood they camped on what Nicollet had boldly labeled the

Coteau Du Grand Bois, a ridge separating the Big Woods from the Prairie. Nicollet's ridge fed the Long Prairie River to the east and the Osakis River to the south.

Morgan rose before dawn, and he was facing the sun as it rose over the horizon. One by one, the other men rose to meet the day. Since the death of young Sofus, everyone wore countenances of solemnity on their faces. Nielson had managed to kill all three Chippewa scouts, so no news returned to the Big Woods, but the absence of the scouts would also raise alarm with whoever had sent them. Waneta suspected Chippewa Chief Sweating Stone.

The men began to gather around Father DeSmet, who served them freshly brewed coffee from his dwindling supplies. Morgan carried Nicollet's map with him and stood shoulder to shoulder with Thunderface and Waneta, who promised retribution for the boy's death. Morgan sat with DeSmet, Lord Erskine, and the Cree chief Crooked Arm who moved stones in the dirt in front of them.

Cairns looked up to see Morgan and explained what had been decided. "It is agreed this is a good camp for staging," he began. "We're halfway to Lake Manitou, and I'll be joining Crooked Arm and Thunderface to scout the area. A decade ago, the Pillagers were thick in the area, and most of those men will remember Nicollet, for better or worse. We need to see what sort of opposition we'll face."

*Opposition?* Morgan had not wanted to be part of the planning, and now he began to wonder if he wanted to continue the mission.

"Chief Waneta will ride south," Cairns continued. "Many of the peaceful Dakota have already settled along the Minnesota River in the new reservations. Among them is a friend of Nicollet, a man named Taopi. With Taopi's help, we could potentially secure a group large enough to take Lake Manitou by force."

*Of course! Renville was Nicollet's ally also. Taopi would be protected there.*

Father DeSmet cleared his throat to speak. "If…you madmen succeed, we'll need an extraction plan. In the past few years, I've learned what Nicollet suspected to be true of the Catholic Church, and with her motives toward the prophecy unclear, I'll contact other allies in Rome. To do this, I'll go back to the headwaters of the Tchankasndata, the Thick Wooded River, which runs straight south into the Missouri River. My appearance on the Missouri

River would be expected, and back at St. Louis, I'd be able to arrange the international transportation needs we have."

*The priest obviously believes we'll find something.* "I should come with you to Lake Manitou," Morgan insisted. "Any sort of relics we find might need interpretation."

"You'll certainly come with us on that day," Cairns said, "but today, we'll keep you here. From what Thunderface and DeSmet tell me, young Wichapi is as important to this prophecy as the Philosopher's Stone itself. I want you to guard over her. All three chiefs will leave a few warriors here to secure the camp. This will only take a few days. It's a sixty mile ride to the lake, and we don't plan on staying long enough to be noticed."

*Once again, I'm being treated as a nursemaid.*

Morgan didn't fight it.

He had plenty on his mind.

First, he had the boy's smiling face on his mind. For months, Sofus sat listening to his stories about Norse mythology, Atlantis, and the Order of Eos. The boy was a better scholar than any of his university students had ever been. For each grand tale Morgan told, Sofus tried to top it.

Second, he could not rid his mind of the black stone he'd seen back at Lake Columbia. *Where had the Order of Eos found such a relic? What was its purpose? How were they going to use it?* For this reason, Morgan didn't mind staying at camp since each step east and away from the black stone felt like a betrayal of his duties. *Before this is all over, I'll need to get back to Cold Garden.*

Lastly, he had his masterpiece to finish.

It had certainly been comical when Sofus hauled a two hundred pound slab of stone back to camp. Nature had molded an almost perfect headstone, it had seemed, and even though the slab of greywacke was far from the supernatural black stone he'd gazed upon, it was an oddity in its own right. So it had become their traveling companion.

Back at Bear Mountain, Morgan first took out a hammer and a few small chisels, intent on marking the grave with a tombstone befitting Antoine Clement, but Clement's winter bride White Feather insisted on giving him a traditional Lakota burial. But the

idea of commemoration stuck in his mind, and he began to inscribe something else upon the stone—a narrative.

They'd traveled over four hundred miles since leaving Bear Mountain, and each evening when the men made camp, he added new details to the slab in tribute to Sofus. Now, while the others prepared to go on their missions, he again returned to his project, intent on finishing before bringing Wichapi to Lake Manitou.

"What's happening?" Vaktar Forsberg asked, looming over the spot on the hill where Morgan had dragged the slab.

"Scouting parties," Morgan explained and told the boy where everyone was off to.

"Could I—" Forsberg began.

"You can stay here with me and watch over Little Star," Morgan intercepted the request before it could be asked. The boy wanted retribution but was in no shape to enter a fight.

Forsberg huffed in resignation. He'd taken the sudden death of Nielson harder than he'd taken the death of Clement. With Clement, there'd been the long goodbye, but with Sofus, it'd all happened in moments, leaving the spirit of the Forsberg boy in tatters. He knew the boy needed good news, so he added, "I think I'm almost finished."

"What is it?"

"It's a tribute to Sofus," Morgan declared.

Forsberg's eyes filled with tears. He wiped them with his sleeve and stepped forward to study the writing. "What does it say?"

Morgan turned the slab onto its butt so that its long, smooth front faced them.

*"Eight Goths and 22 Northmen on this*
*acquisition journey from Vinland far to the*
*west. We had a camp by two shelters one*
*day's journey north from this stone. We were*
*fishing one day. After we came home, found 10*
*men red from blood and dead. Ave Maria save*
*from evil."'*

"He'd like that," Vaktar said. "It takes part of our story and combines it with the story he told to us about his Viking ancestors. I like the part about the Goths."

Morgan turned the slab back to the narrow, six-inch wide side. "On the side, I'll write:
*'There are 10 men by*
*The inland sea to look after our ships fourteen*
*days journey from this island.*
*Year 1362.'*
I was about to add the names of the men Sofus told us about. Do you remember their names?"

Vaktar nodded. "Mikls of Fors, Tao Nielson, Storlum, Fisk, Smed, Lars, um, Marur, and, um, oh, of course, Cnoyen."

Forsberg rattled them off as if taking a test. "Are those the names of the survivors?"

"Oh, the survivors? I thought you wanted the name of the eight Goths who went with Pal Knutson and Bishop Bardson's Northmen."

*He's describing the first expedition from 1354.* "I was going to put the name of the men who came out of the wilderness—the eight who survived a decade lost in the frozen north. The names Sofus added to the tale."

Vaktar smiled his gummy smile. "Do you remember the battle? Sofus said the two expeditions had a great battle out on the frontier. They killed each other until only a handful remained, and then they banded together for survival. The Bishop's men were Cnoyen, Nielson, Fors, Bjarni Olafson, and Father Tveit. Henry Sinclair's men were Drummond, Dobie, and Morrison—if you are to believe him."

*Forsberg can't say the dead boy's name. We never should have brought these young men on such a dangerous journey.* "You should go with Chief Waneta."

"Why?"

*It's the safest path for you.* "He's going to Renville's Cabin, a settlement with men who knew Nicollet. The men who knew Nicollet most likely are the same men who know your Uncle Dagmar."

"You think so?"

"I do. You'll be back in a few days. By then, I'll have finished the runestone."

"It's better than sitting here doing nothing." Vaktar gave him a slight nod and then quietly walked back down the hill.

AN HOUR LATER, the three parties departed in separate directions. Morgan remained, sitting on the crest of the small knoll and overlooking the wetlands below, where the remaining horses ate and drank.

Wichapi remained in prayer outside her tent, and all the young men kept their distance from the beautiful young woman.

*If we do find the Philosopher's Stone in Chagobay's secret cave, will she be the one to wield it? The lost heir of Pierre-Charles LeSueur? It begs another question: whose blood did LeSueur carry in his veins? What made him special in the first place?*

A breeze came up, and white, fluffy poplar seeds, carried on the winds from the nearby forests, filled the air. They covered his faux-runestone, and he brushed them away before grabbing his mallet and chisel.

*Whose name do I carve first?*

Before Professor Corey Morgan had his answer, a shadow appeared from over his shoulder. A rough hand covered his mouth, and a blade swept across his throat. His blood sprayed onto the runestone, and as the strong hand held him steady for a moment, he saw little poplar seeds sticking in his blood.

The hand let go, and he fell beside his work. Before he lost consciousness, he saw a strong Chippewa warrior in full battle attire stride past him to the camp below.

369

# CHAPTER 61

LAKE MANITOU

1854

After the din of battle ended, Nanakonan slipped away from his sleeping bride to peer out the door to the starry sky. The sounds had come from the west, but to the north, the sky was filled with splendid color. His father Chagobay told him that the Northern Lights were created in the days following a Great Flood when the survivors were filled by fear at the sudden darkness of both the sun and moon. To encourage his people, the Great Creator placed great crystals of ice in the north, to capture the light of the sun and then release it in the darkness of night.

His father was always a practical man, but his mother told him that when people die and their soul travels along the River of Souls in the stars, the ancestors dance as the dead are transformed into new eternal life.

After briefly investigating the gunshots in the night, Nanakonan crawled back into bed hoping his mother's version of the Northern Lights was true.

THE NEXT MORNING, Nanakonan loaded his rifle, strapped on his knife, and picked up a hatchet—*just in case.*

When he stepped from the bedroom to the central living room, his young bride Firefly, whom he'd married the previous spring, made a mess on the iron stove he'd purchased for her as a wedding gift. She grew wide-eyed when she saw him armed. "What are you doing?"

"I have to find out what happened last night," Nanakonan said.

Her attention was drawn back to the stove, which produced smoke from the mess she'd made on the surface. Once the crisis was over, she placed her hands on her hips as if trying to draw attention to their unborn child in her womb.

Nanakonan walked over and kissed her on the forehead. "I'll be safe."

After the death of his father Chagobay, Nanakonan went into hiding in Canada for more than a decade, but his duty to his family's legacy led him back to Lake Manitou. His own people feared the secrets his family carried, and for this reason, he kept a low profile after his return. With the support of Nicollet's American allies, he secured several plots of land along the Blue Knife River north of Lake Manitou, where he'd maintained his vigil and built a cabin for his precious Firefly.

But he knew what his enemies wanted.

Evil slept below the waves of Lake Manitou.

He knew it as the Wintermaker, but he knew the metaphors and tales hid an even darker truth—Lake Manitou was a tomb.

Nanakonan descended rocks that served as a great stair on his trip to the river. Natural erosion helped keep the mouth of the cave hidden since his father had brought Joseph Nicollet years earlier. Yet the kindly French scientist had not been the fulfillment of prophecy, a mistake that cost his father his reputation and life.

Along the shore, a few feet above the waterline, a birchbark canoe helped Nanakonan quickly get to the western shore where he'd heard gunfire. He navigated the rocks of the Blue Knife River, and once the current took him into the lake, he began paddling hard.

At thirty-four, he was in his prime—a skilled hunter and fisherman able to provide more than enough for himself and his young bride. During his time in the north, he also learned the way of the traditional Midewiwin religion, which was practiced by the Anishinaabe in Minnesota all the way to their Mi'kmaq brothers left behind in Nova Scotia. It helped him understand the differences between the men who killed his father for being a heretic and his family's own religious secrets.

At the far western shore, he landed his canoe in a patch of cattails. Unlike the granite bluffs on the far eastern shore, the western shore was a field of pink quartzite. From what his father told him, his great-grandfather Wiyipisiw once won a great battle against the Fox Indians and took possession of a relic as old as creation itself—the sacred Water Drum.

Then his great-grandfather waged war against the Dwellers of Spirit Lake for two decades, breaking their grasp on the region at the Battle of Kathio. Finally in possession of the Wintermaker's Tomb at Lake Manitou, Wiyipisiw tried to force the Seven Fires Prophecy into existence, and like Chagobay, paid the price with his life. Nanakonan's grandfather also fled into hiding after the death of his father, yet passed down the secrets of Lake Manitou to his son.

*By autumn, I will hopefully have a son also.*

Nanakonan readied his rifle, knowing the Face of Death could be worn by many of his enemies. Nothing on Flat Rock seemed out of place, so he kept walking, entering the tall, blue-green grass that grew in the swampy land west of the lake.

His father claimed that the magic of the Water Drum—the original drum from the tales of the first men—changed not only the water and rocks to blue-green powder, but also affected the plants and trees that drew life from its ancient waters.

A mile west, he came across a slain Pillager in the grass, dead from a gunshot through his abdomen. He checked the man's vitals and then inspected his body. He was one of Chief Sweating Stone's men from Leech Lake and had been dressed for battle.

A hundred yards further, Nanakonan found the battle scene.

Dead horses and dead men stained the ground with their blood.

It had been an evenly matched, pitched battle where neither side walked away. The attacking Pillagers likely used the cover of darkness to hit the camp of their enemies—for he came across the dead Pillagers along the perimeter of the battle site.

Closer, he found something quite peculiar.

Dead Sioux.

Some he recognized as local Yankton Sioux, who lived on the prairie near the headwaters of the Minnesota River. Others were alien to him. Dressed in ornaments befitting a man of great renown, a fierce-faced elder chieftain lay dead with a hatchet buried in his ribs—right beside the Pillager who'd also died in the fight.

A thick-chested white man, dressed in an expensive vest that made Nanakonan remember the gentle Nicollet, also lay dead with arrows and bullets riddling his body.

Then one of the dead moved.

Instinctively, Nanakonan aimed at the bloodied warrior, who rolled over onto his back still holding a blade.

"Nîpîy," the bloody brute said. Then he smirked and muttered, "Sâkahikanapoy."

*Water*, Nanakonan translated the Cree word, and also *Fire Water*, which was a metaphor for whiskey. "Who are you?"

The bloody brute lifted his left elbow. "I am Chief Crooked Arm of the Rocky Mountain Cree. Are you going to kill me or help me?"

"Let go of your knife and I'll help you," Nanakonan said.

"Are these men your brothers?" Crooked Arm asked, glancing at the dead corpse beside him. Crooked Arm was sliced in several places, including an ear hanging mostly off. The blood on his chin aligned with the fatal wound of his assailant's throat.

Nanakonan answered, "The Pillagers are my brothers by blood, but they are also the men who killed my father. We shouldn't linger here long. The Pillagers will send out scouts to find their fallen brothers. I live nearby. I can tend to your wounds in exchange for your story."

Crooked Arm let go of his knife and raised a bloody hand, which Nanakonan grasped and helped him to a sitting position. Crooked Arm also looked around the battle site, and realized he was the sole survivor. "Thank you," he said.

Nanakonan asked, "How did it all come to this?"

Knowing Crooked Arm's friends and companions were among the dead, Nanakonan gave him time. It was only midmorning, and the blood from the previous night had not yet dried.

With a nod from Crooked Arm, Nanakonan helped the battered warrior to his feet. With two graze wounds on his right leg, Crooked Arm limped a few steps to the slain white man in the fancy vest to mutter, "I tried."

"Who was he?"

"He was once a great warrior," Crooked Arm said. "Get me some food and water, and I will tell you all about him and his fallen companions."

THE END OF PART NINE

# PART TEN
## THE TRANSYLVANIAN ALPS

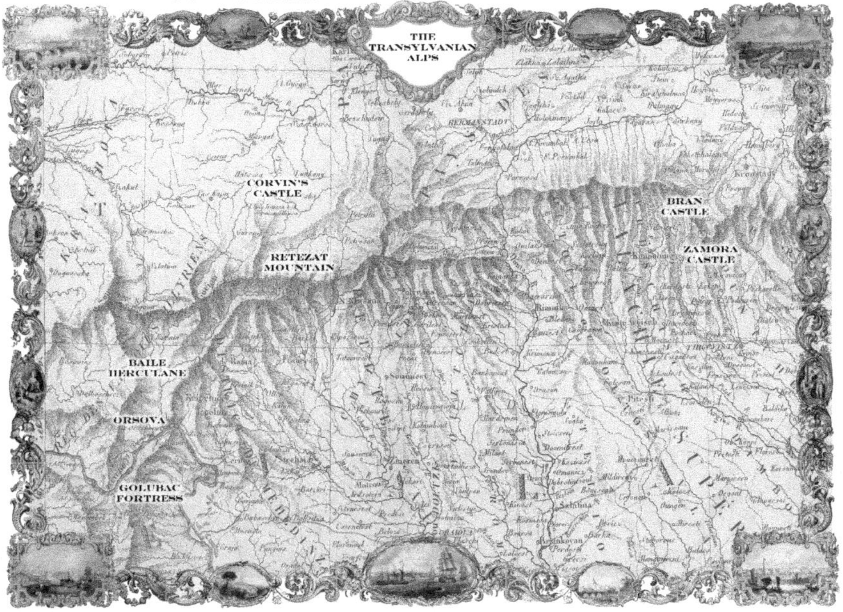

# CHAPTER 62



The room remained dark, and only the heat and smell of vomit greeted his senses. His mind was too clouded with pain to remember where he was. After several labored breaths, he commanded his limbs to move, only to find himself pinned by straps at his wrists and ankles. His attempts to move his limbs woke angry nerves that throbbed with every beat of his heart.

*I am being tortured,* Stewart remembered. The pain came from the finger and toenails that had been ripped out with pliers. From what he heard in the adjacent cell, knives and saws would come next. He'd run out of information to give his torturer, and waking up alive, he began to weep in despair.

*This can't be how it ends.*

In the tales from classic literature, the hero certainly encountered obstacles, and along the journey, pain and loss were to be expected. He'd lost love, that's for sure. He always found a way to push aside anyone he ever loved—for the chase, for glory. First, he'd gone to America to investigate the reasons his eccentric aunt had been murdered—only to find Joseph Nicollet holding all the answers. More recently, he went searching for answers about the origins of the Philosopher's Stone and its purpose in prophecy, only to end up in a torture chamber somewhere in Transylvania.

Knowing his bargaining with his foreign torturer was in vain, he pushed back the pain, closed his eyes, and began bargaining with God.

*Hey, it's me. Do you remember me from St. Louis? I'm the scoundrel who got himself baptized as an adult so that I could impress a potential lover. If my prior sins were forgiven, washed away, what new sins have I committed to warrant such a terrible death? Can you explain that to me? Haven't I been a faithful servant since that day? I set aside Antoine. I stopped drinking. I returned home to oversee my responsibilities.*

Stewart stopped his inner rant when he reflected on the blood on his hands. Prior to his baptism, he committed murder under the umbrella of war, but in recent days, he simply ordered it. *Is that what I must atone for? Didn't your own servants like Moses and Joshua kill their enemies in your name? Am I not acting on your behalf?*

Stewart opened his eyes.

The chamber remained pitch black.

Had it been hours, days, or weeks? How could he tell in the dark?

Stewart counted fingers and toes.

*This little piggy went to market.*

After the Russian cavalry swept into the hills at Baile Herculane, killing and dispersing the wolf pack unleashed on them, gunfire drew them back down the hill as quickly as they'd come.

*This little piggy stayed home.*

He commanded his remaining Austrian mercenary to stay with Karl Geyer while he jogged down the hill to see what was happening. That's when the rag-tag gypsy army caught him. At first, he thought they were just local farmers, for they lacked the flags and uniforms of organized militia, but the longer they held him, the more dire the situation became. Thousands of gypsies came pouring out of the mountains and surrounded the Russian army. Seeing that they weren't taking prisoners, Stewart panicked and claimed "English" status, knowing that the western powers were supporting the Ottoman Empire's sovereignty in its war with Russia. It was the wrong answer.

*This little piggy had roast beef.*

The gypsies cared for him. They fed him. They hauled him back north, and that trip, unmasked by the pain of torture, could still be recalled. Two days through mountain paths brought him to a castle built on a solitary hill. They'd crossed a moat bridge to enter it, and after they cleaned him up, he had an audience with the Countess Simona, a beautiful woman in red. That was his last meal.

*This little piggy had none.*

The beatings came first. Then the needles and pins. Most recently, the pliers began to rip nails from the little piggies. He still had a few nails left on his hands and feet, but metal clippers would soon start taking the toes and fingers off at the knuckles, and from what he heard in the other cell, it would not be quick. So in his waking moments, he enjoyed the simple pleasure of counting his fingers and toes.

Footsteps caused his heart to pause.

*They're coming back.*

The light from a single candle was enough to blind Stewart, and after squeezing his eyes shut for a moment, the single candle was replaced by seven white candles that lit the room. The torturer was not alone either.

The red woman, Countess Simona, followed him into the chamber, inspecting Stewart as if trying to decide between a couple of gowns. Behind her, a short, squatty young woman followed, along with a finely dressed gentleman with Asian ancestry. A thick-necked young man with black hair and piercing eyes closed the door.

*I know him.*

*He's the assassin who took Delhut back in Antioch.*

"I'd like to properly welcome you to Corvin's Castle, Lord Stewart," Countess Simona said, her head held high. "We met briefly a few days ago, but I didn't understand exactly who you were at the time. Now that I know who you are, let me introduce myself. As you are well aware, I had the Russian army to contend with." She turned from Stewart to the chubby young woman beside her. "My first husband was Russian. My mother came from Transylvania, and as a young woman, she was given to my father, a nobleman from Baku. Their arranged marriage was meant to produce a political alliance to thwart Russian interest in the Black Sea region. Instead, it created me."

Countess Simona floated closer to him, hovering like an angel. At first glance, she was the most beautiful creature Stewart had ever seen, but had they offered a piece of moldy cheese, he would

have chosen it over her. Her hand held the torturer whose hand held the pliers. Instead of focusing on her obvious beauty, Stewart focused on the crows feet in the corners of her eyes that could not be hidden by her makeup. Her golden hair was also an expensive wig. By all accounts, she was of similar age as he and Christina, even though her affluence hid her true age.

Stewart's mind tried to formulate a strategy, or even a response, but he was too tired.

"We're here today for some answers," Countess Simona said. "So to save a little time, let me offer the help of my spiritual adviser, Koot Bessant, and his apprentice, whose preferred name is Zenaida."

Zenaida added, "It's a pleasure to meet you, Lord Stewart. I feel like we are kindred spirits who travel the same road, albeit for very different reasons."

"I'll leave you two alone for a while," Countess Simona said. "I have other guests to attend to. Zenaida, dear, come and get me once he's ready to talk."

"Of course." Zenaida smiled.

With that, Countess Simona floated out the room along with the assassin.

"Although your adventure certainly didn't end the way you expected," Bessant began, "I do want to state my admiration for your determination. You are like a single spider bite whose infection spreads and spreads and ends up taking down a mighty elephant—all with a tiny bite. The elephant fought off mighty enemies like lions and crocodiles, never suspecting a little spider would be the creature to kill it. Yet here you are!"

Zenaida sighed. "We want to know about the Alpha."

"Patience, my dear. Lord Stewart has managed to gather up four thousand years of human history in the past…twenty years? I know Countess Simona wants him dead, but why rush it until we have squeezed all his knowledge from him. Then we can toss him away like a dead Russian." Koot Bessant pulled a chair over to the edge of the table, sitting eye to eye with Stewart. "You see, since Countess Simona was all but sold off to a Russian nobleman, she's hated the Russians with every fiber of her being. After she married this Russian Count, the Russians killed her mother and father when they took the Caucasus region. So she killed her husband and used his wealth and power to forward her ambitions and became Our Lady Columbia."

*There it is. Now my enemy has a face.*

Bessant smiled. "That name means something to you, doesn't it? Ah, one reveal at a time. Let me tell you what we already know, so we don't waste any time in the next stage of your interrogation. Zenaida, would you like to do this part?"

"Your God is the villain in this story," Zenaida explained. "Humanity could not stop him from destroying the planet with a flood, but this time, we will not stand by and watch it happen with a fire. Our great prophet discovered that another doom is coming. In the year 2061, your God plans to destroy humanity again, and Our Lady Columbia is going to stop that from happening."

"Zenaida aspires to be the next lightbearer," Bessant said at Stewart's lack of response. "One day, she'll carry the torch now held by Countess Simona, who received the torch from those that came before her. We know all about your Seven Kings. King Nimrod built a tower to wage war against the god-who-brought-the-flood. Then Ramses the Great, another champion of mankind, stood toe-to-toe with the Great Bully in a battle that laid Egypt to waste. Mighty Alexander the Great discovered the truth about the previous defeat of humanity, and it motivated him to learn all he could."

Bessant paused and smiled at him. "In a way, you remind me of Alexander, for in the span of two decades, Alexander learned the answers to most of his questions. The only answer that eluded him was found at the Navel of the Universe, which is where I happened to grow up, but his own men betrayed him, sending him back to Babylon. Antiochus Epiphanes became the next champion of humanity when he tried to use his collected sorcery to stop the unfolding prophecies—a valiant but failed attempt. Emperor Domitian, ruling over the Roman Empire at its peak, believed the destruction of Jerusalem meant he'd shattered the prophecy, only to learn the ultimate power of his enemy—resurrection. Domitian almost burned the corpses of the four kings, like he'd done with Jerusalem, but in his wisdom, he developed a new strategy, which Our Lady Columbia has decided to adopt."

*All my fears are being confirmed,* Stewart realized, *yet I have no one to tell, 'I told you so!'*

Koot Bessant stopped, studying his young apprentice. He was teaching her at the same time he was taunting Stewart. "Tell Lord Stewart our new plan."

"We are going to use resurrection against Demiurge," Zenaida explained. "To save humanity, we are going to raise a champion who can free us from the shackles of our enemy."

A placating chuckle came from Bessant. "The old Greek word Demiurge is her term for your Christian God, and if we let him have his way, the world will be purged with fire, and like those who survive the flood, they will remain his slaves. Our Lady Columbia is a liberator."

*She's the Great Whore of Babylon,* Stewart silently argued. He remembered that moment in St. Louis where Father Brule marked the cross upon his forehead with holy water while Bishop Rosati and Joseph Nicollet bore witness. *Stay strong. These bastards mean to kill me.*

"Our other guest is equally strong in his faith," Bessant said. "Countess Simona is with the torturer right now explaining his choices. You know him. In fact, he told us all about your visit to Detroit a few years ago. Do you know what he believes? He believes in old gods that are simply sleeping, and that with a magical song, the gods will be reborn in the dusty bones of their collection of human heroes. Yes, Eos has the collection of kings you were searching for. It is the responsibility of Eos to find and wake the slumbering gods so that they might cast down a fire god, whom they call Surtr. I suppose that's your Christian God also. Your God is the villain in two narratives, isn't he? We know about it from the perspective of the Christian as well as from the perspective of the Order of Eos. If either interpretation of your prophecies succeeds, humanity will burn. And suddenly, we hear about it from a new perspective."

Stewart held firm. The faces of Joseph Nicollet, Antoine Clement, and all his other friends entered his mind. *Yes, there will be fire, but after, a restoration, a rebirth, a resurrection—that is what I fight for.*

Zenaida nodded. "Those who survived the last purge tried to hide away their secrets and pass them onto their children. All it did was spawn variant religions until only the echo of truth remained. On the lost continent, however, the stories remained as they'd been for thousands of years. Mr. Delhut told us an interesting tale. We want to hear it from your perspective. Tell us about the prophecy of the Seven Fires."

"I never went north with Nicollet," Stewart answered honestly. "Clement went with him into Chippewa territory."

"And yet you sent Clement back to America while you began a search for the other kings of old. Now that we've had time to catch up to your plans, it all makes sense. Obviously, you must know about the Alpha."

"I don't know what that means," Stewart answered honestly, but in the back of his mind, he sensed what she was asking.

"Oh, we think you do. Delhut knew. You were close friends with Professor Nicollet, who seemed to figure it out. If you don't know about the Alpha, then tell us what you know about the Philosopher's Stone."

*What am I protecting if Delhut has already spilled his guts?* Stewart's failure felt complete. If they knew about Clement, he worried about what fate befell the other expedition. *Has my meddling made matters worse? Will it lead them right to Chagobay's cave at Lake Manitou?* First Stewart cried. Then he raged through his excruciating pain. After threatening their lives, he finally came right back to where he'd begun.

To give himself time to think, he told the Chippewa story of the Fisher Cat battling the Wintermaker in an effort to free the Summebirds. Then he told them stories about the Dakota hero Wishwee using the White Egg to battle the shapeshifting monster known as No Soul. While he wasted time, Bessant jotted it all down in his notebook.

"No Soul," Zendaida repeated with captivated interest. "The White Egg must be the Philosopher's Stone. The Summerbirds are the souls trapped by the magic of the Alpha. It makes sense."

*If only I could just kill myself before I ruin everything.*

"Well," Bessant chuckled. "You certainly confirmed Mr. Delhut's theory about the Alpha being found in the Minnesota territory. Why was Nicollet planning to travel to the headwaters of the Missouri and the Canadian Rockies? What did he expect to find there?"

So he told them the truth. "He knew he was being watched by Eos, by the Jesuits, and by something more elusive. So he meant to throw them off the trail by planning to search the headwaters of the Missouri River."

Bessant chuckled. "Countess Simona fell for Nicollet's ruse, too. She sent her operatives to the Rocky Mountains to find the Alpha before Eos or your allies found it. Even the Church sent their men. That was quite a trick."

"So the Alpha is indeed found at the Seventh Stopping Place," Zenaida said with a grin that rivaled Professor Morgan and Father MacPherson's zeal. "Delhut already confessed that he doubted the Upper Missouri theory, but your tale confirms his identity in legend."

Bessant turned to explain to Stewart. "We call him the Alpha, the first letter in the Greek alphabet, since we don't know his name. He was the first king, the one who united humanity against your God. We have no idea how long ago he ruled. Some legends put it at four thousand years ago, and others have it hundreds of thousands of years ago, if not longer. We believe that the Alpha is the key to our resurrection plan, for it was his hands that shaped what you know as the Philosopher's Stone. With the wisdom of the Alpha, we will create our own champion."

The more the mystic talked, the more Stewart wished he had a knife to cut the man's throat—or better yet, his own. He'd sent Clement and the others to their death, or worse, he provided the enemy answers to the great mystery.

"It makes me laugh to read stories about men chasing after it in order to transform lead into gold—when its worth is so much more," Zenaida continued talking in her glee. "The Alpha, just a man, spent his life learning the secrets of the universe from the Archons, the builders of the universe, and he poured all of his knowledge into making his Great Work. He was the original Alchemist, and Solomon's map intended to find his Great Work hidden on the lost continent. The Alpha imbued his Great Work with both human spirit and the magic of creation so that it could act as a key, a key that goes far beyond transforming matter. It can command both matter and spirit, and thus, will become our key to both transformation and resurrection."

Stewart pounded the back of the head against the table.

Zenaida continued gloating. "It's not a coincidence that the legend of the Seven Stars is found in so many of these cultures, and the story about the Fisher Cat chasing the Wintermaker into the stars is only a metaphor for the Alpha's death. We believe his tomb and his Great Work are located near each other. That's why your friend Nicollet hid the location of discovery from his map, isn't it? He knew it'd buy him time so that he could return. Unfortunately, we couldn't risk him returning, whether in Minnesota or in the Rocky Mountains."

*At least I don't know the location of Lake Manitou. They won't be able to pry that information out of me. Only Clement knew that answer.* Stewart's shell-of-a-heart crumbled, yet his despair could not even find tears any more.

"Our Great Prophet learned about the Seven Fires Prophecy generations ago, about the same time he learned the world would end in 2061. Whether he knew it or not, Nicollet confirmed to us the location of the Alpha's tomb. The Great Clock is ticking, but it is my belief that when it chimes again, all will be ready for our Great War with the Creator. It is time to fetch the Countess; I think it is time she explains herself to our guest." Zenaida rose and walked out, leaving the door open.

*And when she returns, she will likely kill me.* Stewart futilely raged against his bonds, and Bessant smirked.

"You're dead already. Don't you know that? All you have left to decide is how much pain you're willing to endure before we allow you to die. So far, you've been quite cooperative, but knowing what I know of our torturers, you have so much more pain to endure. Tell me the exact location of the tomb, and I can promise you release."

The swish of a dress and the click of hard shoes on stone stairs filled the narrow hall.

The open door teased the possibility of escape. *I must be in a deep dungeon.* None of the three were imposing figures, and if the opportunity arose, he knew he'd kill Bessant first before turning on the Countess and mystic.

Countess Simona came through the doorway. This time, she had specks of blood on her face and arms that sullied her expensive gown. "How are things going?"

"Quite well," Bessant said. "I've jotted most of it down for you."

Countess Simona gathered herself. "Mr. Delhut has been quite cooperative also. I'm sending Pyotr with three dozen of my finest men. We'll lay a trap for Eos. Between Geyer and Morrison, one of the parties is certainly going to send Eos into motion."

"We've been discussing Professor Nicollet," Bessant added when she turned her attention to Stewart.

"Have we?" Her face became illuminated by feigned joy. She gestured for Bessant to rise from his chair and she claimed the spot beside Stewart. "I shouldn't hate him the way that I do, for he never did anything to wrong me, but it's just what Professor Nicollet represented that I despise. From what I've read, he was a remarkable man, but I knew an even more remarkable man.

"When I was a little girl, I was staying with my father in his homeland of Baku. A tall, handsome stranger from a distant land called America came to visit. He was a man of science, a man of education, a man of politics, a man with a vision for the future. He was as great as any of those kings of old except he lacked the ego to seize power for himself. He wanted to shape the world into a better place. He was a champion of humanity, and he traveled Europe looking for allies in this fight. You see, he was already a servant of Columbia, but during his time in Baku, he introduced me to her philosophy. I renounced the gods of my forefathers and became a devotee of Columbia, and over the next three decades, this stranger became my mentor.

"Then Joseph Nicollet knocked on the front door of Joel Roberts Poinsett. Was it purposeful or a chance encounter? You see, Poinsett wanted to gather up all these relics of superstition, to keep them out of the hands of Eos or the Church. Your aunt's antique map, for example, was purportedly made by King Solomon to lead them to the lost continent, where the Alpha's tomb and Great Work could be found. Your aunt showed this map to Professor Nicollet days before Poinsett's man killed her and brought it to Poinsett in Columbia, South Carolina. A few years later, Nicollet knocked on Poinsett's door. What are the odds?

"Later, when Poinsett learned of your alliance with Nicollet, he could not let your ambitions continue. First, he tried to stop Nicollet from continuing, but when he persisted, he had no other choice than to strike the shepherd to scatter the sheep. Then I learned that the sheep gathered together to kill my beloved mentor."

*It was supposed to end with the death of Poinsett.* Stewart remembered Poinsett's greenhouse and how they'd made him drink the same poison given to Nicollet. The newspapers wrote that Poinsett died of tuberculosis. "You killed my brother also?"

"The Order of Eos, actually, provided us your names," Countess Simona said, anticipating his thought. "When I learned the names Antoine Clement and William Drummond Stewart, I sent my operatives to kill you. Your brother Thomas, unfortunately, was a mistake. Now, just like Nicollet ended up at Poinsett's door, you end up knocking on my front door. I'm not going to make the same mistake Joel made, and for killing my mentor, don't plan on a quick death."

Countess Simona rose, leaned forward, and kissed Stewart on the cheek.

"Get your answers, and then give him to the torturer," she said and closed the door.

Back at the farmhouse at Hougoumont, the face of death had been a raging French giant. Now, it was a thin oriental man, who terrified him even more. *Now, only one question remains: how long can I endure torture before I submit to death?*

# CHAPTER 63



1 8 5 4

Jamie Anderson now marched to the beat of his own drum—and his curiosity drove him to the ancient stronghold belonging to the Order of Eos. Already, they'd fought off wolves, just as Morrison predicted.

With their remaining Austrian mercenaries flanking them, he and Karl Andreas Geyer led the ascent, with Lachlan Morrison still in handcuffs beside them. Frank Penny kept an eye on Morrison. None of it was according to the plans made in Cyprus, but without Lord Stewart to lead them, Anderson took charge. Knowing what they would likely face, he left Father MacPherson back at Orsova as a witness and last hope at making contact with the outside world. If he didn't hear back from them within the month, he had orders to return Stewart's small yacht back up the Danube to Vienna.

Now, they ascended the rugged ridge to access a mysterious valley in the clouds. Neither farm nor village dotted the mountain range, so unlike the valley, there were few people watching them pass. Unlike the stories from children's books, the lair of the monster grew more open and desolate the higher up they climbed. More and more exposed stone replaced the timber, and the sky cleared to illuminate their way.

Finally, with Morrison's guidance, they came through a narrow pass that led them to a high glacial lake atop the mountains. Below them, a farmer tended a herd of sheep. He raised a hand to wave and then put his hand to his brow.

Lachlan also put his hand to his brow before waving with chained hands.

*A secret gesture.*

*Eos…the brightness of the sun?*

Anderson looked all around the cavity found in the mountain peak. From the valley below, its existence never would have been believed, but an area about a mile wide created several square miles of hidden valley—dotted with white sheep. With the dry grasses and rubble, it looked almost untouched—which was intentional.

The shepherd approached.

They outnumbered and outgunned the shepherd, yet Anderson still filled with fear.

"Sergeant, I want you on that outcropping over there watching the lake and the valley for any sign of trouble," Anderson said.

"It's all right, Little Man," Morrison said. "You have my word. I'm as nervous about this as you are."

Morrison spoke truthfully and seemed nervous. The sergeant listened and peeled away from the men. He had a rifle, ammunition, and a pistol, quite enough to make a stand from above them.

Waiting for the others to approach, the shepherd stopped and leaned on his staff.

"Lachlan Morrison, Albany, New York. I'm their prisoner, as you can see, but we have an even greater enemy on the doorstep."

"Yes, we are well aware. James Farrington, Somerset."

Hearing the man's English accent stunned Anderson, for the chest-length beard and attire made him look like a local. *Geyer and Morrison were right about foreign mercenaries.*

Farrington eyed them. "Our wolves didn't put much of a dent in you. In the days past, a siege would happen to one castle at a time. For the past few years, entire armies have depleted our numbers or else you never would have reached this peak alive."

"That's why I am here," Morrison insisted. "We believed our enemy knows the defensive strategy. If there is a contingency plan for moving the treasures, it must be enacted quickly."

"The Countess has been hunting us for the past decade. Why would she suddenly know about this place?"

"Because I know of this place," Morrison pressed. "Because they have kidnapped one of our three Presiders. The vault is no longer safe. Whatever you need to do, do it."

Anderson felt a bit of relief. So far, Morrison did exactly as he'd promised. Now that they'd contacted Eos, he held out hope that they might rescue Stewart in time.

THE NEXT MORNING, Morrison was no longer in handcuffs, and a dozen shepherds brought their flocks up to the glacial lake to drink.

News was shared of two massive Russian defeats and an army of gypsies camped several miles to the west. By noon, the stones hiding the entrance to a cave were rolled away.

"Apple carts and cheese wagons are being brought into position on various passes in the valley below," Morrison explained about the activities happening at the base of the mountain. He turned to the unearthed cave entrance. "If you want to see one of the true Wonders of the World, this is your only opportunity."

Anderson left half of the remaining Austrian mercenaries to guard the entrance of the cave, and the rest of his team followed the faux-shepherds into the man-made cave structure. *I feel like I am stepping into my own grave.* Geyer and Penny's heads turned from side to side as they descended. For Geyer, it appeared to be earnest wonder. For Penny, it was defensive worry. Eventually, the narrowness of the passageway opened up to a natural cave with an irregular ceiling and floor.

"There are other entrances far below," James Farrington explained, "where the carts will shuffle treasures to safety. This vault was built long before the Seven Castles were built. It breaks my heart to even tell you of the intended destination for the sarcophagi." Farrington continued to lead them through the labyrinth. "The new system will be using museums. Several museums across the world will hold them, under false pretenses, of course. Can you imagine a museum in St. Louis housing Alexander the Great? The audacity of it."

The mountain cave was dry and cool, a better home than any pyramid. *And at least I'm not having to crawl on my hands and knees this time.* Geyer's mobility struggles continued, and despite protection from the sun, he continue to breath heavily.

"During the last ice age," Farrington continue to explain to Morrison, "that valley was filled with ice, and when it melted, this network of caves drained down into the valley below. But, we have lost our castles, and soon, we will lose our vault."

The walk ended. Masonry brought created floors, walls, and even a place of worship, if Anderson had to guess.

*A tomb for the five kings.*

"Incredible," Anderson marvelled. "Are these the actual…"

"Including Emperor Domitian himself," Morrison answered. "Stay here," Farrington commanded, "while we prepare the bodies for transportation."

Preparing the bodies became a religious ceremony, complete with the monk-shepherds chanting for several minutes. Frank Penny grew restless and began to pace around the chamber. Karl Andreas Geyer found a place to rest. Anderson and Morrison sat together. Just like he'd visited Rome at the beginning of their quest, Morrison now also visited a center for his peculiar religion.

After studying Morrison for several minutes, as well as the monks preparing to evacuate the bodies, Anderson held out hope that there'd be no double cross. Yet he figured he'd still broach the subject. "So are we about to kill each other?" Anderson wondered openly.

Morrison chuckled. "No, I assume I'll follow one of the coffins down a tunnel and let you go out the front door at the peak. You've done Eos a great service by trusting me. If I can free our masters, I'll let Stewart live, but I doubt our enemy will let that happen. We've protected the future against the plans of Vendita, but I doubt either of us will live to learn whose prophecy was true."

*I wish Stewart could be here to witness all of this.* "I'd drink to that sentiment if I had any wine."

Morrison raised an imaginary cup. "To the future."

*It's too bad he's my mortal enemy. I rather like this fellow.* "To the future."

The quaint moment was ended by thunderous discharge of a gunshot. It echoed so loudly that it was impossible to ascertain the origin.

And the echo continued unnaturally.

*No, not an echo*, Anderson realized. *Multiple shots.*

Flashes of rifle discharge brought lightning to the thunder, and Vendita gypsies rushed out of one of the drain tunnels, slaughtering Eos men who engaged in song and prayer.

Lachlan Morrison ran forward a few steps only to stop and watch the swarm of swords that followed the opening volley. The Eos guardians were no match for the swarm of gypsies.

*So much for evacuating the treasures. They've found one of the backdoors. We're trapped.*

Frank Penny took off his hat and handed it to Anderson. A moment later, both hands held his six-shooters. He stepped forward, pushing Morrison out of the way. Once in motion, Morrison ran for the glacier entrance they'd used earlier. Anderson took a step in that direction also, but Geyer suddenly dropped to a knee, gasping strangely.

*Dear Lord, his heart.*

Torn between friendship and flight, Anderson stepped back to put a hand on Geyer's shoulder, whose eyes looked at him with a different kind of fear than the one on Morrison's face.

Just as the Vendita gypsies finished overwhelming the Eos men at the shrine, Penny entered the fight. His hands moved like the tentacles of an octopus, firing independently at the closest sign of danger. Patient and precise, his pistols cut a swath through the first squad of attackers. One by one, their swords clattered to the ground.

Then Penny knelt to pray, it seemed.

In those ten seconds, he cracked open the chamber of his first pistol, and his deft fingers produced six more bullets from his belt. Still kneeling, he fired a shot in defense before setting the gun down for another few seconds.

As another six bullets found their way into his second chamber, he could only lean away as a sword came crashing down. His lower leg caught the blade just above the boot, and he fired two shots at the swordsman from his back. He rose with nine bullets and both pistols at the ready.

"A Penny is worth a hundred men!" he shouted back at Anderson and Geyer before entering the tunnel.

*He's going to try to hold them off in the tunnel,* Anderson realized and thought about running after Morrison up the slope. He tugged at Geyer's arm only to see the big man fall flat on his face.

"Geyer! Geyer!" Anderson called out.

Geyer breathed heavily but his eyes only stared out blankly. "I'm sorry. Run! Hide! Save yourself!"

Thunder and lightning echoed in the tunnel.

Six other tunnels remained dark.

And most likely blocked.

*Penny, come back to me.*

*Gah!*

"Calm yourself. Catch your breath." Anderson reached down and held Geyer's hand, feeling the last few pulses of his heart. And then it stopped.

Anderson looked around the glacial cave, trying to determine what to do next.

*I'm all alone.*

# CHAPTER 64



William Drummond Stewart didn't want to die, but dying felt like the only option to protect the legacy of Joseph Nicollet.

Fortunately, Koot Bessant didn't ask the right questions, and his inquisitor was currently with the other prisoner, Delhut.

Telling them about Nicollet's theories would certainly bring an end to the pain.

*No.*

*They have to earn it first.*

So Stewart waited for the pain to return.

To pass the time, he asked himself questions: *Who was the Alpha? What does his existence mean in terms of our interpretation of Genesis? The age of the Earth? Our view of humanity? Of God?*

Twenty years after learning about the *Al Marrakk Map*, he still had no idea how wise King Solomon was able to learn about the "loin of the beast" known as Merak, but the seven stars of the Big Dipper pointed to one unchangeable fact—an eight star, or king, was coming.

For Christianity—it was the great villain, the Antichrist.

For Eos, it was the resurrection of either hero and villain—the Old Gods rising to fight the fire giant Surtur.

For Vendita—

*Why didn't Poinsett destroy the map?*

*Why are they trying to steal the corpses from Eos?*

Vendita decided two centuries ago to destroy the Catholic Church and any other religions that adhered to the prophecies about End Times. Yet their actions were not entirely godless or without belief. Their elevation of Countess Simona as the deified Lady Columbia made them one of the world's youngest religions.

*Yet how are Vendita's actions different than Nimrod's tower assault on God? Did Merak invent the Philosopher's Stone in a war against God? Lady Columbia acts as a champion of humanity, yet what does she want humanity to become?*

Upstairs, Stewart heard Koot Bessant's low voice. Did he have Geyer? MacPherson? Anderson? Whoever he tortured was holding onto his knowledge better than Stewart had done.

The chubby young woman with sinister eyes—Zenaida— frightened him more than the torturers. She seemed keen on anything related to Indigenous lore, yet Stewart held tight onto Nicollet's hypothesis about the connections between the Wintermaker, Red Horn, and an antediluvian king from the Genesis era. He also blocked access to the strange shaman named Shetek who came to St. Louis to meet with Nicollet about the Serpent Star, Halley's Comet. While Delhut's confessions unraveled many of Stewart's secrets, he relished the fact that they did not know the specific location Nicollet had visited.

If Shetek was right and Nicollet was indeed the "star man" known as Wishwee, did Vendita already win by killing him? Did they break the prophecy about Wishwee fighting against the shapeshifting monster No Soul?

Stewart hoped not.

Stewart prayed not.

He flinched at a sudden noise.

*Is that what it sounds like?*

A veteran of war, Stewart recognized the sound of distant rifle fire.

Minute by minute, it grew closer.

Hundreds of guns.

Thousands of rounds.

All getting closer.

Stewart found enough energy to raise his head. His torture chamber remained black except for a crease around the doorway, where the hallway lights illuminated his windowless room.

During his torture, he assumed he'd been kept in a deep, dark dungeon, but from the sound of the gunfire, he reimagined his theory.

Canon fire gave him his answer.

The floor shook, which meant that the cannons placed along the battlements that protected the gun crews and snipers from ground fire were *below* the floor of the torture chamber.

*I'm in a tower?*

His head lifted again.

The light from the edges of the doorframe gave no answers, but he noticed how it cascaded onto the first several inches of the wall—a curved wall.

*I am in a tower—a damsel in distress.*

Soon, the cannon fire sounded on a regular basis, and his heart beat in optimistic unison.

The door opened.

Bessant stepped in. "I'm afraid, old chap, that our time has come to an end. My Lady has ordered Zenaida and I to be on our way. I wanted to say how I do truly respect all that you accomplished, and in a different world, I wish we could have sat around a sofa and smoked and drank into the night. If you're ever in Kathmandu…well… I will think of you fondly in the days to come. Thanks to the wisdom of your rival, we now possess the ability to stop the chaos of destruction that plagues our world. To an evolved mankind."

The door closed and he listened to the retreating footsteps. *Of course, his footsteps are descending. I am in a tower, and Bessant is going into the main part of the castle.*

Instead of feeling optimism at the thought of a besieged castle, Stewart began to feel dread. *They'll kill all of us rather than let us go.*

*Vendita has stolen the five kings from Eos.*

Despair raged in his heart until the battle outside brought a peculiar noise—the sound of horses.

*Have the Russians regrouped to rout the Vendita gypsies?*

*Are they bringing down all their fury upon this treacherous Countess?*

Knowing she'd be brought to justice was enough to let him die with a smile.

*Perhaps in the chaos, they'll forget all about me.*

After hearing the sound of horses for the next several minutes, he suddenly heard artillery fire.

*Field cannons!*

The encroaching army had swept in close enough to the castle to establish firing positions. Six centuries earlier, when the castles were designed, the walls and moats could keep thousands of men at bay, but modern artillery was capable of turning the entire complex to dust.

The focus would be on the gates and doors, he reckoned, but as the cannons continued to fire, he faded in and out of consciousness.

FOR ANOTHER FEW hours, the castle shook with each hit.

When the door opened, Countess Simona stood a wool jacket, trousers, and a cap upon her head. Petrov and two thugs followed her into the room. "I gave thought to bringing you with me, just so I could give you the horrible death I promised. Unfortunately, life can bring you surprises, and it seems I must flee the castle. But before I leave, I want to make sure you are looking in my eyes as you die. Poetic justice for Joel."

She turned to Petrov.

The knife was unsheathed.

And then the room shook in a blinding white light.

As a boy, Stewart had read how Christian martyrs tortured in the Roman Colosseum had found some sort of divine strength as lions mauled them or they were torn to pieces by mechanisms of torture.

But it wasn't an angel that cast heavenly light upon him.

Nor was it a Valkyrie come to take him to Valhalla.

Nor did his soul suddenly float upon the River of Souls.

When the dust fell, he found himself looking up at the afternoon sun and open sky just past his remaining toes. Petrov and the thugs who stood at the foot of the table had vanished along with the wall. Above him, he could see the stonework, for half of the ceiling was gone. A misfired cannon had punched a hole in the tower wall—a miraculous answer to Stewart's prayer.

He had to laugh when he saw his naked body coated in dust and debris without any of the ceiling landing upon him.

When he heard coughing, his heart sank.

Multiple coughs began to sound beyond his head.

One cough, just behind his head, belonged to Countess Simona.

The other came from beside him. A ghastly, demonic figure with a white body and red stripes rose beside him. One wide eye glanced at him while the other cried tears of blood from an empty socket. Fingerless hands lifted, and the remnants of wings lifted. No. Chains dangled from shackled wrists.

It stumbled past Stewart.

"Oh no," the Countess muttered and began to move.

But the monster she'd created was quickly upon her, and their bodies crashed around in the debris behind Stewart. He craned his neck but couldn't see what was happening.

Then two heads appeared below him, turning and twisting in the rubble. When the dance of death finished, Countess Simona stood strong, her fierce eyes looking down at Stewart.

But it wasn't in triumph.

Despite the strength in her legs, a serpentine arm had wrapped around her neck. Although lacking fingers, the creature who'd once been Solomon Delhut managed to get his arm wrapped around her neck and with the pressure of his right wrist, he choked the life out of her.

Solomon Delhut roared like a rabid animal as he mustered his final bit of strength, but when Simona's legs buckled, she stumbled backwards and both fell out the broken wall.

There was no scream, but Stewart smiled as he heard a distinctive thud a few seconds later. Then he prayed for the soul of the man who'd once been his foe.

A few hours later, when troops breached the castle walls and killed the rest of Countess Simona's slave soldiers, Stewart was still laughing about the Countess's facial expression as Delhut choked the life out of her. A soldier found him still strapped to the torture chair.

△<br>398

"Hey," the soldier called out in English. "I found something."

When he stepped into the doorway, he walked past Stewart and peered over the edge of the bite taken out of the tower, then turned around to face him. The soldier wore the uniform of the Highland Brigade. At first he recoiled and then stared in wonder. He asked, "You're Captain Billy, aren't you? You're the Hero of Hougoumont."

For a moment, Stewart wondered if he'd died back at the French farmhouse and everything else had been a dream, but the pain he felt reminded him that he was still very much alive—and rescued.

# CHAPTER 65

VIENNA, AUSTRIA

1854

Lady Christina Battersby Stewart woke to the sound of crying. She slipped on her heavy robe and slippers and hustled to the other small room.

Although it had been Emma Geyer who'd cried herself to sleep, the cries of baby Nicholas Geyer welcomed the new morning.

"Oh, sweet child, is your mother sleeping too soundly?" Christiana swept up the baby into her arms and cradled him, rocking him gently. She hummed a little melody, and all the while, Emma slept.

*Obviously, too much wine.*

More than two decades removed from having her own child, Christina still remembered the depression that took hold of her in the days following his birth. Despite William's promises, she still had to raise the child by herself after that selfish bastard took off on his great adventure to America. At Murthly, the aristocrats hated her for giving birth to a bastard and the servants hated her for being allowed into the estate.

With their husbands still away, Christina made a point of giving Emma everything she needed. So she changed Baby Nicholas, rocked him for as long as she could, and finally woke his sleeping mother with the toe of her slipper. "Someone's hungry."

Emma groaned from her bed. "Ugh, he has his father's appetite."

"Newborns are like this."

"Yuck, my shirt is soaked."

"Your breasts hear crying and respond. Now sit up. I'll fetch you a dry shirt."

Christina felt like crying also. No news likely meant bad news, and without letters from the expedition, they were left reading newspaper accounts of the Russian invasion of the Black Sea region, which made matters worse.

*But I need to be strong for both of us.*

"While you feed Baby Nicholas, I'm going to go to the market to see if any letters have arrived."

As always, she went directly to check mail.

Today, a letter arrived from Bulgaria. Its sender was not who she expected. She took a few steps away from the post office window and tore open the letter.

*Dearest Mother*—it was a letter from George.

*Strengthen your heart, for my letter will not bring resolution to your concerns about Father.*

*Of all the places in all of the world to vacation, Father certainly had terrible timing. When our British forces arrived in the region, the Ottoman Empire was on the verge of collapse, but the French and English navies secured Constantinople, and we quickly retook Bulgaria from the Russians.*

*By the time we arrived, Russia had crossed into the southern Danube region. Our arrival in the war surprised the Russian armies, and their retreat north was chaotic. Many escaped back across the Danube. I received your letter upon the arrival of the 93rd Sutherland Highlanders at the port of Varna.*

*Imagine my despair when I learned that the Highlanders were to be immediately redeployed across the Black Sea to Crimea. Fortunately, Father's heroism at the Battle of Waterloo is still talked about today. Young men who served under him in the King's Hussars and the 6th Dragoon Guards were in Bulgaria to help sweep away the Russians across the Danube. When these men learned about the disappearance of Father—well, Orders be Damned!*

*They rallied for Captain Billy!*

*Our intelligence officer learned that the Mina had also made port at Varna and explained how Jamie the Fool took several of father's companions by land to a place known as the Iron Gates.*

*Our intelligence officers explained a theory on what could have happened. One Russian army retreated through Wallachia and vanished into the Carpathian Mountains north of Bucharest, but rumors of another Russian*

*army sneaking through a western pass in the Carpathians meant that Father might've found himself prisoner of this force.*

*With Captain Billy missing and Russians on our flank, Fate aligned for me to join Father's old cavalry regiments on a scouting mission to the Iron Gates. When we arrived, we were greeted by none other than Father MacPherson, who'd been staying at a river town called Orsova.*

*This is where the news grew grim.*

*Father and Karl Geyer were indeed at the wrong place at the wrong time, and our fears of a Russian flanking maneuver were founded—yet when the battle ended, Father was a prisoner of the local Romanian militia. Bold Karl Geyer joined forces with Jamie, Frank Penny, and the remaining Austrian mercenaries to give pursuit, sending Father MacPherson back to Orsova should their efforts fail.*

*I am writing this to give to Father MacPherson so that he can bring it back to Varna and place it in the hands of the military mail who will send it to you.*

*With the Dragoons on my left and the Hussars on my right, we plan to chase down this local militia and rescue Father by any means necessary.*

*I will need your prayers in the days to come.*

*Ever yours,*

*George.*

Upon reading the news, Christina found herself running back to the cottage on the edge of the botanical gardens.

Her joyous feet stopped running a few feet from the cottage door when she realized she could lose everyone she loved.

# CHAPTER 66



At the end of it all, William Drummond Stewart was reunited with his son. Lieutenant George Stewart now rode beside him on a horse as they neared Retezat Mountain pass. From there, it was another forty miles back to Baile Herculane, the place he'd been taken by Countess Simona's slave soldiers. He meant to give each of his friends a proper burial.

*And now my adventuring days are over.*

His body still ached, even days after he was freed from his torture. He left Countess Simona for the ravens, but he took time to bury Solomon Delhut at one of the old strongholds built by the Order of Eos.

*A fitting tomb for a secret king.*

Even when he was dressed only in a British horse blanket, Stewart tried to get the soldiers to chase after any fleeing Vendita gypsies. But he had no idea how long ago they'd found the vault or where it was located. Plus, the moment his gallant son appeared, he no longer cared about chasing after relics and phantoms.

"Mother sent me to bring you home," George told him. "But first we need to clean you up and get you healthy."

The return ride to Baile Herculane was quiet, especially when the curious officers asked for stories and only received sobs from Stewart. They'd seen enough to know what he'd been through.

First Lieutenant Stewart, his Georgie, also rode silently, although occasionally, Stewart noticed a wry smile on his son's face.

*He's the hero now, and I'm a broken old man.*

Scouts came charging back to the center of the column, and all three officers readied for action. "Sir, we've found others."

Stewart rejoiced, yet only one friend greeted him at the bottom of the mighty mountain—Jamie Anderson. His son had already told him about finding Ross MacPherson back at Orsova No one mentioned Geyer or Penny, which told him everything.

The Fool of Murthly had somehow survived it all.

Stewart's smile almost left when he saw Lachlan Morrison sitting beside Anderson and one of the surviving Austrian mercenaries. Morrison had remained true to his word. Two dozen shepherds dotted the hillside—Eos men.

After introductions to his son, Stewart spoke with the three survivors in private. He learned of Frank Penny's death, holding off the tunnel long enough for Jamie Anderson to hide. He also learned how Geyer's heart had given out about the same time.

In turn, Stewart told Morrison about what had happened to Delhut at Corvin's Castle.

"Vendita's gypsies stole all five kings," Morrison countered as if they were in a competition for who could deliver the worst bit of news. "After Delhut gave away the locations, Lady Columbia sent her men to watch, and once we revealed one of the hidden access points, her army swept in, slaughtering whomever they could find along the mountain."

Stewart turned to Anderson to ask, "Did you see the Vendita gypsies take the bodies?"

"I did. Frank Penny's valiant charge only gave me an hour before another squad of Gypsies came up the tunnel. By that time, I was well hidden in a crevice. The Order of Eos made it too easy to evacuate the coffins. Within two hours, they were gone."

"How long ago was this?" Stewart asked, feeling the hot meal in his belly fill with bile.

Anderson looked to Morrison. "Five days ago? I've lost count."

"I went down one of the other tunnels," Morrison explained, "but by the time I reached the bottom, it was all over. Outside, I found dead Eos men and the wagons destroyed. They'd circled around the base of the mountain killing anyone that moved. I stayed put for a whole day before I dared stick my nose out. I found the watchmen you see in the woods, but Vendita left with such a force that we can surmise that they took the treasure north."

"Most likely to Corvin's Castle," Stewart inserted. "They claimed to be evacuating it to safety prior to the British cavalry arriving."

"So it is truly lost," Morrison bitterly despaired.

"What do we do next?" Stewart asked instinctively even though he knew he could not pursue his enemy.

Morrison had only recently healed from his own wounds. "Vendita is my true enemy, not you Stewart. You were a man of your word. You sacrificed your friends to come to my aid. I can speak for the Order of Eos when I say you can live out the rest of your days in peace—so long as you stay out of this fight."

"When I parted ways with Antoine Clement, we believed Eos was responsible for the death of my brother and the death of Clement's father. Vendita learned about Clement's home in St. Louis from a Sinclair. I cannot attest to what he's done in the name of vengeance."

"Yes, well, when I return to console Solomon Delhut's grieving family, I will make sure all know that the bad blood between us is over, but you must do the same. Is that understood?"

"My son has orders to send me home without my dessert," Stewart tried to find levity despite his broken heart. "I can abide by those conditions."

"Then this is where I leave you, Lord Stewart. You were a ferocious enemy, and an even better ally," Morrison said, walking away with a shake of his head.

His men began to move also, no doubt to shuttle him to whatever strongholds remained that Countess Simona hadn't destroyed. In a matter of minutes, Morrison slithered away into the shadows of the Carpathian Mountains.

"You weren't tempted to kill them all?" Anderson asked.

"You should have killed them all," the Austrian mercenary insisted.

"My quest is over," Stewart said, gesturing to his waiting son.

"Not quite," Anderson said, turning back to the ravine Morrison disappeared into. "Well, looks like he's gone."

"What's this about?"

"Poetic justice," Anderson bitterly answered.

"The bag?" The Austrian asked, receiving a pronounced nod from the dwarf.

Anderson explained himself, "We remained up on top of that damned mountain for another two days before we made our way down, and being strangers in a strange land, we didn't even know where to run. Morrison found us, but he didn't know what mischief I'd been up to when he ran away like a coward."

"Mischief?" Stewart asked.

Anderson led them to a rocky ditch beside the road just a few yards from where they waited. A supply bag held an irregular shape within. When he lifted it, the bag rattled.

"A gift," Anderson said, tossing it forward.

"Your friendship is the only gift I need." The bag fell short, so Stewart went to retrieve it.

"I couldn't bear the thought of abandoning Geyer, and it took me every bit of strength to do what I did. Thank goodness he lost a hundred pounds during the ordeal, or else, I never would have been able to drag him into that coffin."

"You put him in—"

"A place fit for a king. I almost thought about hiding inside of one of the coffins myself, but I feared waking up in some worse place than this. By the time the gypsies regrouped, I had Geyer tucked away for his eternal slumber. They hauled him away with the others."

Stewart picked up the bag, almost aghast, "And this is…"

"Alexander? Ramses? Domitian? I didn't have time to ask, nor was I going to tell Morrison about my theft until he was long gone. If that witch you met plans on bringing any of those kings back to life before the Battle of Armeddon, well…you've got a seat at the negotiation table, don't you?"

"Yes I do. You are indeed the king of mischief." *A place for a king, Stewart smiled upon reflection. I wonder where they'll bring his corpse? Or how long it'll take before they discover Anderson's prank.*

# CHAPTER 67

KATHMANDU, NEPAL

1855

Two months later, Koot Bessant arrived at his home in Kathmandu, Nepal. The support of Vendita had given an escort of gypsies for the entirety of his journey, but at the border of India and Nepal, the British authorities refused to let Zenaida pass.

She was not pleased, but the young apprentice obeyed.

*One day, she'll lead us.*

Even before Bessant left for Romania, he'd prepared a temporary holding place for the tombs, which resembled Retezat and the Shrine of Wuoth. He watched as all five crated sarcophagi were brought into position.

Not only had he thwarted Eos, but now he'd also taken one step closer to steering humanity to a new future. Isaac Newton's clock was ticking closer to 2061, but now, he had a major weapon for the days to come.

"Something's wrong with one of them," a gypsy servant told him as they were leaving the chamber. "One of them smells like recent death."

An hour after the gypsies left, he took it upon himself to deconstruct the crate and then pry open the heavy lid. Inside, he found a recently deceased corpse smiling up at him.

*If this man fills this coffin,* Bessant wondered stepping back, *then which of the kings are we missing?*

# CHAPTER 68

## MURTHLY CASTLE

### 1855

The war was over, yet it continued for another year in Crimea. Lord William Drummond Stewart picked up a newspaper to read all about the tragic "Charge of the Light Brigade" involving his beloved 15th The King's Hussars. The British had been steadily taking away all of the ground gained by Russia in Crimea until a mistake sent the brigade on a suicide mission.

*Russia will see it as a victory, and the war will continue,* Stewart realized. *It will be months before the war comes to its inevitable conclusion.*

His son George continued to surpass him as a hero. After leaving Bulgaria, George arrived in Crimea, where he received honors and a promotion to captain for his part in what the press labeled as "The Thin Red Line," where he repulsed a Russian Cavalry attack, protected a caravan of wounded, and ultimately secured the Port of Balaklava.

*A chip off the old block,* Stewart thought but then admitted he'd done little to raise the boy.

Even though his son remained on the Black Sea, the rest of his family once again resided in Murthly Castle. Lady Christina doted on Baby Nicholas as if he were her own grandson.

While Christina helped with the child, Emma Geyer sat beside Stewart at the fireplace each evening to hear the untold tales of her bold husband. Jamie Anderson joined the storytelling, but he concluded the tale with Karl buried in a high mountain vault reserved for kings. Emma seemed to like the idea of his grandiose tomb.

Ross MacPherson also returned to Scotland, and the two spent their days pouring over obscure texts together, debating concepts like predestination and free will. "I doubt that Vendita's victory will have any more impact than that of Jamie's theft of bones. 'The mind of man plans his way, but the LORD directs his steps.'"

"What is that supposed to mean?" Stewart had asked.

"I don't think Eos or Vendita will be able to stop the prophecies of God from coming to fruition," MacPherson insisted, but it seemed like he was trying to convince himself that their efforts had been a victory, not a failure.

Then one day, a visitor appeared at Murthly.

Jamie Anderson escorted a red-haired teenager into Stewart's office. Anderson prefaced it with, "You might want to sit down for this."

Vaktar Forsberg remained their guest for a month, and Emma found a new storyteller. Vaktar explained what happened on their grand adventure through Scandinavia, America, and Canada. Ross MacPherson charted the adventure on maps, globes, and charts while Jamie Anderson jotted the details down in notebooks.

Antoine Clement was dead.

Lewis Cairns was dead.

Corey Morgan was dead.

And when Vaktar told about the death of Sofus Nielson, Emma cried as if she'd known him since childhood. Stewart cried for other reasons.

At first, the story only made his depression deepen, but when he thought about it longer, he found a surprise detail. "Antoine had a wife and daughter?" Stewart asked with incredulity.

Forsberg nodded and then explained. "By the time I returned from Renville's cabin, Chief Sweating Stone's Chippewa had routed the camp and killed Lord Erskine's scouting party."

"According to Chief Crooked Arm of the Cree," Anderson skeptically clarified.

Forsberg's glare slammed shut any doubt about Crooked Arm's account. "A fellow named Taopi learned that Chief Sweating Stone took Little Star as a captive to his home at Leech Lake. DeSmet

counseled Taopi against taking up arms against the Chippewa. Settlement had opened up, and DeSmet said your enemies would use any excuse to make matters worse for the Native people."

DeSmet had also sent letters with Vaktar that explained from the Jesuit and Periphery's perspective what had happened. DeSmet would remain a champion for Native tribes in the west, but he would not take any personal action in the rescue of Little Star or seek vengeance for Chief Thunderface and the others.

"Can we trust DeSmet not to tell the Jesuits about Lake Manitou?" MacPherson asked.

"The Jesuits are the least of our concern," Stewart said. "Eos lost all five kings to Vendita."

"Four," Anderson quipped.

"My point is," Stewart continued, "Eos will be more motivated than ever to find the Philosopher's Stone and the Alchemist who made it—their Alpha king. It's their final play."

Anderson seethed, "Which is why we should have killed Lachlan Morrison when we had the chance."

"Killing more Eos men would not have stopped this," Stewart insisted. "It's like stomping on a nest of ants. "

"But what about Lachlan Morrison?" Anderson continued. "He knew Solomon's Delhut's mind, and we can't expect him to be tricked by Nicollet's ruse in the Rockies."

"After the battle with the Chippewa, what happened to you?" Stewart asked Vaktar.

"Taopi took me back to Renville and then escorted me down the Minnesota River. I stayed with the Faribault family, who DeSmet said were friends. I was able to meet with my Uncle Dagmar, who had served Nicollet on one of his expeditions."

"Tell me more about your uncle Dagmar," Stewart said.

"He'd taken a wife and had a son, a boy named Sigmund. He'd taken one of the parcels of land and called it Dalleven, after a river near our home."

"In southern Minnesota," Stewart clarified. "Not in the north?"
Vaktar shook his head.

*Then he's drawn no more attention to Lake Manitou.*

"So we have allies in the area if we decide to make another move on the Stone," Anderson added.

Stewart shook his head. "No, I gave Lachlan Morrison my word that my part in the story was over. You were there, Jamie."

"I wasn't there," Ross MacPherson said. "My name is ruined around these parts. What's to stop me from traveling to Minnesota and claiming one of these plots of land near Lake Manitou?"

Stewart picked up DeSmet's letter, "Faribault, Taopi, and Iron Walker felt that no action should be taken until the time is right."

"And when will that be?" Anderson asked.

"It matters not," Stewart said. "Do you remember the custodian saying that to me during our visit with him? 'It matters not.' His response angered me at the time. Now, I understand his wisdom. Do you remember, Ross?"

"I remember it well," MacPherson answered.

"I remember being told about it afterwards," Anderson added bitterly.

Stewart continued his point, "If our enemies are right, Halley's Comet is a celestial clock counting down the final days of mankind. It'll return long after I'm gone…in 1910. Then again, it'll pass by in 1986. When it passes by in 2061, Vendita means to dethrone God and take the world for humanity."

"Of course." MacPherson scoffed. "Which makes me even more determined to have a front row seat at Lake Manitou. Does Eos even know who I am?"

"It likely doesn't, Ross. I remember how the custodian called us men of action. I promised him that as a man of action, I'd go out into the world and thwart the Sons of Darkness. We certainly did that. We've crippled Eos and also held back Vendita from its own goals, thanks to Mr. Anderson's quick thinking. It was a bitter pill to swallow, and the lesson I've learned in all of this is that the custodian was right. It matters not what decisions men of action take, for in the end, what will be, will be. You once counseled me, 'The mind of man plans his way, but the LORD directs his steps.' I believe the Philosopher's Stone should remain at Lake Manitou for as long as the LORD wills it. "

"So it is over?" Anderson asked.

"You are the only friends I have left," Stewart said. "Give me the coming summer. Forget all these other matters. When summer is over, then you can bring young Vaktar home to Sweden, but if

you still feel the need to return to Lake Manitou, then I ask that you heed the advice of the custodian."

"And what is that?" MacPherson asked.

"We will let our enemies be men of action, but if you go, you will go only to nurture the flock. It heals my heart knowing that part of Clement still lives through his child.

WILLIAM DRUMMOND STEWART remained a man of his word, staying at his home in Murthly Castle until his passing at the age of 76 in the year 1871. His remains were buried in the Chapel of St. Anthony the Emerite between the bones of Jean-Nicholas "Joseph" Nicollet and the bones of a man Stewart died believing to be Alexander the Great.

# EPILOGUE

L E E C H   L A K E

1 8 8 2

Big Squeak Weber's dreams haunted him even in broad daylight. He could almost feel his scarred hands shaking, so he stuffed them into his pockets so that his men couldn't see his fear. He hated being this far south, but the chance to make some serious money made it worth the risk of getting so near to his childhood home of Lake Manitou, a day's travel south of Leech Lake.

Big Squeak's biggest man, Blackfish LaBiche, gave him a dirty look as he returned to the boat to grab another case of whiskey.

Standing beside the boat they'd used to cross the big lake, Big Squeak said to LaBiche, "Hurry it up so we can get out of here." As the leader of the Black Hat Gang, Big Squeak had earned the fear and loyalty of his henchman, yet feigning laziness now was better than showing fear.

Each fall, the United States government paid tribal members annuity payments, and in Minnesota, Leech Lake was a designated distribution center at a place called Onigum. Flanked by his thugs, Big Squeak made a killing on his illegal alcohol sales, and they'd cautiously set up out of sight from the few government officials who cared about his operation.

"If you're in such a hurry, why don't you lend a hand?" his other man, Pierre LeDuc, asked as he grabbed one of the last crates. Anywhere else, Big Squeak would've done his part, but he feared seeing his estranged father Nanakonan in the crowd gathered at the distribution center. It'd been more than a decade since he'd run out of his father's sweat lodge, never to look back, but being so close to home made all those memories come back to him.

As he was moving the last crates closer for his men to reach, he noticed a young woman staring at him. She was several inches taller than a typical Chippewa girl, and her face and cheekbones were more angular than the rounder face of the Anishinaabe. Her eyes burned into him without even blinking.

*She's stunning.*

"Careful," Pierre LeDuc, his right-hand man, muttered softly. "She's the daughter of Chief Sweating Stone. He'll cut off your *giinag* and hang it from his porch as a warning to other suitors."

Big Squeak knew enough of Chief Sweating Stone to remember that he'd killed his Grandfather Chagobay for the secrets he'd passed onto Nanakonan and Joseph Nicollet. "He already wants to cut off my *niinag* for selling alcohol to his people."

LaBiche spoke in a rasp. "I've heard she's crazy. Best stay away from that one."

Big Squeak set down a crate, brushed off his hands on his blue jeans, and climbed up the hill to chase off the gawking teenager.

But she didn't run.

"What's your name?" he asked, grinning broadly to flash his dimples.

She stiffened her back and sized him up for a moment. A crease formed in her forehead before she spoke. "Winona, but my mother calls me Winnie."

"Winona," Big Squeak repeated. "That's a Dakota name."

"It means *firstborn daughter*. My mother also told me that it's an old family name. The original Wenonah fell in love with a handsome stranger who did not belong to her tribe."

*This is going better than I'd hoped.* Having run wild for a decade after leaving his home at Lake Manitou, he now felt ready to settle down and start a family. He'd met many woman, but something about Winnie caught his heart. Big Squeak removed his hat and shook out his modern, cropped hair. "As it turns out, many girls tell me that I'm handsome, *and* I'm not from your tribe, am I?"

"No, you're from Lake Manitou."

Big Squeak's smile left his face. He looked around as if sensing a trap. "Do I know you?"

"No, but my mother Little Star told me all about Lake Manitou. She's one of Chief Sweating Stone's eight wives, but the other wives hate her. They even hate her more than his Irish wife because she's Lakota. I've had dreams about Lake Manitou, but my father won't let me go there."

"Told you she's strange," his man muttered behind him.

"Would you take me to Lake Manitou sometime?" Winnie asked.

"You don't want to go to Lake Manitou," he answered. He looked down at the burn marks upon his palms and hid his hands in the hat. Years earlier, during a vision quest, his father Nanakonan had tasked him with holding heated stones. As expected, they burned his hands to the disappointment of his father, who persisted in his belief that Big Squeak was special. The terrifying visions of the demon spirit living under Lake Manitou drove him from home. He didn't even know if Nanakonan still lived.

"My father says I'm an obstinate brat." Winnie shrugged with a smile. "I don't even like living at Leech Lake, but I stay because of my mother. When someone tells me no, I want to do it even more. Why don't you want to go to Lake Manitou? Because of the evil spirit living under the waves?"

Big Squeak laughed aloud, turned back to his friends, and then stepped forward until he was almost toe-to-toe with the eccentric beauty. "What do you know about the evil spirit?"

She stood fearless. "Quite a bit. My mother told me about it from her people's perspective. If you take me there, I'd tell you all about it."

Big Squeak thought of his vision and what Nanakonan had told him about the Seven Fires Prophecy—from the Wijigan perspective. "I'll take you with me today, but we're heading to Fond Duc Lac after this. My father lives at Lake Manitou, and I don't want anything to do with him or his cursed lake."

"Afraid?"

*Who is she?* "No, I'm not afraid. I just made a choice. I rejected the path my father and forefathers set before me. I don't want to have anything to do with their prophecies."

"That's funny. After being taken by Chief Sweating Stone in a great battle on the frontier, my mother gave up trying to fulfill prophecy, yet here you are—the man from Lake Manitou. Perhaps it means we should face the prophecy together."

*That would stick it to my father. Imagine if I came home with a Lakota bride—his ancient enemy.* "No, you don't understand," Big Squeak answered. His men were beginning to gather down at the boat. *Let them wait,* he thought. All the images of his nightmare came back to his mind "If I go home," he spoke softly to her, "the prophecy will find some way of coming true, and if it comes true, the evil spirit that dwells in Lake Manitou will rise and destroy the world we know. I shouldn't have come this close to home."

Reason told him to leave, but his heart made him stay.

"You speak of the Wintermaker. The other wives told me about your Chippewa legend. I heard that he gathered up the summerbirds, which is saying he gathered souls of the dead, and that he tricked the Great Creator, avoiding his fate by staying where he died instead of taking the River of Souls to the Land of Everlasting Happiness."

She told it with such intensity that the hair stood up on the back of his neck.

But then she smiled, "Do you know what would be funny?"

Big Squeak was at a loss for words. "What?"

"We should trick the Great Trickster?"

Big Squeak chuckled at her audacity. "Who are you?"

"Like I said, my father said I'm an obstinate brat. I'm a born trickster, but my mother says it's my destiny to contend with evil spirits at Lake Manitou." She turned and looked down to the boat. "So? Will you take me? I'd like to know what all the fuss is about?"

*This is crazy.*

*She's crazy.*

He took a step away, ready to keep running from his own destiny, but the thought of defying his destiny proved too alluring. He'd been running from his nightmare for a decade, and the thought to standing up to his spiritual bully intrigued him. "How would we trick the Wintermaker?"

"I've had dreams all about it," she said with a flirtatious grin. "But we could only accomplish it if we acted together."

He extended his hand. "Together?"

"Together," Winnie said, taking his hand.

THE END

The story continues in
THE DREAMCATCHER CHRONICLES

Book One: *The Firehandler*

<u>The 1354 Expedition</u>
**Paul Knutson**
**Father Tveit**
**Jacob Cnoyen of Berg**
**Mikils Forsberg**
**Lars Havorn**
**Lars Marur**
**Tao Nielson**
**Bjarni Olafson**
**Fisk**
**Smed**
**Storlum**

<u>The Eight Survivors</u>
**Father Tveit**
**Jacob Cnoyen**
**Tao Nielson**
**Mikils Fors**
**Bjarni Olafson**
**Drummond**
**Dobie**
**Morrison**

<u>The Six Kings of Old</u>
1. **Lamech**
2. **Nimrod of Babel**
3. **Ramses the Great**
4. **Alexander the Great**
5. **Antiochus Epiphanes**
6. **Emperor Domitian**

**Abbaron**—An ancient map made by the Aksumite Kokebi.

**Akhenaten**—An Egyptian Pharaoh.

**Al Marrakk**—An ancient map created by King Solomon.

**Alpha**—the Vendita term for the first king.

**Anderson, Jamie**—The fool of Murthly Castle.

**Arni**—1347 Bishop of Nidaros.

**Bardson**—Bishop tasked with finding 1354 survivors.

**Battersby-Stewart, Christina**—Lady of Murthly.

**Benton-Fremont, Jessie**—daughter of an American Senator.

**Berenger, Gerard**—Order of Eos agent.

**Berig**—First of the Goth Kings.

**Bessant, Koot**—a Vendita agent.

**Cairns, Lewis**—Sergeant of the Cold Stream Regiment of Footguards.

**Carruthers**—Bishop in Scotland.

**Chauvin, Nicholas**—Large Cajun soldier during the Napoleonic wars.

**Clement, Antoine, Jr.**—A renowned frontier hunter. Also known as Brunia and Missabay.

**Clement, Antoine, Sr.**—Retired fur trader living near St. Louis.

**Clement, Basil**—Antoine's brother.

**Clement, Francois**—Antoine's deceased brother.

**Clement, Joseph**—Antoine's brother.

**Clement, Starlight**—Antoine's Cree mother.

**Clement, Xavier**—Younger brother of Antoine.

**Columbia**—a term used to describe the leader of Vendita.

**Crooked Arm**—A Cree Chief.

**Delhut, Étienne**—Order of Eos agent.

**Delhut, Solomon**—Order of Eos grandmaster.

**Demiurge**—The Vendita term for God

**DeSmet, Pierre-Jean**—A Jesuit missionary to the Frontier.

**Dobie, Duncan**—Order of Eos agent.

**Drummond, Margaret**—A Lady of Logiealmond

**Drummond, William**—A Scottish poet with a fixation on the occult.

**Dumont-Clement, Mary Elizabeth**—Antoine's step-mother.

**Edouart, Auguste**—Renowned artist commissioned by Nicollet.

**Erskine, Wesley**—traveling name of Lewis Cairns.

**Faribault, David**—Former guide for Joseph Nicollet.

**Firefly**—Nanakonan's wife

**Farrington, James**—An Eos agent.

**Forsberg, Dagmar**—Uncle to Vaktar

**Forsberg, Leif**—Father to Vaktar

**Forsberg, Vaktar**—A firstborn son from Fors, Sweden

**Fremont, John C.**—Former apprentice of Joseph Nicollet

**Geyer, Emma**—Karl's German wife.

**Geyer, Karl Andreas**—Botanist who explored the American frontier.

**Geyer, Nicholas**—Karl's son.

**Glissant, Julian**—A Periphery agent.

**Gunn, Callum**—Order of Eos agent

**Hyperborea**—A mythical northern island.

**Iron Walker**—Son of Chief Sleepy Eyes.

**Kouzenas, Simona**—Lady Columbia, leader of Vendita.

**Krogstad, Nils**—Bergen reverend.

**Lady Zenaida**—A Vendita agent.

**Little Star**—Wichapi, the daughter of Clement.

**LaBiche, Blackfish**—Member of the Blackhat gang.

**LeDuc, Pierre**—Member of the Blackhat gang.

**MacPherson, Ross**—Former Catholic Priest in Scotland.

**Magni**—Buried Norse god.

**Mahdi**—The sacred prophet of the Seveners, the Nazari Ismailis.
**McBain, Donald**—An Eos agent.
**McGuffin**—Sheriff of Galveston, Texas.
**Merak**—The Phoenician name for a Polestar.
**Miller, Alfred Jacob**—Painted Stewart and Clement.
**Modi**—Buried Norse god.
**Morgan, Corey**—A Scottish historian specializing in Nordic families.
**Morrison, Lachlan**—An Eos agent.
**Mowatt, Mr.** —An Eos agent.
**Nanakonan**—Nicollet's guide in 1836.
**Ney, Michel**—French Field Marshall.
**Nicollet, Joseph**—A French astronomer and mapmaker.
**Nielson, Mathias**—Older brother of Sofus.
**Nielson, Sofus**—A boy from the Faroe Islands.
**Nizari Ismailis**—a sect of assassins.
**Odoacer**—A Gothic king who sacked Rome.
**Ozymandias**—the Greek name for Ramses the Great.
**Pandora's Pithos**—An ancient collection of lost knowledge.
**Penny, Ebenezer**—Former Texan friend of Nicollet.
**Penny, Frank**—Veteran of the Texas Revolution.
**Petrov, Pyotr**—A Vendita agent.
**Priory of Ormus**—The ancient name for Vendita.
**Renville, Joseph**—Early Minnesota settler.
**Rezanov, Nikolai**—A Vendita agent in British Columbia
**Rogers, Henry Darwin**—An American geologist.
**Shrine of Wuoth**—A Gothic shrine in Ravenna.
**Simmons, Conrad**—A Periphery agent.
**Sinclair, Bill**—Hudson Bay fur trader.
**Sinclair, Henry Prince**—Rumored explorer of Nova Scotia in the 1400s.
**Sinclair, Magnus**—Order of Eos agent in Nova Scotia.

**Sinclair, Scot**—Son of Magnus.
**Sinclair, Trey**—An Eos agent.
**Sinclair, William "Junior"**—Order of Eos agent at Oxford House.
**Sinclair, William**—Built Rosslyn Chapel in 1446
**Sinclair, William Henry**—Son of Magnus
**Song-on-the-Water**—Cree Matriarch of the Sinclair family.
**Stewart, George**—Only son of William Drummond Stewart.
**Stewart, Thomas**—William's younger brother. A priest.
**Stewart, William Drummond**—Lord of Murthly Estate.
**Surtr**—A buried fire giant from Norse mythology.
**Sweating Stone**—Chief of the Leech Lake Pillagers.
**Taopi, Jim**—Former guide for Nicollet.
**Theodric the Great**—An Ostrogoth King who pillaged Rome.
**Thule**—A mythological island
**Tun Win**—The Blue Woman, an Oceti Sakowin legend.
**Vali**—Buried Norse god.
**Vidar**—Buried Norse god.
**Wanagiyata**—The Dakota name for Lake Manitou.
**Wahanantan**—Legendary Yankton chief.
**Waneta**—Son of Wahanantan.
**Weber, Big Squeak**—Son of Nanakonan.
**Wintermaker**—An Ojibwe legend about a sorcerer who tried to stop the seasons from changing.
**Wiyipisiw**—Chieftain of the Wijigan Clan of Ojibwe
**Wisakachak**—A trickster god of the Cree
**Wishwee**—A Dakota legend about a young man who battles a shape shifter.
**White Feather**—The Blackfoot wife of Clement
**Winona**—Daughter of Little Star and Sweating Stone
**Zalmoxis**—A shapeshifting god of Romania
**Zenaida**—A Russian mystic.

# ABOUT THE AUTHOR

Imagine the love child of Rambo and Ma Ingalls. That's Jason Lee Willis. Overly nurtured by his Vietnam War veteran father and Lutheran church secretary mother, he grew up in the fantasy realm of South Dakota before his exodus brought him to mysterious Minnesota for college.

His love of mythology and storytelling led him to a career as a high school English teacher, and now, he works as a journalist and blogger as well as a full-time novelist. As a professional storyteller, he's done historical lectures, book talks, radio segments, podcasts, and a video channel on YouTube, The Minnesota Alchemist.

Willis currently lives in Minnesota, where he lives the life of a hobbit by gardening, writing, walking around barefoot, wearing vests, fishing, and going on adventures with his wife, Julie.

As an independent author, he'd also appreciate a star/review on Amazon or Goodreads. That would mean a lot!

Check out his other works at: williswrites.com

www.ingramcontent.com/pod-product-compliance
Lightning Source LLC
Chambersburg PA
CBHW070159310726
48976CB00001B/149